'*Wolf, Wolf* is a slow burn: distressing, subtle and excellent.'
— Rebecca Gowers, author of *When to Walk*

'South Africa's shifting social topography underlies this slow-burn tale of a dying patriarch and his self-absorbed son ... Often caustic, sometimes tender ... [*Wolf, Wolf* is a] textured, ...sition.'
— *Finan...*

'A stark study of arrested ethnicity ... *Wolf, Wolf* is a mesmerising novel. Much as Goldblatt's portraits did in their time, [Venter] skewers his world into place with detail. Matt Duiker rings true – stuck between the old South Africa now passing away, and a new world painfully coming into being.' — *The Guardian*

'At the heart of *Wolf, Wolf* is the confluence of two recurrent tropes in recent South African fiction. The first, which explores the post-apartheid transition in an obviously allegorical way, features the return of an expatriate child, often to a parent's deathbed, sometimes to the farm ... The second is that of queer self-discovery, often in the context of familial or communal resistance ... In *Wolf, Wolf*, Venter's harnessing of both tropes serves to explore the cost of white privilege and the burden of inheritance or its expectation in South Africa's precarious present ... Venter's brave, lyrical novel offers neither consolation nor nostalgia, only a doomed sense of the inevitability of an accounting to come.' — *TLS*

'Very well-written ... Venter has a punchy, vivid style, with a lot of unusual sentence constructions that flow really well together ... A rewarding and satisfying read.' — *Irish Independent*

'A subtle, yet powerful tale of relationships and masculinity, of obsession and thwarted dreams ... A rich, thoughtful novel.' — *New Books*

TRENCHERMAN

Eben Venter is the critically acclaimed author of *Wolf, Wolf* (Scribe, 2015). He was raised on a sheep farm in Eastern Cape, South Africa, and migrated to Australia in 1986. He has won numerous awards for his work, and currently holds an honorary appointment as professional associate in the Institute of English in Africa (ISEA) at Rhodes University.

Scribe Publications
18–20 Edward St, Brunswick, Victoria 3056, Australia
2 John St, Clerkenwell, London, WC1N 2ES, United Kingdom

Published by Scribe 2016

Published by arrangement with Tafelberg

Originally published in Afrikaans by Tafelberg, 2006

Editor: Lynda Gilfillan
Page design by Teresa Williams
Set in 11.5/16 pt Caslon by Teresa Williams

Printed and bound in the UK by CPI Group (UK) Ltd, Croydon CR0 4YY

9781925321135 (Australian edition)
9781925228366 (UK edition)
9781925307351 (e-book)

CiP records for this title are available from the British Library and the National Library of Australia

scribepublications.com.au
scribepublications.co.uk

TRENCHERMAN

EBEN VENTER

Translated by Luke Stubbs

SCRIBE
Melbourne • London

An organism that misses an opportunity for food may get another; an organism that misses an approaching predator is dead.

—— *Paul Whalen*

TRENCHERMAN – *a feeder, an eater (of a specific kind), a person who cadges free meals, a parasite.*

TRENCHER *(Middle English)* –
a cutting instrument, a knife; a person who carves meat.

TRENCH FOOT – *a painful condition of the feet caused by prolonged immersion in cold water or mud and marked by blackening and death of surface tissue.*

I

Only the gloom to the west, brooding over the
upper reaches, became more sombre every minute,
as if angered by the approach of the sun.

THE CALL CATCHES ME off guard: I'm on my knees in front of the sofa. It's late. Outside, the incessant rain has turned Melbourne cold and bitter.

"Marlouw, listen carefully please, you have to go back to South Africa and get Koert out of that damned country. For me." My sister on the phone. "Something's gone wrong," she says, "I know it. In my heart of hearts. For God's sake, Marlouw, he's all I have and he's drifting further and further away. He's buggered," and she draws a deep breath, hard against her palate.

I don't answer Heleen immediately – I realise she's hysterical. And in any case, this is no request: it's a command. One that will turn my life upside down.

The significance of the position into which I had frozen would become clear later. But there I was on my knees, with my cheek flat on the floor, my back hollow and my bum in the air, trying to fish a marble from under the sofa.

"What are you up to? Is that *you*, Marlouw? It's as if she's caught me in this bizarre position and I'm blushing.

"Why are you phoning so late, Heleen?" My voice sounds muffled. I'm upset, not myself. *Me*? Go back to dig Koert out? And who knows where the hell he is anyway? Would Koert bother to listen to me? It's unlikely. That's what I want to say, but you don't second-guess predestination. I already know that I have to go and there's no point struggling against it.

"Do you have any idea how long it's been since I last heard from Koert?" she babbles on breathlessly. She's been drinking.

"I've tried to get him on that number, I don't know how many times: *the number you have dialled is not available*. What's become of him? What are you doing, Marlouw?" She asks again, anxious that I might stop listening.

I get up slowly, careful not to misplace my foot. It's become more tender and bluer in this weather, even though my apartment has underfloor heating. The tiny marble, one from my childhood, remains under the sofa. I'm not sentimental about things like that. Well a little, maybe.

"Why am I saddling you with this?" Heleen's asking. She can't stop: her anxiety is overwhelming her.

I sense the urgency myself; with every word Heleen speaks I am more on edge. My routine's been disturbed. At this time of night I usually warm a bit of milk, wait until it's boiled, then pour it slowly over a teaspoon of eucalyptus honey.

"Every single morning I rush to my computer to check my e-mails," she continues. "Please, dear Lord, may Koert find it in his heart to write to his mother today. I don't even go down to the kitchen to make coffee; my mail is my first priority. When Jocelyn calls from below – Shall I bring your coffee up, Heleen? – I don't bother to answer. Is there any news from my one and only child? For God's sake, can't he even condescend – what's the word – to contact me? It's been how many months now?

"In the afternoons around lunchtime when I used to make his sandwich, smoked salmon and lettuce . . . he *loved* mayonnaise . . . I actually start shaking and run upstairs to check my e-mails again. Nothing, Marlouw, I'm telling you: nothing. And then it starts getting dark and the rain won't stop. Is there something in my inbox tonight? Not a thing. Again. Do you have any idea how it feels? Look, if he were here I'd have boxed his ears long ago. Oh, those ears of his, perfect little shells."

"Please, Heleen." I'm *not* sentimental.

"Listen, Marlouw . . ." she's afraid I've given up listening. "You *must* go and find Koert for me. I'll make sure there's enough money on your credit card. He's still on Ouplaas, he *has* to be there."

It's been ages since I've heard her, anyone, say "Ouplaas." Everything's upsetting me now.

"What on earth are you asking me, Heleen? I've made it clear, haven't I – to myself, to everyone – that I'll never set foot in South Africa again."

"What I haven't done for that child!" she persists. "And he did so well in his German. Bright. Though he's always had a mind of his own. The things he got up to. You know, I realised from the beginning he was worse than wild – there was no way I could control him."

"JP was strict on him."

"Rubbish. His father was never there to help. His father! Please, help me before I lose my mind. Listen, Marlouw, I'm convinced Koert is still on Ouplaas. Where else would he have found a roof over his head? Something has happened. I feel it. Why don't I hear from him? He used to phone all the time, then it stopped. No more signal. Then he mailed every day. Like clock-work. That also dried up. I've got a feeling Koert is sick, and he's on Ouplaas and there's nobody to look after him properly. You know, there's a plague in that land – it's totally out of control. The Lord doesn't hear my prayers any more, Marlouw. What's become of my son?"

"What about JP? Why don't you send him to look for Koert?"

"For God's sake. Please. JP! Not available. As in never ever. Mister JP called yesterday on his cellphone. Can you believe it! He was on the top floor of the Petronas Towers. You know, Kuala Lumpur. Phoned to show off. Tell me what you're doing there, JP, I asked him. Heleen, I wish you were here – he lied through his teeth – the whole city, the whole world is spread out below me, he said. Shame on him! You know, most of the time I feel sorry for him.

"So what do you think JP was doing on the tippy-top of the Petronas Towers? Oh, he was the guest of their minister of edu-cation. He was recruiting students for the engineering faculty here in Melbourne. Mr Bigdeal with his bow tie and all. Feather-ing his own little nest. Heleen, you simply do not understand. It's our bread and butter, man. You know, when he starts calling me *man* I nearly have a fit. I'm his bloody wife, and our child is go-ing to the dogs."

"Maybe Koert's all right, who knows," I try again, though I'm not convinced of what I'm suggesting myself. And as far as JP's concerned – it was only the other day he told me: Don't let your foot bugger your whole life up, Marlouw. Come to the Daily Planet one night – it's a luxury brothel with everything you need. No, I never see JP the way Heleen does.

"To the dogs!" Heleen continues. "There'll be nothing left

of Koert. *Man*. Can you believe it, that's how JP speaks to me in these situations. JP Spies is the only one who doesn't know that the whole of Brighton gossips about us: he's got the sofa and she has the bed. Why did I ever fall for those legs of his? It's hopeless; JP doesn't give a damn about his son. He talks about Koert's *sojourn*." She imitates JP's voice: "Let the kid go if he wants to, Heleen. He's getting nothing more from me. We'll see who crawls back home one day bawling about pig swill."

She slurps at her drink. After all these years in Australia she's clung to the old boere habit of brandy and Coke for a sundowner. She's drunk and hard and sharp as ice, because – God knows – Heleen can be a bitch if she wants to. I suggest I come over, order a taxi. The warm milk will have to wait; I'm willing to disrupt my routine.

"Marlouw, you don't have to come out in this weather. Just promise me you'll go and find Koert and bring him back. That's all. Am I asking too much? Am I?"

"And what about my life? What about my responsibilities? How long do you think it will take to track Koert down? Months and months – who knows? I *do* have a life, Heleen. You're phoning me in the middle of the night." I know right away that I've slipped up: this is exactly what she wants so that she can torment me.

"Your life, Marlouw? God, don't make me laugh. You with all your education – and you end up in Australia selling pots."

"You're full of shit, Heleen." A gust of wind hurls sheets of rain against the wall-to-wall window. My whole apartment shudders. Let her blabber on. She won't wind me up this easily. I'm better off than she is. I'm an agent for Paderno stainless steel pots, and I've never been ashamed of it. Heleen can't even afford them. They're the most luxurious cookware on the market and my clients include some of Melbourne's top restaurants. Though to be honest, there have been times when I've thought that chefs only buy my pots because they feel sorry for me. Because of my foot. But then I tell myself: Don't be silly, Marlouw.

"Don't mess with me and my job."

"Listen, Marlouw. I'll see to your affairs while you're away. Introduce me to your chefs and I promise you, your business won't suffer. I'll twist them around my little finger. You think I can't? You're not the only one with a head for business. If you're not prepared to do it for me, do it for Koert. I know you care about him. Go and get him – dare to do something you've never done before."

"Go to bed, Heleen. You've had far too much to drink."

"And you? You know, I happened to see you one night wandering the streets with a bottle of wine under your arm. On the way to that chic apartment of yours. The loneliest man on earth."

"You're going too far now, Heleen. You're talking about things you know nothing about. Besides, why do you want Koert back so badly? Why? Have you given *that* any thought?"

"What do you know? You've never had a child. Can I tell you something I've never dared say before, Marlouw? Something's eating away at you. And do you know what it is? Do you? You're bitter and twisted . . . because Pappie and Mammie never had your foot fixed."

She's got me now. Always misunderstands me. Deliberately. Been doing it since we were kids. "I'm off to bed now. I don't feel like your shit tonight. Do you have any idea what time it is? It's morning already. I've had enough."

I thought the two of us were far too alienated for her to upset me any more, yet she has. Last night I dreamt again that all I had was a cramp in my foot, and when I woke – the waking was still part of the dream – my foot was fine and I could walk away like any normal person. And then I really woke up. It's an old dream.

For a long time I say nothing. I hear Heleen swallow and breathe. I see her in her jungle room with the zebra skin on the tiled floor and the *kieries* and shields and masks against the wall, and her pedicured feet up on Pappie's stinkwood chair – she got it in the end, I really didn't mind. Her toy pom in the hollow of her knees, her brandy and Coke in her one hand, Courtleigh in the cigarette holder in the other, perfect symmetry. And I imagine creeping up on her from behind and she may as well have been deaf because she's got no idea what's about to happen. I come from behind and strangle her then and there – she *has* gone too far. No one talks to me like that.

The silence over the phone lasts too long for her liking, and Heleen becomes anxious. "Marlouw, please, don't abandon me now. Forgive me, I beg you. Look, I'm on my knees. Anything. For Pappie and Mammie's sake then, please. Martin Jasper Louw," she spells it out to emphasise the seriousness of her call.

"Ask me anything," she whispers, picks me up like you'd play with your baby brother until I imagine her delicious brandy breath against my cheek. "Do this one, last favour for me."

"You don't know what you're asking. Who'd be crazy enough to do it?"

"*I* can't go. How could I, Marlouw?" She's choking on her eagerness to turn the situation around. "I miss you, you know. You never visit me. Don't you know me any more? Marlouw, listen. Just this once, even if I'm not clever enough for you."

She talks faster and faster: "Remember the time you and I

were swimming in the dam and you suddenly began screaming till you turned blue, the tractor tyre had punctured and was sinking like a rock and you were treading water. I paddled out to you on a tree stump and grabbed your arms and put them round the stump and saved your life. Don't you remember that day?"

"Okay then, Heleen. I'll think about it and let you know tomorrow." I don't wait for her answer; I know she's hanging on at her end of the line. At *this* end, I've become motionless. My stomach, though, churns at the way the assignment is taking possession of me. I had never wanted to return to a country where a white skin was seen as a badge of privilege.

"'Night, Heleen," and I put the receiver down to get rid of her, lift my Japara from the hall stand, put it on and let the door slip closed behind me on its quiet, oiled hinges – like all the doors in my lovely white apartment. I walk out into the drowning city, the collar of the oilskin turned high against my neck.

It's pelting, Pappie would have said, although this kind of deluge isn't something he'd ever experienced. I stick to the fence along the footpath all the way down Dandenong Road. Callistemon and lilli-pilli flick against my Japara. The shrubs have filled out, weighed down by water. In wet weather like this I become clumsy, though I don't like to admit it. It's as if the pavement moves under me as the water dams up with nowhere to go. Hobble-hobble. I'm afraid I'll fall, knock myself out cold, and there's nobody to help me this time of morning.

I climb the steps of the footbridge over Dandenong Road. I'm sweating in the Japara; in this rain I won't pause to take off my jersey. Below, cars row along the six-lane highway, their tyres spurting water. The small hours traffic jam of trucks and half-drunk taxis has begun.

The rain falls sheer like curtains, as if the southern heavens are emptying into a trench, spewing out water in a final seething rage. In the gloom, the city emits no more than an unholy glimmer through the downpour. I draw the hood tight, and even have to screen my eyes with my arm to keep the water out.

I'll let Heleen know what I've decided tomorrow. I don't know what to think. It's not the kind of mission one can decide on unequivocally. And here, on this pathetic bridge across this artery of a highway – is there anything here to redeem me? This city has never embraced me, never held me to her bosom. Why not get the hell out of here? At arm's length, twenty years now. That's Melbourne. Heleen and JP and I were young and slim when we emigrated here. The brilliance of the move, we told one another. We all spoke English so well, all of us so passionate.

Sweat runs into my eyes; water gets in after all. My thoughts become less ordered, more fluid, as if in imitation of the surroundings. They flow, my grip on them weakens, my view of the highway ahead and behind dims so that the vehicles now register as whirligigs, each rowing on its waterway.

Suddenly, the shock of a truck with livestock: cattle – sheep in fact. The smell of sodden wool rises up despite the rain; creatures of God, probably terrified out of their wits. I hear a feeble bleat, the remains of their primal language on a piece of open veld.

Lord, let me never see the fatherland and Ouplaas again; let me detach myself from it for the rest of my brief earthly existence. Lord God, help me! The photos of us on Ouplaas: me on Pappie's lap with the starling eggs in my hand. It's all been packed away between blotting paper in the dry-drawer of the nineteenth century Japanese cabinet that I bought specifically for this eternal storage. Why else pay so much for a few pieces of plank?

Pappie's coffin sinking into the cold earth – we were granted a winter's day to bury our father so that we could weep our fill once and for all. I observed the day through my dark glasses, looked over the heads of the bystanders to where a green patch had been planted around the new graveyard: bedraggled cypress saplings. It would take a lifetime for them to cast any shade across the graves. That's when I decided: I wanted nothing more to do with that piece of barren earth.

"Here, please." I took the spade and began filling the grave up myself. Ours was a history that had passed for good. There was sobbing all around, and a mournful gloom. Our father was the last of the generations who'd lived and multiplied there. Then it became even clearer: Ouplaas had long since ceased to be mine and Heleen's. It should be left to the three families who'd been working the farm for the past thirty, forty years.

What did Heleen and I want a bloody farm for? Let *them* take it over – November Hlongwane who was in charge of the sheep, and his two children, Pilot and Esmie Phumzile, and Nombulelo Mildred, the old woman who'd wiped our bottoms, and her son Lehlono, and ouma Zuka and Frans and Sindiswa Zuka and their little boy, Headman, and the rest of their offspring. Let all of them have Ouplaas and make something of it.

Heleen went berserk the day I suggested it. There was a tea at Tannie Driekie's place, and the moment I mentioned it, Heleen threw down her plate of milk tart and dragged me out by my arm. Her pathetic little plan became transparent immediately. Imagine – she wanted the family farm to be put on the market straight away so that she could take her cut, transfer it to her Australian account and redo the en-suite of their Brighton house in marble.

"You're so righteous, Marlouw. Little twit," she said to me that day. By then she spoke mostly English. At first she despised me for wanting to give the farm away, but later conceded.

The Ouplaas title deed was transferred to the three families. That day, Mildred – we didn't call her Nombulelo, of course – dropped the reserve she had towards white people and threw her arms, sinewy as cow-hide riempies, around Heleen's neck. Mildred cried, and eventually Heleen did too.

My heart beats faster. The air I'm breathing in is too damp. Here, in the middle of a bridge over a hellish highway, I realise that I share the fear of the sheep in the truck. It's welling up inside me: the horror of Heleen's charge. Till a moment ago I'd only thought superficially about the mission; but now the reality is bursting open before me, monstrous and malformed.

I will exchange my embarrassingly safe urban existence for a country I'd decided to avoid for ever. The assignment will sweep me away completely. I had committed myself to something I was now becoming afraid of. But if you're afraid of something ahead of time, *and* you are aware of your fear, you are able to conquer it. *I* will. And I *will* believe that I can do it. Yet my heart is faint, my mind shut to the likely outcome of the mission. And what about my disability? I struggle on across the bridge.

What kind of person has Koert become, and what's kept him away from his mother for two years? How can I possibly know? Now I have to go and dig him out of there. His crippled uncle with two pairs of reading glasses: one for reading and one as a back-up. What remains to be read *there*? I no longer know anything about that land. Koert will, in all probability, run me off Ouplaas and I'll come crawling back like a dog.

Despite being polished, my shoes can't withstand the flood,

and moisture seeps into my socks. Water streams down my sleeves from my hands shielding my face. I shudder at the gloom that descends upon me with the dead colour of lead.

Nothing remains but for me to abandon myself to my mission. It has become a matter of honour to me. I've promised myself I will go, even though I haven't told Heleen yet. By now she's probably lying on her bed, worn to a frazzle, with the toy pom to warm her breast.

A truck slams on its brakes below the footbridge, slides to a standstill, and cars splutter anxiously past the colossal object. I glimpse a white knuckle clutching a steering wheel.

I wrap the two flaps of my Japara tightly around myself. I'm drenched with sweat and seeping water, and I shiver uncontrollably. I want to turn my back on the bridge and the city once and for all, and on the terror that the mission has aroused in my life, but this is impossible. It has become a fixed impossibility. My only option is to try and run away, and so I hobble leftwards across the bridge, all the while sliding my hand along the waist-high railings to keep my balance on the walkway.

2

Often far away there I thought of these two, guarding
the door of Darkness, knitting black wool as for a warm pall, one introducing,
introducing to the continuously unknown, the other scrutinising
the cheery and foolish faces with unconcerned old eyes.

NOT HELEEN, but her char, Jocelyn, opens the front door. I'm frozen from lack of sleep.

"Oh, good morning, Marlouw, up so early?" Her top lip lifts a fraction and curls against her nose.

"Morning, Jocelyn," I answer in Afrikaans, "seems you've started early yourself." She doesn't seem to mind that I'd noticed her top lip. I continue our old game, refusing to speak English to her. Jocelyn believes that I'll only have accepted her as an equal once I address her in English. But don't tell me she speaks English at home.

"Your sister is out, I don't think she was expecting you so early. Oh, this rain," she says more kindly. "I discovered mould on my leather shoes the other day." She's got the toy pom against her chest, wriggling and pawing to get at me.

"Stop that, Henrie, stop that now!" Jocelyn commands, afraid that the dog might trample wet marks on Heleen's mohair runner.

"You know where to hang that dripping coat of yours, or can

I take it for you?" She makes a half-hearted gesture, looks down at me, turns without lending a hand, and walks off to the kitchen.

She stops left of the Alexis Preller on the wall and purses her lips: "Mr Spies has been away for more than two weeks. And we're not expecting him back for some time."

In the kitchen, Jocelyn takes her place on one of the stools at the breakfast counter. There's knitting on her lap and she picks up what she'd apparently been doing when I rang the bell. Henrie jumps against my trousers and sticks out a pink tongue.

Jocelyn's skin has become whiter since she first started working for Heleen and JP. It's the result of ointments and creams – I have no idea what miracle potions are available these days. She was originally a brown woman from the Eastern Cape, from Aliwal North, not far from where we grew up. She never breathes a word about her origins. We've both got something we choose to hide.

I walk over to the cupboard where Heleen keeps the coffee and tea. There's a container of expensive instant coffee with a label I recognise. I choose a teabag.

"When will you start drinking real coffee in this house?"

"The coffee here is good enough for us, thank you very much. Can I tell you something, Marlouw? You are a terrible snob, and you don't really give a damn." Her long eyelashes, curled upwards, flicker across her pitch black eyes.

"Jocelyn, I don't care what you think of me."

"That's what I mean, see." She makes me look around at her, and immediately drops her eyes and continues knitting. The wool is black, and she's finished a gigantic piece. It tumbles between her legs and falls in folds onto the sterile kitchen floor. She's using a thick and a thin needle, the thick one pink, the thin one light blue. She stares at me until I sense her gaze, then looks down at her knitting once more. The minute I turn away, she starts staring again. I can feel it.

Waiting for the kettle to boil, I become aware of the slow rising effect of Heleen and JP's underfloor heating.

"There are Hertzog cookies in the cupboard above you."

My left calf relaxes. Since my left foot is turned in and downwards, I am forced to walk on the outside edge of the tip of the foot, so the calf is underdeveloped, even though it has to work hard. It's the most common form of clubfoot, of *talipes equinovarus*. A term most people don't know, and even if they do get to hear of it, they think you've got a screw loose too.

"What's the matter, Jocelyn? Don't you trust me, or what?" Her gaze is so intense that I have to turn around and face her.

Jocelyn has forced her plump feet into two merino wool slippers; she swings them back and forth like a girl. Her ankles have remained a sandy brown.

"Cookie?" she indicates towards the cupboard with her eyes.

"Thank you, Jocelyn." And so, despite all, a measure of empathy arises between us.

"When are you expecting Heleen back?"

"She won't be long at all, she had an appointment at the clinic that she couldn't miss, but she won't be too long. She wants to see you."

"The traffic will be terrible in this rain. I'd rather stay at home on days like this."

"Well, some of us have to get to their work. I stick to the tram in this weather. Much safer. I love watching the school-children on the trams, they're so mischievous." She stops when I don't share her laughter.

"But no, I don't think she'll be long. She wants to see you. She can't wait to hear what you're going to say. Since Koert stopped calling, Heleen hasn't been herself. She doesn't sleep at night. She's got her cigarettes and her drink and not much else. I'm worried about your sister." She turns herself around on the stool. I stand at the window.

The surface of the swimming pool rises and falls: it breathes under the pouring rain. In the manicured Brighton gardens the roses are going black with mildew; Heleen's Just Joeys are rotting from the ground up.

"Nice." I look at the cookie in my hand. Jocelyn cooks all Heleen and JP's food. Her cookies and desserts are outstanding. Though why Heleen raves about Jocelyn's main dishes, I don't know. To me, Jocelyn's boboties are not much more than an excess of sugar and salt. She's utterly devoted to Heleen. Actually, Jocelyn and I are attached to each other in a funny sort of a way.

"Marlouw," she suddenly exclaims from behind, "I've heard about Koert, you know." She startles me – for the first time ever in Australia she speaks to me in Afrikaans.

"Let this remain between the two of us, please. I haven't told your sister, all right. I don't want to upset her any more. She's not well as it is. And I can't see her getting any better. The mental compartment too, you know." She taps her temple with the thinner, blue knitting needle.

"Mr Spies is in Malaysia," she shrugs, and remains silent for me to take in what she apparently dares not say. If JP were home, Jocelyn wouldn't allow herself to sit in the Spieses' chairs like this, especially if JP were in the same room.

"Mr JP and your sister, Marlouw, she'll probably let you know in no uncertain terms what's going on." She's doesn't look at her knitting, watches me intently. Her insinuation has caught me off guard. We've always been careful not to say too much – especially about my sister and JP.

"What have you heard about Koert, Jocelyn?"

"My niece says the people have become afraid of Koert. Krista says he deals in meat and that he controls everything there. If you want meat you have to be in his good books. The whole district is at his mercy."

"Scared? Of Koert?" I fall silent, think about the likelihood of anyone being afraid of a boy like Koert. Koert and I have spoken about fear. What I remember best about Koert is the whiteness of his biceps when he rowed on the Yarra. Sometimes when Heleen had felt nauseated by her friends' glitziness, she invited me to watch the private schools' regattas.

The white, the whiteness of his biceps. It was beautiful. Koert was an exceptional rower. And his father encouraged him, though Heleen maintains that's rubbish. Koert needed support from his father – it was the child in him – he was a boy, for heaven's sake. JP Spies expected too much, though. Then Koert upped and left Melbourne. I'd seen it coming.

One night shortly before his departure, he burst into my apartment. I did feel something for Koert, that I know. "Beer?" I offered, surprised by his visit. I immediately got two beers from my new stainless steel fridge. Koert appeared hesitant in my presence, unsure of what had actually brought him here. It wasn't like him. I could have hugged him. Should have; I should have.

There he was, young and strapping in his Billabong T-shirt, and a little high. He was shrewd enough to turn his uncertainty to his own advantage. He drew me closer with his eyes, still closer, and then dropped me. I must admit: Koert had a power that could unnerve you if you didn't remind yourself that he was only beginning his life as a man. It's not for nothing that his mother called him "my king".

"I want to bum around for a while," he said. "Actually, I've no clue where. And don't ask me what for and why. I have to get out of here. Who wouldn't? Melbourne makes me sick." He downed half his beer in a single swig, looked at me as if to say I should know who he really was, that his uncertainty was merely a front. And that it was only a matter of time before it'd be over. Koert's eyes focused sharply, became glassy, and I recognised something of Heleen's and Pappie's and all our long, distant ancestry in his gaze.

"A horse needs lots of oil on its skin to stand in the rain all the time," Pappie speaks an old, old sentence in my head and gestures with his hands. I see him talk – confident of his views, a sympathetic man – then fade away. Something ignites between the two poles of Pappie's emotion. There is the will that pushes and shoves and seeks to lord it over others merely to survive. And then the faltering sets in, the hesitation and the doubt.

"You don't need to know what exactly you want to do with your life right now, Koert. You're still young. Do what you want. I would, if I were in your shoes."

He wasn't getting anything from me, I could see, but I continued: "You know where you come from, you know what your mother's taught you. She cares about you deeply, man, even if she's messing you around right now."

"You know what? I'm going to look for the old farm in South Africa. See what's up," he announced, all gung-ho. "No one ever wanted to take me when I whinged about going." And then he noticed my expression: "What's there to be afraid of?"

"What, indeed?" I replied and collapsed into my chair as I thought about the land and the farmstead where we all nurtured our own secrets. All of it, even the memories, had long stopped belonging to us. "What, indeed?" I replied again.

Jocelyn knits away on the tall stool, click-click-clack.

"Come on, we all know Koert," I say, "he's far too wet behind the ears – how could anyone be afraid of him? You're talking nonsense, now, Jocelyn. He always played with Henrie on the beach down the road. And cleaned the oil off the penguins and that sort of thing. Koert's a gentle boy. You've got it wrong, Jocelyn."

I know what I'm doing. I want to reduce the remark about Koert to everyday small talk. What is Jocelyn turning my nephew into? A boer with a heavy brow and a thick neck, shocking his cattle into the crush with an electric prod. The thing is, I want to remain normal. I'm leaving in a few days: my life will be turned on its head. That's what I'm trying to resist.

"You'll see, Marlouw. Or rather, you'll have to go and see for yourself. I'm only saying what I've heard myself. Krista is my sister's eldest, and they're not exactly the gossiping type. She's got no reason to lie to me."

"I didn't say she lied."

"We're a decent family. She writes me everything because I asked her about Koert Spies. Krista's been at the abattoir there for a long time. Totally filthy, apparently. She worries about diseases, but there are no other jobs. She hears what's going on in the district. People talk. And she says she was once on your pappie and mammie's Ouplaas. But not a sign of Koert. All she knows is that he's become a man with lots of power. People come and ask him things and he's got all the answers: do this, do that. Seems he's got flocks of sheep and controls the meat that comes into the abattoir. Krista says he's become a different sort of person, Marlouw. And there're other things as well. People who simply disappear when they don't do as he says. Though I'd rather shut up about that. It's not for me to say that it is in fact like this, and then to pass judgment." She plucks at a strand of wool to loosen the ball from where it's got stuck in her floral bag.

"What sort of people are you talking about, Jocelyn?"

"I love your sister dearly. And Mr JP. I feel sorry for him too, I'll have you know. I'd do anything for them, you know it, but I'd never go to that country to find their child for them. Marlouw, you'd have to be crazy to go."

"Where does Heleen keep her cigarettes?" Jocelyn points her knitting needle at the jungle room. Her eyes are big as saucers, and despondent. Next to Heleen's chair – covered in faux leopard skin – is a snuff box, turned by our Oom Willie. I know the thing.

"I'll get you an appointment with my clairvoyant, I can tell you won't take my advice. I look in your eyes and see you've allowed yourself to be caught up in a foolishness beyond words. Don't go, Marlouw, I care about you all, for you too." She's so overcome by emotion that the sensitive toy pom jumps and yaps at her woolly slippers.

Jocelyn had lost it, I reckoned that day. Later, when I realised that she'd in fact warned me against the madness, I revised my "reckoning". A long way into the journey, deep in the interior, I realised how close I'd come to that madness. And although I didn't return crazy in the end, the consequences of that journey would remain with me forever.

As for now – should I visit Jocelyn's clairvoyant before leaving? Mammie had also had fundamental doubts and chose to place her faith in signs. On her deathbed, her skin like bleached muslin, she predicted the number of days Pappie would survive her death. At her insistence I had to write it in her Bible, right there, next to Psalm 23 alongside the "green pastures". She was spot on, down to the exact day.

"Marlouw, come here, let me see your palms."

Slowly I walk towards Jocelyn – she's bundled her mass of black knitting onto the counter next to her.

From today I'm making peace with Jocelyn. My heart had never really hardened towards her. She bleaches herself because people might look down on her. Just think of all the talk when you can't hear them! I lay my right hand in hers as she has asked.

"Oh, I see something like a huge rugby field with players, helter-skelter. There are puddles, there are a whole lot of whirlpools, and you're somewhere in between it all. Look, you get completely mixed up here." She follows a line with her nail, it branches and stops, and a second one runs down from the right. "You can see the chaotic spin right there. All rules have been forgotten."

I know it's to do with my foot, but she can't bring herself to mention it.

"It's Koert's digression, this. Let him get back on track himself," she whispers, her breath full of spittle and vanilla. "Let him find his own way home. You can't force him, Marlouw." She holds her hand in mine, not in the least bit uncomfortable by my proximity. Nor me by hers.

"Jocelyn?" My voice breaks so that I'm forced to look away from the love she shows me. Her heart is so much bigger than mine. Jocelyn Albertse could have been my mother.

"What, my darling?"

"I have to go, that's all I know." I look outside. Rain has pushed the water over the edge of the pool and it is damming up on the surrounding lawn. The grass shines through, slimy green.

She places my hand right against her beating heart and lets hers rest on mine a long time. "It's his own decision; it's his path, he's chosen it himself. All right, Marlouw? Just remember that."

We both look up when the front door opens. Jocelyn lets go of my hand. Henrie darts from the kitchen and barks at the familiar footsteps. It will be Heleen. I stand back, Jocelyn takes up her knitting again. Heleen will see us as she usually does.

"Are you strong enough for this?" She points the knitting needle at my foot. "They won't respect you. It's not a marshmallow land where everyone waits politely for the white master to go in first. Have you thought about how those people will see you?" She speaks quietly so as to finish before Heleen comes in. "I don't want to hurt you, Marlouw." She's noticed my look.

"Shame man, Marlouw, don't think that of me. Those people have so many needs themselves. You know it. And what will a cripple's" – she can bring herself to say it – "what will a cripple's life mean when you're as down and out as them? I want to be sure you know it. Krista says lots of mothers and lots of young girls and lots of children die every day. They've stopped counting their dead."

She looks me straight in the eyes. "Something else: will you cope if you see things inside you that you've never seen before? Have you got the mental strength? I don't know. Who's strong enough for things like that?"

"Does Heleen know any of this?"

"No. And it's better that way. She loves Koert. She adores him more than anyone else. We must give her hope, Marlouw.

That's all she needs. A little bit of hope, so the poor thing can sleep again."

"And JP?"

"Mr JP." She shrugs. Heleen enters with the dog at her heels.

"Oh my God, Marlouw," and she kisses me on both cheeks the way it's done here in Brighton.

"Jocelyn, make us a nice pot of tea. How far have you got?" She looks at Jocelyn's knitting. "Any good news for me, Marlouw? Shall we have something stronger? Rather get the ice, Jocelyn." She's ticking at quite a rate, there's a rash on her neck.

"Aren't those trousers too loose on you, Marlouw – I'm only asking." She tries to laugh, but the hands with the sculptured nails are all over the place. She's shaking. She's reached her limit.

"I will, Heleen. I will go and see if I can find Koert. I'll do what I can. I don't promise anything – how can I? – but I'll go and try."

"Oh, Marlouw," and she embraces me, kisses me like in the old days. Her perfume smothers me. She wipes her face.

"Here, I must show you this so you know the Koert I'm talking about. Before you all think I've gone mad." From a drawer in the jungle room a piece of paper with Koert's last e-mail emerges:

Hey you people down under
There's a max weight auf meine Herz . . . here he comes
I've got doubts bout cumin back to Auzzie, oi oi oi
Boom *** shakalak
I sooo badly want to check you out, the ace family, I love . . . mmm
Mmmisss you and Henrie . . . but right now knoweth
I

I maketh the move cause some people demand this and that, aber es
ist kein muss . . . Count yours Koert–truly out . . . it's 50/50 I say
you brothers, BUT
its just that I sort of got a thingy on the boiler
starting from scratch in Auzzie izze zero option
did I ever confirm I come back one day . . . so why
do some brothers and sisters there by you
menace me
so . . . so confusin!!!
I've got courage for all decisions on my ace
How's that sounding for my JP daddy?
I taketh responsibility for whatever might go wrong
From here on that is THE option
includin includin
takin responsibility for the people right here, brothers of mine.
The people they needeth me like the earth needeth rain
I'm not scared of making mistakes
I learneth from them cause I made them myself
they give me POWER, can youz feel it?
its my 1st time I feel like this
without being plastered
If I come back now I'll clock in a failure
I want to feel good, my confidenz = right up there
love the eternal family. Running out of O²
for xmas an new years maybe I'll be cumin, who knows
you never know, I don't know myself. It's the true.
Koert S♠ieS

Jocelyn and I snort, though it's not in the least bit funny. Heleen
hides her face and doesn't even notice me handing the printout

back to her. None of us can begin to imagine what sort of person Koert has become after hearing that.

"See how he spells his name. And his language. He's not off his head yet, that I know." Heleen looks at me and Jocelyn, and we nod. "See the date, look here. See how old this e-mail is. Nothing. I've tried to reply. Back! All my mails simply bounce back."

Jocelyn covers her mouth with her hand. Slowly, like tar being poured, the black knitting slips from her lap and falls misshapen on the floor. The dog suddenly realises there's a river of black knitting between him and his mistress and tries to wade through it: each time he tries to get free the wool makes waves and entangles him even more. We all look down at Henrie drowning in Jocelyn's wool. The dog wails like a baby.

"Look what's happening to little Henrie!" Jocelyn wiggles the dog loose, gets up, then looks straight at me. Out you go, out, she shoos me off with a bunch of upside down fingers. Right across the ocean.

"Go then, just go." And so she has the last word.

3

*A queer feeling came to me
that I was an impostor.*

HELEEN TURNS UP at my apartment on the last day. She's invited herself. From her handbag she takes travel gifts: a compass, a solar battery torch and a bottle of pills for any conceivable ailment – by prescription only.

Now that there's no turning back for me, she's calmer. "I even sleep through the night," she sneezes pathetically. She chatters away, but her voice is full and strong. She reminds me a lot of Mammie when she's like this.

I pour her a glass of Chardonnay; she drinks it so fast it immediately derails her.

"Take a look at this," and she lifts her viscose shirt. Her perfect navel, in the middle of her tanned stomach, has been pierced by a solid gold ring.

She's delighted: it *is* a lovely ring. Strangely cheerful, like someone on uppers, she stands close against me. One by one I smell her scents . . . I smell all of her: the rubber of her gold and hazel-brown walking shoes, the day perfume I've come to know on her woman's body, and her hair, apple sweet. She can be so impulsive – it attracts me, despite myself. That's what got JP too. Then I withdraw.

"Why the funny look, Marlouw? You think I'm being stupid, don't you? Your silly sister with her marriage in ruins and her only son to hell and gone. I know that that's what you've thought about me all these years. Can I tell you something, Marlouw? You may be clever with all your books and your degree in I-don't-know-what, but it hasn't done you any good. Look what's become of you, I'm *not* stupid."

I step back; it's not my intention to reject her. My reaction has little to do with her. Although she can be very tiresome, and my heart is heavy as it is. "Why should I undertake this insane mission to look for your child when all you do is abuse me?" my voice bounces off the polished surfaces of my kitchen. "I owe you nothing, Heleen. And now you're making it impossible for me to love you."

"You don't really love me anyway."

I don't answer. With her top that's slipped back all rumpled, she suddenly seems run-down. I must get her out of here; I'm in no state to cheer her up. Since I've decided to go, I have too much of my own stuff to deal with. *I* have to get away from here. This assignment has come just in time.

Quieter now: "What do you want from me, Heleen? What have I done to you, man?"

"Sorry, Marlouw. Sorry-sorry a hundred times." She searches for her cigarettes. "I'm going off my mind. I'm not hiding any-thing from you, I swear. Is it a sin to want my own child back? You're the only one who can help me. Who else can I talk to? JP doesn't even know where we keep the extra toilet rolls at home." She starts crying and buries her hands under her armpits. One on each side. No matter how far gone, she maintains her poise in an attempt to preserve herself. It's all she has.

I refill her glass; before taking her drink she scratches around for a pill in her bag. Her tiny Adam's apple moves as she swallows. I wipe her eyes with one of my unbleached cotton dishcloths.

"He doesn't even know where we keep our toilet paper," she giggles.

"Just a moment, Heleen. I'll be back right away – have to straighten my own head. It's getting late."

I turn away from Heleen who remains standing, her hand clasping the neck of the bottle of Chardonnay, her body language reproachful: So what about me, now that you've got a life to live?

I close my bedroom door and stick my hand under my unbuttoned shirt. I'm in despair. The word that marks this journey is taking hold of me in a terrifying way: impostor. A crook. A person who takes on a false identity to deceive someone else.

Heleen and I share the same blood, but she's pawned herself in this country and this self-indulgent suburb for a gold ring and a marble en-suite – she had it done, anyway – and look at her now: a loser. Of course she doesn't see herself like that. And I don't know whether I'm bearing false witness against her with these thoughts. Pappie and Mammie stood upright as cypresses on the earth, stubborn and strong. How could they ever have imagined that their daughter would find it liberating to sit completely alone in an alien city, licking froth from her coffee spoon and planning her shopping – even though she lacks for nothing.

I couldn't possibly attempt the journey for Heleen's sake. And absolutely not for Koert's. On that I agree with his father – this is Koert's choice, let him fuck up if he wants to. I could never wish for Koert's return as passionately as Heleen does, and that she needn't know.

For my own sake and my own salvation. Now *there's* a reason. There is no other way of commandeering the will to go. As long as everyone understands that. Certainly, *imponere* means to deceive deliberately. I don't want to deceive anyone. Not Heleen – and not Koert. That's if I ever find him. Neither of them ever has to know what's inside *my* head.

I may never return. But let me not damn my mission before it's even started. "Give us a laugh, Marlo'tjie," Mammie always tickled and quacked for all she was worth. "Come on, trumpet like an elephant for Mammie, let's hear him laugh now."

If only I could break out, let go of myself until I feel the beat of my pulse, smell the blood; if only I could dance and sing – shock myself into life – and when I've lost all sense, break into laughter.

"Here you have the Paderno series 6100, here the *colapasta per pentola*, the colander for your bouillon pot. Essential for every kitchen. That you know, of course. Simply lift the colander by its two sturdy handles, like this, slowly, slowly." I demonstrate my wares to the new chef at the Italian restaurant on Fitzroy Street.

His name is Rosario, and he has a genuine Roman nose. When I arrive late afternoon with my pots, Rosario has a five o'clock shadow and smells the way a chef should. His name has the sandy scent of rosemary. I like him and do my level best to assure him that I do not underestimate his self-confidence or knowledge.

"Look," I try again, "let me explain carefully. I'm talking about this type of pot: the *colapasta per pentola* comes in diameters of 32, 36 and 40cm. You lift it slowly from your bouillon

pot into which it fits perfectly – that's the difference Paderno
makes – and all your soup bones and vegetable stalks and pep-
percorns, even mustard seeds, remain in the colander, and you're
left with a perfectly drained bouillon. Like this – you know, of
course." And I gently place the beautiful stainless steel colander on its feet and throw my hands up like I've seen Italians do.
"You're not buying pots, you're buying time. Logical, isn't it?"

The young man looks at me in utter amazement as I hold
forth on my pots, and embarrassment wells up inside me.

"You're lucky to have got work here. This is one of the top
restaurants in the city. But you *do* deserve it," I flatter him to win
him over. I've got him now; I can relax. You have to be able to
play with the chef, if he catches on and plays along, you've sold
your pot.

And I, Marlouw, hobble away contented for the day. Though
beneath my vest a cold sweat has broken out, and all the while I
couldn't wait to escape Rosario's stuffy kitchen.

I can sell anything, except the lie to myself. I detest lies. But
what if I lose my reserve on the journey, am able to pull the sock
from my gammy foot and walk about for everyone to see, laughing all the way. And what if I even succeed in returning Koert to
Heleen?

I look out of the window: the rainwater is level with the rim
of my apartment's gutter. The slightest loss of balance could
make it ripple and overflow. The caretaker is aware of the threatening danger of a flood.

"We're living in a bog here, Marlouw," he'd said right at the
start of the deluge. Since then I haven't seen him. He's chosen
to draw his curtains and shut himself up in his ground floor flat.
The whiff of stale, warmed-up coffee filters from under his door.

Heleen walks into my room with a mosquito net.

"Come on, Heleen, you don't get mosquitoes on the farm. Remember? There's always a drought. There aren't mosquitoes during a drought. You *have* forgotten."

"How do you know?"

"I'm just saying what I remember." I won't let her upset me any further.

"Have you thought about sleeping arrangements when you get there? Where will you stay, Marlouw? Oh, I do hope everything works out okay . . . I can only hope and pray."

One by one, I roll my underpants into sausages for packing; I don't bother to respond. Last night I woke up when the rain poured down, it was like a cloudburst. A while before waking – in the deeper domain where occasionally some or other aspect of myself is briefly illuminated – a human figure appeared, dumb and arrogant, bending over an old, sleeping man. The expression in the figure's eyes was so foolish that he couldn't distinguish between life and death. He was capable of anything. And the old, sleeping man's face was highly agitated.

The issue of sleeping arrangements. Surely, once I arrive in Maitland, they'll organise something for me in the house on Ouplaas. No doubt someone is sleeping right now on the very coir mattress I used while I dreamt my ripe teenaged dreams – I can't imagine myself lying on it again. There's the hotel in town, then, or the people who rented out guest rooms in the old days, if they're still around. I doubt it, though. Food and somewhere to sleep – they're the last things I want to think about now.

And what difference does it make how many of our people have remained in the dorp, for heaven's sake. Newspapers here only report the absolute worst. The great explosion was in the news for ever. No end to the overwhelming desperation of the people, the neediness that gets worse until it takes on another shape and enters the domain of fear.

There must surely be people who still eat and drink and sleep and care. I'll definitely find somewhere to sleep and something to eat. The only problem is, I don't know a soul out there any more: into the unknown and home. The joke's already on me.

Heleen's mosquito net is a sign of providence. It's a special one made of cotton. The tight weave won't allow a mosquito through, but is still okay for a slight breeze to reach your sleeping body.

"It's a good mosquito net, Heleen," I call after her. She's walked off again: she can work herself into a state and blurt things out without thinking.

"Well, pack it – I know it will make you feel better. What about your cellphone? Take mine if you want."

"Where will I charge the thing? Is there any electricity after the explosion, can you still get a signal?"

"Heavens, Marlouw, Koert used to e-mail me."

"It stopped," I interrupt her. "There must be a reason for his silence. Have you given that any thought? Can I finish on my own, Heleen? Would you wait for me below in the car? It's fifteen minutes before we have to leave."

"Okay, then. If you really want to keep to yourself like that." She gathers her gloves and handbag and umbrella at the door. "I'm leaving a photo of myself I'd like you to give to Koert. Don't forget, please."

The final moments in my apartment. The only living thing, my fish in its glass bowl, is already in the car. Jocelyn will feed it. I walk through the rooms, my footsteps muffled. I touch and look: the charcoal sheen of the lacquered wooden floor, the rare objects, my library. As I pass the rows of tall bookcases, I hold my breath. I've packed nothing, not a single book. From now on I want to rely on my memory. In the bathroom, I spray on a last few drops, but leave the bottle behind as well. Of no use in the world I'm going to – that I do realise. I bend and touch a kelim I'd recently acquired. Where it had rolled out and come to rest under the sofa, the marble winks its single eye at me.

I rise, pick up my suitcase, lighter than I'd expected, and hang my travel bag over the shoulder of the only jacket I'm taking. The door smoothly slips closed behind me.

The telephone rings. Should I? I'm not expecting any calls from my restaurant clients. Everything has been temporarily shut down; everyone is satisfied with their stock. Touching gifts arrived with their bon voyage wishes: pistachio nougat from Mr Di Stasio, Rosario's boss, a flask of rare extra virgin olive oil from the owners of Cicciolina, other things too. None of it will be lugged along.

Curious – though more because the separation from my possessions is too painful – I quickly open the door and pick up the telephone. It's Jocelyn.

"Yes, Jocelyn?"

"It's not too late to change plans, Marlouw."

"You're crazy, Jocelyn. I'm all packed; my plane's leaving in a few hours."

"Where is she? Where's Heleen?"

"She's waiting downstairs in the car, Jocelyn. I must go, man. I've prepared myself well." What's given the woman such a bee in her bonnet now? She's got nothing more to offer me. I've become reckless. Hearing Jocelyn's damning tone of voice, as if she knows better than me, the final step away from my apartment becomes the most natural thing in the world.

"If you pull out now, your sister won't take it too badly. I've made a few calls – there are other ways of getting him back. Better ways. JP will pay. I phoned him last night in Kuala Lumpur. He's prepared to pay everything. He also thinks it's crazy that you want to go there. You're walking straight into hell, Marlouw. Listen to me now. Heleen . . ."

"I'm not doing it for Heleen." The blinds and curtains are closed, leaving the apartment in glorious mourning.

"I know you care about your little nephew and want to save him," she uses Afrikaans again to steal my heart.

"I'm not going for Koert's sake. I've got my own reasons. I'm going because *I* want to go; I'm doing it for myself, Jocelyn. And you know what – I'm relieved to be able to say it to somebody at last."

To which she has no answer.

"I'm off now, Jocelyn. Thanks for your concern. I appreciate it, man. Take care of my sister. And everything of the best to you, too. Bye, Jocelyn."

"Okay, Marlouw. Hope you manage to keep all your marbles."

I sense her withdrawing and the distance that has always characterised our relationship is confirmed.

When I step onto the pavement – or rather, put my foot down carefully – I smile: I'm surprised at how gently the rain falls into the streaming gutters, into the rivulets next to the streets and onto the water gardens in front of flats and houses, like the tears of old people.

*

I have to get to Fiji to catch a flight to Johannesburg. South African Airways no longer complies with the standards of the International Airways Organisation, and is refused landing rights
in my country.

I board at Nadi Airport, dripping sweat. The cabin is as
sweltering hot as the tropical heat outside and has been poisoned
by the jet fuel that's seeped in. The aeroplane is a rattletrap,
the outbound flight alarming in the true sense of the word. All
around me, passengers in the first class cabin are apparently going through the same experience, and drink more than I've ever
seen people drink on an aeroplane.

When the tail creaks ominously again I check out my neighbour. I have to speak to somebody. The man's already stepped
over me once to go and do his business, and returned with the
smell of cigarette smoke heavy on him.

The name printed in gold letters on his briefcase betrays his
origins. Cautiously, I switch to Afrikaans. "It's a flying coffin
this. Look at the seats. We'd better say our prayers." I wait for JL
Smit to answer. There're not many of us Afrikaners left, and who
knows whether this one can – or wants – to speak Afrikaans.

"Good heavens, man" he says in a dark brown voice, delighted. "Look what we've got here." He offers his hand with the
rings. "Smittie."

He's a Smittie, of course. If your surname is Smit, you're a
Smittie, it doesn't matter what your initials stand for. The famili-
arity almost reduces me to tears.

"Yes, man, the aeroplane, what can you say." He laughs. "Actually, I'm on my way to Lesotho via Johannesburg then on to
Angola," – I wasn't trying to question him – "let me put it like
this: I've been on worse flights than this, and I'll be flying a lot

more, on much worse," and he laughs again. I smell the whisky.

"What do you know about conditions over there? In the interior, I mean."

"Dollars and syndicates. That's what keeps the country going. After the explosion in the south, things deteriorated rapidly. Most foreign investors pulled out. Jobs became as scarce as clean cunt. And the further into the interior you go, the harder it gets to find the things you need to survive. And I don't mean living decently. I mean simply staying alive. Everything's finished, my friend. Except for the syndicates. They're active in the platteland too. That's my experience. They've cast their nets far and wide. Make sure you pick up a few dollars at the airport – you'll need them. The past few years I've preferred to go to Angola. My wife and children live there. This time I need to collect my *tierboskatjies* in Lesotho. Beautiful. Still so young. Dirt cheap." He winks. "Need to make a quick buck."

His posh, flashy rings. The gold chains around his neck. His wild kittens. The raunchy breathlessness with which he talks about them, the saliva on his lips. I do my sums and come to sinister conclusions. Not all Smitties are Smitties, though perhaps I'm wrong. Anyway, if I'm right, I don't shrink back.

"Has anything beautiful survived? The natural environment was always so breathtaking – if I may use that word. Surely something remains? I always used to see a secretary bird along that endless road between Beaufort West and Aberdeen. With its waistcoat and quill pen. Always. And the graatjiemeerkats, what's happened to them?"

"Meerkats?" he gives a sour little smile.

"Okay, let me say what I mean."

"Fuck, man!" he interrupts. "Meerkats, you say. You'll have

to try the London Zoo for those." Smittie laughs and laughs. It's hard to believe anyone could be so cynical.

I want to grab his hands with the rings like golden testicles and hold them tight and say: Look, neef, I didn't mean it like *that*, do you think I'm so naïve that I have no clue where I'm heading?

"I never travel to Africa for the animals. My guess is your meerkats and birds have all been caught in traps and gobbled up by now. If they still exist, *I* don't get to see them. Perhaps some have survived in the mountains. Why do you want to know?"

"Which mountains, do you think?"

"I couldn't care less about that stuff, man, don't you get it?" He becomes rude.

"Hell, I didn't want to upset you."

"Look, man – what's your name again?"

"Marlouw."

"Look, Marlouw, I only see what I want to see." He remains rather surly. "I have no idea what's become of your little creatures. Once you get there, you'll have to look out for yourself. That's the vital thing. Forget about the animals and stuff or you'll never get out of there alive. If you have too many expectations, make sure you get rid of them quickly. Stick to your basic needs: food, drink, somewhere to sleep, and relief for *this*." His mood changes like a mattress that's lifted and flipped in one go, and quickly, playfully, he rests his left hand with the gold knobs on my crotch.

"Have you perhaps heard of someone by the name of Koert Spies?" I ask him simply for the sake of saying something – I'm not at all used to having people touch me, doesn't matter where.

"What does he do, why's he there, where is he? Place him for me; maybe I'll have something on him for you. We whiteys don't differ much from one another – we go there for one reason only."

The man has no inhibitions, it's his profession. I start laughing uncontrollably. During all my years in the city I avoided places where I might have bumped into people like Smittie. There's the Daily Planet in Melbourne. "Come along sometime," JP invited me I don't know how many times. I sat opposite the entrance and watched the men going in and out, satisfied to the brim and without the slightest inhibition, like Smittie. I never had the guts to march in and order a lay. Afterwards I examined myself in the full length mirror in my apartment, a sweet, strong coffee in my hand: not a young cock any more, but fuller, hairier and still horny. I look at the man next to me. Not a single wrinkle: Smittie is smooth and nut brown all over. Lines of sweat dam up between the chains and folds of his neck.

I regain my composure. "I'm on a mission to find Koert and take him back home. Last I heard, he was on a farm being managed by blacks."

"Is it their farm?"

"It is."

"Let me put it like this: the whites who've stayed on, stay because they're not able to leave. They are lower than the poor whites from the apartheid days, remember them? Danville, Bez Valley, Government Village. You *must* remember them. The whites who've remained in Africa have become crafty, always showing their teeth. They creep up on you from behind, and brother, once they've got a grip, they don't let go until you're finished. They swallow you whole. The white rats of Africa. They're usually in the service of some or other syndicate or government faction. They've either got IT capacity or a few bucks left over that they can offer for food, security, transport and the loot they came for in the first place. People like me, in other words – and the guy you're looking for. It's only a matter of time before we'll also have to leave. And in a hurry too, sometimes without getting what we came for."

Smittie calls one of the air hostesses. The sleeve of his jacket slips back and exposes a shirtsleeve whose cufflink is undone. It opens up on his tattoo, wavy and cobalt blue, Maori style. He orders a round of whisky without even asking me what I drink and pays upfront in dollars.

"How do you know the man you're after is still there?"

"His mother believes he is, it's painful to see. She's asked me – I must try to find Koert, to the bitter end."

"Bitter end?" Smittie laughs about everything. When the whisky arrives he leans over to take his. "Play the man, not the card, you have to know who you're dealing with there or you'll lose the plot. The man you come across along your way is your sign. You have to read him; that's how you'll know what the next step is. And where to. If you don't read your man right, you can forget about your Koert. You may as well take the first available flight home."

"I understand."

"Survival, man, that's what it's all about. But I'm a sad man today."

He takes something from his pocket, a gigantic pink lump. "Rose diamond," he says. "It's for the wife, in exchange for my children. If she refuses this time, I'll have to say goodbye to my kids forever. She pushed off to Luanda with her ex-boss, Alex Stavaros. Biggest Mafia bastard in the world. I'm heartbroken, man. You see, my work always came first. They were difficult times, there weren't enough bucks. I'd take her back any time. She's the most beautiful woman in the world, and the unhappiest. If you look into her eyes too long you begin to cry. Her mother died of cancer when she was nine. And she was dropped off at an orphanage. She was raped twice by wardens. Two men. In the end she left me too, children, suitcases, everything. When I got home that day only the boerbull stood there waiting for his food. My throat just closed up. I'll still take her back though. I neglected her, you see."

Smittie tells his story. I sympathise. "Excuse me." I get up to go to the back. I have no idea what else to say to the man.

"How sweet," Smittie guffaws after me, "I don't know when last anyone said 'excuse me' to me."

I want to vomit once I get into the toilet: layer upon layer of slimy excrement and turds of crumpled paper everywhere, even against the walls. I step carefully and hold my breath for as long as I'm able, hobble back panicky, and shake my glass to refresh my nose in the richness of the whisky. The drink smells of grape seeds. I inhale again. Another fume plays between the brown waves, something like children's ice cream. I take a careful sip and give Smittie with his gold chains around his neck a look, and point to my drink. "Something drop in it?"

Smittie licks his lips. "Doctored it a bit. Drink up, you won't be sorry," he reassures me.

The glow of the whisky under the dim night lights, the sense of wellbeing after my first sip. The luxurious effect of the second. I drink without any sense of aversion, trying not to look too eager. Slowly I'm being initiated into the continent we're about to land on. May as well become accustomed to it sooner rather than later.

Time passes, I pass out. The plane falls asleep and glides aimlessly by over mountains without animals, primal forests without
trees, rivers where ancient fish drag themselves towards islands of
drifting oil. Show me the way to Koert, I ask one, a muddy old
barbel. He turns his head without answering, unaccustomed to a
child of man demanding anything other than his life from him.

When I awake, the aeroplane engines are running at their
smoothest yet. I feel quite relaxed next to this man with the exuberant chains on his overripe skin. In the meanwhile, Smittie's
skin has developed a second, smooth skin of perspiration. His
eyes open lazily, he aims a glance at me, smiles, and closes them
again.

Cheers, Smittie, I want to thank him for the drink. Are you
pleased with yourself? I want to say, but nothing comes out. My
words are drifting, I'm losing my grip, not even clutching about
for something to hold onto, and without judging myself for it
either.

I sink right down into my body until I'm level with my feet.
It's hard to describe the good feeling. Smittie's eyes open again,
and again he smiles. *This* time I know what I'm seeing: the smirk
of a pimp. He's a merchant, sure, you can bet your life he trades
in underage girls, no older than, say, fourteen or fifteen years,
and that he offers them to men with needs. The pimp en route to
Lesotho to fill up his treasure trove of girl-slaves – it's no secret.

Here he sits, right next to me, Smittie on his way to work.
Even when he emerges from his drugged sleep for the slightest
moment, he produces his smirk. He exudes guava and whisky
and body-warm silk stockings. Unmistakable: the profile of a
pimp. It makes me want to laugh, to raise my sleepy-dead hand
and shake on it and thank him once again: Smittie has initiated

me and brought the two of us together the way it ought to be. The impostor and the pimp enjoying each other's company.

I must be on my guard. Or else I'll miss the clues Smittie spoke about. Clues that will take me to Koert and perhaps even help me to understand him. What *is* he up to there?

When we land, I'm fast asleep and come to with my neighbour's hand on my arm.

So here I am, is the first thought that crosses my mind, and Smittie will deliver me to the next person, another one like him. I'll move down a river of people, they will determine my route, push me downstream, perhaps even suspect why I've come. Some may know something about Koert. Not everything, of course, just enough to point out the way ahead. Some will detest me and help me from the embankment into the ditch. I must keep my eyes open.

"Good luck, man," Smittie shakes hands, winks, slips on a pair of dark glasses with ridiculously big lenses, and walks down the aisle.

There's nothing to be afraid of. I'm able to gather my things, get up and face the next leg of my journey. Here is my hand luggage, my jacket. My possessions, familiar, and baked by the flight, the last memories of the city I've left behind. I look at Smittie's seat one last time: a harem of unholy scents rise from it.

4

Going up that river was like travelling back to the
earliest beginnings of the world, when vegetation rioted
on the earth and the big trees were kings.

ALL I CAN THINK OF is my connecting flight to Bloemfontein – no time for feeling tired now. Thankfully, the long haul
is safely behind me. "Watch out!" A man in a copper-coloured
djellaba bumps into me from behind. Only my hand against the
passenger tunnel keeps me from falling. Can't he see where he's
going?

My ticket indicates that I've paid for the connecting flight;
there's no departure time or date, only a flight number. The
agent wasn't sure whether such a connection actually existed and
recommended that I don't pay upfront. By then my neck was already covered in a rash, like Heleen's when she gets anxious, and
I insisted: "No, I *want* to pay. There has to be a flight to Bloemfontein."

Except for the Gents immediately to the right, there's no sig-
nage in the arrivals hall. The toilet doesn't have a seat, but it's
cleaner than the one up in the air. It costs a dollar for single-ply
paper, grey and coarse. I get rid of the last food I ate in Melbourne and rise from the toilet rim lighter and full of expecta-

tions about what lies ahead. As I emerge from my cubicle, the janitor flies up. He positions himself in the doorway, eager for business.

"Where can I get information about the flight to Bloemfontein?"

He grabs me by my elbow – I could just as well have put my question to a stone – and pushes me towards his counter. There's a radio on it, and a bunch of plastic petunias and a frame with a photo of his wife and four children and a whole lot of stuff for sale, and that's *his* destination. He shoves me forward; I bump against his table and get annoyed.

"You must have a look here," he gestures insistently, a finger waving over his wares. There's green soap and cheap deodorant and condoms. "Everything you need," he grins with exposed gums.

I shake my head. "Okay, if you tell me where I can find out about flights to Bloemfontein."

"I'll get my brother to take you to Bloemfontein. He's got a van. How much can you pay?"

Forget it, I gesture, and walk out. Behind me he snorts: he knows my type. Where to now? The sooner I get to Bloemfontein and buy my own vehicle the better. There's not a single sign. The arrivals hall has emptied after the landing of the Fiji flight. I check the few people who've remained. And just to make sure, I also peer over my shoulder – like a real baboon.

I'm allowing my mind to run riot for no good reason. There's no doubt about it, anxiety is a form of unbelief. I hobble on in search of a sign to lead me to the right place. And see how Heleen presses her palms against her bedroom window at equal distances from her head and mutters something against the rain that is really never going to stop.

Perhaps she's praying for travelling mercies. And what about Jocelyn? Marlouw, are you planning to get yourself a weapon? No, no intention. Sure? Yes, I'm dead sure. Think about it carefully. Remember, your survival depends on yourself. Consider very carefully: are you going to get yourself a gun? It *is* possible, you know.

I knock at the first office door I pass. The blinds are down, though I hear voices inside. I knock again. Two pairs of hands roll the blinds halfway up so that I have to bow down to talk to the officials inside. Quickly and clearly I ask about the connecting flight to Bloemfontein and show them my ticket: "I don't know the departure time. Is there a flight?" I speak to the stomach of the official to my left. He and his colleague bend down together to look at me. Their clean white shirts give me hope.

"The ticket?" No, they're not interested in the ticket. My neck becomes sore from bending.

"What now?" The officials shake their heads and look wearily at the deserted hall behind me. When the telephone rings, the one with the cold sore on his top lip turns to attend to the call. The other has also straightened up behind the half-rolled blind, and all that remains of him are his hand and white sleeve resting on the counter. I walk away.

My foot's become tired. In a corner I rest on my suitcase and peel one of Heleen's vitamin C tablets from its roll. Two soldiers saunter by, each with a heavy calibre machine gun over the shoulder. Their smokes smell of Gauloises tobacco. They chat on and off, stop when they notice me, inspect me and my luggage as they pass, then look away when I nod.

No doubt about it, I *am* anxious. There. There's a woman with straight shoulders; she looks as if she knows. I grab my suitcase and call after her. The woman's hair is done in a remarkable coil, like an art-deco snail shell. Her gait is measured and straight as an arrow. First she shifts her folders, an open magazine and a plastic bag full of soft sandwiches – that's what it looks like to me – then peers through her eyelashes.

"There is a flight to Bloemfontein, but only on Wednesdays, and today is not a Wednesday, of course." She's beautiful and ought not to be wasting her life away in a job like this.

"If only I knew how to help you away from here," I blurt out. "You look like a model in one of those magazines."

She starts to take an interest in me and becomes much, much friendlier than the earlier two with their white shirts.

"Wait there a moment," and she points. I carry my suitcase to where she's indicated but without losing sight of her office.

All the airport offices are rigged up in prefabricated plastic cabins. They are arranged in a row in the domestic arrivals hall. The remains of the original offices are behind the row of cabins. Bright cloth hangs in front of some; others are covered with bits of black plastic. Some are completely exposed, destroyed by a fire. The ruins of a desk and a chrome chair without a seat, and burnt, bent panels and other rubbish have been scraped together to be carted away.

A tall man bends double to enter one of the low doors and appears in the office of the woman with the coil. He's a West African, purple-blue; the moment he enters her cabin he starts fondling the woman's shoulders and neck. There's no way that he's come to discuss my ticket. After a while though, he does flatten his hip-length shirt, turns his body graciously in my direction without taking his hand from the woman's neck, and calls me over. His fingers flutter, with slender nails like you'd expect on a woman, and loose-jointed.

"There is no more flights to Bloemfontein. We are so sorry, sir." He's got his concord wrong. My ticket is held out to me.

I accept it and our hands touch briefly. Mine pale and anxious, his old and at home, the skin that feels like river mud. The touch lasts just a breath, as long as the short history of our forebears on this continent.

Meanwhile the man has moved closer to the woman again, his hip tight against her thick shiny coil. Now it's their turn to observe me. The way I receive the ticket, the way I fold it neatly and flatten it to avoid making any dog ears before placing it carefully in the wallet with my other papers, the way I snap my briefcase securely shut. The man licks his lips; his eyes mock the fussiness with which such an insignificant task is executed.

"She said there are flights, but only on Wednesdays," I say when I'm done. I swallowed one of Heleen's pills, don't know whether they saw it. My head's about to explode.

"We are so sorry, sir."

"I have to get to Bloemfontein and further, the Eastern Cape. What must I do now?"

"There are buses, sir, we can make arrangements for you."

And then the woman uses the saying I remember about this continent: "Everything is possible. We must just be patient and wait."

She remains utterly composed and asks me to return my ticket. Together they look for a code or whatever. The man massages her neck, seemingly unconsciously. The result is erotic; she's forced to restrain his hand. It seems they've found what they're looking for and the man rattles off a series of numbers.

His voice is loud and clear. It's a long number with many zeros. He makes good progress, but stops and has to start again. When he's done, the two discuss the figures in the reference number. They get stuck on a "nine".

The woman looks up at the man and slips her hand under his shirt. She's reached the point of tedium. Her lips part, she becomes even more beautiful than when I'd arrived. The man now picks up the ticket, licks his finger tips and peels off one of the pages to hold it up to the light. Rising, the woman groans and emits a muskiness that the man obviously knows better than I do, and points her nail at something visible only on the back of the page.

Merely looking at them makes me feel desperate. What's more, I'm tired after the flight, more tired than I'd thought I'd be – thanks to the doctored whisky – but I try to remain alert. There *is* hope, and I don't want to miss the slightest sign.

The woman sinks back gently and flattens my ticket in front of her. She looks down at her watch embedded in a broad, golden armband, and up at me again, indifferent but not unfriendly.

"There is a flight 15 minutes from now to Bloemfontein, sir. We can give you a seat right near the front, it is not the seat indicated on the ticket, and this is not the flight either," at which she finally returns the ticket to me.

"The seat will be available for $200, sir. Sorry for the inconvenience. My colleague will assist you with your baggage." Beneath her lashes her eyes indicate my foot. "Go with him, he knows the way."

The extra money she insists on makes me hesitate and I'm about to object, but remember in time: the woman with the coil and the purple-blue man are the two I must follow for now. They will help me. In fact, they've helped me already. I *have* to pay this money; it's the only way to reach my next destination. That's they way it is, this is how I should view it.

The man walks ahead far too fast so that I'm forced to follow at a trot. It's not long before I have to touch the silky material of his shirtsleeve and point to my foot. He laughs. "If that's what you want, sir," then slows down enough to be able to light a cigarette on the way.

We start zigzagging up a wide escalator. The conveyor belt doesn't move any more and every now and then one of the man's long fingers points to warn me: the belt has slipped from its track and the spikes are exposed. From behind I thank him, but soon realise that he doesn't even notice.

Suddenly a wave of people bears down on us, we're overcome by clamour and colours. The tall man lets me follow in the wake formed by his body. He's become a considerate chaperone.

We forge ahead through a jungle of sensations: the smell of papaya and chicken feathers, of week-old armpits and the flesh of mangoes, rough salt and soapy-fresh clothing. There's every shade of pink, and parrot-bright oranges and the anxious shrieks of little ones from behind their mothers' bottoms. Sweaty hands cling to boxes of spices and sheaves of wild herbs – and to children's hands. This flood of people is welcoming, although I don't know a single one of them. I smell meaty burps, breaths heavy with yesterday's sorghum beer, I hear languages click and comfort and spit – I never knew nor understood these people, even when I lived amongs them.

Plastic crates full of hair extensions and braids pass, thermos flasks are opened en route and sweet tea is poured, chunks of frozen meat are dragged along on trolleys, there's newly starched

African print and perfume on skin, Chanel No 5 – I instantly identify it – and lots of gold jewellery.

Acrylic material shocks my arm and a crowd of businessmen, rowdy in pinstripes, pass, as well as suitcases, mostly battered, and boxes with clever string handles and bundles that appear to contain living things, guns paraded openly on hips, and long objects that look like automatic weapons half-covered in camouflage cloths. And here, right next to me on brown trippy tippy-toes: a child with a cage of twin hoopoes – how could I possibly not recognise them? I'm so relieved that these birds have survived.

"We have to hurry," the tall man urges me. Altogether, $200 and a massive fee for my chaperone, I repeat to myself. No, it's water under the bridge. It's for free. It won't cost me a cent to get to Bloemfontein.

Once again the aeroplane I board has bad air conditioning. I can't identify the model; the engine sounds powerful and the steady drone is reassuring. I try to watch the landscape as we take off, but my eyes refuse to stay open.

At some point children clamber over me, one fingers my ears, fly pads, I'm too exhausted to raise my hand to swat them off. Behind an alto voice chases the brats away. I must remember to thank her. Wonder where she's from? I swear I know that voice. It was short-sighted to have drunk that whisky.

Close to our destination, I order coffee from our air hostess. "Sorry, sir, we only sell beer." A brand I've never heard of.

The mother's voice that had sounded so familiar offers me some coffee from her own flask. The plastic cup is passed over my shoulder. Thermos flasks are *de rigueur* here, I must get myself one right away.

The coffee is sugary sweet and comforting. I turn myself towards the mother amidst her brood: if it isn't our Tannie Piekie from the Eastern Free State, the tannie with the sandstone house, six bedrooms and a red wrap-around stoep. Droplets of fruit dangle from her lobes, miniature bananas and pineapples, complete with prickly leaves.

"Don't I know tannie?" I hear myself dredge up words from a bygone era.

"If you're Ben Louw's son, I knew your pa like the back of my hand. Ah, boetman, the world *is* small." At that point the plane prepares to land. The engines roar as they shift down and the wheels drop out one by one, in disbelief I wonder whether she had in fact addressed me with that hoary old term boetman.

Meanwhile, to a man, the passengers have jumped up, despite the air hostess's yelling. She lets fly a last bitchy remark before giving up. A tussle with baggage and boxes of provisions and 5-litre water bottles and children who have to be stuffed into jackets and beanies, follows. It's winter, and I remember now how cold the afternoons on the Free State veld can be.

"Drink up, meneer," the woman hurries me on. "I must get my stuff out from here." A child grumbles at her milky breast.

And now I'm convinced I've mistaken her for someone else. She didn't hear me properly, nor did she answer me as I'd imagined. It's only on moonlit nights that our Tannie Piekie from the Eastern Free State dances her yearning old woman's dance: "There, in the dip of the road, my son," I hear Pappie say, and see his wicked finger pointing. I could never see her. Pappie's patience eventually wore thin at having to point her out – the blind will always remain blind.

"Thanks a lot, mevrou." My tongue is scorched. I can't help wondering about her again: isn't she dabbing a shiny eye with her jacket sleeve? Maybe she still had something to say, a jewel of nostalgia especially for me. Something about Pappie, perhaps? But she's swept along from behind, and curses as she struggles to prop the flask into her bulging bag. When I attempt to help her, she warily orders me to get a move on. There's yet another suitcase she has to drag along, and her brood dart about ahead and behind her. Like me on my own journey, she too has to keep an eye on all and sundry.

Our beloved Tannie Piekie. Her arms bare and brown and open in welcome, she used to descend the broad staircase with its palm tree on either side. Not a soul was ever turned away. I pull on my jacket and shudder. I'm the last to disembark.

Outside the terminal building I assess the taxis. I finally decide on Rooikat Taxis. My driver is vigilant; he kicks his exhaust as he walks around to me. "It's just from the cold," he says at the spluttering, then switches to Afrikaans. Carefully he places my suitcase in his boot lined with a threadbare floral carpet. I'm happy with my choice.

His taxi is all set up with music – full-blast and surround sound – and crocheted orange-and-blue antimacassars and thoughts for the day, one in the middle of the dashboard and one as a surprise under the vanity mirror when I glance at myself, red-eyed, and immediately push the sun visor back.

"Jaap," he introduces himself civilly, obligingly. He scratches under his dandruffy lapel. "What's made you come back, sir?" he peers at me surreptitiously so that a shadow tempers the blue of his eyes.

"I've come to look for my nephew."

We leave the barbed-wired compound of the airport. "It's my brother, here for a visit," Jaap says to the soldier at the gate who scrutinises me through the window. Is it my smell or something less defined, some sort of discharge, that betrays me as a stranger?

"Don't worry," Jaap says in my direction and holds up a dollar. "Enough?" The soldier folds it in his hand. We drive through, turn right, and push into a tide of pedestrians and open trucks transporting people. It's a snarl-up of the first order, the road and verges full to overflowing. "Where's everyone going?"

"Be patient. You'll see soon enough." Jaap takes the gap and revs up. He looks pleased at all my questions. An engine part starts screeching under the bonnet as if it's about to snap in half. The faster he drives, the louder it gets.

"Fan belt," he mutters. I nod. I haven't forgotten what Pappie taught me about cars.

"Not to worry. We're almost there. It's nothing, nothing at all." Jaap turns up his music, perhaps afraid I'll get out and call another taxi.

A group of teenage boys crowds about ahead of us. The minute a taxi passes they let go of a child of no more than four, five years from their gang, shove him forward, his begging eyes up against the window. I look at Jaap, he shakes his head vehemently.

"Don't. Don't even think of opening. Under no circumstances. Won't help bugger-all. Doesn't matter what you give. No time here for a good conscience, meneer. Get away," he shouts when traders rush at his car.

"You can call me Marlouw."

He smiles rather cynically at me.

Rough-skinned lemons and clothes hangers and cans of drinking water and bottles of Vicks. The traders shout, advertising their wares, and jostle to reach passing cars first. Spit splatters on my closed window. Every now and then I raise my no-thank-you hand, imagining that a residue of their dank survival anxiety sticks to my fingertips; at times I prefer to let the tasselled curtain drop to hide myself from the wave of orphans and people. Look at that tiny scarecrow in front of us, scarcely weaned from his mother's breast.

"Such old man's eyes."

"Hunger. Shrivels them up completely. It's the eyes, isn't it? Avoid them if you can. No point looking."

"I'd have thought you'd have become hardened by now, Jaap."

"To the suffering, yes. Around us every day. Jeez, man, it's enough to deaden anyone. Can't help it. You have to become tough, otherwise you won't make it. Feelings. A few remain. Can't help being human. My wife," he interrupts himself again. "My wife hardly ever leaves the house these days. It's all too terrible for her. Takes it to heart, you know. Worries about our future too much. It's really miserable.

"But me. Jeez, no. I won't allow myself to be holed up like that. Out. Every day. Even if I didn't need to be a taxi-driver – and I do, it must be obvious to you, Mr Marlouw – I'd still go out every day. Last thing," he pauses, the man's thrown. "It feels like the only thing left on earth for me to do. What else can I do? Drive. And look and look. Among the people. Poor things. There's really nothing else left to do. TV reception? Have I mentioned it? Nothing. For ages now. And the radio only works now and then when there's an attempt to establish a central government. Happens less and less now. Meneer, this is a strange country, this."

In one piece, body and soul preserved. It's a miracle I've got this far, that I've landed up in Jaap's taxi adrift amongst all these people. Swallowed up and swept along: I sense the sluggish, desperate force of the poor out there. No need to propel yourself, simply float along. Even finish Jaap's sentences for him. His blunt phrases that often consist of just a single word. Give me a few days and the images of these people won't torture me any longer. If only I could get going in my own vehicle, get to where I must track down Koert.

The route to the city centre of Bloemfontein is shrouded in smoke, paraffin and exhaust fumes. The cloud envelops the taxi and filters in through the ventilation system. Now and then it clears and reveals the single-roomed houses, row upon row, as far as the eye can see. Candles flicker in the dim light and disappear again. Houses, everything, vanished in the gloom.

Close to Jaap and me, in case we've forgotten them: legs and hips and hands pressing on. They disappear into the thick brown murkiness of the smoke, before re-emerging. A runny nose and mouth against the front windscreen. Futher back in the gloom: hands, again and again, masses of beckoning hands. The hand is the one limb that won't be hidden, the hand *has* to ask, and take and lift, and stuff in.

Everything dams up between us and the truck that's stopped to drop off its load. Some of the weaker ones have to be helped down. The moment the truck gets going, the pile-up flows forward. Once again: a handful of old people, grey to their skins, carrying children, or themselves being led by children. There is no will to hurry. Sometimes the traffic is so congested that it's dangerous, and Jaap steers carefully so as not to knock anyone by accident.

"Is it always this busy?"

Jaap nods. He dare not take his eye off the road.

"Destitution. It's obvious, isn't it?"

"Well, I *did* expect it."

He looks at me in disbelief, reproachfully: you who've been gorging yourself on wine and lamb for years, how would you know?

"Immense need. Only relief," Jaap continues, "is to walk along the roads. To get out a bit, to talk. The constant flow of traffic gives them something. Hope. There must be a destination somewhere. Somewhere people can go to. Something still worth driving towards. They know you're fresh from the airport. It's a precious sight to them."

"I've brought virtually nothing with me."

"That's not what I meant. I'm not talking about clothes and cameras and watches and that sort of thing."

I interrupt him: "I didn't bring a camera or a watch."

"I know," he looks at me despairingly. Was I totally incapable of understanding him?

"Another world. That's what they see," he explains patiently. "It's the knowledge that something better still exists somewhere. It fascinates them. It makes them come out onto the streets on a cold afternoon like today. Look there. Look!"

We're close to the mouth of the subway that leads to the city centre. Here the people form a single file all along the edge of the road. I raise myself to try to see the end of the queue; it seems endless.

One hand touches the next, hand to hand with the palms upward, thumb hooked onto the thumb of the neighbour. Weaker hands are supported, held up by the next, less emaciated one.

Palms of hands held out towards us like the fronds of giant river-
side plants. It's impossible to distinguish between old women's
and young mothers' hands, between schoolgirls' palms and those
of boys. Only the very smallest – saucers on twigs – stick out.
Here and there, and stretching into the distance.

Nausea wells up in my throat. Can't stop staring at the endless row of palms that move rhythmically at the taxi passengers'
eye level. Like seaweed, the hands move; slowly they draw you
into the ebb and flow of the human tide and carry you along:
they push and pull, the mournfulness present from that very first
day in the cradle, life cut short, the last vestiges of life slipping
from the eyes.

I bite my lip to contain myself, until I nearly draw blood. My
innards rumble and knot, I have no words to describe the sensation. Jaap looks at me. This isn't disgust: rather it's the difficulty
I have in holding back the flood, in swimming against the tide
and preventing myself from being swept away with it. I may not
give in to it; I can summon more than enough strength of will to
get out and walk away dry-shod to begin the mission for which
I've come.

Jaap takes a pinch of snuff then offers me the tin. "Eyes," he
shakes his head. "Try to avoid their eyes. For your own good,
believe me, it's the only way to preserve your sanity. I can tell
it's getting to you. Happens to everyone who sets foot here. And
they're becoming fewer all the time. Foreigners. Tell me, what's
to bring them here these days? You see, you can feel sorry for the
people. You can try to do something for them, but they've become too many. The numbers are overwhelming." Jaap sighs.

He's desperate to talk. He doesn't understand what's going on
inside me. Nor does he believe that I understand him.

"Have you got any water on you?"

"There ought to be a bottle on the back seat. My wife, you know, she looks after me."

There's a folded blanket and a box full of faded *Volksblad* newspapers on the back seat. The water bottle leans against the box. As I turn, my stomach starts giving trouble again and air, thick, like boiled slime, fills my throat. I gag and swallow loudly to keep the vomit down.

"Not to worry. It will soon pass, you'll see. Doesn't take long to get used to it. Don't let it get to you. Meneer, you're from here yourself aren't you? Isn't this your country too?"

I shake my head, indicate that he doesn't understand. It's not the sight of the people that's making me sick. It's the fear that I'll wash away with them, that I won't find enough strength to resist the tide.

"See that!" Jaap shouts. A mangy dog jumps against his window, bangs his fangs against the glass as he tries to bite. The traffic comes to a standstill.

"Wolf," Jaap informs me. "Lots of strays in the city centre have gone wild. At night they hunt in packs. Rip everything in the streets to shreds. Help yourself." He offers the snuff tin.

"Where are you taking me?"

"You haven't said yet. May as well tell me now."

"I need to buy a bakkie, I want to get going, today still. I'm here to find someone. That's all."

This time he looks straight at me. "Trust me. I know exactly where to take you."

Then he starts up his stories again. "Very little news reaches us. I sometimes pick up snippets at the airport during the day. Thousands of people. Jeez, sir. Can you believe it? Thousands

die every day. Young men, but mostly women and girls. *Nooiens.*
That's what we called them in the old days. Nooi."

My hands grip the sides of my seat. I barely manage to keep
my breathing even. The vomit wells up, subsides and disappears,
and I sigh sweetly for Jaap's benefit. Then a sudden, rancid burp
forces my lips open. I draw my breath in deeply once more, and
try speaking to hold back the nausea. "Don't worry: I wouldn't
dare get out here. I remember the loveLife campaign the government launched to try to stem the tide of AIDS before I left
here."

"Failed. In the end there wasn't any money left in the state
coffers. You have to understand that more and more people
started relying on welfare. Government eventually went bankrupt. World Bank. NGOs. Everyone sick to death of the goings-
on here. Another world, you see. Then," he pauses, takes snuff,
"all hell burst loose. Everyone regarded as more or less middle
class or above became panicky. It was a matter of the hyenas howl-
ing at your gates at night. The good life gone, meneer. Once and
for all. That day my wife came waltzing in with a new pair of
shoes. Started unwrapping them. Beautiful Italian shoes in silk
paper. My wife. Oh jeez, she shook so much she couldn't get the
things onto her feet. Terrible cuts on both feet. Here, and here,"
he points. "Just that afternoon my wife had to run to escape a
gang. Scarcely made it. Barefoot. And you want to tell me, meneer, that you knew what to expect here."

I shake my head. "I'm starting to feel better."

"I've got so much time to think here in my taxi. Forgive me,
sir, but I have to talk to someone. In a quarter of an hour you'll
get out of that door and you'll never have to listen to me again.
Forget your nausea, man, listen to me, just for now." Jaap speaks

more intensely, quietly, "I know what it takes to persevere. Past the filth, the stinking corpses, the rancid breath. Past all the poor, poor people. Been hungry for weeks. Listen to me today." I can scarcely hear him. "You're dealing with life and death here. In the raw. Listen. Look. You've come, and now that you're here, you may as well keep your eyes and ears open."

"Some snuff, please," I stutter.

"Here." He looks pleased with himself, relieved by what he's just said. My hands are so sweaty I can't get the lid off.

"Ants," he says.

"Ants?" I ask after a while when he remains silent.

"Didn't you ever watch the ants when you were little?'

"Well, I remember the flying ants on the farm before the rains came. If you stood on the stoep and looked up at the sky, you'd see them rowing their new wings. Thousands of them."

"No, sir, I'm not talking about little aeroplane ants now. Once you're here you don't get away that easily. I'm talking about the ants that use their mates, their own species, as a bridge to cross a river and to walk out dry and in one piece on the other side. That's what you have to learn here. Survival. It's all that counts. Do you understand me now? Excuse me, sir, but do you have the faintest idea of what I'm saying? Where was I?"

"I have no idea. AIDS?"

"Right. Look, what I wanted to say is: you can't help being human. When you're overwhelmed by poverty and suffering, carnal knowledge" – he laughs cynically – "has become the only salvation and escape. Escape from the horrific suffering. Do you blame them? Will you be the one to cast the first stone? They've fucked themselves to death. Excuse me, unto death. Nothing. There's not a thing you can do about it. The die is cast. Here are your results. All the people here before you are trying to get their hands on something before finally lying down to die. You see how the healthy stand aside so the sick can queue at the entrance to the city? Compassion. Last time they'll come out. Even if they don't manage to get hold of anything, they still enjoy being among the traffic and all the activity. It can't be too unpleasant to see them like this. Relax."

The blood has drained from my hand that's been holding up the tasselled curtain. I let it drop, and rub my pale skin to get the life back into it. My stomach churns once more and quietens down, weak. I sink deeper into the seat. Jaap looks at me and smiles.

"Comfy." He points to the interior of his taxi, turns up the volume of his CD player, and his water sounds surface. Cool droplets and water birds, the exuberant call of the fish eagle, Egyptian geese screeching with pleasure as they land; shrill, lighter sounds beyond the heavy flow of water, plovers perhaps, and other noisy river life that I can't identify.

I'm on course, may as well relax, as Jaap's suggested. Never dreamt I'd travel on a pleasure boat. Jocelyn: Heavens, Marlouw, you really *are* foolish: this trippy is taking you straight to hell.

My taxi driver spoke a true word a moment ago: this suffering mass alongside the road may not take me off course. I've got my own mission, and signs for which I must be on the lookout.

Pine trees, bluegums, karee and wild olives, every single tree that once stood along the road has been destroyed. You should still be able to glimpse a tree top in the brown smog that hangs above the roofs of the shacks, but there is nothing.

"What's happened to all the trees, Jaap? How do you cope with the summer heat?"

"Problem's actually the winter. Firewood. People have to cook."

I have nothing to say. The man's got good suspension under his car, that's something. Why he doesn't put in a new fan belt, I don't know. They're probably not available here. I could easily have brought him one. But Jaap's taxi isn't bad. I blow on my hand – my breath is stale, but not rancid.

"Have you heard of Maitland in the Eastern Cape?"

"Can't say I have."

"Then there's no point asking whether you've heard of someone by the name of Koert Spies."

"Never heard of him." An Egyptian goose calls and splashes down from the back speaker. Jaap smiles in my direction. Around us the line of people thins out, the ones holding their hands up like leaves. We're in the city now. My taxi driver starts talking again.

"I'll miss your type, Mr Marlouw. Let me be frank with you. You see, I talk to lighten my burden. Say if you mind. Koert Spies? No, I can't say that I've ever heard the name. Are you sure he's still in the country?"

"Oh yes, I'm certain." My compass tells me we're continuing south.

"Certainty? In this country. Forget it." Jaap swallows, talks on, can't help offloading more of his woes.

"I was an advocate in my day. My wife had her own car. Have I told you yet? Douw van Heerden. My last client. Prominent case, newspapers full of it. He wanted a divorce. Had houses all over Cape Town she didn't have a clue about. Filthy rich. There were already signs that the Roman Dutch legal system as we'd practised it in this country was collapsing. Ugly, meneer might say, but I didn't hold back. I exploited the system for the last time. Jeez, and *did* I win that case for him! His lovely spouse's money was finished by then. Hands chopped off.

"One night Douw took me to a Japanese restaurant on Naval Hill. Raw salmon in seaweed. In the middle of the Free State. The ultimate in sophistication. Bloemfontein! I ask you. The mistake we made was to withdraw from politics. That was fatal. Look, there was not a single person with expertise left in any municipality. Sewerage and drinking water the same. Government splintered. And the Afrikaners salivated with delight. More poor whites than ever. You saw the poor souls begging at the traffic lights. God help them – I'm not talking about the poor whites now. I'm talking about the middle class and the elite. The ones who wallowed in icing sugar. Fuller fridges. Bigger houses. Staircases and multi-storeys and columns. Wedding cakes, to say the least. And they just couldn't get enough of braaivleis and golf. Became tourists, you see. We stayed on as tourists in our own country. No one accepted responsibility for anything. Meneer, the apathy was mind-blowing.

"Not that I was much of a reader – my wife, yes. In the last days not even the poets made any effort to create original work. Simply plagiarised and published. Stupid. Publisher didn't even click. Just partied on. Wiped the fat from their lips. No one – not even those without brains – imagined it would last. Signs were there. Right in front of our noses – the abyss.

"One Friday the rubbish wasn't removed – no explanation from the municipality. Kikuyu. Directly opposite the house. Planted it myself. When I looked again, a squatter had put up his hut on it. Finished, everything. It started sinking in, for my wife too. You didn't have recourse to the courts any more. I'd already begun with the taxi. Didn't want to be caught with my pants down. Survival. One day I took some leftovers for the squatter across from our house. You know what was the worst for me, meneer? When I looked inside, I saw the kikuyu's albino tendrils trying to reach the sun. No; that I couldn't handle. Jeez."

Jaap's losing hope; he looks forlorn.

"Then came the mouse plague. There wasn't a grain of poison in the city. All Kloppers said was: Sorry. We're sorry. There won't be anything in stock for quite a while. What they really meant was: never, sir. But they didn't dare say *that* to you. I still remember how I stood outside in the sun and thought about phoning my brother-in-law in George. There had to be poison somewhere. I phoned. Oh, my dear sir, by then Bloemfontein was part of the deaf belt. A band as wide as Lesotho cut a swathe from west to east right across the country. No more signal. We'd been struck by deafness." Jaap swallows, he's played out.

"And then? Then the explosion at Koeberg. And the sabotage of the power stations. Boom, boom, boom," he grimaces. "Like cannon shots. Week after week. Across the country. There were too many factions in the government. Even in the provinces. Everyone sat on their own throne like a king. And made sure that they bribed the army and police to prop them up. Each faction prepared to fight for its piece of the cake. You see, sir, imperial history repeated itself here. But this time just with different players. Didn't old king Leopold of Belgium talk about carving up *ce magnifique gateau*? Difference is: the cake that's left is very, very meagre."

He continues, "Me, my wife, well, we swore we wouldn't produce any children in this country. We seldom dare go beyond the boundaries of greater Bloemfontein now. Here at least we still know a few people. Oh, it's been years since we've been into the platteland. I'd say it's become like the dark places of the earth to me. In any case, no one risks the roads at night" – Jocelyn had also warned me about that – "and besides, I'm afraid we won't get any milk and bread and flour. Once you're outside the city," he stops.

It's the first time Jaap uses the word "afraid". The sound of the word is spasmodic and frightening in itself. Japie, my little lamb. At least he manages to eke out an existence: his cosy interior, water music to transport passengers away dreamily, the story about the ants crossing over on their mates.

Jaap's got a few last things to share with me. At times he turns away, I can hardly hear him. I still have some questions, but they're becoming fewer. He's too distressed, and I don't want to torment him. He ought to stop now, really. He's sweating.

If I'd had a camera I'd have taken a picture for Heleen. This is what the advocates look like these days. Ultimately, at the end of my journey, I knew that the man was a minor pointer along my way. He had nothing more to offer. I needed to get one last thing out of him.

"You haven't forgotten about the bakkie? An ordinary one will do. Please take me to the right place."

He shakes his head, wants to say something, but someone suddenly walks right in front of the car, pretends to stumble and fall across the bonnet as if he's been hit. Jaap hoots like mad to get rid of him. The man flies up, ashen, runs and trips, looks for a stone or tin – anything – with which to attack the taxi.

"You see what I mean," Jaap says, powerlessly. "The man wanted to incriminate and judge me. In one go. Then deliver me to the mob for execution. That's how the law operates these days.

You see what I've been trying to tell you the whole time?"

Half past one in the afternoon. In the city centre people hunch their shoulders and walk briskly. It's become gloomy outside, perhaps too late to attempt the drive to Maitland. I'll have to spend the night somewhere. This is not what I had planned, but that's the way it is.

The water music quietens. Jaap's eyes are wide, startled, after the accident. Shivers chase through his body and disconcert me. I point at the heater button on his dashboard.

"Please," he begs, "don't touch anything. I have problems with people who fiddle with my car." Jaap has reached breaking point now. I try saying something to restore the genial atmosphere.

"Isn't there more milk and meat on the platteland than here? Easier to come by? Surely you can still keep cattle. There must be veld left over to fatten sheep on."

"Drought," and he digs another pinch of snuff from his tin. When he notices me staring, he doesn't offer any. "There's a handful of commercial farmers in the Free State. A local syndicate is firmly behind them. If they collapse, there will be no more flour in this country. Nothing. The syndicate ensures that every precious thing that's produced on the farms is brought to the city. Their own soldiers monitor it. Lorries cart the stuff into the city. I see them on my morning shifts. Yes, you *can* keep cattle. Sheep too. But where on earth would you find a cow for sale these days? And sheep? Forget it, man."

My taxi man takes me to a spot at the lower end of the main road, in the vicinity of the station. It's swarming with people. On a street corner a fight breaks out over a soup bone. An elderly man swings the bone above his head, a gang tries to filch it from him. Up and down they jump, snatch-snatch. Ribs protrude from open tracksuit tops, bare bones. They're tough and hungry. The minute the old man turns they're at him from behind. He roars with indignation, scrapes his strength together and lets swing a wild blow. A single compassionate bystander rushes up. "*Voert-sek*," they yell in unison.

"Nearly there." Jaap's voice is weak. "The man will have a bakkie for you. I know him well. Very honest. Not many of his type around. He'll look after you nicely." At which point he simply stops talking.

I lift the tasselled curtain to get a look at the station. Its three gables are still standing, even some of the original pink plaster clings to them. Lean-tos and walls of corrugated iron fill the stoep. The lean-tos are being used as shops, people have fixed chimneys to the pillars with wire. Smoke curls upwards. That's the smell of offal and mealie pap. People are living there.

My poor taxi man. The snuff has brought a tear to his right eye; his left eye is wide open. Presumptuously, I grab his shoulder. "Is that really necessary, Jaap?" And his name sounds brotherly on my tongue.

Tears flow; he's got a whole life to tell. "You don't know what it means to me to talk to you. You have no idea what we have to endure here. Day after day. And now winter's approaching. Hardly any electricity. Long dark nights following close on one another. Candles. Tinned food. Will there be enough? Mamma's at home with us. Oh jeez, sir, one wants to give her one's best in her old age. At least try to keep her warm. The winter. I don't know whether she'll make it."

He grabs my hand that's still on his shoulder and presses it against his lips as if he wants to beg me to help him and his fam-

ily. At the turn-off both hands are back on the steering wheel –
he's pulled himself together somewhat. Ashamed at the show of
emotions, his blue eyes avoid me, not even a glance as at the start
of our journey.

"This is where we have to turn," is all he says. Superfluously.

The compass on my lap reads south-south-west. We swing
into Harvey Street and park in front of Nant's First Luck Cars.
The building has a flat facade with a steel door and not a single
display window in sight.

Almost immediately, a man bursts out of the steel door and
exchanges a few words with my taxi man. This must be Nant. A
note is produced from his pocket, Jaap nods and takes it. When
I pay him, plus a tip and all, he doesn't even manage a goodbye,
merely drives off, a broken man.

"Nant du Plessis," the car salesman introduces himself for-
mally and takes my suitcase. I hobble after him, am tempted to
throw both arms around his boer-belly, a comforting *braaipot*:
here he is, carrying my load, full of assurance. He walks like a
tree trunk, he plants his solid steps straight and secure, a true
war horse, and a car salesman to boot – no time for tears about
the state of affairs.

"Everything in order, meneer?" he asks politely. His eyes
skim across his showroom floor to check that no other rubbish
has slipped in after the meneer. There isn't a whiff of fear anywhere near Nant, with his bald head all shiny and bold.

"I'm terribly thirsty."

With a single movement of his foot, Nant hooks a chair and
moves it under me.

I do not have a single need of which he isn't yet aware. The
front door rumbles closed in its steel frame and locks mechani-

cally. Nant walks over to his paraffin fridge in the corner of his showroom and pours me a glass of cold water into which he plops three ice cubes. I can tell from his shoes that he has big, strong feet. The skill with which his foot moved the chair to under my bottom certainly impressed me.

Over the edge of my glass, I notice the bakkie.

"The white one over there," I say from the cool inside of my mouth. Copper wire, I think when I hand Nant the glass. And with the last drop, pure tannin at the back of my tongue. Maybe he's forgotten to rinse the glass? The precautionary injections Heleen had insisted on in Melbourne were perhaps worth the effort after all.

Nant gets to work on forms and documents. They appear one after the other from the top drawer. He farts when he bends down to take a box of official stamps from the bottom drawer. After a kerfuffle with pens and stamps and books with carbon pages, he asks, "Sweetie for you?" and offers a cellophane packet.

They really *are* peanuts in white and pink candy shells, exactly like birds' eggs. Click goes Mammie's bag on the steps after church on Sundays. Her hand scratches around and places a little egg on the tip of my tongue so that a tiny blob of spit sticks to her church glove.

Nant du Plessis hasn't laid eyes on anyone like me in ages. I sense how he watches me surreptitiously. We get up and check what I've bought.

Nant taps the bakkie windscreen with a thick finger. "Here's your licence, still valid for eight months. Only the jack costs extra; don't even think of driving without one."

And would I like a radio? I shake my head. Nant is dreadfully disappointed, walks back and throws his hands in the air.

"You don't know what you're doing to yourself. Tell me, where're you going? You don't know what it's like out there, I can tell where you're from." He looks at my travel bag. It's nothing fancy, but probably luxurious compared to what you get on the streets here.

"May I have another, please?"

"What?" Nant asks. He's still disappointed. "How far are you going? How the hell will you manage without music? You're stupid, man, if you ask me. Here, take one," and unwillingly he holds out the cellophane packet with the candy eggs. "You know what? I feel sorry for you."

This time I pick a pink one. If you taste carefully, the pink ones are slightly sweeter. The more expensive kind at the movies had almond centres, but we seldom had them, so they haven't left an impression on me.

"Huh-uh," he answers when I ask him about Koert. "I've never heard of the man. Though it wouldn't surprise me in the least if one of my pals knows something about him." Nant talks without ceasing, gets onto flowers. Dahlias. Then it's engagement rings. Then Sealy Posturepedics. He's a man with contacts, can get his hands on anything in the world – and I believe him.

"If you want, call me any time on this number." He produces his card. "I'll try to find out for you. What'll you give me if I pick up any clues?"

"We'll have to talk." I'm not reluctant to pay the man. "Depends on the information. And whether it will help me. One has to be reasonable." I wish he'd given me a last egg for the road, but no. We wave as I drive off.

Drive west towards Church Street, then south to get out of

the city. There's more colour on the streets here. Pink and green and red alongside black on cloth and blankets. *Angel's Mercy available here*. Across Fichardt Street. A row of bottles with orange cooldrink for the little ones. *Dark & Lonely Salon*. A pile of boerpampoens that don't look at all bad. You notice the hunger less here. The bakkie jolts through an exposed drain and drones on. My compass is at hand in case I need it, but I stay on course even though all the familiar signposts have disappeared.

Stop. A pamphlet is thrust through the tiny opening of my window. *Cat Walk Stripshous & Hores Galor*. "Okay, thanks." The child continues to shove pamphlets through the slit. I don't give in to his doggedness. Nudge-nudge at him with the bonnet of the bakkie. He curses like a grown-up and jumps away.

Uphill along Church Street, then Hoffman Square, the heart of the city visible in my rear-view mirror. I've never seen Bloemfontein like this: no lipstick, down and out.

The air that enters through the ventilation holes is laden with petrol and paraffin fumes. It's best to keep your lights on so others can hopefully see you. After the bridge, I come across a sign: Bloemfontein's very own Eiffel Tower. I'm on the last leg out of the city. Petrol's probably unaffordable; few cars leave the city. There are also fewer pedestrians here on the outskirts. I'm glad. Along the roadside, traders hunch behind piles of coal or wood or rows of bottles of paraffin or petrol and the massive twenty-litre cans of drinking water that are for sale everywhere.

How do Koert and the others keep warm on the farm? There were the besembos bushes that Pappie always had dug out, but that was hard work. These days I doubt there's anyone able to hack at an old besembos until its roots are exposed, and then still have the energy to work it loose from the hard, dry earth. A root the size of a ballast basket used to take a whole morning's digging and chopping. Though I must say, it burnt forever.

Krause Street, Nico van der Merwe Drive, old street names preserved on faded boards. Look west across the roofs of the houses to check if I can see the obelisk of the Vrouemonument. Altogether 26 370 women and children died in the concentration camps. I could never fathom why the sculptor created such a voluptuous pietà-like mother and child. Nor why the Queen refused to lay a wreath on her last visit to South Africa before *this* British sin.

Two men sit wide-legged with a bow-saw in the fork of a pine tree – I can count the trees I've seen today on one hand. The smog parts, and I imagine I see the bold point of the obelisk. Can't be sure. Perhaps I'm too far out of the city by now?

The road widens, I pick up speed and allow myself the hope that I'll reach Maitland after all. Then at the Cape Town turn-off where I keep left, the road narrows so badly that it can only take a single lane of traffic in places. Only one headlight works on dim – and both shine on bright. The bakkie rises and falls as the tarred road gives way and later disappears completely, something I'd never have predicted, even if I had wanted to. It's a mess of gravel, potholes and huge, loose stones.

Just in time, I notice the massive rock and swing to starboard, change to a lower gear. An embankment rears up ahead of me and throws the bakkie back onto a piece of surviving tar. Enough to make you seasick. This piece of road is so badly worn that a jaw like a shark's juts out on both sides. If your tyres hit the sharp edges they'll be ripped to pieces right away, then drop to the deep-water mark: both the tar and the gravel upper layer are totally eaten away. The road is so deeply gouged out that I'm driving at window height below the surface. Here I come across huge potholes, big enough to hide an overgrown boerbull in. Once, twice, my chin butts my chest. I imagine myself biting the inside of my cheek and getting lockjaw. I don't have any mouthwash with me.

Back on a higher, tarred stretch, I come upon old farmsteads and veld. Everything has been burnt to the furthest horizon. There's no sign of the fencing that used to mark the farms, only burnt mealie stubble and grass tufts on scorched earth. To the right, the charred finger of a palm tree indicates a garden. The walls of the homestead are still intact. There's no sign of any remaining plant or animal life, only the odd decorative stone that a gardener once placed there. A horrendous, destructive fire must have passed through here. Usually, farmers only burn the veld in late winter, in a controlled way, and always on a wind-free day.

I'll sing something, something to distract me from this scene of destruction. Suddenly there's a gaggle of people ahead of me, old ones and children and a mongrel and suitcases, right in the middle of the road. A man – the father – readies himself to jump into the bakkie and hitch a ride for the whole family, but I'm too fast for him. There's no way I'll pick them up. The man is desperate. Once he's behind me – so far as I can judge, the light's deceptive – I put my foot down. He reaches out and grabs at the wind. He's tripped up by his own coat, down he goes, suitcase and all, kaput. I've got away. In my rear-view mirror I see the case burst open, its possessions strewn far and wide, the father shaking a vengeful fist at the ever-darkening sky.

Slowly now. I reduce speed to 60 km/h. Something's in the road ahead. 40 km/h. It's one of those enormous trucks that's rolled onto its side and burnt out. Its skeleton lies in the middle of the road. There's its chassis, there the hubs on which its tyres once turned. To the left, a detour runs down through the veld, two spoors that climb back onto the road past the truck's bonnet. From its peeled paint you can tell that it happened long ago. The hulk was never removed.

Fires close by, and also deeper into the veld. You might have mistaken them for camp fires were it not for the surrounding desolation, and not a single song comes to me. "My Sarie Marais," come on, give it a try at least. Nothing happens; my tongue cleaves to my palate, dry and swollen. It's getting colder; I may not succumb to it – that would be the end of me. Think the cold away, use your imagination and give it a try at least.

I conjure up an image of Koert Spies: my young nephew waiting for me, beer in hand, by now informed of my arrival by Jocelyn's family. He waits patiently, eager to declare in a powerful voice that he's keen to return with me. Then his beer is finished and he starts spitting. I have my suspicions about Koert, even though I don't know him too well: his moods are volatile. It's the source of his strength, albeit a strength with a false foundation – though you don't notice *that* right away. It startles you. Someone's chucked a bloody butt in my beer, I hear him shout. He slings the bottle away, it shatters, he looks me in the eye: Ice cold, dear uncle, he says. You've judged me wrong. Your pseudo mission is totally fucked. Take it like a man, my uncle.

And this I remember from his visit that night: moody Koert. Without warning. Disgruntled. Sulky. To be honest, I couldn't tell what was going on in his young head. Don't think he knew himself. I was actually glad when he left. What remains? JP's conclusions about his son's sojourn, and Jocelyn's warning. This is not the time to be mulling over these things.

Full of doubt. That's how I journey deeper into this landscape of scorched fields, wave upon wave, where freak islands drift between long-abandoned farmsteads. Not that I want to drive up to any of them. My foot's tired and sore from the constant acceleration and braking. I'll have to stop somewhere.

And above everything, the sombre sky, drought clouds rising and falling with the bakkie. The vehicle reels and clings to whatever's available; I cling to the wheel to prevent the jagged edge of the road from shredding the tyres. At the edge of a hole I hit the brakes, let go the moment I'm through. The steering wheel shudders, shocks my hands loose.

It's foolish to rely on the mechanics of this bakkie. The fears of my taxi man loom large at this late hour. Behind every turn they await me. Phantoms and foul-smelling beasts that slouch towards me and collide with a smouldering poplar bush. Here and there, flames lick the dusk and die down.

Not so the phantoms. I can't discern them with the eye, can't get to the heart of the fear. Here, close to the window I make out only the first layer: the way in which my taxi man sometimes shuddered, his eye forced open, his hands pathetic, alert like a rodent, his fingers grabbing at the snuff, snatch-snatch, and then the salty tear under the right eye.

The road rises once more, and I reach a reasonable patch of tar from which I can look down and survey the damage. Look and look again, pierce the haziness across the burnt veld – there must be an explanation for this destruction. Once upon a time there were blesbuck where the skyline forms on the ridges. Afrikaner cattle with curling horns amid the red grasses. There were fields green with mealies and gold with wheat.

During our last years in the country the commercial farmers

were unanimous, "Come on, let's see what we can do. We're willing to hand over some of our land to you formerly disadvantaged
folk, to share and to give, willing seller, willing buyer. We'll provide advice. One of these days you'll be first-class farmers."

There was a last newspaper photo of the national grain fes-
tival at Bothaville shortly before JP and Heleen and I left: the
big white man and the big black man each held high a swollen
mealie cob, one holding it with his left hand, the other with his
right. White farmers no longer wanted all the land for themselves. They'd share their expertise; sell their land – even give it
away. Pappie told me about these men before his death, friends
of his here in the Free State. The Prinsloos of Smithfield and
the Du Toits of Bothaville. Seasoned and tough, but ready for
change. They wanted to multiply flocks and increase their har-
vests together with black farmers. There were children and grandchildren to think of. The descendants must be assured of the fat
of the land.

Now look what's happened here. Self enrichment and igno-
rance can't possibly have engulfed *that* kind of farmer and led to
such destruction. Did the effects of the explosion reach all the
way to the Free State?

A farm to the left seems to have survived the fire. There's
a bare, trampled werf around the buildings, the space must obviously have formed a barrier against the flames. I slow down
slightly and open the window. The fire reached the outer edge
of the yard; it must have been put out by hand. There are the
farmstead and outbuildings, the barns and lean-tos where lu-
cerne bales were stored, there the stables and chicken runs. A
kennel just to the left of the front door. Yet not a soul in sight.
The house and outbuildings are all basic. There was enough to

live off here, but no extra hands to build ornamental arches in the garden or braaivleis nooks.

The buildings stand as if on an island. There's no movement. The life and the sorrow and the terror one late night in the bedroom – my God help us! – have passed. Not even a stray chicken, maybe just a sparrow or two, at most. Nothing's audible from here. In a few days the farm will be plundered. No one can survive here anyway. One can predict the fate of the farmstead: a man climbs onto the shoulders of another, grabs a gutter, clambers onto the corrugated iron roof. He starts pulling out the nails with the jaws of his hammer, loosens a sheet, lifts it, and passes it to the one waiting below.

Close the window and drive on. The sun is setting. Rays break through the haze and smoke, cast coal-black shadows against the stone koppies. Blue-gold and jet, undulations of grey satin, black-gold and silver granite.

A horse rider suddenly appears on top of a koppie, I slow down. The rider reins in his horse so abruptly that the animal collides with the stump of a wild olive. He turns his head south, then north. He'd seen me long before I'd noticed him. I wave and gesture without thinking of the consequences. The rider jerks the bit so strongly that the animal flinches.

No ways, there's no way he'd dare cross the smouldering veld towards a total stranger. He probably knows exactly why he's there and what he's up to. It's just that for me, the animal and the man had brought unexpected life to the dead veld. It was such a welcome sight to me. To *him*, though, I mean nothing.

The last red of the setting sun is swallowed up, night falls with a sigh. My clammy hands grip the steering wheel. My foot – I try not to think about it. Soon I'll have to pull off for something to drink. I have a sudden need for milk. Around me, the veld and the night melt into one. Rest and peace can come now, night will cover everything like a wide blanket and the damage will become invisible. Tomorrow is another day.

Flickers, like torch and lantern light, approach across the distant veld. In the glimmer I see people waving cloths as if they want to pass something on – it won't be food, maybe it's messages or warnings. Pleas for help. Nothing. I won't respond. I'm not inhuman, but I won't allow them to snatch my mission away from me.

I become aware of a kombi behind me with a red cross on its bonnet and a flashing light on its roof. A crisis, obviously – where can I turn to make way for him? Centimetres to the right, and I'll cut my tyres. Has the driver taken *that* into account? I turn my window down and signal: slower, slower, my arm waves up and down. Anxious. Will he understand the signal?

Now he's right on my tail. The bastard forces me to speed up. Fresh sweat. Am I supposed to shred my tyres and give up everything at the very start of my journey? It's me or them. Besides, if I have to stop here to change a tyre – there's only one spare – I'll be done for. I'm on a mission, too. Reddersburg can't be too far; he'll have to hang on till then.

His siren suddenly blasts. I'm sopping wet. The screech cuts through the bodywork of the bakkie, its dissonance hits the hammer of my inner ear. I'm losing balance. Won't make it and don't want to sacrifice myself for his sake, nor for *theirs*. The sick and dying, who knows how many are stuffed into that kombi. Be that as it may. His headlights shine onto the back of my head, heat burns through to my scalp. I'm going overboard and slipping into dark waters, nothing to grab onto, no one holding out a hand. Hold me, mate. Remember Jaap's story about the ants.

Against all expectations, the driver veers to the left, then sharp right in an attempt to slip past on a road that doesn't exist. I give stick – why not? – my head slams into the roof as the front wheel hits a pothole, a madman on a *mal de mer*, I force myself on, what else is there to do?

The blast of a bursting tyre sounds from behind. I swing my head around in time to see the jaw of the road's edge hit and split his front right-hand tyre. The blow lifts the bonnet and hurls the kombi to the right. It accelerates across the road until it loses its grip, spins, and is thrown backwards and onto its side before gliding across the stubble-veld and disappearing in a wave of ash and dust. Arms bulge from the windows, flames shoot into the air.

I look ahead, take nothing more in. My calf muscles cramp and I force my lame foot down onto the accelerator to speed on at a mad pace. What's happened has happened: it wasn't my fault.

Reddersburg. This must be Reddersburg. Shops crowd the road; grey light falls through empty window frames. I place my hand under the bend of my knee and lift my cramping leg. And so I sail into the town. I stop at a place that looks like a café. Some men are warming themselves around a brazier.

"There's the milk," the café owner says when I ask.

Cartons of longlife. I'm so shaky that I can't lift the container from the shelf. I rest my head against it, my hands grip either side. How many passengers were in the Red Cross kombi? It wasn't my fault. Cockroaches wriggle between the containers of milk – but that's not the worst. Nothing's the worst.

Through the grey light I look up at the man behind the counter. He looks back at me, says nothing, absolutely nothing.

There are rolls of single-ply toilet paper and tins of Bull Brand Pap & Meat – must be a new product. I hobble to the right and take a closer look. No pork, the label states. There are three sorts available. I choose the one that seems most conventional: Beef, Mince & Gravy.

The man doesn't sell can openers. He takes the tin and cuts the lid with a mounted opener. "Enjoy."

Some kids pour out of the room behind the counter. Gathering behind their father's legs, they peekaboo at me. One has a slightly enlarged head, though I'm too tired and distressed to trust my senses. The effort of the drive, then the walk from the bakkie to here, then the steps. Is there nowhere to sit down?

"A fork, I need a fork, please."

The man throws his hands in the air. "Listen, this is not a hotel, my china. You types! You haven't changed, have you?" I hobble away, turn around when he calls.

"Okay, then," he relents, "if you eat your food here, you can use one of my wife's forks. She won't mind." He roars with laughter: he's got the upper hand; his little snotnoses laugh in a chorus with him.

An old-fashioned silver-plated fork, not altogether clean. It'll have to do. The men at the brazier look around when I walk onto the stoep. I lean against the pillar to move my weight onto my healthy leg. I check out the steps. As I sit down, I hiccup. I pause like someone saying a prayer before finding the strength to push the fork into the concoction of Beef, Mince & Gravy. Under the stoep light my hand appears jaundiced.

The men around the brazier go about their business. Dog's food this, salty and cold. Better than nothing. They all have broad shoulders and strong necks. People who get enough food.

That's something, that's a life force, something to strengthen me after the endless dead road. One of the men has unfolded a map on his lap. In the glow of his penlight torch his finger moves from the top to the bottom. They're calm and collected. Each waits until the other has finished before speaking. I don't know what they're saying, yet their voices are like strong water passed from one to the other: they've got something going for themselves, they can forge ahead with it. Look at that, see how resolute their shoulders are, how firmly their heads are planted on their necks. Suddenly they seem like leaders planning something important, people with potential. But first they must warm themselves, fold the map carefully, and then they can get on with it.

Wash the concoction down with the milk, unpeel the last of the vitamin C tablets, and linger until time tells me to go. When I hobble past them, I get an even better view of the men. They *are* leaders. But then I climb into my bakkie and switch on my engine and they get up and move towards me in a tight pack. I'm unable to distinguish one from the other. Apparently they've seen something they want – or have something to ask. They speed up. I pull away with screeching tyres and their hands hit the bonnet, dent the door, the carrier. Clappety-clap, clap-clap.

I shouldn't imagine things. Pause, observe, reflect carefully, then speak. I escape Reddersburg, hee-ha, and thank my lucky stars.

Once in Smithfield, I'm amazed to see the Colony Restaurant from long ago at the entrance to the dorp. Yellow bulbs still wreathe the signboard, even though not a single one is lit. In the old days these elegant gentlemen served champagne with caviar on brown farm bread for breakfast. Perhaps I'll find something decent here, even if it's nothing more than a beer in a tall, clean glass.

The tables inside have been set with white tablecloths and candelabras. There are no guests, only the blond man sitting at one of the furthest tables. He puts down the book he's reading and comes towards me. As he weaves his way between the tables, he stops to light the candles in the candelabras one by one.

"I hope I'm not disturbing you," I say. He's not yet uttered a single word to me – as one might have expected a *maître de maison* to do.

"On the contrary," he stoops to pinch a wick between thumb and index finger. It's burning too high for his liking. In the light, his hair shines like flax on a bleached day.

"Per Strand," he says, and takes my hand in both of his. He's Scandinavian. His left hand is gloved and he wears a white uniform jacket with a high collar, like in the navy. The collar fits snugly, and a nervous Adam's apple moves against it. Golden buttons neatly contain him from top to bottom.

"Please be seated." He leads me to the table where he'd been reading. A groan sounds from somewhere along the edge of the long room. When it comes again, he waves his glove: take no notice.

"Something to drink?"

"A beer would be good."

Per disappears through a back door to the right. I'm not at ease. The tables have been set in two rows all the way down the long room – I can't imagine that any guests will turn up at this time of night. And the candles burning. In these times? Everything so meticulously well-appointed, except for the groans and moans I vaguely hear. There they are again. The long wall just behind me is painted the same grey as the facade of the Colony Restaurant. The groaning comes from behind it. Now and again it moves lightly and billows along its base as if it's not solid. Could be my imagination. Can't be. I lean my head towards it to hear better. Wait, I must take a look. Don't bump against one of the tables now. This way, careful with the foot.

As I thought: it's not a brick wall, but a cleverly painted curtain on which Per has hung paintings to give the impression of a solid wall. I hold my ear against it: a rasping cough – there are people here, you can sense their bodies and breath. Bedding's being lifted and folded, a body turns and changes position. Tip-toe back to the table and open the menu.

"There's offal curry," Per calls as he walks in. He grabs the menu from me and holds it against his immaculately pressed jacket. Inches from the leg of my chair, something like a kick makes the base of the curtain wall bulge.

"What on earth's going on there?" I laugh awkwardly. He's got two glasses of wine, not beer as I'd ordered. He sets the glass before me. Rather fussily.

"You may take a look if you like, but I suggest you first enjoy your drink." He's too formal for words. With the glove folded behind his back he goes off to attend to the needs of his guest. A silver saucer with butter balls appears, a silver butter spoon. He breaks a chunk of homemade bread – the man keeps surprising me. This bread will relieve my heartburn.

The somewhat acidic wine refreshes me. The curry offal he offered never materialises. By the second glass of wine and bread, I know there won't be any food. There *is* no food, not for me, anyway.

"Per," I prod him after chit-chat about restaurants and exotic ingredients that sound strange and foreign and even excessive in this setting, and move my chair closer to his. "What are you still *doing* here? Is it worth the effort for you? How do you get your hands on the food? You manage to keep everything so nice and clean." I look at him and take a sip of the wine. It's eating away the fur that the tinned food had left on my tongue.

"It's not what you think." Per fiddles with the warm wax on the side of a candle. "The restaurant is my attempt to preserve a sense of civilisation. I haven't been able to escape realities here for a long time now. In the old days the restaurant was a kind of bastion – a paper bastion, for sure – against the poverty and suffering on the other side. We all clung so desperately to the Western customs and habits that had been built up here over time. Three centuries perhaps? A little longer? How do you define time on this continent, anyway?" Per's hand lies on the table in front of us, translucent and lifeless. "My country's aid organisations won't give up like the others. Someone has to do something. Come, let me show you."

He picks up the candelabra and walks to the corner of the room.

His steps are measured. In the candlelight he seems so courageous, despite being terribly thin, like a heron. As I weave past the tables behind him, I too become calm, even brave.

Per folds the heavy curtaining back so that the two of us can walk through. There's not much light here either, only three paraffin lamps hanging from hooks in the wooden ceiling. Now I see how the curtain works: it divides the one-time restaurant into two long, spacious corridors.

People lie on three rows of mattresses on the ground along the back corridor, hidden behind the facade of the curtain, everything as painstakingly neat as in the restaurant. They're all covered with blankets. Some raise themselves on the triangle of an elbow and forearm to look at the visitors: at *this* time of night! The lamplight is too dim to discern what their eyes want to say. Not one of them utters a sound.

There: "Here, sir!" a woman calls and holds out a blood-soaked rag. Per brings a bucket and she drops the rag into it. "Thank you, sir, God bless you." There are people sleeping who look contented, others bemoan their lot and toss about.

If it weren't for Per, I'd have turned and fled long ago. Whatever courage I'd built up, has seeped away. In the meanwhile, he's taken my hand in his and is holding me tight. He wants me to stay for a while at least and see what's going on here, see what he's managed to do.

They probably had the offal curry he offered me for supper: there's a whiff of something wafting over the human bodies. It was Mammie who maintained that she'd never touch offal she hadn't cleaned with her own hands. Per apparently senses my queasiness and from a wall cupboard takes an old-fashioned perfume sprayer. Poof-poof, he sprays over the heads of the people.

"Extract of lemon balm and lime zest. Something I'm still able to manufacture myself." He doesn't smile.

Per and I remain amongst the mattresses without anything further passing between us. It becomes so quiet that I'm able to hear the wax drip onto his candelabra saucers when the moaning and groaning stops. Thus we stand for the duration of a Sabbath day, or so it feels to me, in the tender light of his candle and the three lamps. A moth flies against one of the lamps and its wings touch the glass. Per and I watch it, then drop our heads slowly towards the rows of people on the ground, their bodies scarcely forming visible mounds under the bedding. One turns on his mattress near us. Per walks up to him and covers the back that has been exposed. A dog barks in the distance, then stops.

"Listen," Per encourages me, and I listen and suspect he's referring to the silent devotion among his people. He's taught it to them.

At most, a word may sound in someone's sleep, a spasm that makes someone utter a curse, hoarse breathing and snoring, a finger scratching a wart, a leg that cramps and kicks against the curtain wall and convulses. It is done. Night has fallen. Everyone must try to get some sleep. Per takes my hand in his once more. It's warm, a hand of faith.

Eventually, he lets go of me. I look at him and wait for him to say something. He purses his lips in the candlelight. "That's all, we can go." This time he lets me walk ahead and holds the candelabra low so that I'm able to find my way. We reach the restaurant section and Per lets the curtain fall.

Back at our table – he's picked up something sweet along the way from an otherwise bare buffet – he says, "It's a halfway station. People drag themselves here from the interior. It will be the last time they get any food. The last time they can lie peacefully, even though I don't have any medication to relieve their pain. They wait until the kombi can transport them to the city – to the hospital or to a nursing home. Beds are only provided for a single day per patient, sometimes there isn't even medication available in Bloemfontein. There's nothing left of the hospitals, not even the terrible service they provided at their worst. When did you leave here?"

"When patients had to take their own bedding, and families had to come and clean themselves."

"Well, that's history. Filthy wards with bare beds are all that's remained. You'll understand that most people refuse to go there.

They choose to stay here; they choose the pain here with me. Not one of them is deluded. Each and every one knows he's going to die. Did you perhaps see the Red Cross kombi along the road?" he asks out of the blue.

"I did," I say. "No. I didn't."

What am I saying? His question catches me off guard; I felt my heart racing the moment he said the word "kombi." Saw your bus by accident, I talk to myself and smile wryly above the light of his candle so that he doesn't see it. I get up right away – I have to support myself on the table – without having touched his dessert. Syrup has soaked through the cake onto the fine china plate. It looks divine.

"Well then, it will probably pull up any moment. Perhaps you'll help me to carry some of the patients in. No?" Per points at the cake.

"I really have to get a move on." I'm flustered. "I want to reach Aliwal North – it's not too late."

"I understand," he says, almost as if he suspects what's happened to the kombi along the road. What difference will it make to him if it doesn't arrive tonight, or tomorrow, or even the day after. He himself has acknowledged that most of them don't want to be transported to their death on that little bus.

Per does actually betray some emotion. "Pity you didn't come earlier," he says. His voice fades behind me. I've found my own way past the tables and have already reached the front door. Now that the subject of the kombi has come up, I want to get away as quickly as possible.

"Dusk can sometimes last an eternity," he says. "I often walk out onto the burnt veld to go and look at it, things seem more benign then."

My jacket. I take a detour around Per and hobble back, make dead sure not to bump into the corner of one of his tables. There it is, hanging on a chair. Its smell comforts me. It *wasn't* my fault. I couldn't go slower and I couldn't turn off. In any case, the driver was being totally stubborn in going so fast. What for? To force *me* off the road. It's the law of the jungle here: it's either you or the other man. A handful of notes appears from my wallet. Per doesn't want any payment for the wine or hospitality.

"It's a donation, Per." I leave the money on the side plate.

"You don't understand, do you?" says Per. "Money can't do much for my people any more."

"But it's dollars, Per. You have to eat." He shakes his head. I *do* have compassion, if I'm permitted to use the biblical word, for his agony, for the way he strains his body to do even more for these people. The agony of the man moves me.

"Per, listen to me. You won't make it. You've exhausted yourself. Forgive me if I'm speaking out of turn. If I were you, I'd make sure I got away from here. There are too many you're trying to help. This country is devastated. It's over, Per, you're overwhelmed, drowning. You say so yourself. I've been here a short while, but long enough to sum up the situation. Anyone to fund you? Who's there to help?"

"Go," he shouts loudly and chases me through the door, his glove just in front of my nose.

"Oh, Per," I try to stop him. He wants nothing more to do with me.

He's already turned around, closed the door and unhooked the name board with the yellow bulbs and taken it inside. I remain motionless in front of the grey Colony Restaurant. Shame overcomes me, a new kind of shame that has nothing to do with my physical disability. I blush, I shiver, amazed at how the emotion engulfs me.

The man believes in himself and his halfway house in this dorp. And he fears nothing: not himself, his past nor the present power that the sickness has over the people, nor anything that may come to him from outside. And that's more than I can say of myself.

*

It's pitch dark when the wheels of the bakkie hit the bridge over the Orange River and jolt me wide awake. In the late seventeenth century the governor of the Cape of Good Hope handed over a farm along the river to my great-great-great grandfather, its borders demarcated from the back of a horse. Tradition has it that the Orange River was always bountiful then, full to the brim with buck in their thousands trampling the reeds to get to the water. Oupa must have been excited. His hand not far from the trigger of his rifle to ensure that he and Ouma and the little ones weren't plucked from history and denied the belly-full he saw before him: the abundant water, the game and the veld blue with spring grazing.

The bridge has been gouged down to the steel girders. Below, only a trickle of dirty water remains in the middle of the riverbed. I'm so tired I can cry, but my heart rejoices and I'm really happy to have got this close to Koert. Ouplaas is sixty kilometres from here. It's possible that people in Aliwal North know something about him. That's all I dare lay claim to now: information about Koert and his movements.

By then I'd realised that my presence in that land was superfluous and of no significance to anyone. I assured myself that, to survive, my disposition had to be slightly arrogant and certainly defensive.

But first, my foot needs rest. Heartburn plagues me as I rattle across the bridge; I'm afraid the insides of the bakkie will drop out. A porter opens the gate to the parking lot of the Balmoral Hotel. When I turn the key, the bakkie lurches forward without switching off. I remove my foot from the accelerator; it stops with a shudder. I try to restart the engine, but it won't take. I stay where I am, exhausted. The porter peers through the car window.

"So what's the plan?" He points to his lips that are visibly shivering; he doesn't feel like standing about in the cold.

Shipwrecked in Nant's bakkie that was supposed to have lasted me for the duration of my journey. There's nothing for it. My foot needs rest. The muscles of its crooked bridge have begun to contract, you could knock your pipe out on it and I can tell you now I wouldn't feel a thing.

The stairs up to the hotel room nearly finish me. There's a single bed with a down blanket that's lost most of its feathers. I rinse my face in brackish tap water and stretch my eyes: I look ghastly. The porter waits behind me with his torch.

"Is meneer coming down to the bar? Meneer will freeze here."

"Why not? Do you serve whisky?"

"Certainly, meneer." The porter leads me down a long corridor by the light of his torch. The carpet has worn through to the linoleum.

"Be careful," he says when we reach a narrowing. There's stuff stored everywhere; you have to squeeze through.

"Mind the cat. Left, here." He repeatedly aims the torch back so that I can see where to step. Dark right angles of doors pass as we find our way down the corridor. A throat clears behind one, and I hear a shuffle.

"Who's that?" a feeble voice sounds through a chink.

"It's a guest, Meneer Morrees," the porter placates him and lights up a face, grey from sleeplessness, without dentures, and a cup of curdled tea in his hand.

"I thought you weren't taking in any more guests," and he shuts his door.

The other doors in the passage are all closed. Behind them people sleep and quietly forget. If Koert ever spent the night here on the Orange River it would have been at the Balmoral. There can't be any other accommodation in the dorp. Would he, like me, also have noticed the rust on the pipes along the corridor, the dust balls and reek of unwashed people, the grime through which the torch casts its light? Koert? Can't really tell with him.

"Turn right here, here come the steps." What troubles me is whether Koert already knows about my arrival.

"Where's meneer come from?" the porter asks as we walk. I'm not the type he's accustomed to. I speak his mother tongue with the accent of an outsider — that must be what he hears, since I don't wear a watch or jacket that might betray my foreignness.

"Melbourne."

"Oh, that's far." He casts a daft little laugh in my direction. "So meneer shouts for the Wallabies, then. Tell me honestly, sir, is it paradise there?"

"If it is, I haven't noticed."

"I don't believe meneer. Meneer's probably become too used to the soft life to just fib like that."

"Do you ever get electricity here?"

"Not regularly, meneer. The electricity only comes on some days, and never lasts later than five o' clock in the afternoon. You need to have your electric stuff done by then. Otherwise you have to wait until the next time."

We arrive in the bar. It's relaxed and busy. I choose a route past the snooker table to get a drink. Paraffin lamps hang from the roof above the green baize; candles burn on the bar counter. Eyes lift and stare, everyone cosily together. They've marked me as a stranger. I can tell.

And without wanting to, I realised later, I proved that my return to South Africa had caught me offside. The expression on my face must at times have been dumbfounded. The crooked walk with my gammy foot meant that people couldn't miss me. When I eventually returned, I chose – or rather, tried – to re-member nothing of my disillusioning mission. But naturally, that was out of the question. I say "naturally" because it's in my nature never to forget, especially if something has changed me so profoundly.

"Double whisky with ice, please."

Before serving me, the barman mentions the price. Do I have enough? And the ice: "The next ice you'll see will be in Bloem-fontein, sir."

I place myself on a barstool, lift my pants at the pleat and hoist my leg slowly to drop my foot onto the chair next to me. My blood pumps unevenly; I sense prickles like pinheads, pre-liminary signs of a dead sleep that threatens to put my foot out of action for days.

The people seem content to be here in the bar. It's rowdy with sweat and drink and bodies: a stronghold against the outside. A few still watch me through the smoke, dedicated drinkers who cart in old depressions that they offload here. People sit or stand in twos, sharing whispers, or sit on each other's laps stroking and kissing, girls with earrings and coiffures chatting to their girlfriends over their lover-boys' shoulders. Strange how the Afrikaners never established a pub tradition. Braaied at home, left the glasses on the bare paving without a thought, had them collected the next morning thick with flies.

Some life returns to my foot. I sigh: I long to leave the day behind. Something draws my attention. A squeal rises through the dense air. "Buy me a drink." She's got silky black hair, this one. A guy walks up, and with a nonchalant sallow hand separates her breasts; she gives in to him. On the way, though, he bumps against the snooker cue, just as it's about to shoot. Suddenly there's cursing, hands grab him, press him against a chair, too late for him to get a word in.

But the girl with the breasts coos and grabs the snooker cue in both hands. "It's Darryn, darling, please man, you know him. Leave him alone tonight. Do this for me." She kisses the snooker player over his cue. That's the way it goes here. By tomorrow afternoon I'll know whether Koert's still living on Ouplaas and what his story is.

"Sir," I ask as the barman passes, "have you perhaps heard of anyone by the name of Koert Spies? He's my nephew. I'm looking for him."

"Hmm," he says, "I thought you had something on your mind. I watched when you walked in. I know people, see?" He stubs out his cigarette butt and lights another. A revolver hangs conveniently from his belt.

"I won't deny it. But why not ask that guy over there – he'll be more help than me," and he points to a man leaning against the wall. He's watching the snooker game without taking part himself.

"Go on," the barman encourages me when I hesitate. His eyes keep watch over his bar. "He won't bite you. Giel, the people call him."

I make my way through the crowd. Most drink quarts or brandy and Coke. I pass the Gents, from where the smells of urine and vomit filter into the bar. The body heat and the deep red glow of the cigarettes are seductive. Some raise their heads again for a closer look: What's he up to, this guy? Has he got money, is he looking for trouble, is he hiding something that may make it worthwhile to pick a fight with him? He limps, there's something about him, he's got *something*, poverty doesn't look like this.

Then they sink back again, mercifully. Sluts, the lot of them. They forget about me, snuggle up against one another as I found them when I came in. Swallow, inhale, kiss. Grey matter on go-slow. I notice that the Giel guy, on the opposite side in the thick smoke, has looked up at me, limping. I swear he's been watching me the whole time. I walk on.

A whore gets in the way. "I love you." She's fifteen or younger, not a day older. Her tongue passes over her teeth, and she kisses me. Her spit stays on my lips. Instinctively I wipe it off.

"Hey, meneer," she pouts as I try to slip away between two tables. A burly man with a ponytail in his neck has moved his chair so far back that I can't pass.

"Sorry," I say and take a crumpled note from my pocket and pass it over heads to the whore.

On I walk. "Excuse me," I have to say again. I'm forced to lean on a shoulder or lose my balance.

Here I shuffle through; there I touch the cloth of a jacket, hands, feathers on a soft hat, the hair on a man's arm that lifts to draw a lover's hip closer. Looks like they've also started liking me, even want to touch me: a hand comes into contact with mine, rests on my shoulder, "Yes, mister?" Under my jacket, over my two buttocks, the stroke of yet another human hand. Now that I'm among them and can't easily get away, they're looking at me again, and feeling me up, they've got absolutely no inhibitions.

The whore notices I've got stuck and rushes over, hooks her arm around my neck again, pulls the collar of my jacket and laughs sweetly at what might still come.

"Excuse me." I thought I'd managed to get through. Not that easily. No one moves an inch to make way for me. A man breaks a beer wind right under my elbow. I have arrived: I'm here, inside the stale sourness of the Balmoral bar. Let it continue, this blessed night. Perhaps it will teach me something. I hear the mouth organ, see how the men's hands slide between girls' breasts. I *can* make the people in the bar mine. If I wanted to, I could even snuggle up to them, fall asleep in a heap, and wake up still warm from other bodies and order brandy for breakfast. There's an authenticity in this bar that you'd never find in a city like Melbourne. In the dim light they look like the first people on earth to me, unadorned, present and conscious, refreshing themselves and so forgetting all their sins.

Maybe Koert also washed up among people like these. I'm convinced of it. He came to this wretched land to find what he could never get at home. That's how it is: I've landed among his people.

There's an eddy in my worn-out brain, and everything turns

nice and good. Here I am. No need to create order any more, it's cosy enough. Here I can dump all the phantoms. The ashen veld I drove through today, the way the landscape unfolded, preventing me from recalling anything of former times. I journeyed on through the veld, the narrow road my only lead, surrounded by utter hostility. The kombi with its pitiable cargo, everything, the landscape and people, all deliberately hostile. Even now, outside this dorp, the remains of bushes and veld flowers and cold stones taunt me.

Only the rowdiness inside the bar saves me from the looming madness Jocelyn warned me against. There was nothing familiar about the Free State. The images of Koert that I tried to cling to disappeared in that landscape. Then there was the Scandinavian's folly. That's what it was, I now realise. There the man stood, with his white glove and thin body and chased me away, no more than a skeleton dressed in a cloth against the grey wall of his halfway house. He's sacrificed himself. His fearlessness was impressive, but he's off his head. And the more I think about it, the clearer it becomes that ultimately he's got nothing to do with my mission. I won't allow myself to be thrown off balance by him. Over and done with; that's that.

Only the image of the kombi and the flying arms among the flames still haunts me. My embarrassment at my proposal to get Per away from there is also forgotten. It's silly even to think of it. Over and out.

I limp on. Whisky spills onto my hand; I pause and stare at the shiny liquid, wipe the drops off on my jacket.

"Yes, can I help you?" When I look up the face with the hollow cheeks and goatee is right in front of me. It's Giel, the one to whom I've been sent. He speaks softly; I can scarcely hear him.

"I wonder whether you perhaps know anything about Koert Spies. Where he is, and how he's doing? I need to know. I've come so far, you know," I speak in a way you'd normally not dare, to a complete stranger. The man unnerved me from the start.

"We know he's in the Maitland district on a farm."

"I knew it. I knew it."

"If he doesn't say you can come, you may as well forget it. You won't get in there."

"Yes, but I'm blood family, his mother sent me." What's it got to do with this Giel man? I must be out of my mind to blurt everything in this way. My thoughts have disconnected themselves from all logic. This is Giel. Unnerving blasts of breath right against me. He hides his eyes from me.

"Every now and again orders arrive from Koert Spies." He keeps his eyes averted, I can't read him.

"What kind of orders?"

"Look, orders arrive – he's looking for whisky. I have a case packed and I send it with somebody. Or I take it to Maitland myself. And then I have to hang around there until someone collects it. That's how it is: you're not allowed to set foot near the gate of his farm. Yes – I get meat in exchange. That's the way it works, but it's not quite as simple as that."

"I wonder how he's doing?" Giel can't be talking about Koert. A case of whisky? Giel's off his trolley.

"Personally," – and now I *do* get a glimpse of his currant eyes – "I've never seen him. Sometimes we hear this or that. Also my man who transports the whisky when I can't, never gets to see him. That's the way it is. A clown, this Koert Spies. But we'll get him."

A second, new whore joins us. I honestly don't feel like her, but here she is up against me. Negligee with shoestring straps, weary bronze shadow around the eyes.

"Let's go up," she invites me. Giel's goatee jerks as he relishes this turn of events.

"Meneer, I can see meneer's cold and needs cosy baby," she persists. One of the Balmoral's bouncers shoos her away, and for now she's gone. He brings me a chair, and before sitting down I look over the heads at the barman who signals: don't-worry-I'm-keeping-an-eye-on-you.

"Look, we hear he's a laaitie, but man, he's built himself an empire in this district," Giel continues. "And he's stirring big shit, just doesn't know it yet. Right now, no one can touch him. But everyone meets his Moses sooner or later."

He leans forward so that his goatee nearly touches me, his countenance indecipherable, "Koert's got way too much say over meat around here. Why? Who does he think he is?" He bites his lips. He looms above me and my chair, suddenly massive. I try to move. I must get away now.

"I'd like to see the man myself. I want to speak to him here. Right here. Let him come out of his bunker. He knows we send him booze, why the hell doesn't he come here himself? Is he scared to show his face, or what?" Giel pulls away, his eyes cold. "Send him here if you can get hold of him."

When Giel stands back a little, I'm relieved. It looks as if he's bitten through his lip. My doctor warned me: Avoid all contact with blood. Four out of every five people are infected. I must get a move on.

Giel keeps his eyes on me. "Yes?"

"No, I didn't say anything. I'm just wondering how he manages to get hold of all that meat. You know, I really don't think we're talking about the same guy." The first whore slinks out from the shadows.

"So why ask me about him then?"

I shake my head. My whole body, from head to toe, trembles. Dust scratches under my eyelids; must go upstairs and get to bed. I've found what I wanted here.

"Let me tell you something tonight. What's your name again?"

"Marlouw."

"Well, Marlouw. There can't be too many people around here with the name of Koert Spies. If you've come looking for Koert Spies, then this Koert Spies is your man. Let me tell you, that man's sitting pretty. We hear he buys sheep from here all the way to East London. He runs the whole show. There was a story the other day of people who disappeared at his place. But who can prove it? And who cares? Go ask him yourself how he runs his show. One thing's certain: if you want meat around here, go find Koert. People tolerate the set-up, but I can tell you now, no one likes it. His little empire won't last. People will get tired of his shit. They'll go and take him out one day. It's just a matter of time."

The young whores keep a safe distance. Now and then they say something silly. Another whisky arrives from the barman. I shake my head. "Who is he? Who *is* this Koert Spies you're talking about?"

"Why do you want to know? Why do you keep harassing me? Who are *you* by the way? Fuck off," Giel snarls at the one with the purple lips who's caressing me from behind.

"Family. I told you, it's the honest truth. I've been sent to fetch him. His mother wants him back, she doesn't trust his silence. Look, here's a photo of her. Koert looks a little like her, doesn't he?" Giel is startled by the picture. Koert's got his mother's eyes and low brow.

"Don't trust the calm!" he ridicules me, but quickly pulls himself together. I swear the photo rattled him.

"You know what, Marlouw, or whatever your name is? One day I'm going to take him out myself. And he knows it. He knows someone's coming. One day, just as he and his gang start partying. That man's playing with fire. Last time he didn't send back a fair share of meat. Don't tell me he doesn't know what he's up to. And he won't listen. When are you going over?" he wants to know.

"Tomorrow, I hope, but there's a problem with my bakkie."

"What sort of problem? I'll get it fixed. I'll pick you up here in front of the hotel – tomorrow morning early. I know a mechanic."

"What are you drinking?" He's climbed out of his hole, now that I've started talking about the bakkie. "Brandy and Coke?" I push myself up. Giel shoves me back onto my chair. I try again.

"Where do you think you're going? You owe me more than a brandy for all that information."

"A quick drink, then," I can't imagine where I find the courage.

Suddenly he becomes passive, nods and leans against the wall. "I only wanted to help," he says quietly, just as he'd spoken at first.

Far too ready with his information – and too opinionated. Doesn't quite know how far he can go with me. Why would he lie about Koert? No reason. The drink's talking, as they always say. I sway. *This* is my last drink. Must get upstairs. Delirious with exhaustion. It's a pure feeling, the golden whisky in your veins. Must press on. Complete my journey.

The air is thick, the bar even more crowded with loudmouths and swindlers and women who'd been pretty once upon a time. One's earring sparkles as I limp past, stop, listen. Everything is possible here. And I can believe anything I tell myself, as long as I believe it myself. In fact, I'm convinced I hadn't spoken to the man the way I spoke to him. I know nothing about this Giel and his opinions about Koert. Nor did he press his goatee into my face: absolutely nothing happened between us. There's an infinite distance between me and someone like Giel. And that's the way it ought to be.

"Just a moment," the barman says, putting my glass down. "I've got something to show you."

He takes a piece of paper with a painting from a file. He places it on the counter in front of me and pulls a candle closer, careful not to let any wax drip onto it.

"This once arrived as payment for the whisky. Old Giel was furious, walked up and down swearing. Wanted to jump in his car and fuck Koert up. Later I said to him, Giel, take it easy, man, let me pour you a drink. You're going to come short; Koert Spies has got too many men. Besides, where will you get petrol money to drive out there? Then I took the painting for myself. Maybe it'll be worth something one day. It's him," and he presses his finger on it.

It's a small sketch in oils of a little girl, draped and blindfolded, walking on an endless surface, something like the salt pans of Namibia, with her hands stretched out in front of her. The sketch is covered in an opaque white layer. If you look at it long enough it seems as if the little girl is disappearing back into the grey-blue from which she'd appeared.

"Who painted it?"

"Koert."

"Koert? Did Koert paint it himself?"

The man nods, snatches away the painting and locks it away carefully in his drawer.

With an effort I pick up our drinks. Where's Giel got to? Nowhere to be seen. It's because he's been lying the whole time. And he also had mixed motives, none of which I can quite work out. I'll ask Koert about his sketch. At least I know what he's up to now. Certainly not meat. Should I entrust my bakkie to Giel tomorrow? And if he doesn't help me, who in this dorp will?

*

A knock sometime in the middle of the night, my sleep done for. The voice of one of the whores at my door. She enters and sits at the foot end of my bed, hides her face behind one hand, peeps at me through her fingers and sees the glass of whisky I'd brought upstairs. She helps herself.

In my drunkenness I do nothing to stop her. She pulls her leg up to her knee and whispers sweet nothings and smiles, her tongue smooth from my whisky. Next thing, she's got my sock off and is working my foot, the normal one. She becomes more daring and starts on the other, with the sock still on. I nearly have a fit.

No one has ever touched my foot like that, except for doctor Symington, during my final examination. There's nothing more we can do for him, he caucused with Pappie and Mammie that day. Mammie sobbed, I could hear everything. "But hasn't the built-up shoe helped, doctor?" Pappie asked hypocritically. What a nerve. Fools! They'd delayed and delayed, I should have been operated on ages ago.

The whore's fingers crawl over the crooked bridge of my foot, down the sock, and massage my instep, inch by inch. When she starts pulling off the sock I throw her out. She coaxes me, waving the glass of whisky.

And she returns, hoarser, more determined, the glass refilled. When I open, eventually, the old gentleman croaks through his door, "Have you lot got no decency left?"

She lets me have a sip of her fresh whisky. I'm overcome by exhaustion. Then she's on my bed, both socks off, wham bam. She must like me, to be persisting with my foot in this way. I turn away to avoid her eyes at all the things she's getting up to with the foot. She rubs it and it becomes deliciously painful – how should I put it? – bigger, pulsating between her deft hands so that I want to scream and laugh from deep within my belly. And I do: I can't believe my ears. And she laughs with me and holds me tight and keeps busy, and in between she fills her mouth and then her wet tongue gets to work.

It was a dream, I thought afterwards. I'd never felt like that about my foot before. I'd never *felt* like that.

Giel's standing on the stoep of the Balmoral the next morning. He's wearing the same hooded jacket and shifts from one foot to the other while he waits for me, no less sinister in the daylight. When he sees me he puts out his cigarette and drops the butt into his jacket pocket for later. We push-start my bakkie and he jumps in with me.

"You'd better get out, I'm not having the thing checked now. I'm pushing on to Maitland." He remains in his seat, stiff as a poker.

"Out," I order.

Reluctantly, he opens the door and points at my foot, "Born like that?"

5

The silence of the land went home
to one's very heart – its mystery, its greatness,
the amazing reality of its concealed life.

THE HOME STRETCH brings me to the dorp where I grew up. As I enter memories multiply and overpower me so that I'm unable to think about Koert any more.

Tears, nearly; heartache that I'm almost able to touch in my chest. *Bossieveld* stretches around this dorp, as wide as the vulture flies. In rain years the red grass pushes up. The veld surges and flows, with koppies of ironstone and mountains with cliffs where animals find shelter during the cold winters, where ewes search out the warmth of besembos during the lambing season. Elsewhere it breaks open into rivers and streams and vleis full of platannas and bullfrogs and wild geese. But only when the water runs, when the eyes of the springs open. I want to remember it like that one last time.

The night before the millennium, I recall, comrades from the Landless People's Movement arrived on Ouplaas. They planned to incite November and Mildred and the Zukas: "Your baas stole the land from you."

But the workers of Ouplaas were already too merry for such

talk. Mildred took in some of the poison, as Pappie afterwards referred to it, though not enough for the LPM. And Pappie wouldn't listen to a word of her nonsense once the comrades had driven off to the next farm in their minibus.

"Can you believe that they – *they* – dare to call us *amaYuro-phu*, Europeans." And he showed his hands, hands that could sift the soil to test its colour and fertility. And eyes that could read the clouds: the ones like cigars that roll the cold and rain in their sheaths, the broken haze that announces the coming of the west wind and drought.

"Who can survive without God's grace; does any farmer know how to keep sheep farming going during the seven-year droughts?" Pappie asks. "Show me the farmers who are the men among boys." He shakes his head in the pale yellow light of the table lamp. Despondent about the future of the country at times, but not always, he went to his grave firm in his faith and convinced that he had lived a righteous life.

Past now, I must journey past the memories, they have all passed and have nothing to do with me now.

I remove my foot from the accelerator and glide breathlessly downhill, under the railway bridge and into the dorp. Martin Jasper Louw. Never heard of him. Never seen him. Delete his name. I arrive anonymously, shy about my intimate bonds with the dorp. I peer about, almost hoping for a greeting. No one steps out of their houses, straightens a dress, a tie, approaches with outstretched hand of welcome, my goodness, it's Ben and Kotie Louw's son, it can't be!

Back to my memories, then, for the last time. I have to undertake my very last journey to Ouplaas. So: to the south of this dorp lie *bossieveld* and koppies and vleis that together constitute the farm Ouplaas, where fleeces and meat grew in abundance and earned money that enabled me to gain an education.

And now a word comes to me, disturbing, just like "impostor" on the day of my departure. "Funk" jumps into my head. The word means "cowering fear" a condition of panic or terror. Hopefully, I'll find Koert on Ouplaas today so that I can complete the mission. As far as funk goes, we'll have to see how I deal with it as and when it comes.

Koert's waiting for me, at least, that's what I suspect. He's awaiting the arrival of his uncle, but not as a scaredy-cat with the heebie-jeebies – God forbid – he's merely waiting.

Here's the school to the left, the grounds deserted, the children inside, who knows. The pine trees that used to line the fence are all gone. By now I know what to expect: wood is fuel, not even their summer shade could save the trees. They were there to be used; now they're all gone.

Here's a tree after all, behind high wire, here's a seringa, its winter arms pointing upwards; here on the dorp square an oak has remained, and so have the monuments. Here's the post office, its doors and windows boarded up with corrugated iron. To leave the town I must turn left onto the southbound road to Steynsburg.

The Dutch Reformed Church has a razor wire fence around it. Dominee can sell off this stinkwood chair and this painting. It was my late mother's – it means nothing to me any more, the congregant stutters about her contribution. The day of the auction has arrived. And likewise the next offering, the one the farmer brings: take my old Massey Ferguson tractor, let the people bid for it, the highest bidder can have it. The dominee plays auctioneer, he does it with aplomb, with growing urgency.

Funk must have reigned in the church hall that day. The handful of congregation members who've remained look up at a strip
of light from the highest window, straight from God. They're
the ones who feel the creeping fear most strongly. Will we raise
enough today to put up that razor wire right around the church?
As long as we can protect the House of the Lord against the su-
perior numbers, they think and tremble. And: another cup of tea,
Dominee? Here's one of my nice thin pancakes for you, I know
Dominee's got a sweet tooth. Let the trees around the church
go if they have to, as long as our place of worship survives. We'll
even share the church if needs be. On Wednesday nights and
Sundays, a service for this lot in the morning, a second one for
that lot. But then the people who're asking to use it, who want
the extra services – because they are *different* after all, for God's
sake, forgive my blasphemy – must also contribute to the security fence. It's only fair. Put it to the mayor, Mr Mervyn Jantjies.
When the request came, the mayor straightened his polka-dot
tie and asked if he and his family – he has so many people to
support – could have the church trees for firewood the coming
winter. Then the congregation got a fright: they realised that the
world had changed radically, and how, and that the request for
shared responsibility was quite out of the question. It backfired
on them. Oh dear Lord, just let Mervyn Jantjies have the trees.
Let's get that fence with its razor wire up and save our church.
Look what's happened to the stately Reformed Church, it's been
turned into an orphanage. Children lying all over the place on
the pews – that's to say the pews that are still there, we hear the
last are about to go – the pulpit, dear Lord. Can't bear the sacri-
lege. Pass me a tissue, please.

Here's a bottlestore. On the pavement people lift their heads.

Apathetic, eyes and mouths that open and mutter about me. I slow down to take in more of this alien yet familiar embankment of buildings and parked cars, not many, I must say, mostly wrecks without tyres that have washed up here; and women emerging from shop entrances with bags of flour and sugar and mealies.

Here, the woman with the slovenly headscarf, gazing, where to, at what? The eyes have become dim, the hands claw at bags of food. A child helps her across the road, past my bonnet. All that remains in the dorp of the years of plenty with their red grass and fattened ewes is resignation – well, it was never quite as simple as that. My journey is, so to speak, at its end.

Booze? For how many on the farm? I can't sit and drink alone there. I've got the scarf for Mildred, woollen socks for November, Ouma Zuka's getting extra thick pantyhose. She must be very old by now.

Forget the booze. See which way the cat jumps first. The rules of the game have changed so much that I have to relearn everything from scratch.

Closer to the turnoff to Ouplaas, the veld has remained pristine. Not a sign of fire; even a piece of fencing is still intact. There's grass behind the jackal fencing – as if the veld's been saved for winter grazing. I take courage.

At the farm gate a young man with a gun stands guard. He approaches the moment he notices me. Though the sun isn't sharp at this time of year, he's wearing dark glasses with shiny, reflective blue lenses.

"You are Marlouw," he identifies me right away.

I put out my hand to greet him. He shakes in a triple movement as is the custom here, his name is Pilot. He stares at my suitcase on the seat next to me.

"And you must be November's son. Do you know how big you were when I left?"

Pilot doesn't answer; his eyes are hidden behind the glasses he's not going to remove.

"You were too small to remember me." I want him to know my background. His father used to be an important man on the farm, he knew everything about the sheep, he could identify every ewe with her lamb.

"Who *are* you, then?" I ask mischievously to get a reaction from him.

"Who are *you*?" he imitates me. He's got a gold ring in his ear and small drops of sweat form on his nose. It seems there's nothing unusual about me: my suitcase and clothes are too ordinary to admire, he stops peering.

"Your father?" I start.

"*iTopi lilapha*. My father is here."

"And Mildred, Lehlono, your little sister and Ouma Zuka?"

"They are all here. My little sister is a big sister now. Esmie Phumzile. She is number two on the farm. Ouma Zuka is the *umthakathi*."

"What's that?"

"It is a witch. Ouma Zuka has become a witch, and she lives there, in the koppies, that way. You see there? We do not talk to her any more." He swings his gun to the other shoulder.

The gun's an out-of-date thing. Do you still get ammunition for something like that? There must be heavier weapons here on Ouplaas; though perhaps an old gun like that provides enough protection during the day. Pappie kept hunting rifles, nothing else. He believed the Lord would protect you and that the time of your death was pre-ordained. When he began to weaken –

Heleen and I flew here for the funeral – the few remaining farm-ers slept with machine guns and magazines of ammunition, all illegal, in their bedrooms.

"May I get out?" My request seems reasonable to Pilot and he stands aside for me. Once again he scrutinises my clothes and suitcase on the front seat.

"Who are you? You are Koert's family. We know you will be coming, we wait for you every day. Along this road." He points down the road, in the direction of Maitland, and beyond to Aliwal North, and over the bridge across the Orange River, and further north all the way to Bloemfontein. That's how the news is embroidered, he means. I know how it goes. Pilot doesn't say much more. He waits for me to ask and tell. He wants to know more about me.

"Does Koert know about me?"

He waves his finger in my face, "Who are you?" he teases me. His skin is the colour of nutshell, his shoulders straight, and his teeth sparkling white. Pilot has grown into a handsome young man. He still doesn't allow me to see his eyes properly. I must give him something to get him on my side.

I load my suitcase onto the back of the bakkie. He lifts his leg over the side and nudges the toe of his gold Nikes against my case. I assume he'll drive back with me to the werf at Ouplaas.

"I knew your father, you know. Well, in my own way, that is. He probably knew me better than I knew him. Then my sister and I emigrated and never heard from him again. How's he do-ing? Is he well?"

"What have you got for us?" His only interest is in opening my suitcase. It's locked. "I must see what you have got in here." He fiddles with the lock.

"Listen, Koert and I are blood family." I cross my two index fingers – does he understand the sign – is it still in use here?
"This farm belonged to my father and mother. I know your father
and Mildred and Frans Zuka and Sindiswa and Ouma Zuka.
Even if your father and the others don't talk about us any more.
Why would they? I'm not here for funny business. I'm clean," I
show him my open hands. "You can search my stuff if you want –
but it's not necessary."

Pilot laughs. There are two Marlouws in the silver-blue
reflective lenses of his sunglasses. "Clean," he laughs again. It's
my choice of word and I have to smile at it myself. Pilot feels my
suitcase from left to right like you'd examine something soft in a
rolled-up towel.

"We have to search everyone's stuff. He did not say I do not
have to search *your* stuff. He did not say I must not look."

"Who are you talking about now? Koert? How's Koert doing? Is he okay?"

Pilot clambers onto the roof of the bakkie and digs a pair of
binoculars out from his trouser pocket – one of those trousers
that hang extra low at the crotch – and uses the opportunity to
fine-comb the farm. His shoes are new, the rest of his clothes are
dusty and patched, their colours like the winter veld around us.

"Pilot," I ask gently, "is it going all right with all of you here
on Ouplaas? Do you have enough to eat? Does the farm still support you all?" He's young and vulnerable, a mere boy – I can per-
suade him to tell me what I want to hear.

"It is going well with us; it is going well with my father. He
is an old man. My sister and I look after him; my father knows
every single sheep on this farm. Ouma Zuka stays in the mountain, that is where she stays now. *UMaGrace Zuka uyathaka.*

Ouma Zuka is a witch. We do not talk to an *umthakathi*. No one wants to see her. Now there is a problem with all the sheep.

"*Ngamakhalane aluma iigusha ebusika*. The ticks that bite the sheep in winter. The sheep fall over and they are going to die. We need to buy dose so we can inject them, or all the sheep on this farm will die. Koert knows about the ticks, but he is not talking to me now. He is not talking to my father. The ticks only come with the winter." Like a springhare, he hops from the roof of the bakkie.

"Did you bring us something to drink?" And he makes a boozing action with a funnelled hand in front of his mouth.

I throw my hands in the air to show I've brought nothing. He laughs in disbelief, shakes his head, and displays his own empty hands.

"You come here to our farm today and you say you bring nothing. We must get something to drink."

"What about Koert, is he okay?" No, nothing. I can't get him to say a single word about Koert Spies. It must be an order: can't believe he'd clam up like this of his own accord. "May I drive in?" I remain polite.

"You can drive, they are waiting for you. But when are we getting everyone something to drink? Promise?"

"Okay, I promise."

Along the farm road I travel as if in a real dream. I sail, gently-row-your-boat, and think of the texture of velvet pudding. I should never have come, too sentimental: I sit on Pappie's lap, fall asleep against his heart in the khaki shirt, hop-hop, see the springhares hopping ahead of us – ho, caught in the headlamps of the bakkie, us boys, brazen and horny, ready for the hunt with our .22s on the back of the bakkie, the springhares are knocked over one by one. The oldest one is Ouma Hasie. Ouma Hasie sits on a flat soapbox cart. Like two little horses, her two grandchildren pull her through the veld. Every now and then she looks back; her rabbit eyes are very scared. We must get off here, Ouma Hasie says, we're the last of our family. She sings the way for her two stalwarts. They pull bravely, they're not going to make it. Oh dear, Ouma Hasie. Sleep, my child, sleep, you're with your Pappie now, you don't have to be afraid of anything in the whole, wide world – and out on the veld there are still lots and lots of hares.

We drive past the koppies to the south, the koppies have ridges, ridges like the shoulders of Afrikaner oxen. Bottle-green *besembos* bushes grow on the shoulders right through winter. Stop, crush a twig in the palm of your hand and smell the spittle of a young girl. I drive towards the dip in the road where the water flows during the rainy season.

Pilot sings and looks straight ahead. All I see is his profile, his shiny teeth, his tongue when he licks his lips before starting his chorus:

> *Lala lala lala mntwana*
> *Lala lala lala mntwana*
> *Lala lala umama uzo'buya.*

Here's where Pappie planted round poplars to provide shade for the flocks during the hottest days. Here at the gate there used to be rows of battered bluegums that withstood drought after drought. I turn the window down to be able to hear the veld, the dry scrub that still clings to life, the bitterbossie that no mouth ever touches.

As I approach the werf, I hold my heart and my breath against the horror of the nakedness. God forgive the axe: there's not a single tree left.

Pilot sings louder, he carries me all the way to the farmstead. I won't cry. Take in the farm air: it is light, smells slightly blue, like the sky, and is utterly pure. At least nothing's changed up above.

This is where Pappie kept his stud rams with their ballbags full of seed; here are the troughs where cows quenched their thirst after milking, here the gate you had to open before you could drive onto the werf. I dedicate my arrival prayer to Pappie and Mammie and to little Heleen. Sing for me, Pilot, sing, man. So where's Koert?

Children run up to me. Koert's nowhere to be seen. Mildred – that must be her walking towards me – she's become old and small, not like the full bodies of the mamas that I once knew and still remember. She's got something with her. She crosses the werf where Mammie's rose garden once bloomed, dappled pink and antique apricot and red like family blood.

Nothing. Not a single tree, like in primal times, when the veld lay untouched, without homestead or kraal. I look up: the sky is grey and light blue, beautiful over the winter werf. Koert hasn't come out to greet me.

"Mildred, is that you?"

"Marlo'tjie," she sobs over me – little Marlouw – the one who has returned. She folds her blanket around my shoulders as I get out. It's a kind gesture. I look down at her hand, the same hand that wiped my bottom, washed my nappies, later made my bed and puffed up my pillow so that the hollow left by my head was invisible when I got into bed again. I cry.

Marlo'tjie, you must walk with open eyes. The time for tears has passed" – she'd always taken over Mammie's sayings and twisted them. "This isn't your mammie and your pappie's farm any more. We live here now, sack and pack. Happy as can be." And she laughs away her tears and takes my hand in hers so that I too stop crying. I accept: this is Ouplaas now.

"*Abantwana mabalumkela unyawo lwake*. Mind his foot, you children," she shouts crossly at the children shoving and pushing.

I look around helplessly. Children and grown up girl-mothers and poultry and mangy mongrels and skinny cats mill around, or simply stand without purpose. What in God's name do you do when you are so poor that you have nothing and have nothing to do? Everything's finished, everything destroyed: the farmyard is almost unrecognisable.

Off the children and animals and poultry go, crowd together in a sunny patch, wait and look and look and finish looking and saunter away to something: a game with the broken halves of a tennis ball. Mildred and I walk down the dusty pathway with our arms around each other's shoulders. Look, a shard from a cup. Bend and inspect it: Mammie's blue tea cups with the red-breasted robin on the branch of the birch tree.

"Mildred," I say in the absence of anything else to say – I had never wanted to see any of them again, I'd never wanted to see *this* – "I'm here now."

Here come Sindiswa and Frans Zuka, they've got a child with them, November's khaki figure comes over from the barn, there's Lehlono's too, with more children. The people of Ouplaas. We shake hands. They stand back to look at me. I look at them.

Esmie Phumzile is introduced to me. She withdraws her hand from mine. It hasn't seen much farm work. I notice how the children look at her clothes, new and fancy, different to all the others, her skin chocolaty, a shade darker than Pilot's or their father's. She walks slowly, not like a young person.

"We've been expecting you for a while now." She speaks fluent English, full of self-confidence. "It's good you came back to Ouplaas. That name! Can I tell you something – I've never liked it. Ouplaas, what sort of name is that? He," – and she points to her father, November Hlongwane – "he won't let us change the name." Esmie walks off, disapproving of those standing around the stranger.

"We'll speak again. Later tonight or tomorrow night," she says. Everyone looks at the pink glass beads tinkling on her silver sandals.

"*Mahle*. Pretty," a little girl whispers. Esmie is the princess of the farmyard.

November comes forward to greet me. He's turned into an old man with old bones. He starts singing, my hands in his:

Lead, kindly Light, amid the encircling gloom,
Lead thou me on;
The night is dark, and I am far from home;
Lead thou me on.
Keep thou my feet; I do not ask to see
The distant scene; one step enough for me.

"I've been thinking about you, Marlo'tjie. Koert told us you were coming. Then I thought: you must sleep here in our house because it is also the house in which you were a child. You can't go and sleep in the dorp like a throwaway lamb." He laughs at his own joke.

"We spoke a lot about where you'll sleep. We're giving you Ouma Zuka's mattress," Mildred now says.

"So where *is* Ouma Zuka?" I ask to hear what they say about her.

"She had to go to the mountains, she's living there now." Mildred tilts her head towards the koppies to the north-west. She takes me aside. "Koert told Ouma Zuka she had to get off the werf. He said she's a witch, that she keeps making trouble. We never ever see her any more. I send the children with food every Monday. Recently they've come back with a story that Ouma Zuka's walking on her hands like a baboon. And they taunt her: *imfene, imfene.* I smack them when they do it. *Andiyazi into engene lo makhulu.* I don't know what's going on with the old woman."

"She's not an unchristian person, that old woman," November chips in. "We should go and fetch her. It's not good for her, walking around all alone there, that's what makes her head go funny."

Pilot taunts from behind, "*UMaGrace Zuka uyathaka,* ouma Zuka is a witch, Marlouw. And she brings trouble. Look, this time it is the *amakhalane* biting the sheep to death. Big-time trouble. When?" He makes the boozing motion again.

Esmie stayed put when she heard the talk about Ouma Zuka. "Koert will have to say. We can't just go and decide to let Ouma Zuka live here again." She looks at me. "It will not be our decision to bring her back. We can't decide anything on our own any more." She walks off and disappears around the side of the house.

Mildred leads me into the house by my arm. She talks non-stop now, like the *boere-anties* of long ago, complete with heaving bosoms and over-the-top hospitality. I simply *must* hear about everything, see it all. The house has been divided into four living quarters to provide for the needs of three families, as well as for Koert Spies.

"Does he live alone?"

Mildred nods. "More or less." She tilts her head again. "Esmie." She rolls her eyes to the roof.

"Oh, Mildred, if his mother ever gets to hear this." I catch myself in time and say no more. Mildred knows what I mean, she was never stupid. She takes my arm and we walk on.

"And November Hlongwane, Pilot and Esmie Phumzile live here. Sometimes she sits in the sun here with Pilot, but she doesn't really live here. This is their section, here," and she waves her hand to point out everything I should see.

This was our sun room. Half of the sitting-room has been added to make their quarters more spacious. Down the middle of it a partition of cupboard planks and cardboard has been hammered together. Closer to the window they've simply hung curtaining. I fondle the material: little aeroplanes tumble, red ones with green wings, spectres; I used to fall asleep with them behind closed eyelids every night.

Mildred notices. "Yes, weren't they smart in your old room. Shame." She's in high spirits at the excitement of having me in the house, hers, and at the privilege of being able to show me everything, to surprise me, even shock me a little. She secretly enjoyed my reaction to the curtain.

"What on earth's happened to the furniture, Mildred? We *did* leave everything for you. The dining room table and chairs and the fridge and all the stuff from the sitting room, the sofas and coffee tables. Where is it all? Did you have to sell it?"

"No, not sold. All gone to Koert. He asked for all of it and

we lugged it into his quarters. That was quite a day! Screaming
and fighting. Pilot had too much drink in him; he smashed some
stuff to smithereens. Take, take. That's all I said: Let him take
the lot." Mildred strides on so she doesn't have to say anything
more about the furniture. Behind us, Pilot bursts out laughing.

"But Mildred, it's your furniture, isn't it? After the funeral
you got everything. Everything."

She cuts me dead. "You get Ouma Zuka's mattress. But you're
sleeping in November's house, you'll sleep next to him. He gets
rheumatism in the cold of night. He needs medicine, doctor's
pills, Marlo'tjie."

"That's fine, Mildred," is all I say. "You're making my heart
sore." It's clear they spent a lot of time speculating about my
sleeping arrangements, and they've planned everything down to
the last detail.

I wanted to ask more about the missing furniture. The carpets and curtains and bedding, the scatter cushions to push behind your back when you watch television, the television. All
gone. Koert's got everything. I'm becoming increasingly uneasy.
Heleen suspected he was sick. I have to get to see the man: he
must explain what's going on here.

I start walking towards the furthest part of the house where
Koert's quarters ought to be, but Mildred hasn't finished with me
yet, not by any means.

"You have to see everything, Marlo'tjie," and she draws the
"everything" out.

I'm tired, impatient. "Why can't I see Koert now, that's what
I want to know?" Mildred's hand supports my elbow. Pilot and
Lehlono and the Zukas and all the children and dogs draw
closer.

"Take your time, Marlo'tjie."

And then I click: Mildred will be my guide from now on. Her body, gestures and explanations will provide the signs that I must follow until I reach Koert Spies. I must do as she says: first I must understand how Koert's influence has penetrated even their private spaces; after that I can prepare myself to meet him. I'm still uneasy.

Sindiswa and Frans Zuka live in the remaining section of the sitting room and the first bedroom – the one with the blue ceiling that Mammie used as a guest room – with their son Headman, who hasn't come to greet me yet, and the Zukas' other children as well.

"Headman has just returned from initiation on the mountain, he was a very good *umkhwetha*," Mildred tells me. Chuffed, Sindiswa and Frans nod, and smile to show how proud they are.

"Headman, where are you? Come out of your hole," she shouts. He's been lagging behind us. Back there somewhere. The way he avoids looking at me exacerbates my unease.

"He didn't want to go at first," Sindiswa reveals. "That's how they are. Afraid of the knife. But he knows a young boy who wants to become a man doesn't have any choice. He was naughty, the boy child, but now he's a man. We need him on the farm; he knows how to fix the windmill. Headman," she calls and blows her nose on the hem of her dress.

Headman's hand is on his brother's head. He doesn't utter a single word. He averts his eyes, and just as the procession comes into motion, looks at me again. I extend my hand – no? He's not going to greet me.

To the kitchen now. I feel uncomfortable, like after an indulgent Sunday afternoon meal. It's so late. A meeting with Koert

Spies – His Honour – is not on the cards for today; by now I can predict how things will turn out.

Mildred shoos some of the children away and points out what I've already noticed: the kitchen table is also missing. There's an emptiness in the kitchen, and there is not much in the cupboards. Empty cooldrink bottles, a flour bag filled with the coffee and chicory mixture, the stuff that's always been drunk here, and ghoe-ghoe mealies soaking in an enamel dish. The stove has been lit. Everyone aims for its warm heart. Me too: I can't struggle against this stream. Hands and bottoms must first be warmed – there's time for everything here.

I move aside, my chest is closing up. My disquiet doesn't leave me. Still, I have to laugh: a child spits on his finger and nimbly touches the stove plate, "siss" it says, and he lets out a little shriek.

"Come on, you lot, Marlo'tjie, you too," Mildred calls.

"I'll take a look at your house later, Mildred. I need fresh air."

"No, no," she urges, "it's not that bad. You're a boerseun. Quick, quick," Mildred orders, and gathers everyone to continue the tour. Together, that's right, there's no time for turning back now. Watch out for signs. Take your time. My skin's started prickling under Mildred's hand.

The bathroom is shared by everyone. There's a shard of sunlight soap, smooth from use, and a towel, and everything's spotlessly clean. The toilet door is firmly shut.

"We take our shits outside in the veld," Mildred explains. "The children messed in your toilet. Honestly. They don't know about aiming properly or pooping down a hole, then I come here" – she pinches her nose, laughs at me – "and it stinks all the way to my house." She points down the passage to the last two bedrooms where she and Lehlono and their family live. "So I said: We must all agree that the toilet is locked from today. We'll shit outside in the veld like we did in the old days when we lived in our huts on the koppies. Nice and far away, you remember, don't you?" and she nudges me. "The olden days, dearie, dearie me." She clutches her cheeks and doubles up with laughter.

She's proud of her own little place. The second and third bedrooms are shared by her – that's Mildred – and her son Lehlono and his children. Three, she counts on her fingers, her grandchildren, milling about our legs.

"Lehlono's wife is dead," Mildred tells. "You know what from?" she asks. I nod. "Lehlono's taken himself another girl now."

A hole the size of a small window has been broken through the wall between the two rooms. "I held the bottle for the babies when they screamed." She demonstrates how she aimed the bottle through the window with the teat at just the right angle.

There's an old glossy paper almanac on her wall, open at May 1997 with a picture of a naked beauty on a Toyota Hilux bonnet. To the left against a grass-green wall there's a Formica and chrome kitchen dresser which she's turned into a clothes cupboard. The partition behind the glass door has been arranged with a jar of Vaseline, her hairbrush and old magazines, a pencil and tins, and boxes filled with personal stuff. The mirror at the back has gone, and Mildred has papered the side neatly with pilchard tin labels. Absolutely everything is shown to me.

"And here?" I ask about the furthest part of the house where Pappie's study linked up to the garage and meat room. That must be where Koert stays?" By now I'm grumpy, really irritated.

"All his," Mildred answers. "All three of the rooms and the

garage are Koert's. But not the way you white people used it. Ja-nee," she sighs ironically. "Here you'll see that the door has been plastered up so that we lot can't just drop into Koert's house from this side at any old time. You see?"

"Is Koert here, Mildred? I ought to say hello to him."

"He is here, but you can't see him now. You may only see him when he sends for you. Oh," she calls out, "*andifuni inkhathazo tu*, I really don't feel like trouble."

Pilot moves nearer when he hears Koert being discussed. In the gloomy interior only his teeth and gold earring flash in the light. I frown. He comes even closer; now I see he's pulling faces at the door that's been plastered closed. And he wants me to notice what he's up to.

"Some tea for Marlo?" The tour's finished, Mildred suddenly sounds deflated. She's no spring chicken any more. No, she's tired of the hospitality game. It wasn't all that exciting after all. And the only thing I harp on is Koert, Koert, Koert. Mildred sighs again and lets the others guide me along.

"Some tea for Marlo," Pilot mimics her. "In the little cups with the little saucers," he continues.

Laughing all around me. The atmosphere's changed here at the wall of Koert's quarters. Mildred's cackle rises merrily above the others as if she's enjoying herself again. I must get out of here, I never *was* part of this. The presence of the white outsider has awoken memories of the old order. Tea for the white baas, everyone blusters, the air stuffy from the heated breath. Thankfully, the procession starts moving once more. People, children, a mongrel against my legs, all clogging the passage to the kitchen. The ceiling seems lower than I remember it, as if it's collapsed, the mongrel's warm tongue touches my hand.

"Wait," I call out, hemmed in and afraid that my foot might get hurt. Mildred also intervenes half-heartedly from behind; but no one hears or understands why they need to be careful. This is excitement of the first order.

"Tea and biscuits," one shouts, and Frans slaps the child so that his head hits the wall. Some of his other children who are also becoming unruly dart out of reach.

There's no need for them to behave like this in the narrow passage. I must get out. "Wait a minute." I'm flustered by all the pushing and shoving. Oh my goodness, I must get out of here. I choke on the stuffiness, when Headman reaches out his arm and half strangles me from behind, cocky as hell. His armpit, rank with the smell of venison, opens right in my face. I duck – but the smell gets to me.

"Tea," I call out too to prod everyone on a bit and break the knot and hurry them down the passage. "Mildred, where are you, man?" and I shrug off the blanket that she'd folded over me earlier, I could just trip on it. Luckily someone behind me grabs it, so it's not trampled on the ground. Mildred immediately says what must be done with her blanket. She's also angry.

"Wait, give it here," and I take the blanket that's being passed to me over the heads and wade on through the bodies. I've never been overwhelmed by people in this way, everyone all around and right next to me with arms and hands and legs and feet. I must get away from here before I pass out completely.

The herd of breaths presses forward together, we battle past the toilet door, where an unholy smell seeps through, out, to the outside, but people block me at my sides, ahead and behind me. Lehlono talks about the year when the tractor ploughed so nicely and when there was oats for the lambing ewes, and enough of it too.

"No, we must get that tractor going again, Marlo'tjie. Hey?" The children to the left and the mongrels to the right. We're too tightly bunched up to loosen ourselves from one another; all we can do is to try to move forward together. Bottoms, I'm particularly aware of the round shapes of bottoms pressing against me.

We push on down the passage to the door on the right that opens onto the stoep. "Open it, please, Mildred," but I no longer get anything from her. Mildred easily gets into a huff. The blanket episode made that clear enough. Here *they* are boss; it's *their* house. If anyone's going to be saying how things will be done around here, *they* will be the ones to do so. To Koert's quarters for a breather, away from everyone – you must be joking. A visit to his quarters is out of the question, and no one can say for how long. The bastard! He didn't even bother to welcome me.

I must let go. The people of Ouplaas have been expecting me, and here I am among them. At last. Tea and biscuits on their way – and they're hoping for more – and there's a twittering and a yackety-yacking and a fluttering in my tummy and a tune played on a *trompie* for me. Marlo'tjie has arrived!

We're outside now. Everyone's still shoving me around: there's more, more to see. Before I know it we're back inside, back in the sun room so that November can show me the mattress that's been carried in for me. There's a single blanket folded at its foot end. And now they're all watching to see how I look at my bed.

*

It's evening. My suitcase has been carried in and placed next to my mattress. Someone has arranged my toothbrush and toothpaste and comb and torch and compass in a row at the end of the mattress. The biscuits that had excited the children never mate-rialised. At least Esmie brought me tea and a slice of bread on a tin plate. I sit on the mattress to eat and expect her to leave, but with her hands on her hips she watches how I greedily swallow the bread down with the hot tea.

"Nice," I say, even though there's no butter or jam.

She smiles. "You're hungry, Marlouw." I look up at her thin legs and the triangles of her arms on her hips; she's changed into long pants for the evening.

"How did you know I was coming?"

"News always reaches us. We hear everything. Which one's recently died from the virus, and why, about the availability of coffee and tea and flour and sugar, about everyone who comes and goes." She doesn't evade the sickness. I won't ask her about it at this stage; it's clear she's got AIDS herself. She's ominously thin.

"People get totally excited about fresh news. We fill ourselves on it during the empty nights when we have nothing else to do. It's the one thing poverty can't take away from us and that won't make us sick. Tell me what it's like on the other side."

I launch into an account, my words too fast and too numer-ous. I sketch a rosier picture than the reality I know, without any heart. My thoughts are elsewhere. With Esmie keeping me com-pany – I suspect she's been instructed to do so – and with the tea soothing me, the tiny hairs on my arm have settled down. I've become calmer. I can now admit that I haven't yet reached my destination. I still have to advance to Koert's quarters, all the way to Koert himself, and it will involve much struggle and effort. For that I'll have to rely on myself.

"Kangaroos, clubs, shopping? What else do you want to

know?" I ask Esmie. "No, there are very few black people."

When she notices the time, she bites her lip and taps the fingers of one hand on the palm of the other. "I must go, I'll have to run. Koert will punish me; he can't stand it when I stay away." We walk out together to one of the open fire places. There's more than one on the werf. The direction of the wind determines which one is used.

"Wait here," and she walks towards Koert's quarters. It's the fastest I've seen her move today. She touched my hand lightly before going, "Thanks for everything, we're in business."

In the west the last light is fading. I'll wait for my chance with Koert. It's obvious he's gained himself a special place on Ouplaas. Merely seeing him is a privilege in itself. He's untouchable. It's not for nothing his mother called him "my king".

Lehlono has stacked the fire in a shelter where the wind won't disturb it, and I feel its heat flow through me. Later Esmie Phumzile shows up outside again and ensures that she stays close to me. There's always somebody near me. Esmie's wearing a gossamer-thin cardigan with her jeans. Her skin contrasts deeply with the turquoise of the cardigan. She walks about spiritedly, even showing off, but doesn't say much. I suspect she's too tired most of the time. In the light of the flames she appears darker, even more unhealthy than before. The moment I as much as peep in the direction of Koert's quarters, she's right next to me. When I go off to piss, I don't return. I take a wide berth around tonight's fire in a direction that will lead me to Koert. If only they'd let me get to his door.

"No, Marlouw, you can't go there," Esmie calls when she sees what I'm up to, and comes trippling along, breathless, blocking me off from the door. There are bars in front of it.

"Why not, what's going on here? Why can't I say hello to Koert? Why hasn't he come out to me?"

"He'll let me know when he's ready to see you. I'll bring the message. Come," and we walk back.

"I know," I say despairingly, "I know." Esmie shrugs her shoulders.

Pilot arrives, without his dark glasses now. He's noticed that Esmie has had to keep me away from Koert. It's the first time I've noticed how bright his eyes are, how alert he is. He greets me with his smile and shiny white teeth. His shift at the gate is done, he may rest now. The night shift is Headman's.

"You're not allowed anywhere near Koert's door," he adds his bit. His eyes are larger than his sister's, and slant upwards slightly at the corners. He stands up close against me.

"I feel like a beer," I say to him.

"Wait, I'll ask Koert," Esmie scampers across the yard and disappears behind us where the darkness is deepening.

It's getting late. We wait, thirsty. Esmie doesn't reappear. Pilot sits so meekly that I decide not to mention anything more about the beer. We could drive into the dorp with my bakkie and buy beer, but it seems no one may do anything without Koert's permission. Best be patient and wait and see how things operate here.

Frans Zuka sits opposite me on a tattered old office chair that hadn't belonged to Mammie. He rolls Boxer tobacco in a scrap of newspaper. He watches the fire intently and gets up only when it burns low and looks as if the coals are about to die. He pulls a *besembos* stump from the pile of firewood, weighs the precious fuel – yes, that's right, yes – positions it on the fire, and smiles.

He doesn't have much to say. They're keeping the fire going specially for me.

Supper is ready. A three-legged pot of mealie meal is placed near the fire; a saucepan of tomato and onion sauce is brought from the kitchen. Mildred and Sindiswa dish up. Two little girls hand out the tin plates one by one. Bright-eyed, they concentrate on their task – they know they're dead if they spill a single scrap.

There's some meatiness to the sauce, the pap just stiff enough for you to roll a little ball between your fingers. Esmie and the children watch to see if I can do it the way they do. Esmie manages without even looking at her fingers, though she doesn't eat heartily like the rest. I don't feel too uneasy. It helps that Headman has gone. He must be dying of cold standing guard out there.

The saucepan has been made to stand on flat stones at the edge of the fire. No more than a mouthful remains after supper's been measured out and dished up for everyone. Mildred sees me eyeing it surreptitiously.

"That's right, Marlo'tjie. It's the saucepan you had your Sunday dinners from." She gives a hearty laugh. One of Sindiswa's little boys looks for leftovers, and is immediately chased off. "*Sukuphatha apho mntwana, yekha Headman.* Get away, child, that's Headman's, that."

"How often do you get sheep to slaughter per month?" I ask. The speech rhythm falls easily on their ears, a familiar manner of speaking that I unpack from my basket: the wind is biting, the sun is westering, our old miesies has a heart of gold, oh my goodness.

"Koert says when we can slaughter sheep," Mildred explains. "Sometimes he says today we must slaughter for everyone. Even on Sundays, when everyone's dressed for church. Then Esmie is

sent: yes, yes, yes, you *have* to slaughter today." She avoids looking in Esmie's direction while speaking about her.

Esmie puts down her plate, makes a sucking sound with her
tongue against the back of her teeth, and marches off. Instantly
Sindiswa Zuka picks the plate up and shares the leftovers among
her children.

Mildred doesn't take much notice of the princess. "I'll be
in my church clothes already, November's got his jacket on,
Sindiswa and Frans too, we're ready to walk to church and for
visiting afterwards. Esmie Phumzile," – and she whispers so that
Esmie can't eavesdrop on her way back to Koert's quarters – "yells
at us. She's still a child, after all, Marlo'tjie, and now she yells at
her own father: No, we have to slaughter today. She even hit November once when he refused to slaughter on the Sabbath."

"Yes," November adds, "she slapped me right here on my
cheek. I get very cross with Esmie Phumzile. No, she's not behav-
ing like a child of mine."

"And then?"

"Then Pilot takes the dog and he and Headman go off to
collect the sheep, and Pilot slits a sheep's throat and hangs it up
on the two poles and his father skins it, and you see, all the time
we still have a bit of meat left over anyway. There was no need to
slaughter today, I mean that Sunday, like Esmie kept insisting,
and Koert too. My meat, my meat, he always says. Some days I
have to bite my lip, you know. And we always have to make sure,
even now, that there's some cooked meat left over for him, even
though he's stuffed himself silly, or else he'll go into a frenzy."
Mildred has mellowed in the low orange light of the fire. There's
not a trace of bitterness in her words.

"I take my Nikes off before I go out into the veld when I have

to slaughter sheep," Pilot adds and holds his gold left shoe close
to the fire so I can see – but not too close, in case a coal shoots
out and damages it.

"And then there're times when we go without meat for a
whole month," Mildred continues. "Esmie Phumzile, I say to
her, you go and tell Koert we're short of meat now. No, not a
word from him. We're not allowed to slaughter. Everything belongs to him. *Ingathi ziyamshiya ingqondo.* He's a bit crazy," she
points at her headscarf.

"Surely they're your sheep? It's *your* farm. What's going on
here, Mildred? November? Has he become your new baas? And
how will he ever know if you slaughter a sheep?"

"It is, it is," November says, "the Lord bless us, Ouplaas *is*
ours." And then he falls silent and looks at Mildred who in turn
gazes into the distance.

Pilot notices I'm watching him and beats his open palm with
his fist. He hasn't stood still for a moment – even during the
meal he walked around with his tin plate in his hand. He keeps
looking at Koert's quarters where it's too dark now to distinguish
anything.

"You people will not believe me when I tell you: *UMaGrace
Zuka ungumthakati.*" He looks at me: "Ouma Zuka is a witch.
Look, there is her fire." Pilot points to the darkened west.

"She is the one who makes all the trouble for us. She makes
Esmie sick, she makes Koert difficult during the day; and at
night when everyone is sleeping, he gets angry, you do not want
to see it. Ouma Zuka, she is the one who does it. She causes all
the trouble on the werf. *Ihilihili,* that is what she is, the one who
wanders around aimlessly. She has got many names now, Marlouw, you would not know. Everyone has got a different name

for her. Why? Because she has got something on everyone. Some nights when my father cannot sleep because of the rheumatism that makes him moan and groan, he hears her coo, so now he calls her *ihobe* – that is the turtle dove." Pilot spits. "She is *not* a turtle dove. Turtle doves are not like that."

"Frans?" I address the man sitting on the drum. "This is your farm and your sheep too, why don't you slaughter when you need to? And what does Pilot mean about the *umthakati*?"

"No, it's true. Marlo'tjie, things are different now. The farm has changed. And Koert can tell if we catch a sheep and want to slaughter it. He knows the numbers. He's got his spies who tell him what's going on. No, it has changed on this farm."

"How has it changed here on Ouplaas, Mildred?"

Pilot adds something in isiXhosa. He speaks urgently: "*Um-aGrace Zuka ungumthakati. Anifuni uku-understanda.* She is a witch, you refuse to believe me. If one of us puts a foot wrong, she hears everything. Who do you think tells her? Think about it carefully. It is Headman!" His voice rings out and falls on the fire, petrol on flame. He's on a roll, shouts about Headman who carries lies to his Ouma Zuka in the hills, and about Ouma Zuka who's jealous of Koert because he gives the people lots of stuff. And look what's happening now.

"The *ihilihili*," he now screams about Ouma Zuka, "the one who wanders around aimlessly. Do you see, now?" He wants to order his thoughts, but all we hear is the rasping edge of a narrative that's out of control. No one wants to listen to him.

"*Suka!*" November reprimands his son; Pilot is all the more inflamed. They don't hear a word of what he's saying. He's enraged. His face contorts and words spew from his crop as his golden Nikes dance around the fire.

Frans hears something and jumps up. The darker the werf, the more tense the adults become. Esmie Phumzile returns from Koert's quarters. In a single action Frans grabs the *kierie* that he's had at his side all evening, swings low, and hits Pilot full on his stomach so that he cries out and bends double. His eyes flash white at us.

"Leave Headman out of this," Frans orders. He's proud of his son; he won't allow him to be insulted. And nobody wants to hear another word about the *umthakati*, about Ouma Zuka.

"Oh dear," Mildred sighs, and takes my hand in hers and caresses it. "Let's keep off the business of the sheep in case Esmie Phumzile carries stories to Koert." She whispers in my ear. "We're still living nicely here off the fat of the land on your Ouplaas, we've got more than enough."

Esmie Phumzile must have noticed what was happening on her way back to us. Heading for the fire, she passes between Pilot and Frans Zuka and gives her brother a box on the ears. Of all the drinks imaginable, she's got a bottle of Jägermeister. "Koert says you must have a good time on his farm." She turns to me.

Pilot, still clutching his stomach, sticks his face into Esmie Phumzile's and slowly curls his lips from his teeth. "Graa," he growls from deep within his innards. She slaps him.

"You'll see," he says. "*Lo maGrace uzo'nifumana entanyeni* one-by-one. The witch will get you by the neck. One by one."

"Your cups," Esmie Phumzile requests, and I and the other adults hold out our tin mugs for a tot of the dark brown herbal drink. Through the darkness, someone else comes towards us. Frans and Sindiswa, with the children on their laps, have already noticed him, and wait for Headman with his raging armpits – I too smell him now– to enter the circle around the fire.

"What are you doing here? Your shift isn't over yet," Esmie snaps.

"It's cold and there's no one. I'm not sitting there waiting for nothing," he snarls back. Everyone looks up, surprised that Headman would speak to Esmie like that.

"His *umkhwetha* days are over, you see," Mildred whispers. "He's Mister Big now. He's a handsome boy, isn't he? Since his initiation he's become very jealous that Esmie sleeps with Koert."

Headman points to the quarters. "Why does Koert buy Pilot Nikes, and I walk around like this?" he slaps his boots with their holes at the toes. "That man, Koert, only does what *he* wants."

"What are you doing here?" Esmie goes for him again. "You're supposed to be standing watch at the gate. What are you doing at the fire, keeping yourself warm like a woman? I'm going to tell Koert."

"Go. Go tell him. What can he do to me?" Headman prances in front of her and rubs his genitals against her thigh. Pilot's there in a flash. He grabs Headman's arm and twists it behind his back, shoves him aside. Headman chokes with anger.

Esmie and Pilot take turns to pour the last of the booze down their throats. In the meanwhile, she's attached herself to her brother as if nothing has happened, touching and stroking him – you'd think they were lovers. It's to taunt Headman. He stares at them with red eyes, turns away from the people and remains in the background, heavy with indignation.

Those who have things with them collect these; I take my blanket – the one Mildred gave me – and we walk away from the last of the night's glowing coals towards the house. Some of the windows are broken and covered with hardboard and black

plastic – which I hadn't even noticed before. Tonight winter will
gnaw at the house.

Esmie Phumzile assures me that she'll talk to me again tomorrow. She shivers slightly. The darkness envelops her as she
walks away from us and the fire and enters Koert's quarters to
spend the night with him. We all head for our quarters, I follow November. It's my first night on the mattress next to his.
Everyone will lay down their heads and pull up their bedding.
Everyone's got pap and tomatoes in their bellies, me too. Thus I
become one with the people of Ouplaas.

*

I'm too exhausted for deep sleep tonight. I'd crept under the
blankets just as I was, with socks, jacket and scarf. At least I've
got two blankets; next to me, November Hlongwane only has
one. His old man's shoulder forms a small mound. A silent, steep
mountain. Sleep now, sleep sweetly. Sleepy dust in the eyes.
Rock-a-bye baby, little child, see how the night dons her pitch-
black cape. See the barn owl drop, drop down when he sees the
field mouse. See the night sky drop, drop her stars one by one,
two, three, from her black cloak, see her hand the shiny stars to
the children of men. Mammie's child must sleep now, Mammie's
hand closes my eyelids, brushes my cheek and tiny chin. Her
ring finger touches my dimple – mine is a little shallower than
Heleen's. She's folded the blanket double over my lame foot.

There *must* have been some guilt. The splints at night, the
leather bands and buckles tightened in an effort to force the foot
up and back; the comical orthopaedic shoe by day. Show us your
foot, Marlouw, the girls taunted me during school breaks. They

lifted their dresses and exposed themselves, tried everything and giggled. I'd rather have died than show them. Then the arguments crept down the passage to my bed from Pappie and Mammie's room when they thought I was asleep. The few words I could make out were enough. The splints and the shoes hadn't worked, you see. The foot needed to be operated on, and soon, too. I think they were short of money. That was the root of the problem. Mammie got so furious with Pappie that some nights she went and slept with Heleen. Early in the morning I found them there, rosy-white with sleep, girls' breath, their smell that of women. Then Pappie sold the car, some of his rams too, and kept back just enough to keep the stud going. There was a drought: that I remember. On Sundays there was no longer a carafe of Muscatel with its doily on the table. I do believe Pappie would have done everything in his power to make the operation possible. Listen to me now, you Ben, yes you, Mammie would shout down the passage . . . They never explained why my foot wasn't operated on.

Now everyone in this house sinks into the deep sleep of the early part of the night; the breathing becomes languid and slow. November snores, sighs, and moves his hipbone so that it doesn't touch the floor through the mattress. He sends a last arrow prayer up to his Lord who will lead him into green pastures in his latter days.

At midnight it becomes busier. The sleepers rise slightly from the pit of deep sleep. One reaches a caring hand towards the little mites next to their mother, Sindiswa; Headman's dreams are prickly with anger; the bodies of Lehlono and his new, shy girl slip into each other effortlessly and they release sounds of love. The doors of this house could never muffle the passion of so many bodies.

There were weekends when our house was full to overflowing. I remember mattresses in a row along the passage, nephews and nieces under Pappie's winter coats when we ran out of quilts, but there were never as many as fill the farmhouse now. Two on a bed, four in the corner, a tattered piece of muslin to separate the lusty pair's cries. May as well let the children get to know the calls of life, the short, thick spurt of fresh sperm that the girl feels against her receptive walls, that makes her cry out in delight at this single heavenly moment on earth.

Late night is sombre. Giel's face in Aliwal North rears up. He glares at me with poisonous reproach. If he'd had the opportunity, he would have finished me off. He is slime. Why are his eyes still haunting me? It's Koert who's driving him mad. Koert, with his power stretching from farm to farm and dorp to dorp, like birdlime ensnares the wretched of the earth to himself. Giel's also trapped, and he hates it like the plague.

"Take me with," Giel screamed even before I'd driven off in the battered old bakkie, "I'll help you find Koert. Two's better than one." He began gnawing at the inside of his thumb. Out of the question, I didn't even give it a passing thought.

Everyone's under Koert's sway. Mildred, November, Pilot, Lehlono, the Zukas. Esmie too, even though she plays the princess. Headman hasn't got a snowball's hope in hell against Koert. "Someone has to keep the whip in hand," Mildred had remarked.

I swallow my spittle, dive into the shallows, and dream of Mammie's pretty curtains that lift and billow on summer Sundays, and let in geranium-scented air. I wake up and touch November's arm. It startles him, he wakes too, his old man's sleep light in the depths of the night.

"November," I whisper, "what's happened to all the curtains? They help against the cold, you know."

"Go to sleep, you." His words are harsh for someone who's just woken up. "Jackets, dresses, we used the cloth for everything. Don't you know how we do things? Look at that rich man's belly of yours." He turns his back on me, but the words were too severe, he won't fall asleep easily. He's a Christian.

I fumble for my shoes in the dark, half-fasten the laces, and walk out onto the werf. It's filled with the shadows of dancing, dead things, and it is profoundly beautiful under the sickle moon. I pull my jacket tighter and undo my zip to piss on Ouplaas's one-time garden, right where Mammie had her bed of ranunculuses.

Fuller and deeper shadows fall on Koert's quarters. I'll have a look, continue my journey until I reach him, get right to him, because I have to. I have to find out who Koert Spies is before I leave Ouplaas. There, there's a thread of light coming from his windows. I get closer: just a single step – perhaps slightly more – to go. "Damn it!" Two men with balaclavas pounce on me. One hits me through the face, the other grabs my elbows, holds my arms from behind, and presses his freezing cold body against my back. "*Sizakukubetha uthambe*. We'll fuck you up."

The shock gives me strength, I react instinctively, duck, and slam my head into his chin – they mustn't think, "mmm," because "mmm" – a hand covers my mouth – that because I hobble, I'm a cripple. I try to free my arm from his grip and shove my buttocks to get him hard in the crotch. His hand shoots away from my mouth; I'm amazed at my success.

Imagine, right here at the window that was once Pappie's study. What's worst is the isiXhosa in my ear, slopping like pap from a man's mouth. It nearly drives me berserk and makes a sense of ownership well up inside me: that I'm standing with my feet on this werf where the cold is rising from below; that I know this kind of winter's night all too well; that I know this house built on this ground better than anyone else; that I was suckled here with milk, milk that tasted of bossies – that I still have a claim to this ground. How dare they creep up through the night and attack me like this.

"Let me go, I wasn't doing anything. Fuck the lot of you, why can't I say hello to Koert?" and I head-butt the one holding me again. A candle is lighted in Koert's quarters. "Koert, come and help me, man, I'm your own bloody family."

They let go and stand aside, each lights a cigarette. I look through the window down a passage deep into the mournful gloom of Koert's quarters where the flame is still visible. Not a soul moves. I step forward to get a better view, and the two men are immediately at my side, though this time without touching me. Then the candle is extinguished and only the dark square of the window remains, with or without Koert inside.

One of the balaclava-men holds out a Stuyvesant to me, coughs dryly, and speaks to his mate. He sounds incensed, put out. The claim I made on my relationship with Koert, one that's supposed to protect me, has apparently touched a raw nerve. *"Ukuba uhlobene kutheni engenakungena? Ingaba abantu abali-hloniphi na igazi?* If he's family, why can't he go in? Don't people respect blood?" they wonder. My claim on our relationship has confused them. Now they nudge my shoulders. "Come on, back to November's room." I return to my sleeping place.

Some of the bodies in the other rooms have begun to move, loosening themselves from the grip of early-morning sleep. I hear a groan, a breath that draws in and out, shifts and lightens. My mattress has lost all body heat. I lie down, my shoes still on, and wait for the frost that will announce the hoary morning. I won't fall asleep again.

*

"Dose" is the first word I hear when I walk out onto the frost, teeth chattering. Pilot is dancing about. "We have to dose," he waves his arms; "the sheep are all dying. It is the paralysis tick, our meat is dying, and everyone's sleeping. Dose." He kicks a chicken to hell and gone. Today he's wearing brightly polished boots. "Dose!"

"Why the hell didn't you buy dose a long time ago?" I shout at him across the werf, playing baas.

"No money! We told Koert. Every day I say to Esmie: tell Koert to give us money, the sheep are all going to die, we have got fuck all meat for winter, we are all going to die here on Ouplaas. Koert says nothing, fuck off, he says. You give us money," Pilot demands of me.

"Come, the pap's ready," Mildred calls from the back steps at the kitchen. There's a strip of sugar on the slap pap. Only Koert gets milk.

"Don't you go and let all our sheep die today. Don't you dare." She's grumpy. "You men there! Frans, November, where's Lehlono! She screams at the three slowly making their way across the werf.

"What are you men doing to us? The time for beating about the bush has passed." She addresses me. "It's the men, it's their fault. The ticks come every year, every winter. Your father showed them how to kill the things to prevent the sheep from dying."

Frans and November keep their heads down, take their pap and squat to one side. Headman walks up too. He's not wearing a jersey under his overall like the others. He shivers under the bare cotton, his knuckles chapped, blue with cold as he takes the tin plate.

"Ten," he mutters, "there are ten dead at the Damkamp."

The Damkamp. The Springbokkamp. The Tweewindpompkamp. They've kept Pappie's names for the grazing camps without a single change. Do they still practice rotational grazing to save veld for the drought? What's the condition of the windmills? And the troughs? Is there water in all the camps? You must ensure that all the troughs on your farm are clean or you'll end up with diseases.

"It is Ouma Zuka's fault, this." Pilot wolfs down his pap greedily. "She is the one making our sheep die. *UMaZuka ebeyi-thethile lento*. Ouma Zuka predicted it."

When Headman sees me looking at him over my plate, he lifts his shoe, bends his foot inward, downwards like mine, starts hopping about on the other foot. "Koert, it's Koert. It's not Ouma Zuka," he chants.

"Stop that," his mother screams, and he freezes with his fake lame foot in the air.

One of the mongrels slinks up and Pilot throws down his cleanly scraped plate for the animal. Everyone watches the dog pushing the plate around trying to find a morsel, and hears him yelp at the smell of food. No one responds to Headman's allegations. More mongrels move in.

"Jeez, Mildred, don't you feed the poor things?" And I attempt to scrape some of my pap out for them.

Mildred grabs my wrists. "You eat that pap yourself. This

pap is for the *people* on Ouplaas. Eat your food and say thank you God."

Her words prick like needles, so early; her grip leaves my wrists sore. She pushes me aside.

"You will not fatten the dogs like you used to do on this farm, mutton and gravy overflowing from their bowls." She spreads her arms out. "That's what your dogs looked like and you dished them more and more food and said" – she imitates Mammie's voice – "oh, Mildred, please make sure there's enough pap for Kaptein and the other dogs, I don't want to have to go into the pantry on a Sunday and find there's not enough pap for the animals."

November looks up. "Sisi," he placates her and shakes his head. "God is watching."

"More food for your dogs than for us and our children on the farm, your dogs ate more meat than we did, you think I didn't notice?" she refuses to stop.

I draw away from the people and remain silent. It's difficult to digest Mildred's crap so early in the morning. Their newfound authority has to be balanced with old grievances. We neglected them; they neglect their animals. Their sheep are dying in droves in the veld.

November is getting angry because he sees how angry I've become. He waves his arms. His hands wave until the dust whirls up at his shoes; he's worried that the situation has got out of hand. One must be careful here. He sinks onto his old haunches, despairing. Has Mildred completely lost her head? Somebody they can use to their advantage has arrived on Ouplaas. Why go on about the dogs and all their bloody food? That's old, rotten stuff that just hurts everyone's ears. Now the paralysis ticks are

attacking their sheep, beyond this werf the ticks are walking up
the ewes' feet and into their arseholes where the flesh is naked.
The ticks burrow their tiny heads into the folds, grip tightly,
bore in and tap delicious blood and swell bigger and bigger just
like the white people's dogs in the olden days. Please let someone care now. See, the ticks get fat and their sheep drop dead.
Look, Marlo'tjie, the sheep lie about like ant heaps. And there's
no dose. But that's not the way I want to put it – *this* is what I
want to say: we need money to buy dose in the dorp. Mildred,
shut your mouth, he waves his arms across the earth until the
dust rises. He gets up slowly and gestures for me to come closer,
into the circle of Ouplaas's people. I must stand among them,
pap in my belly like the rest of them.

Inside the circle it's quiet. Pilot rubs his hands and holds
them out to warm in the sun. He dances about. He wants to remain here, comfortably at that, and catch the good times every
night at sunset, in god's name shut your mouths, please, stop
talking rubbish.

The sun is feeble so early in the day; *I'm* definitely not going
to say a thing. I'm not here to listen to this sort of stuff. I'm here
for Koert, to take him away. That's it.

"Marlo'tjie," November says at last in a pious tone of voice,
but with all the authority he still possesses as an elder. "Don't allow Mildred to make you angry."

"Oh, don't worry." Mildred, sweetness personified, holds her
stomach that was round once upon a time. There are furrows
about her lips and eyes. She'd forgotten for a moment: she is the
matriarch. "Coffee?" she asks.

"Wait a minute, Mildred," November interrupts, "we must
finish this first."

I know, I know what's coming.

"Marlo'tjie, do you remember that day at your pappie's funeral when I whispered to you: Don't throw us away, Marlo'tjie. Now that you've returned to Ouplaas, we want to ask you please to help us to buy some dose, because if the sheep die on this farm we'll have to trek, and where to? There isn't enough food or wood in the dorp for everyone. Enough sickness for everyone, yes, that's all."

"I knew you were going to ask me for money. Listen carefully now, November: I'm not your father, right. Nor am I a bank. I'm not your patron. Do you understand the word 'patron', Pilot?" He looks at me, his face pure and unpredictable.

In the meanwhile, Esmie Phumzile appears on the kitchen steps. She looks down on all of us in the back yard. Today she's wearing silver tights and a loosely knitted mohair jersey. Koert clearly favours her and stuffs her with money. Guess it's not my business. She looks bad, ashen. She's got something in her hand.

"Who was at Koert's door last night?" She swings a dead lizard by its tail.

Mildred snorts. "What now?"

"I'm asking: Who was at Koert's door? This thing didn't hang itself there."

"Why don't you ask his balaclava guys?" Mildred hits back. "How well can they be doing their job if *that* ended up on his door? He pays them doesn't he?"

"They've gone back to the dorp. They're not here to ask."

"It is Ouma Zuka. It is the *idliso*, the black poison." Pilot paces about. "I told you so. No one listens. She came down from the mountain last night and put that thing on Koert's door. It is *idliso* to make him sick. To make the sheep sick. We are all going

to pay the price because of Ouma Zuka. And you won't listen."
Esmie looks at her brother and flings the dead lizard towards
him. He ducks.

"*Idliso*," Pilot rubs it in.

"Shut up, Pilot." Then Mildred looks at me. More than anything, she, all of them, wants me to respond.

"Why should I help you? Why don't you ask Koert?" My
voice is already capitulating. "Okay, then. I'll make a deal. Tell
Koert to set a time for me to say hello and speak to him. Then
I'll help you and we can buy the dose. Why doesn't *he* help you?"
I suddenly flare up again. "What's going on with him?"

No one answers, it's not the kind of question they want to get
involved in. It will make matters worse. What's more, it's point-
less raising the issue of a financial donation from Koert Spies.
Everyone knows by now what's what.

"Pilot?" I turn to face Esmie Phumzile, "Esmie, do you hear
me? That's my condition, right? I want to know that I can speak
to him before I'll help you."

They all look at Esmie, she's got the key to the outcome. And
the mongrels persist. Low on their haunches, hollow chests on
the ground, they aim for the lizard that Pilot has crushed under
his feet.

"Yes, Esmie?"

"Come here," she gestures familiarly and I stand closer. "He
is sick," she admits for the first time. "He won't be able to speak
to you now. Koert is very ill. He is very low, very low. He'll see
you once he's better. I promise you."

"*Inyosi amafutha*. The fat bee," Headman mutters when he
hears Esmie talking about Koert. She ignores him.

"Then we have to get him to a doctor, Esmie." No, she doesn't answer. "Mildred? November?" They turn away from me.

"*Voertsek*," Pilot snarls at the mongrels. He's annoyed that no one believes his story about Ouma Zuka.

Silently, Esmie goes into the kitchen and returns with a tray covered with a dishcloth. She heads for Koert's quarters, and shakes her head as she walks away. She knows I'm still waiting for an answer.

"He won't talk to you now. We must all wait until he feels better. He has to improve before he can talk. He's only human, you know. He's weak. And he totally refuses to call a doctor."

The dishcloth covers something: perhaps a cup of warm tea, a bowl of stock. Esmie Phumzile's bottom and legs are perfectly formed, like Pilot's teeth. There she disappears around the corner of the house with the tray and bottom and legs that belong to Koert. Everyone on the werf knows and accepts it. Only Headman hasn't digested and spat it out yet. He can't: see how he licks his lips as his eyes follow her. Pilot lifts his foot so that one of the mongrels is able to get at the lizard.

"Marlo'tjie," November draws my attention to the dying sheep again, "you mustn't throw us away. The Lord has sent you."

"Let's go, then." I tap my back pocket for my keys. "Are you coming, Pilot? Do you know what kind of dose to buy?" I ask impatiently.

"I know the dose." He rushes inside to change into his gold Nikes for the trip to the dorp.

"It's Koert's foot," Mildred whispers as she passes me the bottle of water.

"Are you having me on, Mildred?"

"No, no, no," she protests, "it's not like your foot. He hasn't got your sickness; I'd never tease you, really I wouldn't. Koert's got a different kind of sickness that changes the colour of your toes. His foot has gone grass green."

"Gangrene?"

She nods. "Here." She's dried the bottle of water with a dish-cloth. "The water in the dorp turns your stomach upside down." She doesn't let me go right away, but cups her hands around mine and the bottle of borehole water.

"Don't believe everything Pilot's going to tell you. Koert is sick, but it's not because of Ouma Zuka. Koert is a strong and clever man. He's helped us a lot; he helps everyone, near and far. I have to say it, even though I don't care much for him. Now-adays he's helping a little less, that's certainly true. He's prob-ably too sick, like Esmie says," – then she lets me go. She always wants me to believe *her* side of the story.

"What's going on, Mildred? Between him and you people?"

Mildred flatly refuses to answer my question. Or deliberate-ly refuses to understand me. She's in present time now. Simply wants Pilot and me to hurry up and fetch the dose so that the sheep can be saved and peace and quiet descend on Ouplaas once again, dear Lord help us.

6

It was an inextricable mess of things decent in themselves
but that human folly made look like the spoils of thieving.

THE FURTHER WE DRIVE, the more annoyed I become at
returning to Maitland without knowing what's going on with
Koert. I'm forced to traverse ground I've already covered.

Neither of us turns down the window, nor do I feel like talking to Pilot. He doesn't mind. He stares through his window
that's covered in moth wings and dust. The veld passes by, dried-
out livestock dams, the ridges with *besembos* bushes along their
spines. Poles stretching boundary wire between veld and road fly
by. One and two and three, one's missing here; there's an opening people have used, they've trampled the fence right down.

"Where are all your sheep, Pilot?" At the mention of his
name he turns round and his lips open onto his pure white teeth.
What does this man wearing glasses and all want, and what kind
of way is that to look at us?

"November herds them into the Damkamp where the veld
is good; problem is, the windmill is out of order. The sheep are
grazing there now."

"How many do you still have?"

"There are a hundred ewes and a few lambs left. And then the weaned lambs here in the Huiskamp where the windmill does work, a total of forty-seven lambs."

"Is that it?"

"Koert has sold the rest. He even sells off pregnant ewes, he doesn't wait for them to lamb. He sells as he needs money or when he wants to drink. November has told him that we need rams. The old rams can't do their job, their balls have dried up. Esmie says Koert knows about the rams, we must not buzz about his ears, he is too sick. But he does nothing, to this day.

"How many of the farm's windmills are still working, and is there water in all the camps?"

"One windmill here in the Huiskamp still works, the other one in the Damkamp only pisses. Its pipes leak; I can tell that is the problem. We have to dig them out, but where will we find the money to fix them or to buy new pipes or soles?"

"Only one windmill!"

"Only one windmill," he imitates me. "We do not have the money to fix the others, and one needs new soles. Why are you asking all these questions? Do you want to come and live here again?" he smiles.

"You must be joking. I'll never live here again. I don't even know why I bother about you and your sheep, but I do. I care about you, Pilot. What will you do when your last windmill breaks down? Where will you get water? How can you survive on a farm where there's no more water? You'll have to leave. Aren't you worried about that?

He spits on his index finger and buffs his Nikes. "No," he answers abruptly. He spits again, pauses with the glob on his finger. He looks at me. "Yes, we are," and licks the spit.

"You aren't, Pilot. Not one of you knows what you're up to," I say softly.

He hasn't heard me, or couldn't care less if he has – he does not bother to answer. He folds his hands and stares ahead at the road, at nothing in particular. His bum has formed a hollow in the seat. He's snug and content for the first time today, or this week, or this winter, in fact. This brief moment in the bakkie purring and rocking him gently, *this* means something to him. He couldn't give a damn about anything out there. Not even the implications of a farm without water.

Hell, what's it got to do with me? I've lost my way, impatient with myself, irritated at my concern. In any case, what am I doing on a road that's taking me away from Koert? I'm battling upstream for the sake of sheep dose – is this why I've come to this country? To be swallowed up by other survival issues? To exercise my compassionate heart and eventually to succumb: Here, have it all, my real mission is to help you.

I must penetrate Koert's quarters and take his hand in mine: Koert, I don't really know you, but I've come for your sake, my nephew, my blood family. Get up now, take your things and for heaven's sake let's get away from here. As you know, the two springs on Ouplaas dried up long ago, your windmills are on their last legs. You can't live on whisky and Jägermeister alone. The windmills will break and be left just as they are, the people will bundle up their meagre possessions and hit the road, Mildred will probably hire a bakkie to collect her stuff. They'll abandon you before you know it, Koert. Once your meat is finished, you'll mean nothing to them. Believe me. I'm no baboon. Come, Koert, trust me, give me your heart, let's escape this hell while we can. Meanwhile I'm listening, all ears for the sentence, for the word that will reveal to me what happened here, what's going on, what's going on with *you*.

Out of the blue, Pilot says, "It's been like that for a long time."

"What?"

"Koert's foot; it stinks and it's rotting off."

"Do you know what gangrene is, Pilot?"

"That man cannot stand any more. Lies on his bed the whole time."

"Because of his foot?"

"No, Marlo'tjie," he picks up his taunting again, "don't you know by now?"

"What, know *what*?" I scream.

"Koert is too heavy. *S'dudla*. The fat one." He makes a giant circle with his arms, past my left hand on the steering wheel.

"Koert is a heavy man. Mr Big Boy. No, he cannot, he cannot get up from his bed any more. Too heavy." Pilot's eyes fill with tears, he's laughing so much. "*Indlovu*. Do you know *indlovu*? Elephant. He cannot get up and walk around any more. Then the thing with his foot happened, now he has to lie in one place. It is all Ouma Zuka's fault, she is jealous. Jealousy. She wants Koert to leave the farm. Ouma Zuka looked Koert in his face on his first day. Who are you? she asked. Koert Spies, my mother and my grandfather and my grandmother lived here, he answered. Ouma Zuka watched him and she said: You're not staying here on our Ouplaas. You're not welcome. Go before there's trouble. *Ukhawulele iinkawu ziyakusela*. You will get between the baboons and their drinking hole. She meant Koert is interfering in something that is not his business, and that he will get badly hurt.

"Ouma Zuka pestered Koert, even though he bought coal for

the kitchen and dose and coffee and jeans for Esmie and Nikes for me and lots of stuff that nobody on the farm had ever been able to buy. And Headman went to Koert's room every day to play Mario Kart. Do you know Mario Kart? You play it on a Nintendo, you play with two little men, Toad and Joshi, they fight. Headman liked it so much that he did not want to do any work on the farm any more. Then his mother and father chased him to the mountain to do his mountain school and the *umkhwe-tha* time. And Ouma Zuka also went to live in the koppies. She never slept in the big house any more. Never, never. Mildred said it was Koert who caused Ouma Zuka to go to the koppies, and it was for the best. But then Esmie said, no, Ouma Zuka chose to go to live in the koppies herself. Ouma Zuka asked everyone, can't you open your eyes? Koert is devouring all the meat before your own eyes. Then she went away. Then I saw that she is an *umthakati*, Ouma Zuka, and it is a good thing she left because she is a witch."

We've reached the outskirts of the dorp. Thin smoke from morning fires drifts towards us. That's Oupa and Ouma Rhynie's farm on the left. Môreson. I slow down and my eyes follow the turnoff to the house where the two old ones lived until their end. Other people have moved in since: it's conveniently close to the dorp.

"Pilot! My grandfather and grandmother lived there." It's as if he's snuggled himself into a bliss of down and fluff, and his eyelids droop every now and then. Like a child.

My eye follows the road to Oupa and Ouma Rhynie's house and its stoep. I can't see further. The stoep's been boarded up with corrugated iron sheets and cardboard for extra sleeping place. Children jump up and down, an early morning game right on the spot where Ouma's magnolia tree used to stand in all its splendour.

My gaze is so intent that Pilot stares in the same direction. On Sunday afternoons we used to drive over to Oupa and Ouma for tea and cake, and the giant magnolia cups cast their scent over the stoep. Sublime, Ouma exclaimed at the mystery of the scent. And as if startled by her word that threatened to take us beyond the temporal, Ouma then made a simple remark about the cake: It *has* to be eaten, people.

All things must pass: the floral plate with its cake fork is graciously placed on a side table where somebody will collect it later. Per Strand was right. It was a culture that never suited this land; from the very beginning, it was impossible to maintain it. Marlo'tjie is upset. Why then, Marlo'tjie? You don't own a scrap of land here, do you? Upset about the cake fork that will never again be placed on the edge of the cake plate? Tainted memories, my dear, dear Marlo'tjie. All gone. Just look at those children skipping away on your Oupa and Ouma's stoep.

"I've seen enough," I say to Pilot who's pointing out the next sight: our family graveyard with its circular wall.

"No." He shakes his head and grins. "Look there, there on the other side, look!" It's not our family graveyard he wants me to see; that too, yes, but he actually wants to focus my attention on something else.

"The township on the other side, other side your graveyard," he laughs, his mouth wide open, his teeth white.

My stomach churns. The shacks, the tiny shacks. Each with its own cloud of smoke. Grandmothers wrapped in rags, babes in blankets on the backs of teenage girls who piggyback the little things and hum away the cold, back and forth in front of the houses, each with its own patch of barren earth. There's also a donkey, his ears, caked with sores, flip and flap. Look, there's more to see, keep moving, always further from Koert's quarters, upstream between rows and rows of shacks that link up with the second township, which in turn joins the first, Mzamomhle, the oldest township bordering the dorp. Row upon innumerable row – incomprehensible that so many homes are needed in a town that's never had any major industry.

"How many?" I point to the houses.

"Fifty thousand, this side of town."

"Where do all the people come from, were conditions so bad in the places they've left? What's there to eat here?"

"We never have any difficulty selling our meat. It is all gone before you are able to smoke your first cigarette. We can slaughter seven sheep, fourteen, fifty-five, hundred and fifty-five," he enjoys giving the tally.

"And what about the windmills, Pilot? What if your hundred and fifty-five sheep don't have any water to drink?"

At this question he withdraws and snuggles back into his seat, just his finger points through the windscreen: drive on, white child of your Oupa and Ouma Rhynie, you who have opened your mouth about us once too often, drive on through the outskirts of the township far beyond the periphery of Maitland where the shacks have crept up right against the wall of your family graveyard.

I cry. I'm at an utter loss for words. I could wring my hands at my beloved Oupa and Ouma Rhynie, restless under the ground, and Pappie and Mammie, even more restless. Oh, I can't bear thinking about them, their eternal resting place disturbed. I hear Ouma's little cry, she's anxious as a bee caught under a drinking glass: Marlouw, she squeaks, it's all finished. Surely you've got a plan? Pappie? I imagine I hear him whisper something in my ear. His distress would know no bounds.

The spectacle leaves me gasping. There are houses as far as the eye can see, filling the plains where once upon a time sheep grazed. And on the grass verges on both sides of the road, people are moving alongside the bakkie, big and small carrying and helping one other, a procession. And nothing with them, not a thing in all the world.

"How can this be? Is there no respect for the dead? Nothing? Don't you people believe in the ancestors, that the graves of the ancestors must be maintained, Pilot? How could they have gone and thrown their foundations right against my grandparents' graves?"

Pilot mocks me: "At night your Oupa and Ouma get out of their graves and sit like owls on the wall and look and look and the people come running along to hear what they have to say."

"And what do you think they say?"

He cups his hand behind his ear. "I am trying to hear." And so we enter the dorp.

"Where do we get the dose?"

"Close by," Pilot says, and climbs out in the main road. I drive on and park under one of the remaining oak trees. At once I'm surrounded by children: a picture of a calf drawn with a Bic ballpoint pen is offered; do I want the bakkie washed? They touch me, grab my jacket.

"Where're your cloths? Have you got a bucket and water?"

I slap their hands away from me and stride on stiffly. It's not at all pleasant. With my bottle of water in hand, I look for somewhere to rest.

Three men sit talking close by. Two are white. Besides these, there are not many white people to be seen. I unscrew the bottle and drink some of the farm water. Pilot will fetch me here when he's finished and I have to pay for the dose. The sun is pleasantly warm, I keep my foot relaxed. Pilot mustn't waste my time today.

Every now and then, pigeons settle on the square in front of me. A hunchback stalks the birds. When he's close enough, he slips a blanket from his hump and tries to net them.

For his sake, I hope he captures one or two. My Ouma Attie had a delicious recipe for pigeon pie. It was whispered to Heleen and me when we were reckoned to be old enough, that Ouma Attie was actually an adopted child. From then on we looked at her with new eyes. She had an elegant neck enhanced by exquisite stones. Heleen and I both sat on her lap. It's because she's adopted that she loves children so much, Heleen said. Garlic and a dash of Cape Muscatel, raisins and bacon – I don't remember the rest of the recipe.

The three men sitting next to me on the step chain-smoke Stuyvesants and talk non-stop; the butts are made to stand in a row, and they laugh themselves silly at it.

From a distance, the gang of children keep watch on us like vultures. They point at me and the other adults but dare not sneak up. They're like the dogs on Ouplaas. With a malevolent flick, one of the men throws a half-smoked butt at them. A child scoops it up and takes a puff. There's a scuffle, kicking, one's got a penknife.

"Fat pig," I pick up the words from the three men nearby. They are incensed. "It's the last time. I swear," one says. I listen attentively. The pigeons flutter and descend again, agitated by the attacks on them.

The three have taken out a bottle of Klipdrift. There it comes again: "fat pig." Without a doubt, it's my nephew who's being discussed. It's Koert, this. Koert is the one being called "fat pig". The three are outraged at his inability to provide meat for all the thousands of people, and equally outraged that he dares mouth off about meat that is coming in from Bloemfontein, and in the end you can't get your hands on any meat at all. One moment there's a glut, the next a shortage in town that lasts for fucking weeks. And messages turn up from Fat Pig that he's got enough meat for everybody, people must just be a little more patient. Koert is never mentioned by name, they call him Fat Pig or Fat-fuckingpig, or simply "the Fucker". After the last name, they laugh even harder and try to think up more, but Fatarsefucker is not a name that sticks. The one guy, himself rather overweight, throws himself back in an uncontrollable fit of laughter. His head hits the granite monument. His pals wet themselves; it's the funniest thing.

"The last round," one says, and offers his packet of cigarettes. It's completely empty. He hadn't realised it himself, honestly, he made a terrible mistake. They start slapping him about, it's gone way past a joke, this. Fuckit: he's taken them for a ride. And come to think of it, hadn't they heard that he's been brown-nosing Fat Pig? Collaboration. Is it true? Yes or no? The empty cigarette packet was the excuse they'd been looking for: accusations flow thick and fast. The man covers his head, the other two beat him senseless.

I get up quietly and hobble towards the headless marble woman, the old Afrikaans *taal* monument, for shelter. The hunchback with the blanket is there. "*Voertsek,*" he hisses. Then he slinks as low as his legs can carry him towards the pigeons.

His eyes flick back meanly at me. The pigeons coo and peck in front of him.

Where to now?

So many times during this journey I've landed up in undignified situations. That's how it began: kneeling in front of a sofa. Laughable, completely out of place. Off-side. I always had the sense that I did not belong in that country, that my people, my forebears didn't belong there either. Watching the people streaming along the roads made me feel like a voyeur. What the hell are you looking at? Who do you think you are? I never fitted in anywhere. It would take me years to overcome this strange feeling. To be honest, I still carry the scar.

In the meanwhile, the men on the steps of the monument have collapsed, tired out by the fighting. The two give their bloody-nosed mate a last kick.

The three men here, Pilot and Esmie Phumzile, Mildred and all the others on Ouplaas waiting for the vaccine and the bags of flour, coffee and sugar that I must still buy, all who have stepped out of the confines of their existence to speak to me or offer advice – I'm now able to place them. They have all crossed my path to point the way to Koert. All their words and explanations, often false and with hidden agendas, were preparing me for my meeting with Koert. Even these three on the steps of the monument are part of it. I'm getting closer. My journey to this country, the dorp, the farm beyond the dorp, to the house and the quarters in the house – nothing will have been in vain.

I see Pilot's golden Nikes amongst the townsfolk. He beckons me, I'm relieved.

We walk down Retief Street, past the stalls with their meagre hawkers' wares. Pilot inspects every item. Hardly stalls, no more than odds and ends of cardboard on which they squat and call out to buyers. "Here," one grabs Pilot's hand, "razor blades, try them yourself."

The woman behind a row of cabbage heads seems to have lost all hope. Her eyes are closed, she's praying. Her cabbages are lined up at her feet, mould between the leaves. There's also a stall with three brown onions, 5-litre cans of water, very clean, nice *dimmas* – sunglasses – and fan belts. There's a pyramid of Oil of Olay bottles. Another stall sells shampoo for hair loss in case you've picked up the virus. More blades, cheaper. We come to a man with religious tracts, green ones and pink and light blue, arranged in a pattern. *Ngoana Jesus oa Prague* – the Baby Jesus of Prague. Each booklet comes in its own plastic packaging, it's spotlessly clean when you remove the wrapping.

"Where does he come from?'

"This man?" Pilot lifts one of the tracts with the toe of his Nike. "He comes from Lesotho. Smell him, he's walked a long way."

Now the seller gets up and whispers something in Pilot's ear – they know each other – which makes Pilot smile broadly. He sucks his spittle the way he likes to do. I shudder, look up and down the street: I have to get away from here as soon as possible. Can't entrust myself to Pilot or the people of Ouplaas, not even to Mildred. It would be an error of judgment, a sign that I'd misread. It's not a matter of distrust; trust doesn't even come into it. As far as the farm goes, I've seen enough: the veld has been overgrazed, the water table is low, everything's worn to the bone. There's not much left for the people of Ouplaas to live on, and what little remains won't go far. If anything goes wrong, they won't stand up for me. They'll try to save their own arses. I'd do the same.

Two women want a word with Pilot. "Aikona. Nothing, there's nothing. And he's not available."

"So where are Koert's sheep?" they want to know. "Koert's always got meat. Won't you ask Koert for some meat and send a bit to the dorp, Pilot?" Both women wear African print, with a double wrap of silk around the hips. They look as if they've got money.

It strikes me again that whenever Pilot speaks of Koert, he refers to him as "him" and "that man". He refuses to call Koert by name. And meat? Don't come asking Pilot for meat. Never associate Pilot Hlongwane with Koert Spies – that's the way it is. Pilot calls me closer: we must get going. He turns his back on them. They're at a loss.

We slip into an alley between the former post office and the old co-op. Can't see much, must watch my step. There's a rustle below, must be rats. Pilot slows down so that I'm able to keep up – perhaps my judgment about him and the rest of them on Ouplaas was too harsh. At a door along the right-hand side of the lane, Pilot warns me to duck. The doorframe is low.

We arrive in a badly lit storeroom with bags of flour piled to the roof. I smell mealie meal. A second low door leads us into a smallish office with a plastic table. Behind it, a woman sits on a plastic chair with a radio on her lap. She's listening to Youssou N'Dour. A globe casts its yellow light on her headscarf.

No notice is taken of me; they shake Pilot's hand. The woman's got gold rings on all five fingers. Various 1- and 5-litre bottles of sheep dose are on offer.

I look at Pilot. "Is it the right stuff for the paralysis tick?"

"That's it."

I nod: he must take over now. The extended negotiations begin without the music being turned down. Koert's name is mentioned six times during the conversation. Only the woman mentions him by name, Pilot continues to refer to "he" and "him."
He's playing the fool. It's Pilot who is Koert's man here in Maitland, not Esmie or Mildred or November or any of the others on
Ouplaas.

"She wants some of his meat, not money," Pilot explains.
"What good is money to her, her children have to eat. She may
accept American dollars. Maybe."

"I don't have many dollars on me; does she want me to be
stabbed around the first corner?" Pilot does not interpret my remark for the woman. Shut up, he gestures to me behind his back.

"Okay," Pilot now says. The two come to a new agreement.
It's an underhand business, a messy transaction. The woman's
hand is extended again and Pilot gives the three-shake greeting.
The deal's done. "You'll get your leg of lamb tomorrow. Trust
me," he promises.

He's talking shit. How would he get hold of a leg of lamb
on Ouplaas? The things are dying like flies and Koert is flat on
his back. Youssou's voice dies away and more music from Sen-
egal starts up. The woman flutters her hands in her wide sleeves,
the decision is revoked. No, something's gone wrong. There's
whispering and I step back, it seems the best thing to do – even
though my money's paying for it.

Pilot reports: No, now she wants seventy-five percent in cash;
the rest in meat. And some sheep offal thrown in too; she wants
a nice well-scraped sheep's head. It's her birthday, see, and she
thinks we have been sent to her.

"Like angels," comes from the woman, her deep voice makes a sweet curve upwards.

Only now am I included in the conversation. Like most people around here, this woman is able to use English – it just depends on whether they choose to or not. She chooses to. No; now she insists we buy an extra 5-litre can, and for that we'll get a free tin of Frisco coffee. She groans and picks up a tin behind her chair. She taps the lid with the nails of all five of her ringed fingers.

"Is that the final deal?" I ask impatiently.

"Oh, your white friend should not raise his voice here with me. You should tell him, Pilot."

Pilot responds in isiXhosa. "*Ngabantu bakulo Koert Spies.* Koert Spies is his close family." When she hears that she looks straight at me and the tap-tap on the lid stops.

This is the very last time I will allow myself to be drawn into the farm's business. Those sheep can die as far as I'm concerned. I place my hand on Pilot's shoulder and am amazed at how sturdy he is, even though there's so little food on Ouplaas. I draw him into a dark corner, full of rats.

"I'm sick and tired of this game. How long do you have to wheel and deal just to get your hands on dose? We've still got to buy flour and sugar and coffee. I suppose I'll have to cough up for that as well. Here – here, it's in my hand, I'll slip you a little extra. Will *that* get me what I want now? Pretty please?"

"Marlo'tjie," he taunts me, "it is *our* country this. We have got our own rules. Don't get all uptight now, Marlo'tjie."

"Tell me, Pilot, what are you going to do when you can't get hold of meat any more? Land up even deeper in the shit, if you ask me. Finish up with that woman, please. You may call me Marlo'tjie and mock me as much as you like in that voice of yours, but listen to me once and for all, Pilot: I'm not here to bail you out. Tomorrow I'm speaking to Koert, and then I'm done here. I'm off. Do you realise that?"

"We know about you, Marlouw, don't worry. I will make sure Esmie Phumzile talks to him, or I will go in myself. We will get meat, don't worry. I'll grab one of his sheep behind the koppie and slaughter it right there, he won't even know." Pilot is self-assured and makes all sorts of flamboyant signs with two index fingers, too presumptuous for words. Does he honestly imagine I believe him?

I go to a building that's being used as a bank and draw money. The transaction takes an eternity and involves a bribe to get the cash. And then we leave with three 5-litre cans of dose and the tin of coffee.

I'll go and buy the food myself that I'd like to contribute to the kitchen provisions. I'm more comfortable on my own. Pilot is splayed across the bonnet of the bakkie, cigarette in his mouth, conversing with everyone who drifts past. Big mouth. Not only about his golden Nikes, but also about the person who'd bought the Nikes for him. About the power he has to be *able* to buy them for Pilot. Koert's power and influence protect Pilot's arse. And he uses the name as he pleases. That's how he gets hold of goods, how he swings things in his favour.

Old Mr Wesley comes in groaning from a back room. Someone's apparently let him know a white person has come into his shop. Tears begin to fall when he sees who it is. He wears a wide scarf around his neck that he starts undoing to show me his tumour.

"Your mammie was the purest I ever knew in this dorp." His tries to be polite by speaking to me in Afrikaans.

"Shortly before her death she made a chicken pie and brought it over herself. With the butter pastry the farmers' wives made so well. Delicious." More tears. "I already had this then," he points at the growth and shudders.

"Mr Wesley, I'm shocked at the state of this town," I whisper. "There's absolutely nothing left. I could cry when I think of the shanties, Mr Wesley, right up to our family graveyard, right against the encircling wall. You must know where it is. You know where my Oupa and Ouma Rhynie lived."

With an effort he stretches across the counter and takes hold of my shoulder. His touch evokes further emotion in me.

"Oh, Mr Wesley, I never expected anything like this. It's the worst thing I've ever seen. It fills me with fear. Why does it frighten me? I don't know. I am in a constant state of readjustment as no answers and no solutions are apparent. I feel as if I've completely lost my balance, Mr Wesley."

Mr Wesley fiddles under his counter. There's something he wants to give me. "Don't talk too much about it, please. I'm nearly in the grave myself, and till then I have to live here. All of you left long ago. That's not my business, but what happens here is not yours either. Just remember that. What's your sister's name again?" he changes the subject.

"Heleen."

"Of course. Heleen" He gets up, red in the face, from where he's been scratching around. He's found what he's looking for. "Here." He gives me a handful of flat pink sweets. Love hearts straight out of our childhood days.

Then Mr Wesley's emotions overwhelm him. Old, oh, he's

quite finished. Tired to the bones. His voice breaks. "I have organised my own cremation. I know who's going to do it, I have paid half, the balance will be paid when he takes the cremation notice to the bank. All organised. I trust this man. There are always people left you can trust." He waves disapprovingly. "Oh, it's a sin against God what is happening out there. No one wants to be buried in the graveyards any more." He weeps gently and indicates that I had better go. If Heleen were to see the state of the poor man's nails . . .

"Vaseline," I remember before I leave. My skin is drying out just like the others' on the farm. I'm becoming part of them, right down to my skin and bones. One pot of Vaseline I ask, not from Mr Wesley. He's disappeared. I pay and put the pot in my bag with the other stuff.

*

We're back at Ouplaas. The winter sun is at its warmest, and everyone's basking on the back stoep. Mildred has an enamel bowl on her lap, she's picking stones from the dry sugar beans. Sindiswa plaits one of her children's hair; separate from the rest, November and Frans Zuka and Lehlono sit on the ground, each with a cup of chicory coffee. I don't see Headman or Esmie Phumzile. As Pilot and I walk up, the dogs blink at the sun, then drop their heads and doze off.

November peers over his coffee. "You got the stuff." He puts his mug down and quietly rolls a Boxer cigarette, one for Mildred too. She doesn't really smoke, though on the stoep in the sun like this, she likes the odd puff. No one's much interested in Pilot and me.

"Is there any more coffee, Mildred?" I'm unsure whether I'm allowed to go in to get my own. "I've brought a tin."

"Headman's in the kitchen. He'll give you some."

My head is spinning – I need coffee and sugar – I have to support myself against the wall and sink slowly down onto my haunches. A chicken scurries from under me.

"Cheep cheep," Sindiswa calls out in high spirits. One foot at a time, the chicken comes stealthily closer, then aims: the remains of a dorp cockroach are stuck to the sole of my shoe. Pilot also sinks to his haunches; the sun shines on us all. I *am* dizzy.

"Headman," Mildred hollers inside, "bring kleinbasie his coffe-e-e," and she crescendoes so that the others on the werf cackle like witches.

May the Good Shepherd have mercy on me; tonight I'll be sleeping somewhere in the dorp. Is November jeering like the rest of this scum? No, here he comes, the sun on his grey beard. He reaches out to pull me up. Why must I get up? How's that going to help?

"Leave me alone," I say. To my own ears I sound exactly like their Marlo'tjie. Now they're really laughing: the little man has returned to waggle about the werf with his gammy foot. Oh dear, miesies, your child is too cute. Repetitive, high-pitched shrieks alternate with a spatter of laughter, while Mildred's beans plop into the bowl one by one. The turkey cock takes the rousing sounds as a signal to dance. He drags his wings, he twists and turns and tilts forward, his wattles dragging on the ground.

They don't really accept me. My presence has opened up the past. I represent the bad old days on Ouplaas: oubaas Ben has returned; see there, the oubaas strides across the werf with his *kierie* and hat. He thinks to himself: a boer doesn't work with his hands, but with his head. November, you and Frans go off now and collect all the sheep, the ones that can still walk. Do it properly and make sure you don't miss any. When I return from the dorp with the dose I want to see all of them in the kraal. We'll take the bakkie into the veld and collect the ewes that can't get onto their feet any more, the ones the ticks have got to, and we'll bring them home. Check where they're lying so you can show me. We'll inject them. They'll live, they *will* make it, you'll see. I know everything. Go now. There's not much time.

Time's the thing, not so, Marlo'tjie. You white people always have so little time and so much stuff. While we have such an awful lot of time, and nothing worthwhile to show for it after all these years. Fuck all. Look, there's still a whole day to tend to the sheep. There are days, weeks and years for them to die. We're all going to die here. Let's enjoy the heat of the sun while we can, tonight we're back on our thin, cold mattresses – is that you, November Hlongwane, are you talking to me like this? Is this how you speak to your own people? Is this all you have to offer them? Dying sheep, empty stomachs?

November had offered me his hand again. I pushed it away. Once more the laugh from many throats. I'll lose my mind here. I had a thorough examination before I left Melbourne; when I get back it will be easy to check whether I've become demented. Medication is the only solution. Marlouw, you'll have to take a break before you're ready to sell your luxury stainless steel pots again. Pot hawker. That's my life. That is the most pathetic significance I'm able to bring to my life. God give me strength: tonight I'm going into Koert's quarters, tonight I'm getting the hell out of this damn place. I'm thinking of you, Jocelyn, working on that long piece of knitting. Now I know what you were doing, Jocelyn, you were knitting my demise with those needles of yours. You said it yourself: I should never have come here.

I struggle up. "Come, Pilot, let's go and collect the sheep."

Now they all look at me, their mouths shut. Suddenly they see Pappie's hand in front of them. The hand of the patron, always open, always giving. Why shouldn't we sit and wait for time to pass? Marlo'tjie's returned to help us. Nothing will ever make him angry, he'll never throw us away. Here's the dose that will save the sheep; tonight we slaughter and make merry.

"Headman," Mildred screeches into the kitchen, this time even more excessively, "get Marlo'tjie some coffee to make him s-t-r-o-n-g. Oh! he was always such a beautiful boy, my Marlo'tjie. Esmie Phumzile should have asked him to marry her. They'd have sent you lobola from that faraway land, November Hlongwane. You'd have become so rich that you'd be shitting golden eggs. Now Esmie Phumzile has taken *that* one," and she flicks one of her sugar beans in the direction of Koert's quarters. "Ugh."

I go into the kitchen to get away from them – even though Headman is there. The kettle is on the wood stove, boiling for all it's worth.

"Esmie?"

She's also been there the whole time, must have heard every word slung at me outside. She wraps perfumed arms around my neck. "Don't let them laugh at you. It's not worth the effort, Marlouw. They are all stupid, every single one of them. If it wasn't for Koert, there'd have been nothing here on Ouplaas long ago. My father thinks he knows everything about sheep. Well, look what's happened now. He knows nothing. None of them knows anything. The day you and Koert leave, we'll all be done for. I don't belong here. I despise them all except for my brother. Take me with you, Marlouw." She shows me her hands, the result of years of dedicated care.

"Does Koert love you, Esmie? Does he?"

She turns to the stove and pours coffee into my cup. "Koert is too sick to love any more. I look after him because I care about him, because I know he cares about us, that's all I can say."

Headman has been wrapping food in newspaper and packing a basket: bread, coffee and a bare meat bone that's he's found who knows where. He does it quietly, trying to follow our English.

Esmie Phumzile looks at the basket. "That's for Ouma Zuka in the mountains. See what Headman occupies himself with."

He shakes his fist at her when he hears his name. She laughs.

"He was the *umkhwetha* just the other day. See what I mean. They still believe you have to cut off your foreskin before you can become a man. He was cheeky when he came down from the mountain. Big mister. Even tried to order me around."

"What did you do to Koert? That's what I want to know, Esmie. How did he get so sick? What on earth has happened here? He was so healthy when he left Australia, he used to row, he went to the gym, took the dog walking, everything. How could he suddenly have become so sick?"

"It is the madness of this country. And the madness in Koert's soul. One day he arrived here and said he wanted to help us. He'd do anything for us, we must just tell him what. He can collect wood, chop it for the winter, Mildred said without thinking, he's nice and strong. We laughed; we didn't really know what help he could be to us.

"Ouma Zuka said after the first night already that we mustn't allow a white man to interfere here. Not under any circumstances. It was summer, and Koert slept outside on his blow-up mattress. Then he took a taxi to the dorp and returned with food and booze. Baked beans, real milk, toffees, whisky, all that stuff no one knew any more. And he carried on: he wanted to help us. Then it dawned on him that the people wanted meat, and he arranged for meat here on Ouplaas. Cautiously at first – he had to see how things worked. Of course, he had his computer with him, and he's sharp, that Koert. It went well for quite a while. Later on he bought sheep from other farms and fattened them here on Ouplaas to deliver meat to the abattoir. It went very well. There was money for everything. Pilot got his golden Nikes, Mildred and November could ask for anything they wanted. We partied on Saturday nights with wine and whisky and braaied meat. Headman also got what he wanted. Hey, Headman? You can't come with your blame now," and she looks in his direction where he stands with a grin on his face.

"As we produced more and more, Koert started seeing the power of meat. Let's face it, everyone likes a chop. Soon we were supplying the abattoirs in Aliwal North and Queenstown, sometimes even as far as Bloemfontein, when there were shortages. Koert always wanted more. He discovered the power of bargaining, and he was very good at that. People started talking about him. Everyone knew about him. Koert's the man who's always got meat. If you want something, meat, anything, why not have a chat with Koert? Perhaps he can work something out for you. So it went. His meat business became very big in his region. His power and success were extraordinary and he liked it very much. It did not last. He's sick now and his sheep are all dying. Will you take me back to Australia with you, Marlouw?"

"It's impossible, Esmie. It's totally out of the question." And more to the point: I don't want you, though that I'll never ever say to her. I like Esmie Phumzile and she likes me. She knows I can tell her English is better than anyone else's. That she's different, a cut above the rest. But taking her with me to Melbourne – she must be off her head. She overestimates her own worth; she's apparently picked this up from Koert.

Pilot sticks his head through the door. "Are we going to fetch the sheep? Where are you hiding?"

I don't look at any of the stoep-sitters as I leave and no one dares make any more remarks. Pilot, Headman with his basket, myself and three of the mongrels head for the veld. We keep going north-west towards the Damkamp where the last of the sheep are grazing, that's where the windmill still spits a bit of water.

Pilot takes long strides and hums tunes full of nostalgia. He's the only one who didn't laugh at me earlier. Here's my hand of appreciation – I'd like to offer him my thanks but he doesn't give me the opportunity. Perhaps *he's* the one I need to trust – I just wish he'd say or give me something so that I can do so with conviction. His loyalty doesn't necessarily have to lie with his own people. His sister must have left him with that thought by now. Pilot won't find his salvation here. He's young; he can escape before it's too late. Botswana's still doing well; he could make it up to the border and try to skip across it.

I'm shocked at the sight of the first sheep we come across behind the koppie. Bewildered, deathly thin and peeling wool, they dart away to a bunch of *besembos*. They don't have the energy to go any further. Dose or not, they're going to die. I lift myself onto one of the round ironstone rocks and look across the veld: death's lurking there. The bossies are bare, and chewed down to the stem. Not a single animal will survive this winter. Further away, another group of sheep congregate. They lift their heads towards the people, these mongrels. Some won't even make it into the kraal.

The sun has withdrawn, and fleecy clouds gather in the south. More cold on the way. What's Pilot up to? I must tell him everything's done for on Ouplaas. The dose was a waste of money. Shielding my eyes, I look at him and Headman, who are chatting together. When they see I'm looking at them they signal to me to remain where I am. I don't want to be in the veld, I don't want to be here on Ouplaas any more.

Headman walks off on his own in a westerly direction. Once again he looks around and I can just make out his sneer. *This* thing, he points to his basket. Am I too stupid to understand? Here, he gestures again and points wildly at the basket. He must first take the food to Ouma Zuka. He starts climbing the koppie.

There the old woman emerges from the *besembos* to meet him, a blanket folded over her shoulders. It must be freezing at night. Perhaps they didn't burn down the *umkhwetha* hut, and left it for her. I hobble through the bossies in their direction. I *will* speak to Ouma Zuka. She can't do me any harm, I don't believe in her witchery.

Despite her fear, one of the ewes walks towards me. I've got nothing for you, old girl. Like me, she's panting. My eardrums start humming. Now even the animals are making a claim on me, and I can't do a thing about it. I can only respond with silence. A terrible silence, one that goes to my heart. I felt it coming yesterday. Walking here now, I fear nothing. By tonight, though, as surely as darkness will fall and find me struggling to sleep on my mattress next to November, fear will return.

The ewe bleats pathetically and squints at me with her flat, brown pupils. The memory of Pappie's supplementary drought feed lies in the hairs of her ears: at daybreak the bakkie is already delivering hessian bags filled with mealies. Buckets of mealies are emptied into each camp, depending on the number of sheep. Here, Marlouw, pour it into the trough. I'm on holiday on the farm, and Pappie doesn't notice how my foot's battling to get a grip so I can tip the mealies into the trough properly. Or perhaps he does see and wants to toughen me up. Don't miss, he admonishes, every kernel counts. I got November and his men to build the troughs in good time, he explains, drought is endemic here, you know. You must be prepared; you have to save for the lean years.

I walk on.

When Headman and Ouma Zuka notice that I'm heading for them, they almost have a fit. Ouma Zuka shoos me off with rowing actions of her hands. Her blanket forms two horns around her shoulders, she's a real old witch. Headman goes berserk. He curses so loudly that I can see his gullet from here, then drops the basket and chases me away with stones.

The old woman starts up a low, unholy chant, "*Mzungu, mzungu, mzungu.*"

"*Voertsek!*" Headman rants.

I turn round.

There's no need to anger them any further. Poor souls. Ouma Zuka's song stopped me in my tracks, the droning of the word. *Mzungu*, do I know that word?

Here are Pilot and the mongrels. He shakes his head at Ouma Zuka and Headman's performance. "I told you, didn't I, she is *umthakati*, you refused to believe me."

"Pilot," I take him by the shoulder, "what on earth have you people done to this farm? How can I help these animals, what are you expecting from me?"

"Nothing!" He jerks free from me, whistles, and shouts at Headman, "*Ngxama wena ngenonsensi yako okanye ulibele sizaku-landa iigusha?* Stop your nonsense, or have you forgotten we have to collect the sheep?" His shouts bounce off the ironstone of the koppie and the mongrels prick up their ears at the shard of life that is cast across this piece of earth.

I reach a patch where not a single bossie or tuft of grass re-mains. Hard earth, brown stones and gravel, skeletons of plants that once were, the sun-bleached spine of a millipede. I bend down: it has become a desert. I pick up a stone, put it under my tongue, drop it. The spittle on the stone evaporates immediately. I dislodge a twig. Pilot shouts as he drives the sheep on and his echo enlivens the veld, a flicker of life, its energy infectious. A veld locust hops from a *perdekaroobossie* into the patch of desert.

Below, Headman makes a wide circle to herd the runaway sheep back to the larger flock. Pilot moves in the opposite direc-tion to round them up, the mongrels snaffle at his feet.

I come across five ewes that must have collapsed days ago and are now caked with blowflies. I kneel, stroke each one's head as you'd do to a feverish child. The animals' breath is rasping. There's scorn in Headman's eyes when he sees what I'm doing: old mommy priest with dried out tits. Pilot grins.

Slowly, the sheep form a flock, find direction, and plod along within the horseshoe of people and mongrels to the kraal. Once there, Pilot gets things going. He made himself a whip and he calls and whistles, it makes your pulse race. It's cheery and I'm grateful, but Pilot's message has sunk in: like the others, he'll crush me if things come to that point. He's one with them, no doubt about it.

November has also closed in and whistles and stiffly blocks a lamb that tries to dart away. Frans swishes his own whip through the air to force the mangy flock into the kraal. As soon as the kraal is shut, the sheep are herded into the crush and the inside gate is closed for the dosing to start.

The orderliness generates a sense of wellbeing in me, and I return upbeat to the house, determined to speak to Koert, even if it means I have to break into his quarters. I've regained my courage.

*

By early afternoon of the next day, I've still not had a chance to foist myself on Koert. In the meanwhile Headman's gone to ground. Everyone is agitated by this.

"It's Ouma Zuka's doing. Definitely. You saw the two of them plotting on the koppies."

I await an opportunity to speak to Koert, but am repeatedly prevented. Camp, cook, sleep, strike camp, march. My life is reduced to a primitive existence, like that of the pioneers. There's nothing I can do about it until I get to see Koert. Memories of the farm overwhelm and confuse me. Pappie's agricultural methods come to mind; at night the names of Mammie's roses keep me awake.

Mzungu, now I've got it. In the silence I am able to penetrate the meaning of Ouma Zuka's abuse. She must have contact with bone-throwers from further north: *mzungu* is the word the Chewa of Malawi use to describe Europeans. It doesn't relate semantically to the term "human". Only Africans qualify as *abantu*, as people. I with my white skin, and also Koert, fall outside the human category. To Ouma Zuka, Koert and I are *mzungu* – a non-being, a kind of non-human.

Thus my days pass with the opening of old drawers. I remember things, sort them, and make meaningless annotations. The history of the dorp, our own family history on the farm come to me in bits and pieces, come adrift from the greater whole, disappear into forgetfulness. When I look back I see my memories untangle like driftwood and float on the stream without will or direction: the founding date of our dorp, the sack-races every year on athletics day, the evening when Pappie spoke – quietly, he wasn't one for gossiping – about how Abraham and Tossie were caught one night loading the farmer's cattle onto their tenton Mercedes truck to take to market. Both sat in the elders' pews, imagine how they must have fought off their Christian conscience to commit such a deed against their *own* people. The story was so terribly upsetting that he had to excuse himself and take a piss on Mammie's manicured lawn. He returned to predict that this signalled the end of our people in this land: the writing is on the wall.

Do I hear something? No, nothing. The drone in my eardrums has ceased. Nor do I know what's happened to the fear I was so afraid about.

Today November is wearing a jacket stitched together from Mammie's mohair curtains. Whoever made it floundered when she got to the sleeves, the left shoulder puffs up and sits higher than the right one. The lining of the former sitting room curtains have been left as is; so when the jacket blows open in front, it's not too bad. At least it keeps him warm. He prances past my nose to show it off and makes sure the others see what he's up to. I suspect November's attitude towards me is changing, like Mildred's and Pilot's.

Meals have been cut to two a day: pap for breakfast, and at night pap with a sauce. It's made from fat, a tin of tomatoes, and strips of spinach that sprout next to the old drain. Last night there were bits of meat in it. I kept to myself: hell, isn't that mongrel a descendant of our old Simba? The eyes that flirt with you like that, the little sock on the front right paw.

"*Voertsek*," November shouts when he sees the mongrel bothering me. But it's nothing more than habit. Pretence. A bad attitude is being cultivated towards me, they're becoming spiteful.

Where does the meat in tonight's sauce come from? Has someone slaughtered a sheep? The woman in the dorp was supposed to get a leg of lamb and offal. It's not my business. I honestly don't want to know how they do things on this farm.

A kind of emptiness descends over the werf in the late afternoon. The only evidence of life is a whirlwind that pushes the poultry this way and that. A suspicion assails me: is someone creeping up on me, is my life in danger? Am I losing myself completely? I've never been suspicious before. I *must* get hold of Esmie Phumzile.

I walk around the house to Koert's quarters, but this time approach it from the back. Shall I? I check over my shoulder. There's nobody around, not even the children. I slip around the corner to the window that looks into his living area. The werf has been evenly raked with a *besembos* broom. I try to leave as few tracks as possible.

It's exceptionally neat in front of Koert's quarters, and gloomy inside, as I'd expected. I peer though the window, down the passage, and notice how Pappie's study has been enlarged, the back wall demolished so that the garage and meat room are now part of it. A curtain hangs at the back; it seems to partition off the furthest part of the room. My nose is flat against the window. Hidden behind the curtain, a cumbersome shape like that of a boar rises, slinks further back, slowly, until I'm only able to make out the grotesque formlessness. A darker embryonic figure is visible on the bed behind the curtain. Motionless. It must be Esmie Phumzile.

I swing around. Safe. I've seen enough for now. I amble to November's living quarters to doze for a while. The white I saw was nothing like the white of Koert's biceps, the way they used to be. The colour of this unwieldy lump is different. It's a grey, transparent larva white.

I'm whiling away the time when a child bursts in. "Come you, come," he shouts and jumps up and down. I pull on my shoes and walk out onto the werf. There they are, the child points.

At the gate of the kraal where the dosing is continuing for the second day, there are two policemen with Mildred. She gestures and clasps her hands like an actor trying to express shock on stage. When she sees me she becomes even paler. The two policemen walk over. The sheep that had been huddling in a corner disperse. The two men's rank insignia flashes in the sun, demands respect.

"Mr Martin Louw, is that your bakkie parked over there?" The policeman points a crooked finger at my white bakkie.

"Yes, it is."

"It is a stolen vehicle. The bakkie belongs to Mrs Sofie Radebe of number 3430M, Botshabelo. It's been missing since

May this year. Her husband is dead, she herself is sick. The grandmother and children look after her. The bakkie was stolen from in front of their house, but now we've got it back," and he punches the air.

"I bought and paid for it. I can prove it."

What a farce. I am becoming demented; I can tell this from the number of calcium deficiency spots forming on my nails, the drone in my eardrums the moment I set foot in the veld, here comes the fear. What fear, my friend? What are you talking about? Let me meet their madness with madness, it's the only language they know.

"Is that your bakkie there?" both point to my white bakkie.

I nod. See, you *are* mad. You've asked me already. All of you, completely crazy. They notice the loathing in my face.

"It's our job to make dead sure," one says, and taps his insignia.

"Forms, papers," I stutter. "In my bakkie, in the cubby-hole." I point. Words come from my mouth; I have lost my sentences, my sense. I step back and stumble across the rubbish dump at the kraal, fall and plunge my hand into a rotten pumpkin peel, slip and try to get up. The two think I'm trying to get away and trot up to me, pistols in the air. The dosing at the kraal has stopped, all eyes are on the spectacle.

"Mr. Louw," Pilot crows, his legs wedged between two sheep.

The policemen lead me to the bakkie by my elbows so that I don't have a chance to wipe the rotten pumpkin from my hands. At least they allow me to fumble for the bakkie keys in my back pocket.

"Here." I stuff their hands with the documents Nant du Plessis stamped for me and gave me in Bloemfontein. One, two, three, one of them pages through the papers, hands it to the other. November, Pilot, Frans and Lehlono resume their work with the sheep. Pilot's whistling as he pushes sheep into the crush echoes across the werf, rises, and becomes dissonant. The mongrels yelp.

"Sirs, please."

"Sergeant. I am Sergeant Dixon Ndude. This man here is Constable Sandile Khowa."

"My apologies, Sergeant and Constable. Please, you must give me a chance, I'm only here to collect my nephew, then I'll be off. That's sister Heleen's first-born and only offspring." I let go, all familiar: "Sergeant, Constable, you must have known my father, you surely know what our family's made of. Robbery doesn't figure in our world. Don't we sit in the pews listening to the Ten Commandments every Sunday? Heavens guys, give me a bit of leaveway."

"Do you mean leeway?"

"Leeway, yes, that's what I mean." I blush terribly. I'm afraid. Here it is. This is the fear I'd seen approaching.

I'm losing ground. "You must know that I've earned every dollar I spend in South Africa on the other side. Pots and pans, I sell the most wonderful cookware over there. Let me know, I'll send my brochure, mail-order post, and I'll send you a beautiful pot. On my account, it won't cost you a cent, to delight your wives. Your children, gentlemen, I mean Sergeant and Constable, imagine what a pot like that will mean to your children. Stainless steel with a thick base, will last until the fifth generation. You're actually getting an heirloom thrown in on the deal."

Sergeant Dixon Ndude drums his chest: Is the white man losing it? What's he saying, he doesn't understand a thing. "Pots?"

He stares at his colleague, Constable Sandile Khowa. "What's he on about?" The sergeant opens my international driver's license and holds it out to me. "Who is that?"

"It's me, it's me, that. It's my birth date. It's me in the photo. You have no idea how bad you look in those photos. But that's what I look like. It is. Compare the nose on the photo with mine. It's me, that. And it's my bakkie. Fully paid for, I don't owe a cent on that vehicle. Don't, man." I try to snatch back my forms and papers when I realise what Sergeant Ndude is about to do.

But he's already begun to crumple up the pile one by one. He sticks the last – a narrow pink one – into his mouth, then chews and spits it out in an arc over the werf. A chicken runs up to it.

"Mr Martin Louw, you are coming with us to the police station right away."

"To the dorp? I'm not dressed for the dorp. Look, give me a few minutes. One should at least look a bit presentable on dorp days. Pappie wears his going-to-the-dorp hat with the pheasant feather. Mammie slips on kid gloves, with her matching handbag and Extra Strongs in the left pocket. Okay, I'm coming, I'm coming." I am crazy.

I slide behind the steering wheel and start the engine. "It's my bakkie, this," I say to myself and observe my nose in the rearview mirror. "It's my bakkie, this." My lips are blue with tension. If they throw me in pison, I mean prison, I'll have had my chips. Things will grab me by my ears like a rabbit and screw me to a pulp and I'll catch the virus straight away and Jocelyn's prediction about me will come true. I could weep that I've come here. The monstrous white back of the white boar. It wasn't Koert Spies. He is not here any more. I'm on a wild goose chase.

We're on our way.

If only Sergeant Ndude and Constable Khowa would drive a little faster, I wouldn't have to put up with their dust. Inconsiderate. I don't know why I didn't check with Nant du Plessis that the bakkie was dust proof. My nice jacket. Look, they can beat me to a pulp, but I didn't steal the thing, and I won't sign away my innocence – never ever. I don't owe anyone on this earth anything. Not Heleen, not Koert. Koert can fuck off as far as I'm concerned. And I'm not going back to Ouplaas either.

In the rear-view mirror the farm gate disappears – I hadn't noticed the guard there today – and the gate posts become two stones, smaller and smaller, a last glimpse for the very last time, hooray.

We stop at the police station. EASTERN CAPE PROVIN, the remaining letters have fallen off. Arms folded, the two men come and stand next to the bakkie. They wait for me to get out. I lock the vehicle, notice how Constable Khowa eyes my sunglasses on the dashboard, so I unlock again, remove the glasses, and put them in my inside pocket.

"Okay," Sergeant Dixon Ndude's lips move soundlessly and his constable sidles up to me, inspects my orthopaedic shoe, smiles, and holds out his arm to escort me up the stairs.

It's like sweaty, warm tea inside and people are sitting on all the available chairs, breathing in this air. There are at least four babies that are tied to the backs of their grandmothers. They're being coaxed to keep quiet. Kwaito plays above the talking. Sergeant Ndude clears a path to the counter.

When someone refuses to give way, the sergeant pinches her on the groin. She shrieks, but stays put. She just shoves her breasts and forearms onto the counter with even greater purpose to claim her space.

"I'm here first," she protests. Sergeant Ndude grabs his revolver from its holster and pistol-whips her. She stumbles in front of the grandmothers with the babies, grabs her head, there's blood. Some of the chair-sitters start screaming as if their lives depend on it.

Constable Khowa waves his pistol about above the people's heads. "Shuddup."

In the meanwhile Sergeant Ndude has gone behind the counter. He pushes a form towards me. "Write here and here and here, sign on the dotted line with the date and everything, Mr Louw. And here's the bag, you can put your bakkie's keys into it." He passes me a plastic bag. It's a zip-lock. Wouldn't have thought you'd still get them here.

"Ballpoint," Sergeant Ndude shouts over his shoulder to one of the subordinates. The pen arrives and he holds it out to me.

I want to take it; he doesn't let go. Instead, he pulls me by the pen across the counter towards his face. His lips curl to make way for the tongue that now wags right in front of me. "If you pay $400 by five o' clock today, here at this office, you can go back to the farm. I'll even arrange for Constable Khowa to escort you. Special security."

"Sergeant, I don't have that kind of money on me." The thick tongue almost pokes me in the face. "You can do what you like, but I didn't steal that bakkie," I say more firmly, determined to clear my name.

"Six months behind bars," he spits out. His tongue licks the sweaty air of the charge office, curls back, and disappears behind his lips. I remain there with the ballpoint pen in my hand.

"I must phone the consul of my country. Consulate," I repeat to make sure he understands. "I'm not a citizen of your country,

Sergeant, you may think you can do what you like with me, but I have rights. You know: rights, basic human rights."

The sergeant looks past me. Two men have arrived to cart away the bloodied girl. One of the grandmothers struggles out of her chair to wipe the blood from the girl's head with a cloth. She's kicked away.

I bite the end of the pen, realise what I'm doing, then immediately pluck it from my mouth, wipe it and spit out. Spittle, sweat, blood and other body fluids, the police cells will overflow with it. I'll have to watch my step. I can't allow myself to be taken beyond the counter and the waiting room, deeper into their hell. Let me think a moment.

The sergeant watches. "Write," he points to the form. "You're wasting my time."

This man has no time for me. My family history in this dorp means nothing to him. He doesn't know me. He'll chew my passport to bits and spit it out too, just like that pink form. Then I'll have nothing to save me. I don't even wear an expensive watch. My sunglasses? I take my sunglasses – LA Eyeworks – from my inside pocket, and slide them across the counter to him.

"Could Constable Khowa take me to the bank, Sergeant, I'll draw the money and exchange it for dollars."

Without looking away from me, he takes my sunglasses and slips them into his pocket.

"Okay, he'll escort you. Everything's going well now; you'll go with him and come back. You're co-operating nicely, Mr Louw. I'll wait for you right here," says Sergeant Ndude. "But first you must write down everything. On this form." He slides the paper under my hands. "Write, then you'll go with my constable. Write first, then sign."

I scribble on the bottom left-hand corner of the form. "Your pen doesn't write, Sergeant."

He grabs the ballpoint from my hand and scratches long strokes across the entries in the big charge book that's lying open on the counter. The page tears under the pressure he's applying to the empty pen. He chucks the thing aside and shouts for another pen. The subordinates can't help him.

Do not provoke your children, that's also a sin. I feel in my pocket. The best solution is to provide a pen myself. Sergeant Ndude is already worn to a frazzle, has been tested and found to be desperate. He's capable of anything now. He paces about behind the counter, roaring for something to write with. I can see him swinging around and bursting out of the seams of his rage, then hitting me to hell-and-gone in a single blow, having me dragged out of here by my feet like that poor girl, my socks and shoes already stripped from me and being looted by his minions; I can see hundreds of fingers quivering and gnawing in a cell full of polluted air that invades me and makes my head swell uncomfortably, makes my eyes pop out of their sockets, makes my eardrums burst by the time midnight comes – and I am afraid, afraid like I've never feared anything before – until I bleed to death from inside through enlarged, violated orifices. The next morning a cock will crow somewhere in the dorp and the people will continue their lives in their shanties.

"Here, Sergeant, here's a pen for you."

The man turns to me. The hold-up has driven him to the edge. I'm definitely not going to make it; it's far too late already. Lord, I pray – the body hairs on both sides of my spine trembling in pure anxiety – give me a word, one single word that will make him release me. $400 is nothing, no more than two 34 cm stainless steel pots with lids – and the rats of hell will pass me by.

The sergeant looks past me – there's somebody behind me. I turn around. It's Pilot Hlongwane, gold Nikes, teeth white from ear to ear. There he stands among all the waiting ones, with a cardboard box balanced on each forearm. Must be meat he's got with him there, the base of one has started to give way and blood, sheep's blood, seeps onto the floor of the charge office.

"Pilot," I could almost cry. He stares, amazed at the emotion.

"Yes, Marlo'tjie!" He is triumphant at his entrance and at the two heavy boxes he holds up high, so effortlessly. "Koert said I must bring the meat so that you do not end up in jail. You thought we had forgotten you," he whispers in my ear and slips one, then the other box onto the counter.

"At your service, Sarge," Pilot says and salutes as he points at the bribe, two boxes of mutton. The sergeant steps forward with outstretched hands. If it wasn't for the counter he'd have hugged Pilot.

"Koert! It's Koert?"

"Of course. Who do you think still has enough meat to fatten all you guys?"

"Koert Spies and I have a good understanding," the sergeant says without even hearing Pilot's effrontery.

He taps the two boxes possessively and winks at me. I wink back. Why not? His professional aggression is something of the past. Benevolence washes over Sergeant Ndude's cheeks. Slowly he wades into the cool waters of the promised land of meat until his head is completely submerged. When he pops out again, his features have been purified. Humane. He sits on his stoep, watches his mutton chops braaiing on thorn-tree coals. Harmony – he laughs with his wife and gives her a little pinch. He has moved into the formerly white residential area of Harmony, Maitland along with some of his colleagues. Now there's meat, too. His children are happily eating chops right down to the bone, their cheeks running with fat. He himself will lick the fat from his fingers. Abundance has arrived; they will eat and drink, and then have a snooze, flat on their backs. All thanks to Koert. He and Koert are pals, thick as thieves.

I cry. "Pilot, did Koert send this? Did he get up and tell you to slaughter?" I whisper so that the sergeant and the other wretches can't hear me.

Pilot can't stop smiling. "I brought the meat, Marlo'tjie, am I not the one who has come to fetch you?" His teeth are whiter than white. Without him saying it, I hear him: you must trust us, Marlo'tjie, or we will beat you to death, the peace is past, you will be walking in the veld and we will be upon you, a thunder-bolt out of the blue. Do not say I did not warn you. Look, man, at the very last moment we rushed to your assistance with meat still warm with blood. Look at yourself, your face contorted, your eyes popping out of their sockets and your lips blue, your lame foot in spasms and your hands shivering. You have pissed in your white man's boxers. You – you, Marlo'tjie – thought that we on Ouplaas had completely forgotten about you, didn't you?

I sob. It's true, Pilot, I never trusted you. We Louws never trusted you or your people on Ouplaas, not for a moment. Though there were some occasions, that's true. Mildred mixed our pudding with her own hands, day after day, peeled quinces and cucumbers and we ate without giving it a second thought, the remnants of her fingertips still clinging to our cucumber rings. However, the minute a packet of Marie Biscuits disappeared,

fingers were pointed at her. Loot, Mammie thought right away.
Like the stuff I saw for sale here on the pavement along the main
road. Plundered from somewhere. And all the while the Marie
Biscuits had rolled behind the sugar bin. We should have trusted
you, Pilot. Even if you pinched a thing or two here and there, we
should have trusted you as people, you were and are true to your
flesh and bloody humanity, you're just like us.

The two boxes bulging with fresh mutton stand on the counter between me and the sergeant. The people sniff the charge
office air. "*Inyama*. Meat," says a child on his grandmother's lap.
"*Inyama*," another mimics him. The chant rises to a chorus, "*In-
yama-inyama*."

Sergeant Ndude grabs his pistol from its holster and twirls
it around his finger at the hungry gathering. "Shaddup." At the
same time he picks up the two boxes even more flamboyantly
than Pilot did, and hides them behind the counter so that only a
whiff of meat remains. He hands over the zip-lock with my keys.

"Thank you, Sergeant." Pilot steers me away from the counter with its charge book, without the sergeant saying anything
more. My pen, I think, does he really have to get away with that
as well?

"Pilot, wait."

"What?"

"No, nothing," I say, and then, "okay, okay," as he leads me
away, too fast; he knows only too well that we have to get away
from here.

"He can take back your keys before you know it, the sergeant
can change his mind any second and grab you and throw you in
the cells, before you know it," he speaks close to my ear. "Come,
hurry up."

Is the sergeant watching us, can he see the rush we're in? I dare not look back. The people in the charge office hadn't missed a thing. As we move through, the grandmothers and grandfathers and children, all look up to take us in and envy us one last time. They look at me, the redeemed, the ransomed one. And Pilot? They know Pilot, make no mistake. The whole dorp knows him. The limited power and influence he has is thanks only to his connection with Koert. In himself, he means fuck all. Can he read? Can he add or subtract? But his time and his day will come. And you, white-skin, last of the meat eaters on earth, you'd better tread lightly. We saw how you passed your pen over the counter to the sergeant, your arse cramping in fear. And lo and behold, you were about to turn back to claim your pen and risk your life all over again. The sick greed of you white people. You wanted to stay behind and bicker about a ballpoint pen. Are you completely mad? Gather your skirts and run as fast as you can, your meat has saved you from a disaster – it could have been life threatening. You'd have been infected with AIDS before the cell doors had slammed behind your arse. Shame on you and what a shame. Look what happened to that poor girl just because she complained about something, and quite justifiably. As sure as we're sitting in this office until who knows when today, old Ndude will be off, now that he's got his meat. And here we remain, poor shits. Go, run away while you can, and count your blessings one by one.

We go outside; the smoky air of the dorp suddenly smells refreshing. In the charge office one of the waiting ones is overcome by a coughing fit. There's a thud like flesh being hit with a plank and the coughing turns into a gurgle. I stop in my tracks.

"Why are you stopping?" Pilot sounds surprised. He's started rolling a cigarette from his pouch of Boxer tobacco. He's at the bakkie, is ready to get in and drive back to Ouplaas.

"It's not fair what's happened there. Nor is it fair what happened to me. I *bought* that bakkie. Why don't you care?"

"Yes, Marlo'tjie. Yes. What is right? What is wrong? That right and wrong stopped here with us a long time ago. Do you not understand? Is it because you are a white man? Open this," and he taps the bakkie's door. "We must get going, man. Do you not understand?"

I get in and we drive off in a cloud of dust. Pilot quickly looks round. "Do you see now?"

In the rear-view mirror Sergeant Ndude and his constable are standing on the police station stoep. They're staring at the bakkie.

Pilot is enraged. "Look there," he shouts. He's been drinking. "Koert sent the meat for you, and I brought it to the dorp. What besides do you want?"

"What more do you want," I correct him. He looks at me, uncomprehendingly.

"You are free. The meat has saved you from prison. As long as we have meat on Ouplaas, as long as we have Koert, we can do what we like in this dorp. They will not mess around with us."

We reach the last row of shops, Wesley's General Dealer and the muthi shop. For the first time I notice that the side of Wesley's has started to collapse. Some of the corrugated iron roof sheets have already been pulled off; bricks have been loosened and carted away.

"Will not mess with you," I mimic him the way he does me. I'm angry.

"You make me laugh, Pilot. Your sheep are all busy dying.

And Koert? Where is Koert? Sick! Sick! What can he still do? Does he have any money left to help you? I doubt it. What will you do when the house windmill breaks? Then there will be only one left. It will also break. Don't come running to me. I refuse to help you again. In a few days I'm off. I'm just waiting to speak to Koert; once I've seen him I'll have done what I came to do. You're a fool, Pilot, I'm afraid for your sake."

"Koert knows what he is doing." That's all he has to say about Ouplaas, nothing more. He's drifting away, away from my threatening tone, from my anger, my concern about their day after tomorrow, my empty warning. And in fact I've got nothing to do with him or his people.

"Pilot, won't you listen to me?" I beg. "It's not too late yet, you can still save the farm. Your father knows how. November knows everything about sheep. He's cleverer than my own father was with sheep sicknesses. He knows where the ewes hide with their new lambs. He knows exactly which lamb belongs to which ewe. Pilot?"

"Here! Stop!" he screams. In front of us lies a flattened hare – I'd thought they'd all been exterminated. I stop. Pilot gets out, grabs the hare by its ears, and chucks it into the back of the bakkie. When he gets back into the cab he rolls a cigarette.

"A bit of meat," he says.

"I thought you slaughtered a sheep. Is there nothing left? Isn't Koert going to give you something too?"

He flashes his white teeth and lights a cigarette.

"Pilot, tell me something: why don't you ever mention Koert by name in the dorp? Why don't you?"

"The people must not come asking me for meat."

"But they know you're not the man with the meat. They

know Koert's the one who has the sheep slaughtered and sends it off. He's in charge. And they know you're the link with Koert. Everyone in the police station knew it. I could tell."

"Mmm."

"Don't you want people to think you're Koert Spies's confidante? Do you understand confidante, Pilot? It means you're the man Koert trusts most. That's you. You're the man who knows all his private things."

"It is not safe," he mutters.

"What isn't safe?"

"To be Koert's man."

"Since when hasn't it been safe to be associated with Koert? He's had it, hasn't he?"

Pilot looks out and tap-taps his fingers on his knee.

"No more safe. That is all. No more safe. Aah, Marlo'tjie," he draws deeply on his cigarette. "Nice."

Boxer tobacco, the bakkie's full of it. It smells of hands that have been working with a spade and soil all day long, of khaki trousers.

"It is nice," I say, because a spot of sunlight has entered through the back window. Pilot's singing. His golden Nikes rest on the dashboard.

"Do you like driving, Pilot?"

"My whole life long, Marlo'tjie."

I look at him, enjoy him. We're driving towards Ouplaas. Pilot and I alone through the potholes. "Hey-y-y," I shout as we land in another deep one and bounce out on the other side, heads against the roof.

"You see these holes? Your tyres drive through them. Right through. Holes worry no one. I like it, I like it the whole day and the whole night. You see these poles?" He points to the telephone poles that pass by one by one. In places the telephone wire hangs right down to the ground, sometimes there's nothing.

"What are the poles still doing here, Pilot? They don't serve any purpose. There isn't even a telephone service any more – you can't phone anyone on this earth from here."

"I like the poles. Here they come, here they come. Do you know why I like them, Marlo'tjie? Because we do not drive into them. You can turn that wheel slightly this way then slightly that way, and we pass them by. You can step on the brakes with your shoe for me to pick up the hare. I like that."

"And when I leave and you don't have a car to drive in any more?"

"Then we simply walk around the holes. Then we walk past these poles. Do you understand now?"

"I'm beginning to understand, Pilot," I say, envious that anyone could feel like that.

7

There were moments when one's past came
back to one, as it will sometimes when you have
not a moment to spare to yourself.

"November," I say to the old man before turning away from his snoring, "you know about windmills. Shouldn't we check the one that's still pumping tomorrow? See whether it's okay? We can't afford to let it break."

"You're just bothering yourself with all this stuff in your head."

"I'm only saying."

"I'm tired, Marlo'tjie. Look at my legs." He pulls the blanket away and shines the candle on his naked legs. They are cramped up with rheumatism and full of bumps where there shouldn't be any. "That windmill needs a leather washer, I know that. But who will pay for a new one? You?" He puts the candle down and bandages his leg with a woolly cloth.

I don't have the heart to ask why he presumes that I'm the one who's going to pay.

"Here, take this for your other leg." I hand him one of my two jerseys to wrap around his leg. When he takes it, his rough hand touches mine but he doesn't thank me.

Sleep now. Sleep sweetly. Mr Sandman is coming. Rock-a-bye baby, child of mine.

No, I don't trust this kind of sleep, it unsettles me. I had a dream, I remember now. It was one of Pappie's dreams. As he's about to fall asleep, Pappie feels as if a sliver of ice is pricking against his skin, moving down and cutting a straight line. Even the blood that spurts out is ice cold. I'm so afraid of it (I'd registered the fear in my dream). I look and look: a man with a knife in his hand, his hand is so real that I can smell grass and dust on it. A man next to Pappie's bed in the middle of the night, a man as rank as ploughed soil, his knife shiny like a river fish. It's a butcher's knife. Pappie screams for help. I support him under his armpits and try to drag him away; we're both dripping with sweat. I achieve nothing, I can't budge him. I sit bolt upright. It was no dream. I don't remember it as a dream, but as reality, as a piece of history. It is the source of my mistrust. I'm afraid, and I experience a raw anxiety in my dream. The man with the blade over Pappie, over me, the blade pointing at my temples. Naked fear. It is Pappie's fear, and it is his dream, now I remember, now I know. I've inherited it from him. Fear finds its most honest expression in the dream, and it isn't only Pappie's fear. It's mine too. I remember very well how he told me about that dream. The sweat stood out on his temples. After the telling he had to get up and pour himself a drink. Poor Pappie. He sensed the horror of his dream. He knew what it was about, where it came from, and what it meant. Poor, brave Pappie, so burdened by this mountain of fear.

*

The pap is lumpy this morning.

Three days have passed and I've still not seen Koert. Today everyone's celebrating Youth Day – it's the sixteenth of June – and this tradition hasn't died out yet. Young friends of Esmie Phumzile and Pilot have turned up from the dorp with booze. Headman is also back. He's changed; he's friendlier towards me. At last he's become a man, he says, now he's ready for the thing.

"What are you saying, Headman? What are you ready for?" Mildred confronts him on the kitchen stoep. His own father and mother are too cowed by his new-found bravado.

"I was with a girl. She's made me clean."

"Oh dear Lord, don't tell me you've also gone and picked up that virus. We've buried Lehlono's wife, and Esmie's sick – when I see how she fades away day by day, I don't know how much longer she'll last. Now you're coming with this story. Who did you lie with?" Mildred insists on knowing.

"I had to, I had to. Ouma Zuka said my water, my seed, has been fiddled with. She can fix Esmie for me, but before I shoot my water into her, I have to sleep with another young *intombi*. So I went to look for one. I found one with a red cloth around her body. And she had a soft neck. I told her I wanted her beauty, I wanted her. Then she gave in and I put my water in her. I got rid of my bad water. She won't get sick, because see, Ouma Zuka said my bad water was never meant for her. Only if it was meant for her, would she get sick. Now I'm back, now I can sleep with Esmie Phumzile, I can put my good water into her. You'll see."

Mildred slaps him through his face. His mother has begun to twirl around on one leg and moan. "What have you gone and done now, you fool's paradise, you." Mildred screeches one of

Mammie's sayings all mixed up and slaps Headman again with the back of her hand so that he spins around.

"Ouma Zuka said I had to," he lets fly, his fists clenched.

"Who did you lie with? Who is she? Don't you know everyone in the dorp is carrying the death virus? Where did you find her? What troubles have you brought on another family?" Mildred steps closer, she's sent one of the children to fetch a knife, she's actually going to stab him.

Headman dare not resist Mildred and her knife. He curses the matriarch and withdraws across the werf, away from everyone. "I'm a man, I don't have a foreskin any more, I've spilt the bad water," he cries, furious at the humiliation. "Bring Esmie to me," he screams, "I'll show her who's the man on this farm."

And now everyone on Ouplaas speaks at once. The young people who'd come to celebrate with boxes of wine retreat. Lovingly they stroke the booze, keen for the taps to be opened. Pilot has gone to speak to Headman's mother, trying to calm her; November supports Frans Zuka and offers him tobacco. Mildred clasps her head, she's tired of all the trouble Ouma Zuka stirs up. They can't afford to care for another invalid on Ouplaas.

"Where is Esmie?" she asks. "Pilot, find Esmie, she has to speak to Koert. I've had enough. And that lizard on Koert's door. No, this nonsense must come to an end right now."

"Esmie's sleeping," says Pilot.

It's none of my business, this. I walk to the east side of the house where the vegetable garden used to be. For the past three mornings I've been coming here with the spade. First I shovel out the weeds, then I turn the ground over and prepare the beds for sowing. I've already finished three, for carrots, pumpkin and tomatoes. I'd stuck my hands into the rubbish heap next to the kraal – it was rather nasty – and fished some peels from it. And so I discovered fourteen boerpampoen seeds. They're drying on the kitchen windowsill where Mildred can keep them away from the children's hands. What else can you do with pumpkin seeds apart from growing them? On the other side, where I come from, yes, restaurant chefs serve them with tagliatelle: roasted pumpkin seeds, arugula leaves, smoked salmon and baked pumpkin shavings.

I walk to the barn – only the walls remain – to see whether there isn't any hessian lying around. In the mornings the water is frozen in the pipes; it takes until eleven o' clock for a few drops to piss out. The pipes should be wrapped. I'm concerned about the water situation on Ouplaas. It worries me even more than the dying sheep. And I'm afraid of the image of Koert I've put together from all the stories and that single stolen glance – was it him?

When I return – there are no hessian bags – the young people on the werf have gathered and become jollier. The issue with Headman has been put aside. He too stands nearer when he sees the wine flowing from the boxes, blood red. The children sense the excitement and chase one another between the legs of the big ones and fall and hurt themselves and get up without any squealing.

I'll wait until they're wasted, then I'll knock on Koert's door. No one will notice me. Only I will know what I am up to. I'll walk to his door and knock. I have to battle against myself, my heart is full of despair: I'm afraid I'll never get to see him. If I were honest, I'd have to admit that I'm wondering whether to avoid the meeting altogether, to willingly accept the disappointment, and return and dish up some or other story for Heleen.

"Here we are, Marlo'tjie, why are you so down in the mouth?"

Mildred hands me the axe. Her breath is still warm, she's been on her knees blowing at the coals of the stove. "The young people won't be collecting wood for my stove today. The wood in the house is finished. You see now, Headman is a tomcat, I can't tell him to fetch wood."

"In the old days the women fetched wood, the men worked with the sheep," I protest.

"Then give the axe back. I can see you don't want to help me. No."

"That's not what I meant. I'll get the wood, I'm just saying how it used to be."

"Everything is the way it is now. You've slept here how many nights already, aren't you getting used to it?"

"Yes, Mildred. Or rather, no."

I try to avoid Pilot and the others, but they spot my axe right away and come sauntering across in a group. The boxes of wine have been opened. Pilot lifts his above his head and a hand turns the tap for him. Red wine flows into his gaping mouth. Without closing the tap he passes the box to the next man. With his head thrown back and mouth open – glistening from the wine – Pilot looks at me and laughs.

"Give Marlo'tjie some wine." Some girls hold Pilot from behind and the whole bunch sways forward together.

"I have to collect wood."

"Can you collect wood, Marlo'tjie?" Pilot turns to his people: "Do you think this man can collect and chop wood?" And back to me: "Show us your muscles, Marlo'tjie." A girl's hand emerges from the group and closes his lips. A ring flashes in the sunlight. I convince myself that it is Esmie Phumzile who's come out to stand up for me. I like Esmie.

"I'm off," and I walk away as fast as I can. It's years since I last collected wood. It's common sense, you don't need much more than an axe. String? String's handy to tie up the bundle.

I keep to a north-westerly direction towards the top of the koppie. Ouma Zuka must be up to something there. If I hear a human sound I won't be afraid. It can only be her.

Here, a *besembos* branch that's been prepared for cutting later. Firewood for heat, pap and sugar for the stomach, and a smile. It's the least that you need for yourself, without it you won't get by. Mildred and the others must make sure they preserve the basics for themselves here on Ouplaas.

Besembos branches wave about me and give off their berry-like aroma, something between thyme and pepper. Scattered between them are tufts of frost-hardened grass and stones large enough for a big bottom, and smaller ones like tortoise backs, rounded and uneven. And mountain birds, berry eaters that have always kept to this place and avoided the open veld.

It's dead quiet. Something rustles, as if there's a presence among the *besembos* bushes, then silence again. The clipped chirrup of a bird, and silence. This is how it will start playing with my mind, this is how the terror will come to me in broad daylight. I squat, the handle of the axe gripped firmly in my hand. The buzzing begins in my eardrums again. From under the *besembos* I observe the world: to the south-east lie the house and the werf where there's drinking and talking. They'll certainly have something to say about me. Or absolutely nothing. Please don't let me presume that I still have a place here on Ouplaas.

Without thinking, I run my thumb along the cutting edge of the blade. To collect and chop wood – it's an old and comforting phrase. That's what I've come to do here. I don't have to be afraid of this or anybody, not even of Ouma Zuka. She's only human. I must search the koppie carefully: you have to look for dead *besembos* branches, then hack away at their ankles, chop them down and lay them aside until you've got a solid bundle. Look carefully, some branches have been snipped by human hands to dry out and cut up later. The branches that have been worked in this way will be here – just open your eyes and you'll find them.

Open your eyes, Marlouw. I too came here often to escape the hurly-burly.

Pappie? Years later in Melbourne I could still repeat that conversation between my father and myself word for word. The reality of it remained as clear as daylight. Not that I didn't know Pappie well enough in any case to have imagined it.

Yes, my child, his voice blows like wind in my ears.

Let me be, Pappie. I didn't come here to talk to Pappie.

My eardrums hiss. Let me hide under the thickest *besembos* and wait there; nobody will be able to sneak up on me. I've got the axe. I run my thumb lightly along the edge of the blade once more.

Marlouw?

It's his voice. Milky with age. It's my father keeping to the *besembos* here on the koppies. He had ants in his pants when alive, and in death he can't stop wandering. Strangely, Mammie predicted it.

My knees creak as I get up, and above the sound the wind belches, satiated by all the days and nights of people who have lived on this patch of earth and have never stopped living there. Pappie too. When the farm attacks and the land claims began, Heleen and I repeatedly begged him to sell the farm.

Draw your thumb across the axe until the blood runs, Marlouw.

What are you saying, Pappie?

I must do something to wake you up. You refused to believe
me. After '94 it was a foregone conclusion. In fact, I predicted
it even earlier. Remember how I tried to bring it home to you,
Marlouw, that Sunday under the old poplar tree. Listen to what
I'm saying to you today, Marlouw, this country is sinking. Goodness, I wasn't stupid, you know.

But Pappie refused to concede that the old government did
wrong, not even on one single point. Stephen Bantu Biko, all
those men were murdered. And Pappie was part of the generation that kept saying, even when the truth had been made public:
No, I don't believe the police would have committed crimes like
that. I never wanted to speak to Pappie about these things. That's
not what I wanted from you, don't you understand? It's my foot,
I attempt to say again, but he never gives me an opportunity to
raise the subject.

Were we supposed to sweep everything we'd achieved from
the table? Just like that? There are the foundations on which I
built my life, Marlouw, my identity. I simply could not accept
those allegations. Not during my life, nor over my dead body.
What do you think would have happened to me if I had? I'd
have become a nothing, a bloody nothing.

You're still angry. And scared.

The Lord has punished us all.

Oh, for heaven's sake stop it.

Fine, I'll do as you say, Marlouw – I love you very much. You
are my flesh and blood, thirteen generations of Louws of whom

not one remains in this land. The Lord has blessed us here for thirteen generations; you and Heleen are the last.

Pappie, I have to go, I've got too much to do here on Ouplaas. It's all good and well that you brood on these things; dealt with them long ago. As I've said, I'm only here to fetch Koert, no matter what Pappie thinks of him. He's also our flesh and blood. He is. And I'm still here, I live off this land, I have to collect wood so that we can eat. We have bodies that need looking after. Pilot and November and Mildred, oh well, Pappie, they've got their ways, but they're not a bad lot. Do you know what? Deep in my heart I care about them. November's old legs, oh dear, Pappie.

The wind comes up and dies, then blows again between the *besembos* and tufts of grass. Restless. The wind carries him on its back. How does he feel about it, the bitter wind against his sides? Pappie never liked the wind.

There was a dream, Marlouw, a dream, I hear him murmur. My grandfather dreamt this dream, and my great-grandfather Daniel, and his grandfather before him, thirteen generations of us had this dream until it no longer felt like a dream. Let me tell you about it – that is if you don't yet know it yourself. Someone sneaks up in the night with a butcher's knife, the blade is shiny and smooth in the sliver of moonlight. The knife glints like the body of a mermaid. He glides through the house filled with the breathing of the sleeping grown-ups and children. Without bumping into anything, he slinks right up to the side of the bed where the man is sleeping. The knife takes on another form. Now it's the body of a crocodile, sharp and sleek. He's chosen the correct side of the bed, the side where the man sleeps . . .

Where the father, the progenitor, sleeps – I take the words out of his mouth.

You see, I knew you were familiar with the dream. As I was saying, he sleeps on his side, this patriarch with his hands strong like stone, his feet strong like stone. And suddenly he sits bolt upright. Then the knife-bearer bends over the bed with his rancid breath and body, heavy like an ox carcass, black like ploughed soil, and in his claw: the white blade of the knife. The patriarch screams until the whole house is awake. Everyone sits up, bewildered. The primal call echoes and re-echoes in their ears. They lurch towards the main bedroom, weepy, the little girls panicky. The patriarch sits with his head in his hands and sweat drips from his forehead. One by one the little boys step back, bump into the doorframe and return to their own beds. They know what the dream was about. Quickly they pull the sheets and blankets over their heads and weep sorrowfully at the terrible burden of their inheritance.

Listen carefully: it's easy to misinterpret the dream. I'm not afraid of dying, or even that I'll be killed in some cruel way. Even if it's with a knife in the night. My fear goes much further and deeper. I was afraid we Afrikaners would be wiped out roots and all. That's the heart of my fear.

That is the heart of Pappie's dream. It's the source of the primal fear. I understand, Pappie. The fear is rooted in your amygdala.

What would that be, my child?

It's a small almond-shaped segment deep inside the temporal lobe of the brain.

I'm not so sure, Marlouw. That's your way of putting things.

We're talking about the same thing, Pappie. At the precise moment that the man bends over his bed with the blade of his knife, the patriarch jumps up. He's sensed the icy beat, the heart of fear. The primeval fear rises in the patriarch's head, in the core of his grey matter, and throws him from his bed like a chewed bone. He sits upright, wild-eyed; the inherited fear has taken shape. He's ready to fight to the death for as long as he can protect his own. That's how it must be understood: the dream that we men have all dreamt repeatedly is passed on from generation to generation in our genes. It's the effect of the conditional stimulus on the amygdala, the almond deep in Pappie's brain, that makes the body react instinctively. Pappie knows how fast your heart beats, how geared up your body is after you've had that dream. It's the amygdala telling your body what to do. The next thing Pappie does is fight or run away. The stimulus on the amygdala makes you respond in the appropriate way – it's the basis of the survival of the species. Of our species.

It is as you say, Marlouw. I'm glad you understand me at last. I believe that we've had this dream since our first forefather stepped onto these shores, to warn us against life-threatening danger. It's exactly as you've put it. It's been handed to us so that we can get up, defend ourselves and survive.

But now the amygdala has fallen asleep. We didn't listen, we didn't read the signs accurately and that's why we didn't begin fighting in time, nor did we leave in time. We threw in the towel, we engineered our own demise.

What about Pappie's grandson? Pappie knows I've come to fetch Koert. That's the only reason I'm here.

Oh, he's an abomination who's abandoned his mother tongue. His generation has trampled their inheritance. Into the gutter. I don't regard him as a Louw. Let him keep his father's surname. Our lineage has come to an end with you and Heleen. The thirteenth and last generation. Don't they say thirteen is an unlucky number? This is how the Lord has willed it. All that remains of us are the dregs, like that nephew of yours. A bastard-Afrikaner, scum.

Oh, please, Pappie. Heleen so badly wants me to find him and take him back.

Marlouw, my dearest son. If only you knew how much I always loved you. My dear, dear child.

Then why didn't Pappie and Mammie ever have my foot fixed?

It's late in the day. Time's running out for me, I'm talking to lighten my mood. There's nothing left to salvage, that's all I meant.

Good, I respond, because I don't want to harp on at my old reproaches any more.

I now hear a footstep crackling over the dry bossies. Overwhelmed by the conversation, I step back into the embrace of the *besembos* and let the axe fall to the ground. My body is shaking from the inside. I cover my face with my hands. I have seen what I never wanted to see: primal fear in its pure form, and it's been part of me all my life.

Marlouw, there's one last thing I want you to do for me, otherwise Mammie and I will never be at rest. I want you to go back to the graveyard on Oupa and Ouma Rhynie's farm. Destroy everything. Everything. Burn the wreaths, flatten the whole graveyard. I don't want a single trace of me or Mammie or our family to remain in this land. That's my last request.

Is that why Pappie can't find rest? Pappie always had much faith in the heavenly destination.

I'm almost in reach of it. Almost. But there's one last thing we have to finish off. Marlouw, at night they come and tamper with our graves, during the day they hang their underwear on the circular wall. The other day someone stole Ouma's photo, the one behind glass, the one where her eyes look at you so joyfully. The children come with unwashed bottoms, disgusting, and piss right on our graves. It's the holy truth. I know you're uncertain about the reason for your visit to this cursed land, but here I'm giving it to you. Go – go today – and flatten that graveyard to the ground. It's the last thing I ask of you, my child. Let me rest in peace, in God's name.

Pappie?

Yes, my son. Below I hear someone clambering up the koppie. It can only be Ouma Zuka.

Pappie. He's off. Easiest way out. Can't really blame him at his age. I forgot to check whether he looks any older.

The wind has died down. The *besembos* branches breathe lightly, otherwise there's no evidence of his presence. I shove my hand into my trouser pocket and wipe my face with my last clean hanky. I can still hear Pappie's words; I can repeat them one by one. I remember every syllable and inflection. In the end, Pappie was my master and I his unwilling student. I have inherited his word and his dream. And now I'm also burdened with his task.

There she is. "Ouma Zuka?" I hesitate. She walks on all fours and maintains the distance between us. It can only be Ouma Zuka. She's squatting; her rough hands dangle across her knees. Her nails have become ingrown from all the digging for roots. She raises a forepaw, is she waving? I wave back. I step closer and she hops to the right, ready to run off if I move any nearer. She's taken on the appearance of a baboon, just as the children described. *Imfene.* The hair is knotted and has a reddish sheen. Must be the constant hunger. There are the eyes now. Even from here, I can see how poorly the iris focuses. If there was once distrust in the gaze, there's little of it left. And no trace of the cunning of which Pilot speaks. She hasn't even got the blanket with her. I inch forward, she immediately withdraws, moves even further back on her haunches, almost to where the koppie falls away to the plain below. She keeps jerking her head back as if she's got her eye on something.

I ignore her, keep myself busy. Collecting and chopping the wood. Here's a nice branch. Chop it down, twist it around its sinews, and stack it with the others. Another, this one drier. It will burn nicely. Make fuel to cook food. Eat and sleep, rest well. Tomorrow you'll walk out onto the werf and repeat what you've done today.

That's enough for the moment. This bundle ought to keep the stove going until tomorrow. I'm no longer today's child, how much wood does Mildred expect me to bring home? I look up: Ouma Zuka's still squatting there in the cold.

"Hey, you," she screams in my direction: she wants to communicate after all. She extends the fingers of both hands and makes two duck beaks talk-talking to each other, then rises slightly on her haunches and gesticulates wildly behind her back: go, go and look, down below on the plain. She imitates some sort of bird, a crow-like screech in a shrill tone. It echoes across the veld but breaks off almost immediately. The woman's strength is spent, she couldn't harm anyone. I must speak to Mildred and November about Ouma Zuka; they can't allow it to go on like this any longer. Someone must take pity on her. She needs pap and sugar every day. More: she ought to be fetched and brought home. A witch doesn't look like this.

She points in a northerly direction a few more times and then makes tracks. I hear her hop once more. She'll be hiding some-where, like a wild creature, keeping watch on me, always the first to know my movements.

There's something down below. I'm curious. It's a horse rider on the plain that stretches to Ouplaas's boundary fence. I note the spot where I leave my bundle, and then clamber down the koppie. There's wind on the open veld, and its sharp coldness makes my eyes water. In places the bossies and grass have disap-peared, the veld has turned into compacted, hard ground. Stones lie strewn like dry bones. Resin brown, ochre and a clayish baux-ite flash briefly in the winter sun before merging into a uniform nothingness through which I walk.

I hobble along faster to generate some warmth. The rider comes closer, too. It's a woman; I reckon I know the face. I wave my arms, a scarecrow in the middle of nowhere. I can't deny it: I am glad to see her. She tightens the reins so that her horse doesn't bolt at the sight of me. My breathing is uneven.

Make sure you stay tough, Marlouw, or you won't last in this world, I hear Pappie again.

Oh, Pappie, I wish you'd stop.

The rider allows her horse to prance, its feet lifting high as if to avoid aardvark burrows. She sits proudly on the dappled horse; she wants to impress me, together with reins held in gloves, but-tocks firm in the saddle, back straight, chin pulled in by the strap of the riding helmet.

"I think I know you," I shout as I hobble along.

She yanks the bit and halts. Stirrups forward and tight against the flanks, a real saddle-horse. At first she doesn't re-spond to me – she must think I'm raving mad.

"Never mind," I shout, out of breath, and start walking, but

I have to stop and bend over to catch the phlegm that's pushing up. When I've finished, I remain standing with my hands on my knees and look at her through half-closed eyes.

High up on her horse, etched against the horizon, she is imposing. She seems hesitant about the encounter and remains motionless in the saddle. With her bright red riding coat and the pitch-black velvet cap she evokes an era of whisky on the rocks, springbok hides on polished stoeps, and orange blossom perfume as the hostess bends over to offer last winter's finely cut biltong.

She jumps down from the saddle, riding crop in hand – I don't know why I thought I knew her. From closer up I notice the pistol on the belt of her jodhpurs. I don't know her from a bar of soap.

"You're probably glad to see a white person," she says and gives me her hand. "We heard you were coming to Ouplaas. And why."

"I can't tell you how relieved I am," and I grab both her hands in mine. She allows this, then withdraws her hands from my ice-cold grip. I must first be inspected.

"It's cold this year, isn't it?" I remember how people always started off with the weather. She waves off my observation. "Do you know about the old woman who lives here in wind and all weather?"

"Who knows, she may outlive us all."

"But the way she walks on all fours, and the eyes that have lost their focus. It's starvation, you know."

"Marlouw," she rolls the "r" and my name sounds precious in her mouth. Now I know that she also values the meeting. "None of us who remain can afford to play the Samaritan. There's not enough to go round. Besides, she's lost her mind, alone like that

in the mountain. My husband and I, we simply try to keep ourselves going. Marlouw, if I may," and she pulls me closer with
gloved hands and kisses me right on the mouth as the custom
here always was.

"Please don't expect more from me than what you see." I'm
flustered by the kiss. "Do you know, my father . . ." I stop myself.
The task I've been given of destroying the graves is too personal
to share with a stranger.

"I know, I know. I only wanted to feel how another man kisses for a change. Come on, make me a sentence with the word
'*minnekoos*'."

"Minnekoos? To have and to hold?" And then I sense what
she's after. She knows us Louws. She knows our habits, our ways,
the life we lived here, what kind of people we were. So too with
the people from whom Koert is descended, JP and the Spieses.
If she doesn't know them herself, she ought to be able to place
them. In those days there was a school principal from Bloemfontein with the surname Spies. An exceptional example of upright
homo sapiens. Meerkat eyes behind glasses, never overlooked
the slightest wrongdoing. There definitely must be a thread running from her to JP's people with their sturdy thighs. In the old
days there were golden threads that connected most people with
most others: this one went to school with that one's brother,
that colonel was so good to this young soldier in the army – he
rather favoured him (laughter) – all because he knew his uncle,
they were like brothers, hunted together outside Bloemfontein
where herds of springbok grazed, if I'm not mistaken they got
married on the same day in the same church. And wasn't the
colonel's oupa one of those black Labuschagnes? Heavens, that
oubaas had a quiver full of gorgeous girls. And each and every

one of those Labuschagne girls knew what was good for them: they all married so well. June with a thoroughbred horse breeder and Suzie – oh, she was a shrew if ever there was one – with a fellow whose people owned that big supermarket chain, and later she divorced and married a diamond magnate, they say they had a gold dinner service – and the third girl, the strawberry blond, I've forgotten her name – anyway, she also married into money. Bonds of blood and bonds forged by marriage, information about close family and distant family, knowledge handed down by great-grandparents, hearsay chatter about inbreeding and infidelity, about brothers who shot one another in the presence of their own father, pleading with an open Bible on his lap. The woman in front of me is aware that she and I must fit in somewhere in this great, golden tapestry. She knows it as surely as she stands before her horse, and she wants me to be equally sure of it. Golden threads connecting us so that all of us from the Cape knew all the people in the Transvaal or at least could have known them if only enough of the right questions were put to family experts: tannies with crochet on their laps who had the ability to embroider wonderful threads that ran through this land like rivers from one person to the next. They could babble on about silver tributaries and shining branches that flow on, further and further away from the main river, but – they'd quickly add – we still hear of course how they thrive or go bankrupt, shame, their memory won't be lost as long as we're alive (make us a nice pot of tea, please, our throats are bone dry). There will always be connections, always the golden threads. But nothing remains of them today. Like the Jews, the Afrikaners have forsaken themselves to a mighty diaspora and left the blood river for good; though unlike the Jews, they even cast their language on the waters like stale bread, drifting downstream rapidly so that some of the words of the language, words that everyone remembered and used once upon a time, floated away, faster and faster, and disappeared under the water. Under, then above, like fingerlings, sometimes you could almost see their splashings, but like miniscule traces of water life they eventually disappeared, never to be seen or heard of again, faster and in greater numbers, so that their presence became ever less noticeable, ever vaguer, until no sign whatsoever remained of the existence of these words.

"Minnekoos," I repeat when I've gathered my thoughts.

She smiles, waves her hand. "No, forget it," she smiles again. I see you've lost the thread. I was joking. My dear man, I simply wanted to hear you speak."

"Say shibboleth," I manage a bit of repartee. She must know that the threads of blood and words to which she's alluded have passed. The only comfort now is the three of us together. She and her steaming horse and me with them.

"Where are you staying? My house is open. Any time, just say the word."

"I'm happy enough on Ouplaas."

"Don't tell me you're staying with that rabble in your parents' house. A garbage dump. Oh, the shame." Icily, she continues, "Your father and mother would be turning in their graves if they knew what was going on there."

"What business of yours is it where I stay, and with whom?"

She recoils. "That's true, that's true. Forgive me." The sense of warmth between us wanes; she tries to win it back. "Times have changed so much, I was swept away for a moment, I'd forgotten that the old days have gone forever."

"What do you mean?"

"That I can't assume any more that we all share the same feeling about the rabble. That I can't simply assume that you are a brandy-and-Coke man. Or that you watch rugby. Oh, the rugby days, the Saturday afternoons with braaivleis and beer."

"I'm not nostalgic," I lie and use the opportunity to take a good look at her now that the moment of magic has passed. Her outfit is not at all as I'd imagined it from afar. The tips of the gloves are threadbare and the shoulders of the riding coat perished: poor boer woman tarted up on an old grey horse.

"I know, I know," – she's noticed what I'm looking at. The fingers of her glove are spread out in front of me. "Holes wherever you look. For everyone to see."

There's something about the woman that won't go away, the paleness of her eyes, her straight back in the saddle. Something. "*Do* I know you?"

"You want me to tell you? You won't like it, but if you insist. You look like your father, you know. You've got your father's lips."

I shake my head.

"Of course, your father believed a man ought to ride a stallion. Oh, he sat so well on that horse of his. What was its name again?"

"Prinsdom." I don't want to be part of this conversation.

"We only met here in summer. When the heat made the air shimmer. You know how days like that feel – I don't get it any more, you know."

She's playing cat and mouse with me, gives and then snatches back. Sympathy is what the poor thing wanted. She shouldn't have told me the story.

I don't know why I didn't walk away from her and her horse

that day. The veld was flat, I could have escaped easily.

"Almost without making a date, we sensed each other across the veld. Your father was horny, if I may say so, and my eyes became moist. I always brought an extra saddlecloth along, I'd spread it out on the hard ground for us. Dust and saliva, we didn't mind – it was part of the fun. And afterwards, when I lifted the saddlecloth, I made sure that the bossies were pushed back into shape. Odd how I remember these details. And the sudden white flash when I opened my eyes under him and looked straight into the sun. Oh, the sun, the sun and the extravagant whiteness of those days, I can still smell it. I don't know why your mother only had you two, your father had a lot of spunk."

"The progenitor," I mutter. "Why are you telling me this?"

"Marlouw, it's the truth." She says quietly, echoing me.

I nod. "Maybe."

"Don't you see what your father meant to me? Can't you value what we had just for a moment? Oh, man, it was heavenly. I could feed off the memory for days. His hands cherished me, he . . ." she takes a hip flask from her inside pocket and shakes it. "Empty! I carry it on my hip for old time's sake. Nothing warm or comforting remains for me."

I continue softly. "And now you've spilt your memories too. Like seed on the ground."

She laughs at my expression, her lipstick smudging. She's become a mess.

"Now you've betrayed your intimacy with my father. And *him* too. Why did you tell me? I mean, it's true as you said. But now there's nothing left for you. You've spent your memories. How do you manage to make an existence here, how on earth is it still possible?"

She pulls herself together; this time she is truly icy. "We farm rabbits. That's how we get hold of meat. Every night my husband brings the whole colony into the house so that they're not stolen. We have some pumpkins left over from last summer and we grind meal from some mealies that my husband's managed to get. Times are hard, but what do you care about us?" and she taps her heart under her red riding jacket.

"Do you still keep sheep?"

"Sheep. Don't make me laugh. Your family here on Ouplaas has the monopoly on mutton. If my husband gets hold of a few ewes and lambs and hides them away somewhere, they're stolen the same night. We can't defend ourselves any more, we hardly have any ammunition left. On top of that, my husband had a fallout with the rabble in Maitland who sell ammunition. Let me put it like this: until recently my husband was part of a syndicate. They loaded sheep everywhere at night – they stole them, that's what it boils down to. That's the way it goes. Either you play the game by today's rules, or you go under." She looks at me to see if I'll respond.

"I don't care how you make a life here. Don't look at me. You're the one who has to live with your conscience."

"There isn't such a thing as conscience in this land, Marlouw. My husband and his crowd went as far as Ficksburg to load sheep, that is, when there were still sheep to steal. They worked with sheepdogs. Petrol for the trucks was always a problem. My husband lay awake at night about it. He detested it, but there was no choice: they had to pick up child prostitutes in Lesotho and transport them in exchange for cans of petrol. There was no choice, believe me. My husband ensured he always took them to the closest dorp right next to the border, Ladybrand or somewhere like that. He insisted on it. Some of the girls weren't much older than twelve.

"Dear Lord."

She ignores me. "That's how it went. We didn't live too badly; I almost thought we'd make it. At that time my husband often dealt with Koert and provided him with sheep. But Koert always expected more from him. And he spoke to my husband about his final plan. Grand final, he called it. He wanted to provide meat to the whole of the Free State and the Eastern Cape, to establish a monopoly on meat in this part of the country. And how do you propose to manage that? Show me your plans, my husband said to him. There are too many syndicates and factions already. It's impossible to control what happens in the northern Free State or along the coast. Then he'd say to my husband: Just think of the palace we could build ourselves here; we could lay on water, doesn't matter where from. We could have Roquefort and real coffee and Turkish Delight flown in. Don't be crazy, my husband told him. Then Koert would lose it and order his guards to throw my husband out.

"Of course, Koert still owed him money, and he had to crawl back to try to get it. When he arrived on Ouplaas, Pilot and that sister of his put a spanner in the works."

"Esmie Phumzile?"

"I couldn't give a damn what she's called. We want nothing more to do with them. The humiliation my husband had to endure. And if you ask me, Koert doesn't have any money left. Not a thing. He's gone through it all, that nephew of yours. Everything. My husband can't sleep at night. His rage has made life unbearable for him. There've been times when his screams have driven me mad, but I'm sure you don't want to hear about that.

Why should you care about me?"

No, I'm not going to answer. I want to be off, get my foot home so that I can rest it.

"That's how we've been stripped of everything," she says. "I'm not even talking about our earthly possessions, my carpets and dinner service that I had to barter to put some meat on the table once in a while. Our humanity, that's also been sacrificed. Koert's made sure that he took that from us too. What makes me most bitter is the fact that he's nothing more than a snot-nosed kid."

"I can hardly believe that of Koert. Who are you talking about? Koert Spies?"

"Who do you think you've come here to see, Marlouw? A high school boy who blushes when he touches a girl's breasts for the first time?"

"How should I know? I'm here at my sister's request."

"Let me tell you what you've come to find here: a colossal monster. A man who lacks restraint in the gratification of his vile desires." She lifts herself back into the saddle, the grey baulks at her weight. I notice for the first time how weak the animal is. He's obviously fed the bare minimum. I must get going.

"May I ask you one more thing: Why have you stuck it out for so long? I mean, without ammunition, how . . ."

"You mean why haven't we been attacked and shot dead yet?"

"Yes, I suppose."

"You know what, Marlouw, I should never have bothered with you. You're not the person I'd hoped you were. Your land of plenty breeds a type of character I'm not familiar with. I can't rely on you, God preserve me if I'd hoped I could." Ruddy from the cold, she turns her horse.

"I'm here to fetch Koert. It's not my choice, I'm not mad like everyone here."

"Koert!" she barks. The horse refuses to budge. She waves the riding crop over its hindquarters – it's obvious that she wouldn't flick the animal. "The last we heard is that Koert has had it. I thought you knew. And that *that* was the reason for your visit."

She succeeds in getting the horse to move. The woman's energy is almost spent, her back is bent. Wisps of hair hang from under the riding cap.

"Why are you only telling me now? I don't believe it," I scream after her.

"What does it matter if Koert's finished? It's a relief to us all." She turns slightly to say it. Every now and then she lifts her gloves and wipes her eyes. She's crying.

"I don't believe that Koert is dead," I shout when she's already gone some way, her horse stumbling along. I bitterly regret our unfinished farewell. And feel sorry for the woman who's bent double on her horse. The meeting had briefly enlivened her, given her hope, who on earth could imagine for what.

"Come back, please. I've got something else to ask you. I wanted to . . ." She's done with me.

So it's back to the koppie to collect my bundle of wood and then rake a walk to the werf.

*

I've made my bed today and tidied up November's living area. I folded up a piece of clothing, placed Pilot's Nikes next to each other, shook out his bedding and aired it, then swept. Butts and sticks and gravel carried in by walking, a dead *stofdakkie* bug.

There's not much in the room to gather dust. I walk across to my vegetable patch and pick up the spade I'd left stuck in the ground – Pappie couldn't stand it when a spade was thrown aside at the end of a work day – and I try to turn the soil with the weight of my normal foot. I'm soon tired out by it. I walk to the koppies to collect more wood. I keep to a south-westerly direction, away from Ouma Zuka.

Pilot laughed at me as usual when he heard that Ouma Zuka had ostensibly appeared to me seemingly on all fours. "Ouma Zuka has caught you out, ha," he drools and capers about. He's not sober, must get the constant supply of booze from Koert.

"*UMaGrace ubenza bazimfene.* Ouma Zuka pretended to look like a baboon. And you saw her and thought she is a baboon," he hoots. "She knows she cannot speak to you like an *umthakati*. You are too clever to believe her magic tricks. Now she is suddenly a baboon. She gets up and walks upright the moment you walk away, then starts her plans again. Look at Esmie, she has been shitting non-stop since yesterday."

"Diarrhoea?"

"Yes, she says she has eaten something bitter. Like the karkoers lying around. You know, karkoers, the bitter melons? You see, it *is* Ouma Zuka."

The muscle under my lame foot has gone into spasm since returning from the koppie, my foot's contracting into a horse's hoof. Even with the orthopaedic shoe it's pulling down more than usual. She has deceived you again, Pilot echoes in my ear. I don't even want to begin to think that there's a connection between her tricks and my sore foot.

Dusk draws across the werf; for the past hour a child's been whining without being fed. Night envelops us, it's slow to become dark. I know what it's about. I've been unsettled since the horse rider suggested that Koert is dead. I'm going to find out what's going on with Koert. This instant. First ask Mildred if there's chicory coffee. The brew keeps me awake. Okay then, drop the coffee. It's only an excuse.

I reach the door that leads to Koert's quarters. A heavy chain with a lock has been placed around the security door since the night I tried to break in here. This is how they try to protect him against troublemakers. They're afraid I'm going to take him away from them, that things will get even worse.

The curtains are completely drawn. I lift my hand to knock. Even if he only opens a chink, I know what I'm going to say: Hell, Koert, I've been here for who knows how long. Are you making a fool of me? My knuckles touch the door through the bars. I'll knock until he answers. Wait, check if the door is locked. If not, I can swing it open and just talk through the bars. Maybe Koert doesn't know that I'm still on Ouplaas.

"Koert, I know you're there." I look back across the werf: don't care if they hear. Any of them. "I know you're still alive, Koert. Come out, man, come and say hello to your family. You must decide for yourself, okay. I'm getting ready to leave," my voice thinner, ever thinner.

I've felt it coming: it's not that I don't have the guts to rage at Koert, it's a half-heartedness that's taking possession of me. A merciful release from my mission. Heleen never needs to know about it, I don't want to see Koert any more. I'll finish the vegetable beds over the next few days, and all my responsibilities here will be completed. I'll be able to pack up and leave.

"Koert?" I thought I'd heard the shuffle of slippers. I press my ear as close to the door as possible. "Koert, are you there, man?"

A hoarse voice sounds from inside. So he is there after all, I knew he wasn't dead. I hear it again, a snort. Maybe he's been drinking and smoking and has only just woken up. This has been my problem with the mission since the beginning: speculation. I shake the chain and lock. Immediately, someone comes running up.

"Koert, have they imprisoned you? Is that why you're not coming out? Talk to me, man."

Esmie Phumzile coughs behind me. I'm startled at how bad she looks.

"I don't care what you do to me – I have to speak to Koert before I return. Are you keeping him behind lock and key, or what? Answer me, Esmie."

She shakes her head and folds her arms across her chest. A full-length tartan jacket hangs from her shoulders. No cloth of any colour can hide her illness now.

"Esmie, is there nothing that can be done for you?"

She uses my hand to pull herself up the three small steps and stands between me and the shut door. "I'm okay," she whispers. "I just have to get over the diarrhoea; it will take me a few days. Pilot's got hold of some Lomotil; I'll make it, I've been worse." She collapses against my chest. "You have to take me with you, Marlouw."

I'm intensely aware of the croup in her breath against my neck. I don't reply; she pushes me away. I climb down the stairs and walk away.

Finish my business, pack up and drive off. That's what I'm going to do. It's callous, but I have to put a stop to my involvement with Esmie. I'll be leaving in a day or two; she shouldn't invest any hope in our relationship. I'm convinced that Koert is still alive, and that's what I'll tell his mother. Pilot can have my extra trousers and shirts. I'll take only the clothes I'm wearing, drive to Bloemfontein, leave the bakkie there, and fly back. Heleen need never know that I didn't see Koert. All that remains is Pappie's charge, the responsibility that it entails. Here comes Mildred, frowning.

"Is Koert being locked up there, Mildred, is that what's going on? Let him go, and you can have all the money I've still got."

"Your wood is still wet. How can I make a fire with wood like that?"

"You know what, Mildred? I'm tired of the whole lot of you. The farm is full of people much younger than I am, and you ask *me* to collect wood? Not one of you wants to help me to see Koert. You're all protecting him like a baby. What's going on here, Mildred?"

She stands erect and marches off to the kitchen.

8

We penetrated deeper and deeper
into the heart of darkness.

THE HOUSE IS PEACEFUL. I shiver on my mattress and try
to keep the cold at bay. My foot is unusually painful. Pilot hasn't
come to bed yet. In a moment I'll get up and pinch his blanket
for myself.

It takes an eternity for me to force myself to actually get up.
I pull Pilot's blanket from his bed and bundle it against me. It's
ticklish against my cheek, and slightly smoky. And there is the
smell of offal, exuded by the one who crawled on all fours on the
koppie. Visions and smells come to me at night: Ouma Zuka,
Giel. I shouldn't allow them to make my mind run riot, shouldn't
let them lead me astray. They are merely the chance encounters.
The figure of the horserider, the shrunken little bundle that rode
off, that's a different matter. I regret not having hugged her and
holding her tight against me, despite the conflicting emotions
during our meeting. If only she'd given me half a chance.

It's time to sleep, to bear the heavy burden of Pappie's dream.
To register the stimulus of the fear, respond, and jump up and
run. I must listen. I have to observe the signs. This sign of the

inherited dream is the chevron, enormous, with yellow and black stripes, you can't miss it.

Next to me, November's mouth has fallen open in his sleep. Tobacco breath and rheumatism rattle the old man's body. I'll listen to him, to the yelping dog further away that's been locked out of the house. Further away still, winter's frosty blanket drapes over the farmyard and the veld. Tonight I won't be getting any sleep.

I saw myself in the mirror yesterday and stepped back in horror at the image with its hollow cheeks, blue lips and bewildered stare. See, I told you so, Jocelyn will scold me. I've become like the people around me, smoky like Pilot's blanket and wild-eyed like the people along the road. Come inside, you out there, you're one of us now. Stiff with cold and a splodge of porridge in the stomach.

Nothing. Free me from these thoughts, Lord, let me sleep this one night through. Stiff muscles all along my foot, even stiffer now that I'm lying down. Ouma Zuka's doing? Is it?

"Where are your nails?" Pilot asked me this afternoon. "I saw you sitting there with your scissors cutting your nails. Where are they, have you checked? Let Pilot tell you what has happened to them. Or take a look at your comb next to your bed. Go on, take a look where it is lying so neatly next to your toothbrush and other things. All the loose hairs on your comb have gone. Your nails, too. Headman collected them for the baboon in the mountain."

I had looked. The half-moon nail clippings on the step where I'd sat cutting my nails had vanished; my comb looked as if all the leftover hairs had been stripped away by a thumb and index finger. Now Headman has also started something against me.

He can't get to Koert; he's been banned from his quarters. Now he's taken my nails and hair so that Ouma Zuka can make *idliso* and he can play out his resentment.

During the pitch-dark night the victim flays about on his mattress and obsessively considers this row of causes and effects, and a yellow-green knob of vengeance grows in his throat. The *idliso* comes in many forms. Now it's become a creature that worms its way into the gullet and clings there; I become feverish at the mere thought of it. I choke back my fear – in every respect, I've become like the people around me.

Hear something – *there*. Where? I heave myself up. A candle burns next to Pilot's mattress: he hasn't come to bed yet. There are no fires outside on the werf and he wouldn't be in one of the other quarters at this time of night. He and Esmie Phumzile could only be with Koert.

In the east wing of the house I hear the kitchen door open and close. The yelping stops. Someone's bothered about the dog. The candle at Pilot's bed flickers against the wall and ceiling. I try counting the shadows, the faint images that walk the ceiling and sail the walls like hunchbacked animals.

The house is quiet. The candle flares up, throws a last greyness against the furthest wall, and a blind darkness envelops me. The candle wick and wax have burned away and Pilot isn't back yet. I fold my arms across my chest to preserve my body heat and nod off – when I open my eyes again there are two figures next to my bed.

"Put on your jacket," the one orders.

"Is that you, Pilot?" What's happened to my voice? My words are smothered against the sleeves of the one who pulls me from the mattress.

"Your shoes," and the other shoves my shoes in my hands. It takes a while to get the orthopaedic shoe on. They wait patiently – must know about my foot.

The moment my laces are tied, they pull me up and lead me out of November's quarters, not via the outside door – that would have been the easiest and fastest route – but through the house. Our quest has begun.

I screw up my eyes – they refuse to get used to the dark. I sense the sleeping people as I walk past them, the jacket sleeves of the guides on either side of me. I already suspect they are taking me to Koert. The hour has arrived. At last my journey will come to an end.

We move past trapped pumpkin farts and through Boxer tobacco vapours, musty socks and stale feet, all mixed together. I have to smell my way; my sight hasn't adjusted to the dark. Shadowy blurs rear up ahead of us. It becomes so impassable that I freeze and jerk away from the arms of the two men. Suddenly I smell nothing. They sense my fear and a match is lit: we're in the passage that passes the Zukas' quarters. Headman coughs, we stop and listen. "Headman, is that you?" We shuffle on.

This is what Jocelyn was on about while knitting: that I'd be cut off from any comprehension of my surroundings. I smell rust and something like brewed tea. Walls and a billowing ceiling become visible in the darkness. And children's bodies. Little bodies in need of a bath, frail from the cold, afraid of the Iceman who creeps around at this time of night and forces your eyelids open and plays tricks with your mind. This is what I mean, see? someone says. Mammie? My voice no longer carries very far. Come closer, says the bogeyman, my name is Iceman. Gather around so I can grab your skinny bums. I've come to collect you for the kiddies' graves, the little mounds on the farms and the little mounds in the towns. Poor things. Your blue dreams are queuing up for me.

Lord, if only I could help them. I want to. Just show me how. I'm being held as if my life depended on it. And now I know: they're keeping me alive until I get to see Koert.

I'd guess we've reached the last quarters, the ones that belong to Mildred – I encourage myself with this thought. Here, near the southern wing of the house, there ought to be a door to take us out and around to Koert's front door. Quite close now, I'd say – and I try to calm my heartbeat with the thought. Quite close? Terror is driving me off my head. Must increase my vigilance, count our steps. Or my breaths. I recognise the dimensions of this door, the edges of this corner. If only I could reach out and touch it. One, two, three. Question four. Put the following sentence into symbols: anyone who consults a psychologist must have his head read, where

Px = x is a person;

Cxy = x consults y;

Sx = x is a psychiatrist;

and Ex = x must have his head read.

Three minutes before the exam ends. Subject: Informal Logic. Can't control my pen any more, my answer pad is smudged with the drops rolling off my anxious forehead. Professor, I'd better close my answer pad, save what I've managed to write so far. Yes, very well, I appreciate your dilemma. Although you have to answer that last question or else it's tickets as far as your distinction goes. My ticket? Professor, I can't breathe any more. Wait, don't take in the answer pads, I haven't finished yet, give me another minute. My voice has ceased to convey any meaning.

"Mildred, answer me, tell me if it's me walking past your mattress." My two guides don't silence me; I begin to doubt my own words. "Mildred," I repeat, to make sure that I can hear my-self deep in the darkness that's becoming tangible at the end of our night march.

There he arises: the Prince of Darkness down the passage, a fire eater, incensed by the night-time disturbance he slams doors as he fulminates and swears just ahead of us. That's all I'm able to hear. Doors that keep slamming in my face and suddenly, the swish of wings. My body shudders and jerks back so that the two men have to grab hold of me: I feel the sticky claws of their hands on me, around the bones of my joints. Tomorrow I'll go to the source of the spring and check the eye. I'll carry out my deci-sions tomorrow and see what happens next. Tomorrow I'll feel my blood pump as it should again – carry on talking, talk the fear away. Here, here's our route, guys, we must go through here. A wing, a bit of down, a thistle, strike my cheek; someone pulls something over my head and the shred of sight I'd won is finally lost. At times I even feel light on this short, eternal, nocturnal expedition. Hold me, I'm falling, I'm falling, and the two on ei-ther side of me carry me forward; they make a bridge with their arms beneath me and I fall:

Atishoo, atishoo
We all fall down

They're kidnapping me, I am powerless. Until a sensation in my neck provides the signal and I make myself heavier, too heavy for them.

"*Myeke azihambele.* Leave him, let him walk himself," the one says.

They let go of me, and I'm temporarily left to my own devices. If only I could get myself to, Professor. Yes, but then you mustn't become panicky, your blood pressure's rising, man, you need all the blood in the world to think clearly. Difficult, it's too difficult, the symbols drift up as I sink, sink continually so that I have to drag myself forward, my bowels also full now like after a midday meal. I have to go to the toilet. Sorry, mister invigilator, I have to relieve myself. (Anyone who consults a psychologist must relieve himself before the consultation: if Ox = x relieves himself.) Well then, a man will have to accompany you to ensure you're not hiding a note with the answers in your underpants to cheat – that's forbidden. I smell excrement and old piss: we must be close to the toilet Mildred's locked up. Could it be that our family's still seeping through and causing the stink? Mammie's was almost pleasant, apricot-like. No, I've lost direction, I'm losing my head. Here follows the report on the patient (it doesn't look too good, note well, he's not so terrified that he's going to shit in his pants, he's too advanced a species, evolutionarily speaking, to respond so primitively to the stimulus of fear): all the physiological indicators suggest that Martin Jasper Louw (yes, the patient with *talipes equinovarus*, shame) finds himself in a state of fear. His heart and pulse rate have quickened, his temperature has risen, he is breathing rapidly, and there are signs of muscle contractions. Should his body find itself in a genuine life-or-death situation, it would be ready to respond down to its very last cell: it would either defend itself or flee. By way of an appropriate response, it will attempt to ensure the survival of the last of its species. It's interesting to note that the fear response takes place without any language-processing in the cortex; the subject's response to the fear stimulus is a reaction he's been conditioned to both genetically and historically. In fact, the subject engages in action without conscious recognition of the fear stimulus. He must and will get out of the situation.

I count my breaths and my pulse rate to retain my sanity. I must get out of here. The last part of the journey takes a long time, it feels like years of stumbling, of seeing nothing and speculating about what will come. Come here, the children call, you can clean yourself here. Fuck it, there *is* something in my underpants, I couldn't hold it in. I feel a hot sense of shame. Come here, the one with a head like a caterpillar larva shouts, and I look into his two round worm-eyes. Without a doubt, this is a prophecy: the larva head is Koert's. Touch it, touch it, the children taunt – the one with the swollen head taunts the most cruelly – and then they shove me in so that I can begin cleaning myself. I have shat myself all over. Go away, leave me alone! I roar; shame at my condition has given me strength. Only now do I see where they've brought me. It's our spring, it's the drinking water for the house. I can't possibly clean myself here. Pappie threatened us with death if we dared mess in the spring. That was sacred water, that. Look! Nothing has remained of the springs of Ouplaas. Thistles and stubble and seed that bursts and releases down that rides on the wind. I'm so light that I am dissolving, my blood translucent and too thin to congeal. If the terror descended upon me now, I'd be light enough to run away quickly.

The two who are with me sense something of my condition and lift me up. Suspended above the earth, I feel threatened anew. The sensation reappears in my neck; gravity drags me down, I collapse with force. Will it ever end? No, it will never end, not tonight, never, not in my lifetime. Let me meekly fold my hands and pray for the end of the abomination, let me pray, lessen the impact of the larva head I'm about to face. "I beg you,"

I say weakly. They hold me tighter as we move forward. Potato yeast. That must be Mildred's bread rising in her room.

Again I want to utter something, this time to ask for my compass which is lying on my mattress, but I can't possibly endure the return journey. It will take me years. What will I say to Heleen when I stand at her door, old and shrivelled: my dear sister, it took me one hundred years. Here's your compensation: silkworm blankets that I had spun for you with your child's name on them. Look, K O E R T woven into the rich yellow circles and twirls. Oh, my sister, look at your hands. How they've aged. Your tears fall like leaden drops on the little silk blanket. Touch it? Please do, my dear Heleen, I'd no idea you'd lost your sight. Grief and make-up – it must be the make-up, its toxicity.

The wind blows against my face under the stocking, fresh and icy. My nose starts running. We're outside. I see the light of the stars through the stocking that covers my head; I'm even able to imagine the Milky Way. Such a clear sky will bring frost early tomorrow morning. As long as I make it through this night journey. Even if I *am* filled with terror. We are outside.

"Move," one of the guides says.

I instinctively use my strong foot. The stocking is removed from my head, a match is lit. Slowly, my sight returns in the circle of the flame's light. I make out solid objects. I'm so grateful. The man's sleeve is right in front of me; two hands snap at the lock, another match is lit. There are the steel bars and the security door. I can see again.

The man picks the right key from the bunch, and in a single movement the door opens. The chain clatters; steel rings touch my hand. We're at the entrance to Koert's quarters. I am awake.

Once inside, the two loosen their grip on my arms and leave me to go towards the smudge of light.

A glow passes through my body. I'm warm and relieved from the inside, mortified by my happiness, it's so excessive. And there's no one to share it with. I have reached my destination. I squat and bury my face in my hands and sob. Here I am with your son, Heleen. You have to grant it to me: I was able to get this far. I've no idea what lies ahead, yet I *have* reached Koert. At least I'm able to say *that* without deceiving you or myself. I have reached the sole purpose of my journey and I am still alive to experience it.

Ahead is a passage that disappears around a bend. There's not much light. At the entrance, the sides of the passage consist of piles of boxes and bundles stuffed into hessian bags. Pappie's study has been turned into a storeroom, depressing to say the least. I have to pass through here.

As I wade deeper down the passage my eyes become used to the dim light: it's Pappie and Mammie's furniture that's been gathered and stacked here. Old familiars, all of them. I touch here and sniff there, drift about among the stuff and try to use my remaining senses as efficiently as possible: it's a sorry sight. Browns, greens and pale yellows, I try to guess the hues. The north sun always shone on the corner of this old sofa. Here's the wobbly table leg. Koert doesn't know the stuff the way I do, or he'd never have stored it like this, easy chairs on top of the imbuia dining room table, bedside tables and cake tins stacked on top of the armchairs. The stuffing is coming out of all the cushions. They must be saved, or it's to the bonfire with them. Must and mouse droppings, mice nesting in the stuffing and covers. Here's the patchwork cushion where Oukat died, here're Mammie's hat boxes, her Singer sewing machine – so this is where the contents of the home have washed up. Koert has bloody well made sure that Mildred and the others got nothing. I saw it the first day I walked into the house. They've been robbed, though I didn't say it then. That's not what I came for. Look at this: the gravy boat simply discarded. Here's Jan Pierewiet's cage, oh, how I loved that sea-blue budgie. One morning when I brought the jug from the bathroom to refill his water, he lay there with his stick legs in the air. I never liked the Munich Beerfest jug, though – a knobbly nipple-pink thing.

When I see Heleen again, I'll tell it as it is: along this wretched passage I could see what her son had been up to. This is how he planned it: I refuse to pussyfoot around his spitefulness. Mice are nesting in Mammie's bedspreads; he's removed and stored useful things like brooms – even the brooms. The wood isn't being oiled; the mice are gnawing at the golden-threaded tassels. It's blatant. The display cabinet – how could I have forgotten where the display cabinet stood in the sitting room? On top of it, the carpet has been rolled up into a sausage. Here are more carpets, the dining room chairs, the bookcase where Mammie kept Langenhoven's *Versamelde werke*. It's inconceivable why Koert wanted to take everything for himself. Dust on the mirrors, cracks and splits where the wood has dried out; this hoarding testifies to neglect and pathological greed. It's a disgrace.

I drift down the passageway formed by the household goods, and can't stop myself from touching and feeling. I even push my hand between the sofa cushions to see if anything has survived from my childhood days. The desolation overwhelms me, I must get a move on, out of here. The gleam of a lamp comes into sight and the smell of paraffin clogs the musty space.

What will I say to Koert? Here's Mammie's fridge, oh, in the end it kept food lukewarm, like an old man's behind. Koert, I'll say to him, I've never felt so awful about having to meet another person. Why do I still want to see you? Man, I can tell what you're like. Rust and moth and mildew and burn marks from cigarettes. Why, why?

Exhausted by the anticipation, by the grimness of everything, yet relieved that the final destination is in reach, I could collapse in a heap on the floor and fall asleep. It's nice and warm here. No, I *must* push on, must hurry further down the passage, abandon myself to this whirl of emotions that I've long since lost control of.

Here, under my hand, the texture of one of Mammie's chair covers. Twists and turns like the roads of a dorp, that's what the fabric became under my hands when I lay awake as a child and heard the grown-ups talk about the dead. Always deceased ooms and tannies to be mourned. And always it was said that they wouldn't have harmed a fly.

I'm in Pappie's garage that leads off his study now. There's furniture stacked to the ceiling here too, arranged to form a circular room in the middle of the garage. The space has been partitioned by a see-through curtain with a mermaid design, and behind it burns the lamp that has led me this far. There's a table with a primus stove, a pan, cans of water and a sack of mealie meal on this side of the curtain. Shadows of people are visible on the other side. All activity is focused around the silhouette of a double bed where voices murmur as if administering to the sick. Some people sit or lie on the bed, others walk around it or bend over it and then stand upright again. One of the shadows will be my nephew Koert. Not a single voice is raised.

I look around. A disc of lard floats in the pan on the primus. There'll be frying again tonight. I've reached Koert, I've moored and disembarked onto *terra firma*. My journey has ended. From now on everything will run smoothly. I remain on this side of the curtain, waiting with a pounding heart for one of the shadowy figures to tell me what to do next. I stick my hands in my pockets to stop them from shaking. I'm sweating like hell.

"We know you're there," Esmie Phumzile says from behind the curtain. "Stay right where you are. He's not ready yet."

"Koert? It's me, Marlouw. Your uncle, man," It's the first thing that comes to mind; I'll say anything to get rid of this anxiety. "You have no idea what I had to go through to get to you," I now let rip. "I don't know what your intentions are; I'm at the end of my tether, man."

Right away, someone gets up from the bed, walks to the edge of the curtain, and pulls it aside. It's Esmie with an open tin of Heinz baked beans in her hand. "Shut up. He knows it's you. Wait your turn. I told you he'd talk to you as soon as he's ready, didn't I?"

"Ready for what, Esmie?"

She jerks her head and shouts at one of the shadows inside: "*Yizoshaya le ndoda ingathi indawo yayo ayiyazi.* Come put this man in his place. He's far too white."

"Okay." I'll wait. *Too white.* Didn't think Esmie would know the expression. "I understand," I say. "Your guards don't have to hold me down. Why are you treating me so badly? Do you have water for me, please, Esmie?"

"What?"

"What's he doing? Is he sick? I can smell Deep Heat."

"He's playing Mario Kart and he won't speak to anyone until

he's finished. He has to score enough points first."

"Mario Kart?" but Esmie has pulled back her head and the curtain is hanging in its place again.

I stand where I am, patient, sweating. My bladder is bursting. Prance around, prance around. I refuse to budge until I've seen him. Thirst assails me again as if I've landed in a nightmare. I am in one. Sheer blank fright, pure abstract terror. The shadows of the people busy with Koert dance in front of me. An arm, a torso, the movement of a body from left to right – it looks as if there are four people behind the partition, and one on the bed.

"What's going on with mine brudder?" the one on the bed shouts. It's Koert. It's him. "Mine Oncle hast announced himself for an official visit." The voice of a retard.

"Shove off, you shysters, leave Koert's site," the voice commands. It *is* Koert, with a mouth stuffed full of porridge, his words jumbled and childish. "Thou, too, miss Esmie," the voice says. The shadows disappear to the back and I can't make them out any more. They use the door that leads from Pappie's garage to the meat room. It closes tightly.

Thirsty, full bladder. While I wait anxiously, a burning sensation pushes up and I want to be sick. My throat fills, I can't throw up here, can I now?

"Where's the mensch who's come to sniff me out? Step in site, brudder of mine swister."

I draw the curtain back myself.

A figure sits on the bed, covered from head to toe in a blanket.

"Koert?"

There's a movement. Slowly, the person under the blanket turns towards me. A loose edge lying against the living mass vibrates. Has my presence unnerved him?

The being inside the woollen husk turns some more and a groan emerges. A massive, lardy arm appears and grabs at the blanket as it slips down. A cyclopean head on a stump of neck emerges, the eyes, nose and mouth squashed and deformed by translucent embankments and bulges.

"Koert, is that you?" I mumble, and falter stupidly at the sight of this king larva. "It can't be, Koert. Is it?" I bow before the massif, the master of masters.

A gigantic puff of a hand clutches feverishly at the blanket; wool gets caught in his long nails and at the corner of his mouth, then the blanket slips down until only one leg and a foot are covered. I look up, alarmed, and try to shield myself with my hands. My jaw drops.

The flesh of all flesh rises in front of me, flesh consumed by flesh that has multiplied and swollen into a malformed colossus of human dough with pink folds hanging from its sides. The giant rounding of the shoulders, the ox-like shoulder blades that shimmer with the secretions of fattiness, the droop of the breasts, the belly that shudders and is stretched to bursting point at the navel.

I get up and hobble gingerly out of the light to hide my expression. I dare not provoke him.

"Look adit, look adit, look adit," he shrieks when he notices me retreating. "Oh, ye be rats, all of you. Straight from the sewerage. What to ekspek? Whooz gonna blame me for comin' to this hell hole? In this place waren nog etwas, som'pin to salvage, but, but by you were zero possibilities. Youz all too far gone. Middleclassy shitroaches, each and every one of youz. Mammie sips her baby cappuccinos. Mammie wears bling-bling sandals. And pappie whores after is job. An whaz left for Koert, a little something? Fuckall-hole, actually."

The two puffed-up balls of his hands bounce on the mounds of his thighs as he emphasises the words. He fishes for the piece of blanket that is folded under the right shin and foot, apparently to keep the foot hidden. He can't reach it. "Nothin' remains here, nothin' left to salvage. All hope gone to hell-and-gone, okay?"

I shake, grown man that I am. Physical sickness and psychological disgust. Here is the embodiment of the fear of all our forebears. The fear that the man with the knife beside the bed of the forefather will gain the upper hand and that nothing will remain of us: here it is now, the nothing, writ large. An abomination that has retained merely a splutter of the original language. But it's not the man with the knife who is the father of the monstrosity – it's us. He came forth from our loins. *That* Pappie would not have understood.

The voice booms from the body: "Hast thou heard what Koert tunes you? That nothin' remains here too? So why brudder, why did you cum, why do you disturbeth me? What izzit that you want to bite from me, mine brudder?" His tone now sulky, now strident, a stallion.

He spits: "Cum straight to tha point 'cos I'm waitin' not much longer for all you lot's shit."

"Koert, your mother sent me. It was a huge sacrifice for me to come here. You think I wanted to come? Do you know how long I've been here already?"

"Wacht, wacht, wacht." He raises his arm and makes an immense gesture: "Not one snot makes sacrifices for me, mine brudder. I am the one who does the sacrifices round here, right? Since I've arrived, I've given these specimens in the middle of nowhere eine Leben. For them I brought in the music, music from das Welt, for them the DVDs, an we watched it night afta night, mine brudder. Terminator and Rambo and romance shit so tha' there can be love all over. So much, too much. I waz the one that brought the Bells and tha Jack Daniels. Do you think for a instant any of these wretched specimens had ever tasted Bells? Huh, huh, huh?" The torso lifts itself up, doubles over, keels forward, throws its shadow right onto me.

"Sag mir, izzit truly human to propel yourself all the way through this miserable life without ever sampling a taste of Bells? Einer nach dem andern I made them come and plunged my fingertot in de Bells and let them taste. Baptised with Bells, brudder. Gold in de grain. Do you realise everything I managed to do on this Platz?" The effort of the monologue makes waterfalls of sweat run down his lobes.

"Koert, your mother is sick with worry about you. Don't you know it? Can you imagine what she feels like? It's affecting her health. You know how much she loves you. You're her only child, man."

"Mammie's stopped loading mine credit card. Right? Right! Love is reality, brudder. If you don't experience it, wez the charity now, madam? Do youz realise how many little sheep I graze on dis farm, do you realise how many little sheep I myself got for de town an de districts an de global province? Meat fo' de people. Right? Right! Wij hebben gedansen an celebrated on thiz liddle Platz. Bells ran like syrup. I showed them Mario Kart and we gamed. You think any of them knew Mario and Luigi to the day that I let them race with it? Then they refused to brake. They gamed an gamed till their brains were soft. Headman lick my arse till it shone. Even cultivated a miniature mustachio to look like Mario. Peware, I warned de mudfucker. Laughing ends in shit. Now his ouma-love has tuned him a hole in Kopf. Ouma-love blames yours truly for their crap. Koert has become the bête noire. Ouma-love wants to kick him off here. But the people will decide. Ha, my brudder, the people shine and their hearts beat for their very own Koert. I delivered poetry to them, everything. I have access to dollars, to Mario Kart, to wisdom. They've got like what?" The eyes peer through the eyebrow-ridges to make sure the blanket's still covering the shin and foot. He definitely does not want me to see what's going on under that piece of blanket.

"Troops of 'em come to thiz Platz, brudder. They hail from Maitland and Aliwal Town and East London and Bloemfountspray and once even from de Emirates. Only difference was dem little brudders from the Emirates presented genuine valuables to Koert the Kingk, beautiful rings that I gegaben to Esmie Phumzile right away. Other specimens also come, but with their's pathetic morsels: seriously underfed chicken like rubber and pieces of carved wood and blue-crane fedders apparently oh so scarce, things have all dulled out. Do ya' kno' what I mean? Everyone brings theirs gifts, shit or snot. They all come for a sip of Bells and their bit of meat from this man here. This here Koert Spies. Sing for the Kingk and they sing. Dance for the Kingk and they dance till it shits. Read a little something for the Kingk, come along, please, what-its-name, they can't read. Oh deariefukkinme.

"To the women and meisjes I give extra aid because they are starten to go extinct. Extra loose coins if I have, extra meat dat I let them carry off in plastic bags. Most are on last legs. Finished. Let them enjoy a piece of sheepie for ol' times. Do ya realise tha', mine brudderkie? Het meisjes and the women are first to be felled by the virus and who's gonna bear for the future, who's gonna help the nation multiply? No Esmie's auch krank. The shits. Anyway, I had the people come, got the queues stand here right up to Koert's quarters. In de bitch of de sun they wait with folded hands for the cup of aid. And I dish it out, make me think of my late ouma upright at Sunday lunch. And I never sleep. Day in and day out, I'm busyman, oh man. Human people forms behind me human forms crowd before me, this way, that way they stand. Little sheep, the lot of them. I confirm, it's true.

"One day I question Pilot, I question November, I question Headman, I question the majitas on de farm. Mine brudderkies, says I-ze to youz: how's it going with the sheepies? You know about dem. Wha do they hang out, wha do they graze, wha's their babies? Are your entire lives not busy with the little creatures? Or am I lying now? Tell Koert, brudderkies, while I counsel my butt skin off like this, are you looking after my sheepies nicely? How izzit going with all of dem? No, reply is with-holded. Thula forever, amen.

"Okay, says I 'cos I know the people insides outsides. Lets make a Bells. Esmie pours the tots all round. Gold, only the best. Tongen kwamen loose. I ricketitick on their Kopfe: brudders, where're Koert's sheepies? Are dey okay? Are dey in condition? Are dey glowing? Are dey having babies? Twins? Even triplets? Are you caring specially for the mudder ewes who give titty to the triplets?

"Then I notice they suddenly go blank. I notice they frighten themselves into fits. They held party, mine brudders, they ordered silky shirts and shiny boxers, televisions galore, music systems, all such classy consumer shit when there were still power lines that operated, when there were still dollars tinckling from de hand of de lords, our father Koert who art on Ouplaas.

"Take notice, Koert: it's not a matter of a prank, there's max attention needed, I realise on thizz Platz of yours Koert-truly. Our sheepies is neglected, they go down to the valley of death like on a foefie slide. There's not enough babies to replentish, the flocks are a-dying an a-dwindlin', I scream at them till they put corks in theirs ears, an I realise I have sinned. Forgive mich, mine brudderkies. Esmie Phumzile cum an lick-lack paddy-wack my wounds. I sink. I stink." He draws breath.

"November an Headman kommen sie on the double. Bastards! They's the main men who know the sheepies like their own children. Du wist, brudderchen, November ist mine man who's able to tell you, thiz baby lamb goes with that ewe-mother, those two babies, where's their mother? Oh, there she is, the ewe-mother with the pathetic udder, she won't be able to raise those twins of hers, not a damn. Needs Milch. Now November mine man looks, he looks around, he's already schemed his scheme. Look, there's the ewe-mother who's geverloren hebbe her baby-lambkin. Now he feels in his panties: where's mine pocket-knife? He skins that deceased lambkin-baby and pulls the skin beautiful like a little jacket over one of the twins and gives it to the ewe-mother who's lambkin's deceased, she's got her little lambkin back. She sniffs and snivels, her lambkin has been resurrected from the dead. Miracles on Ouplaas. Now November mine man chases the ewe-mother with the pathetic udder and her one baby lambkin to one side. The ewe-mother still looks for a while: where's my otha child? But after some while she gives up, just like everyone on thiz pozzie. That's November for you. Right? Right!

"Here, check the master in his eyes, I says to November, I

nearly shouts again. I notice the man recoils, starts glaring other ways. Zero wish to mix with Koert when he's a-screamin' an a-shoutin like that. Look adit, look adit, look adit. I know themmens, zwei Jahren on thiz farm of mine and I can say them like nursery rhymes. Tot of Bells all round. Now they feel charged up. Okay, tactics, plan of action.

"These sheepies are the people's livelihood, brudders. If they appear te wesen on the way to hell, gaat wij samen with them to hell. There it is. An inkling of understanding is a-dawning. Responsibility for tha day of today, that my brudders have, read me never wrong, November has responsibility for today. But now he has to put his Kopf around tomorrow, an tha week afta, an the week afta the week, an the month afta tha month. An that's the Achilles spot of November, mine brudder. But now the understandin has dawned, an I celebrate. Another tot of Bells all round. What are yours needs, mine brudderkies? How do we salvage what's remained of the flock?

"Just one dous an de sheepies will be okay again, November announces, Headman also chips in, little stoepshitter. In agreements. Now they only need the eine kleine dingske: dollars. They need dollars for de dous to inject into my sheepies mouths. They need dollars for supplies of all sorts, dollars and dollars, because the sheepies need extra feed. There's everlastin' drought, I who'm Koert Spies realises. Can the sheepies fatten themselves up on stones and dusts? No ways, brudder. Too much short supply, reports November. Too much, we need everythin' reports Headman. I's believe him and I's don't believe them. I wanted to get them aid. I wanted to get them supplies, future tense, get my drift? Supplies cost bucks.

"And dawn the day that I connect with Mammie'tjie and ask

for an advance on master Koert's his credit card because of mine supplies were low an ya know wha she proceed to do? Mammie spit me from her mouth. Snake poison. Uh-huh, won't help me. Mrs Spies snaps her handbag tight as a tight-arse. And then, what then? Now you drift into my quarters like a piece of vomit and big mouth big boy with love and charity from seine Mammie. Whadda ya expect me? Just because mine Onkel is supposedly family the Onkel expects favours? I know you who hail from down under, I know how you walk and how you sit and how you misbehave. Snakes and adders."

"Understand me clearly, I don't want to interfere in your life, Koert. As far as I'm concerned, you can do what you want. Heleen asked me, begged me to come and look for you. I came for her sake. And yours."

I lie. I lie. And I know Koert misses nothing, not this false note, not a thing. Within two years Koert Spies has became chief counsellor, interpreter of people, leader of the underdog, entertainer, fucker, great liberator on this planet. To lie to him is to insult him.

In the lamplight, the neck fat pushes up and squeezes the ears and folds them double, the ears Heleen was so besotted about. A movement comes from deep within the grotesque body: his upper arms start quivering, the inner tyre around his waist starts vibrating and pimples swell up everywhere.

I'm too dumbfounded to utter another word. I'm afraid of, or rather hope for, a stroke.

"All you hypocrites united, ganged up against me. Do you think for a moment ich bin mashugana?" he roars.

Behind me I hear his stalwarts stir in the old meat room – what are they up to, butchering a sheep?

"Are you okay, Koert?" Pilot calls.

"Shuddup," he shrieks, enraged. "Stay put, deine Schweine!"

The right foot and shin, now also begin to protrude because of the quivering and vibrations. And for the first time I see the shin and foot, an enormous column of meat rolled in bandages and pinned with nappy pins, almost a work of art. Immediately he notices what I'm staring at. He's going to kill me, there's no doubt about it.

"Stand. I can't stand up any more," he surprises me with his admission. He's one step ahead, so I won't know when the attack's coming. Everything seems to have been carefully planned. I shudder.

It seems that he wants to slap his shin with his hand, or else he's trying to reach the bandaged stump. His body starts vibrating involuntarily. A grimace appears between the puffs of his cheeks, his lips press together, relax, and open around the sick swelling of his tongue. A stream of spit spurts out.

"Laugh till your whiskers drop off, mine brudder. Laughing ends in shit, you see what I can still remember. Your lot's language that you shaped and dressed and propped up so. What for? For nothing. Snot brudder of mine, let Koert truth-say for you: I am he, I am the *taal*, the volk, I am your destiny, your fear, das Ende des Lebens, the one who shits last, the very heart of darkness who has remained. I am he whom you've come to sniff out. You're lookin' fo' the man," he sings in a soprano voice, quite sweetly, then tears well up, they're trapped.

"Here," he points obscenely between his legs at something under the double bed. "Bells. I've had to start hiding it; it's no longer as in days gone by of plenty. The people have already started to gather forces against Kingk Koert, shamefully abandoned,

I'm not stupid. No one can hide nothin' from Koert Spies. Come here, schmuck, come and fish the Flasche out for us. Or are you also afraid of me as if I've deviated to become an animal?"

I bend down between his legs that reek of sweat and the rancid remains of food to fish out the bottle of whisky – just to get it over and done with. Under the bed, my mate, whether you like it or not. Rubbish. What the hell? Magazines, half-open boxes of Heinz baked beans and torch batteries, empty whisky bottles, meat knives, dried-up puddles. I think of maggots, of maggots' eggs that burst open to produce baby maggots – I can't control my thoughts.

I tremble as I press my elbows to the floor. Here I am: on my knees, my cheek flat on the floor, my back concave, my bottom in the air. Back in the position in which I'd begun my journey. The uncle with the lame foot had to come all this way just to assume this position before King Koert, the one who's laughing so much he can't hold onto his stomach. Lord, if he closes his legs now, I'll smother right here. Pray, Marlo'tjie, pray.

More vapours through which I discern things, subspecies that drag their transparent bodies behind them. Slowly my palate clogs up so that I grab the bottle of whisky under the bed and roll backwards until I land back in the shadows where I have to breathe hard and rhythmically against the stench in which this person lives.

"Look adit, look adit, look adit, cool it or I'll cool it fo' you, brudder, on your behalf. You want me to let you cool down? I've got my methods, I haves. Tha power an the glory. Tell me, brudder, have you come or do you want to *voertsek*? You tell how me want to treat you. Otherwise itz CWOT."

Complete waste of time. He still remembers his SMS jargon.

A language used miles away from this burrow, so far away I can scarcely associate him with it. I try to remain as alert as possible, swallow back the sickness, quickly unscrew the bottle, and take a big mouthful. In the meanwhile, Koert digs something out from under his almighty bottom.

"Gimme, gimme," his voice breaks into a bat shriek. He grabs the bottle of whisky from my hand. "Shyster, who paid your ransom, who paid for your stolen bakkie so that you don't get buried in the sacred halls of prison? Here he sits," and his fingers drum on his chest.

"Do you know Mario Kart? I've got brand new Mario Kart 64. Racing tracks have got the 3-D panels." And again he tries to dig something out from under his leg. It's his Nintendo machine. The thing isn't switched off, and every now and then a pip-pip escapes.

"What do you want? Wha' did you cum for, brudder? To blow my brains out? Come to play with yours truly's Kopf, have you got it, have you?" Filthy breath rasps in and out of his throat. "Do you think I know not your game, brudder? I manufactured a zillion games in the country an they all fell for them, every single one of 'em."

"Koert I need . . . where can I go to the toilet? Didn't there used to be a . . ."

"Shuddup over tha past, brudder. There's no past and no future here, right? Right! Underneath the bed is deine pisspot."

I turn my face away. Can't make the connection between the person in front of me and Heleen and JP's son. The white biceps that played their part so well in the rowing team, the young man on a bright Melbourne afternoon on the Yarra River. The chains have once again been twisted decisively around the security doors behind me, the quarters placed under lock and key. I won't in any case be getting out of here, I don't care what I say in the presence of this white idol.

"What's going on here, Koert? What do you expect me to think of you? What has become of you, Koert? What has become of *us*?"

"You wanna piss or not?" Saliva dams up in his mouth that he still hasn't tried to close again.

I don't move. My bladder is about to burst.

Then I make a slight movement. And quickly, without thinking twice about it, I bend again and lift the blanket just this side of one of his stompers. It's finished with Koert, it's finished with me, with us all, but who cares about the all right now? I'm the one who has to preserve *himself* in the presence of the hulk, I'm the one who ultimately has to get out of here – that's all I keep telling myself.

"Here's the pot," I say, merely for the sake of saying something. I pull it from under the bed – it's half full with dark green urine – and walk across to the furthest, darkest corner of the room. And if I have more piss in my bladder than the pot can hold, that doesn't matter either.

"Whaaat?" he snorts.

Only the two sounds remain in the room: Koert's heavy breathing and me plink-plonking against the rim of the pot. It was Ouma's pot, this. Now it's full to the brim, urine splashes onto the hand with which I'm holding it. I put it down and turn around.

Koert has sunk back again. The Nintendo machine is visible from below his bottom. The bandaged shin and foot are in full view. In the murky light of the lamp, I notice that the bandage is coloured red and green. Above it, the knee is spongy and full of pus.

"My question," he babbles. "What to say, brudder of mine?" He's very tired now.

"I can't remember what you asked. Why are you talking so much, Koert? You owe me an answer, you know. Why have you waited till now to allow me in? Your mother's sent me to fetch you - in God's name, Koert, that's all. I'm not here for any other reason." I can't see his head behind the mountain of his belly and move closer so that I can make out his eyes.

"How dare you, you piece of white shit. Koert Spies owe you somethin'? Your arse is stuffed full of jokes." He puffs up with rage. "Fucking disgrace, that's what you seem to be. Do you think, do you think I never noticed mighty embarrassment about your club foot? Mine Onkel's Kopf bobbing up and down next to yours Koert truly as we walk together on the pavement, piece of shit bobbing on a stream, shame."

They buzz around my head, blowflies from Koert's mouth. Here they are with me. Sweat. It's the blowflies' work, this sweat, they make me anxious. I hear them, can't keep them away from me. I smell them, yes. Remember one thing, Marlouw, I tell myself, the words of a sick person have little punch.

He moves into another gear, without warning, the voice on high-pitched toes, "How goes it with Mammie'tjie?" he giggles.

"Badly, she wants you home."

"The family minds what's happening with de verloren zoon?"

"Yes, Koert." For the first time I feel a measure of sympathy for the man.

"I'm dying, die, die." And he whimpers like a dog, the rump

jerks, the puffy hands clutch the edges of the mattress. The nails are badly chipped.

"You all right, Koert?" Esmie Phumzile calls from the meat room

"Yessum, mine baby."

"Is there anything I can do for you, Koert?"

"I've got gangrene, mine brudder. They have to come and saw my little foot off of me. Gangrene, my brudderkie. I tries so hard to be something for the people here. So hard, and they despised my efforts. My kingdom came and went. I sense it now, they're starting to lose respects. Dollars are gone, meat is finished. Nintendo's batteries almost flat. I gave everything to them I could, everything. Esmie still supports me, I've got a few loose coins that she gets. She loves fashion. But she's on her way out. She's got the virus, you know.

"One dark night she dreamed of a plate of food delivered here to her. Esmie get so weak from tha dream that tha next morning she couldn't even get up to prepare mine breakfast. Koert's breakfast. Koert is upset, verstehst du? Pilot, come listen to you swister. To her diseased heart, 'cause she's a closed book with me. Won't share with Koert, not a damn.

"Pilot comes tellin' me: it is not the heart, God's truth, it is the lungs, shame. Esmie coughs severe. *Ukhohlokhohlo.* Coughs her lungs out. Coughs and sneezes. Slime and goo collect, run out of her mouth. Her skin colours schwartz. Now she's a true darkie. More slime and goo. It didn't want to stop.

"Esmie can barely manage to talk bits and pieces. And shares her secrets only with Pilot. The two whisper. Okay, okay. They will come to report. Koert Spies must know everything. Koert Spies knoweth everything. Pilot reasons the reason for Esmie's major cough started with Ouma-love. Ouma Zuka is the cock-roach. And Esmie's got a story to tell.

"One dark night she dreamt a big plate supper stand before her. Whatz that on my plate? She lifts herself, she's very weak, mine top girl. Whatz this for supper? It's meat and pumpkin and other tasties. Esmie is so hungry she eats it all up gerade wie eine Hund. If you check out the plate, you never say there had been any supper on it.

"Next morning she starts the *ukhohlokhlohlo*, can't stop. Coughs and coughs. Cum here dream girl. Hug her. Koert hugs Esmie tight. I press my meaty breath in her neck. Here, here. It's food. Not that shit you dreamt. No ways. All in vain. Esmie and Pilot belief what they want to belief. And it's not white man shit that constitute their beliefs.

"From then, Esmie cough blood and shit every night. Then she and Pilot know for sure, Ouma Zuka delivered *idliso* on her plate of supper in her dream. My big toe, here, off. Gone one morning. Headman's dirty trick. Koert's quarters is forbidden territory for that jackal. He and ouma-love are both-together cockroaches. Ouma-love wants to bury Koert. No doubt 'bout that. Pilot? Will he still side with me? Pilot will eat from the Kingk's hand for a short while only. Lost all belief in Koert Spies, I can tell. Koert talks a load of shit. And he's the sort who doesn't mind. Belief waned, brudder. The Kingk tells fibs, and the sheep die. That's the true. And the true has come to stay."

"Listen, Koert, if we leave here tomorrow morning early, I can get you to a doctor in Bloemfontein. There have to be doctors who can help."

"Lack of understandin', brudder. What do I have in exchange for the aid, for the operation? Meat is finished, I knoweth, don't

I? I don't need to cruise around on thiz Platz to know its poegaai with everything."

"I've still got money left, I can help you, we can get out of here. It's not too late yet."

"Lost me now in peace and quiet. Where's my's blanket, pass it here and let me be. You're talking past your mouth, stuffed with a *taal* and an attitude that don't belong here any more. Lack of understandin'. Mine blanket."

I pick the blanket up from the floor and spread it over the body. A mustiness rises from it, I dare not touch Koert.

"How do I get out of here?"

"Go your way now," he mutters.

I'm standing at the curtain with its mermaids, the back of my hand against the cloth, but I haven't pulled it aside yet to let myself out.

"Listen, Koert, there's one thing I have to do before I fly back. I have to go to the graveyard where Pappie and Mammie and my Oupa and Ouma Rhynie are buried, your oupa and ouma and your great-grandparents. There's a job I have to do. I'd appreciate it if you'd come along too, if you can." He says nothing. His mouth has fallen open, his lips pressed grotesquely against the bed.

"I don't know whether you can. If it's still possible. Seems to me everything's possible for you – well, till recently at least. Who can really fathom you, Koert? What do you gain from this situation? And how did you get so fat, man? It's goddamn impossible to cope with you the way you've become. Your position here on Ouplaas, here among Mildred and the others. Your language. Did Esmie perhaps pick up the virus from you, Koert?"

I may as well have been speaking to the dead. He's not listening at all; he doesn't have the strength to say anything. The bulk on the bed – the man can no longer be transported, a long journey isn't an option for him. I have to start thinking about my report to Heleen. It will be a bother to scrape something together.

"I'll be back tomorrow." No movement on the bed. "After that, I won't disturb you again. Could someone let me in tomorrow, please, Koert?"

"Go, scheisse, go." The last words from the pink mouth. "I know your motives, I know what sort you are, mine brudder. Go, you don't belong. Never ever. Baby," he calls weakly. The door opens immediately, and Esmie Phumzile appears.

She frowns, looks at me, and then at the master. Concerned, she picks up the tube of Deep Heat and squeezes a blob on the open pores and begins massaging the skin above the bandage. After only three rubs she has to rest, then turns her head and coughs.

"I hope your family hasn't upset you, Koert, he'll be sorry, won't he?" She rubs again, but she doesn't have any energy.

"You feel too hot to me. Why are you so hot? I'll have to take your temperature."

"Let him go," he orders, a disconsolate fart his farewell. I pull the curtain back to let myself out and trudge off down the passage between the furniture.

9

He became instantly
the prey of an abject funk.

THE NEXT MORNING Pilot informs me that Koert wants to go to the graveyard with me. "You must sort out your business there. Koert wants to supervise and make sure everything goes okay." Pilot's all charged up.

On the werf a stretcher is being made for Koert. Two long steel pipes are placed three metres apart, with thinner crossbars at equal intervals. Pilot and Headman secure the crossbars with wires and pliers. The king size mattress will be placed on the stretcher with Koert on top of it, then the whole lot will be loaded onto the back of my bakkie.

Headman is handy with the pliers. He wants to get the job done. Doesn't respond when I greet him.

"When do you want to go?" Pilot asks.

"I guess it depends on Koert. Doesn't everything depend on him?"

"Koert said I must go with."

"Then you'll be going."

I fetch the axe behind the kitchen where the bundles of wood are kept for Mildred's stove and stuff it into the carrier bag I've brought specially for the purpose. I beg the sledgehammer from November. There *is* still one on the farm – I'd seen it with my own eyes. He wants to know why I want it, but when I remain tight-lipped he lets me be. Not so Mildred with the axe.

"You bring my axe back, Marlo'tjie. How will I chop wood for the stove? What are you going to do in the dorp? Cause trouble? They'll take all that stuff from you."

"And if Koert's with us?"

"Koert always takes a gun to town. You don't need all that other stuff to protect yourself. So what are you up to? *S'duhla.* That fatty," she laughs nastily, "he can't drive too far any more, you know. What *are* you up to? He has to stay in bed like someone who's always sick. Pilot is his nurse and Esmie Phumzile is his doctor."

"Doctor Esmie."

She takes me by the arm, "Tell me honestly, Marlouw, what are you going to be doing? It's better for you to tell Mildred, I still know what's going on here and in the dorp. He," and she points to the stretcher that's being prepared, "knows nothing any more. He might think he does. His head," – and she taps her index finger against her temple and makes a circular movement.

"Fine. I'll tell you if you tell me how Koert got so fat." Everything, including information, is bartered. That's the negotiating principle; everyone knows it, myself included.

"Pap and meat, you can see for yourself."

"You all let him get away with it. I don't understand."

"I don't understand you either. How long have you been on this farm and you still don't know what goes on."

"Come on, Mildred, you're talking nonsense. You say it's your farm, but Koert orders you all about."

"What do you mean, orders us about?" Suddenly she looks like a toad to me.

"Drop it, Mildred. Forget it. I don't need to know what's going on here."

Now she has a go: "Your bag," she points, "where's it going with that axe and sledgehammer?"

"We're going to the graveyard where Mammie and Pappie are buried."

Mildred is startled. "No, Marlo'tjie, no. Don't go there. Stay away from graveyards. You don't play around in graveyards; you'll meet your own death there."

"They open the graves, Mildred. They sit on them, they piss on them. The shacks are creeping closer to the circular wall around the graveyard."

She holds her head in her hands and climbs the kitchen steps, "Listen to your *nkosikazi*, your mama. You know nothing. Leave the graves alone. Don't go there. Not today and not tomorrow." The door slams behind her.

By a quarter to four the sun has disappeared behind clouds, and the little warmth there was has disappeared. The stretcher's been ready for a long time, but there's no word from Koert yet. Everyone sits and waits, the cold's creeping up.

At last the garage door swings open. The two with the balaclavas who'd led me into the quarters last night carry the mattress out and place it on the stretcher. As they walk back, they call Pilot. November and Lehlono follow listlessly. Pilot is called again to come and help. It's time to go now, and final preparations have to be made for the master. After an eternity, the mighty lump of flesh appears among his helpers. The two guards, Pilot, November and Lehlono all support his limbs, as they propel him forward. Esmie walks ahead with his travel bag as one would lead a donkey with a carrot.

Everyone on the werf stops to look. Some of the children recoil and moan when they see the deformed figure between the cortege of helpers. Koert is wrapped in his blanket. Two support the body by the armpits and elbows, Lehlono prods from behind, Pilot and November manipulate the healthy leg, moving it forward step by step, and Esmie, shouting instructions nonstop, stoops down at every step to help the gangrenous leg along. Once at the stretcher, Esmie stands on her toes – Koert is a tall man – then reaches up to where the little ear must be and whispers a cue against the blanket.

Now the blanket drops and folds double, there's a hullabaloo, and the whole caboodle collapses onto the mattress. The two guards go down with it; like a hot sausage, Pilot quickly rolls away to avoid the falling mass. Esmie tucks the blanket in all around, including the head, so that no part of Koert remains visible. The effort nearly finishes her off. Everyone – Headman included – helps to lift the stretcher with the human mass onto the bakkie. We break our backs. Finally, boxes of bones are carried from the meat room and packed on either side of the stretcher.

When we're on our way I can't resist the temptation to question Pilot, though I say nothing about the sheep. There's no trace of any sheep on the section of farm we're driving through, and nor do I want to know anything more about them now that the dosing has been done – or at least I assume this is the case.

"This man's got all the power in the world. In his two years on Ouplaas he's built up an enormous power base. The strangest

thing of all is that the people the farm belongs to, the legal owners, allow him to do as he pleases. Why? He wasn't like this when
he left us. He was a normal young man who spoke Afrikaans and
English – he was good at languages. I must know what's happened here, Pilot. Do you know?"

Pilot rolls a Boxer cigarette and gazes out across the desolation.

"Pilot?"

He's not going to answer. I'll have to approach this in some
other way. A donkey cart approaches carrying sick or dead people
covered by hessian bags. As we pass it, Pilot turns his head.

"Can I buy you something in the dorp?"

That's got him interested. "What?"

"You say."

"You will not find what I want in this dorp."

"What is it? Tell me."

"Nintendo. I want to play my own Marion Kart. Mario . . ."
He sniffs indignantly and keeps his eyes on the veld. "I hardly
get to play before he takes the thing from me. He always hides
it in his bed. Now the batteries are finished. I see Koert does
not play so much any more, but he will not let *me* have it to play
with."

"Why does he treat you like that?"

"He likes my sister more, she gets everything."

"And so? What are you going to do about it? And what will
Esmie do when she can no longer get what she wants? Besides,
she's really seriously sick."

He falls silent and I slow down, because we're not too far
from the family graveyard and I'm dying to get something out of
him, a final word of revelation, as they say there.

"You ask, ask, ask. You white people never stop with your questions. Why do you want to know? Why are you asking me? Ask your own people. What does the word '*flater*' mean?"

"*Flater*? Blunder. Who said that?"

"Koert. This morning he said he has made a blunder. He said his whole life is a blunder. What is a blunder?"

"Now *you're* questioning *me*."

He laughs. His shiny white teeth and his expression move me. Soon I must leave all these people behind. Pilot with his defiant smile, Mildred with her sad eyes like a ewe's. What had I in fact come looking for here with all my questions and nothing to contribute?

"Blunder," he laughs at Koert's word. "Koert gave me this." He pulls a 9 mm revolver from his pocket.

"Is it loaded?"

"It is."

"Do you know how to shoot?"

"Koert showed me one day with tins that we put in a row on rocks and then we stood back, one, two, three, and then I shot. It is a double-action type, this."

"I don't think there'll be any more tins to shoot. I hope you're able to use it if we need it. Here we are now," and I swing onto the dirt road leading to the graveyard with its circular wall.

"Pilot, tell me one thing, please. Why do you all bow down before Koert?"

I just can't stop myself. I refuse to believe what I see. On that wretched day as we were driving towards the graveyard, I did not grasp that I had already understood everything there was to understand. Koert had dishonoured Pappie and Mammie's earthly heritage. That's what he'd done, that's what he had turned into here. Though I did at least comprehend then that even the story about the furniture that I intended to convey to Heleen was oversimplified. Koert was always one step ahead – that I must grant him. All the old furniture had been piled up specifically for someone like me. In this way it lost all its original function, all value. That passage with its walls of household chattels checked my gushing sentimentality. Koert intended this specially for me; that's how Koert wanted me to experience our old home. How he thought I should see it.

When I was safely back in my apartment in Melbourne – after that journey I began to drink heavily – my understanding of those past events did not ease my spirit. I felt unsure on my feet, and I'm not trying to be funny when I say that. Meat would never taste the same again. When I took a bite of a lamb chop, I saw things worming their way out of it. The expedition left me permanently unsettled. And I couldn't get the people of Ouplaas out of my mind. Not that their neediness ever produced an iota of altruism in me – for *that* I was too self-centred. It was the vision of desperation, a wretchedness like no other, that I couldn't put behind me. The sight, sound and feel of their extreme need haunted me. And beside that nightmare, there was also the enigma of Koert Spies, the knowledge that he, his kind, were the last of our descendants who remained there – that was the reality I couldn't come to terms with.

"Esmie says he gives us hope. The only one who can still do that," Pilot says.

"And you, what do you say?"

"I also say so."

We've reached the shacks on the outskirts of the township; Pilot grips the revolver on his lap. It is late dusk, and whatever light remains is pushed aside by the smoke from the evening fires. Koert must have realised that we're almost at our destination – I now accept that he's all-knowing – because every now and again his movements on the stretcher bounce the bakkie.

When the graveyard's wall comes into view, Pilot puts his hand on my arm. "Wait, there are people inside."

"Where?"

"There at the graves on the opposite side," he points to the west.

I indeed see them myself. The wall hides their bodies so that only their heads stick out. A spade comes up and throws, behind the spade a head, then the spade as well as the head dive down and pop up again from behind the wall.

Children play and fool around on the other side of the wall until the cold drives them indoors. I hear dogs, I hear adults calling, I hear water thrown from a slop bucket into a yard and want to hide away right there in the bakkie's cabin when I think of the gravestones that have to be smashed with the sledgehammer. Maybe it's not necessary after all. Perhaps the grave robbers, the coffin thieves, have beaten us to it.

"Stop," Pilot shrieks. He refuses to go an inch further.

I look at him: he's afraid. The eyes are fixed, the body vulnerable: a stick that could be broken in two across a knee. His finger keeps guard on the trigger. I hope he knows how to shoot.

At the back, Koert weighs the bakkie down almost to the ground. I switch the engine off and wait and wait, and look on as my spirit rises high above the scene where no harm can be done to me or to Pilot. That's how he saved himself, people will say about me one day. Fear made him light, his blood flowed faster and thinned out, his sweat uncommonly pungent.

"He must get up," Pilot says about Koert.

"Why, Pilot?" I ask amazed, so high above it all that I've transcended everything. And I endeavour to rise even higher: there's the bakkie with the lump of flesh, there's the circular wall with the gravestones, and there are the coffin thieves with their spades sending clods into the air. They don't even have the decency to wait until dark. Brazen, they dig up the skeletons right before our eyes. How much will they make per coffin: fifty, a hundred and fifty, two thousand in dollar notes? If a beloved young daughter of the family dies, every last cent will be scraped together for a respectable funeral.

Pilot speaks, I don't hear him. He shakes my shoulder, screams in my ear, "Koert must help us, he must."

Well then, let's see what he can do. I tap against the back window, the blanket rises and the form appears from its folds. Look people, children, coffin thieves over there, see what's rising up here on the back of the bakkie. His hand leans on the roof, the metal caves in. A sound emerges that could only have been wrenched from an animal's belly.

It's Koert. Koert Spies cries out, and the whole dorp listens. They know that voice; they know the body that can bring forth a bellow like that. From their shacks people come running, old aunties and children gather on stoeps and listen in awe. And slowly, spontaneously, they put one foot in front of the other without realising that they are heading for the graveyard. More figures roll up through the smoke of the evening fires, some covered in blankets. Closer they come, in tens, twenties, too many to count.

Pilot remains dead quiet and rolls a Boxer cigarette, the 9 mm at hand. At first he says nothing. Then, "I don't trust what's going on here, Marlo'tjie. Do you know what is going on?"

I hear him and don't hear him. On what side of the fence is he sitting? Is he with me in the bakkie, or is he with them, surging towards us like a wall of mud from the township.

"Trust nothing," he finally says and shuts up, then draws on his cigarette in anticipation of what's about to happen. He's in the bakkie; next to him is the one with the lame foot, and behind, the big, heavy-footed body. Will the people streaming from the houses be able to place him, sitting here with his gold Nikes and his Boxer tobacco – they may think he's got something *they* don't have.

The coffin thieves look up from their work, spades over their shoulders. They're totally brazen now – but as soon as they see the enormous torso on the bakkie they withdraw. Away from the flood of people, further and faster to the back section of the circular wall.

Some of the children have already scaled the wall; a barefoot child has landed in front of the first grave. It belongs to my great-great aunt, Hendriena Louw, born 1844, died 1921. Another child hops over the wall, then another, some of the older boys lift one leg over the wall, stick out a hand to help the aunties. Hitching up their dresses, the women mutter and groan. They're over.

And the whole time Koert Spies produces his noises. A series of short, high-pitched shrieks, bellows from deep within his innards, inciting sounds that the mob understands. When the blanket slips, he again plucks it back and struggles with the recalcitrant piece of woollen cloth. Then he lets it all drop again and spreads the wings of his arms and beckons the noisy mob to come still closer, calling them from their shacks of cardboard and corrugated sheets and planks.

"Turn off youz primuses," he screams, "put aside the pap-spoon for the time being, rub-a-dub-dub on the Voorkopfe of youz invalids, say: we's be back soon, sing hallelujah songs fo' us, poor blesseds on your last legs like pick-up sticks. We's must answer to the call of da great white master, lullaby until, until. If youz got hounds chained up, let loose, let slip the dogs of war, grab thy iron stake next to the wall, the loose spanner, the ham-mer, youz use them all. Come all ye people, my pap guzzlers, my sheepies, if youz suffering or got injustice or anger or your death's a cumin, itz now thy chance, mine brudders and swisters."

The coffin thieves drop their shovels and bolt. They jump over the furthest, western section of the wall, one, two, three, and streak into the night veld. Fleet-footed, they scarcely touch the ground. Who will round them up and hold them account-able? How many coffins haven't been dug up on farms, on Bot-terfontein and Smaldeel and Ontevrede and Vaaljasfontein and Die Vlei, and from dorp graveyards in Venterstad and Maitland and Burgersdorp and Aliwal North and Colesberg and Smith-field, it depends on the demand, with specifications, the price the family is willing to cough up? An imbuia coffin with silver handles, a red-painted pine coffin with imitation gold latches and hinges . . . how are you supposed to know what's under the ground – white people have such weird taste – dig away and hope for the best. But now: leg over the wall, look back at the white master and his troops bearing down, scoot.

They look back – one last look at the scene of the crime – straight into Koert's devilish eye. He barks the order: "Get 'em, mine hounds, take him, mine boerbulls, pavement specials, rip 'em to pieces. Rip theirs panties right off, dig youz teeth into theirs thighs. You too majitas without foreskins, catch the coffin thieves, grab your spades on da way, use de flat sides, fuck up the Dummkopfen."

Behind the furthest wall where Pilot and I can just make things out amid the smoke and the throng, two of the coffin thieves are thrown to the ground. People and dogs get to work on them. An old auntie is lifted onto the shoulders of a young one, they stand just this side of Oom Ray Louw's sandstone tombstone. Oom Ray was Oupa's brother, and he adored everything English – even English on his gravestone: *Passed away* it says. And fancier: *beyond the swelling flood, we'll meet to part no more.*

The auntie introduces a drawling hymn for the children, to save them from the trauma of seeing the two coffin thieves being brought down, and the bloodthirsty jaws of their own mongrels. It's the most poignant hymn I've ever heard and I turn my window further down.

"Pilot?" He's not saying anything more. He's expecting the worst and sits petrified on his nice warm seat: Lord, please have mercy on us.

The last phase of our little expedition has arrived. It sounds as if Koert Spies is running out of steam. Every now and again his bellow turns into a cheep; only we in the bakkie notice this. Pilot shakes his head: the absolute worst, that's what he's expecting.

With maximum effort, Koert revs up the incitement once more. The cheep grows into a squawk and he manages to shout out the order, high and clear so that it can't be said afterwards: No, but we misunderstood Master Koert.

He eggs the crowd on: "Smash the grave-tombs to bitz, inna hundred pieces. Whole slot, to piece till fuck allz left. Lift ye spades and stakes and hammerz; destroy de sacred build-

ing works, level it with the bloodhound. Bloodground! Finish
an klaar, then skedaddle. Here's youz long-awaited meat bones.
Juicy, cumin fetch. Indulge youz, wretched of the earth."

The people look up at Koert in unison – to make dead sure –
it's late and they have to start gathering children and carrying
them home, to warm themselves at their fires. Let the mongrels
finish off the two coffin thieves. At least *their* tummies will be
chock-a-block.

I bang the bakkie's light switch on. We may as well watch.
And watch. What's the point of closing your eyes to desecration?

"Put those lights off," Pilot hisses.

"They know we're here, what difference does it make?"

The two headlamps bore through the smoky blue light.
Heads and shoulders move, bend down; they're busy, the legs and
hips of the people hidden by the white circular wall. Some hit at
the gravestones with difficulty, reluctantly; others smash with intent as they join in the old woman's hallelujah chorus.

There's the one with the meat cleaver. He chops away at one
of the children's graves. Here lie buried the earthly remains of
the firstborn of Mr Antonie Bothma, born 2 June 1918, died
2 June 1918. Tannie Annatjie Bothma was Ouma's oldest sister,
this little boy her only son. After the Great 'Flu she bore two
more children; they were both girls, and Oom Anthonie never
forgave her for only giving him the one dead son. Black hair and
dark eyes, he'd have looked exactly like his father.

Bits of marble and slate shatter, finger-thick splinters shoot
from the wooden cross on boetie Neelsie's grave. Pappie absolutely refused to have the cross erected there: nobody can tell me
it's Protestant. That time Mammie stood firm, she had the cross
made anyway. Later, when they put fresh chrysanthemums on it

after church on Sundays, I noticed how Pappie admired its simplicity.

Closer to us the marble angel on Great Ouma Driek's grave goes first, then Oom Andries and his wife, Tante Marjolein's granite graves. There are no problems with Oupa and Ouma Rhynie's – the tombstone had already cracked from top to bottom, you could stick your hand through it. There goes the glass dome on Oumatjie Attie's grave, too. The flowers inside, brittle from sun and age, had survived miraculously. We called her "ouma'*tjie*" because she wasn't really our ouma – neither from Mammie nor Pappie's side – she was always just *there* in our house. Pappie thought it was only right for her to be buried in the family graveyard. Besides, in heaven it doesn't matter who's connected to whose bloodline, there everyone is one big happy family.

An exceptionally brawny guy strolls towards Pappie and Mammie's graves. I turn the lights on bright. "Over heres," Koert calls for the last two graves to be dealt with. The guy jumps over the wall, and the next minute he's right at the bakkie.

"We are all going to die in this hell-hole," Pilot whispers. He ducks down on his seat so that only his beanie is visible. The guy looks in through my window.

"Good evening," – I'd better say something. He doesn't make the damndest response.

Koert hands him the bag with the sledgehammer, but the guy *does* have something to say before he gets going, "*Bendingenakuligcina na elilitye lesikhumbuzo ukuze ndilithengise ngelinye ixesha?*"

He pulls the sledgehammer from the bag and walks back to the graveyard. In the light of the headlamps his eyes look back, white, at us, and his forearm muscles gleam with Vaseline.

"Could you hear what he wanted?" I ask Pilot.

"He asked if it is all right to keep the two gravestones to sell later. They are still new, they can be sanded down and new letters engraved."

"The cheek."

"We must drive, we must go back to Ouplaas."

"Koert will decide when we can go."

The two most important stones, right in front of us, have been left till last. The guy is about to begin. There: his first blow falls on Pappie and Mammie's grave. Heleen, you may as well pour your brandy and Coke, light your Courtleigh. Cigarette in one hand, drink in the other, keep your balance. It's better like that. That way you'll be spared this hell: no need for you to see this, nor ever to know anything about it. Only that your son helped us today. Koert's so helpful, Heleen, you wouldn't believe it.

I pull up the collar of my jacket, sink my head and neck into it, and pray, "Trust in the Lord, Pappie and Mammie. May he lead you to his eternal dwelling place. You may rest in peace. Let your hearts rejoice, you have come to him, trust in his holy name. And forgive us the desecration, Lord, and may we forgive ourselves." I glance at Pilot, his head pulled in like mine. "Amen," I say. It is done. I'm so glad I didn't see it, Heleen. Now Pappie can rest in peace.

"Pilot, it's finished."

"Shut up," Pilot hisses.

It's over. Everything happened so fast. Two minutes per grave. Pulverised. I'm glad the brawny guy had the sledgehammer for this.

Koert is ecstatic. He stomps about on the back so that the

whole bakkie shakes. "You can jetzt skedaddle, hometowards. All of youz too sweets for words, you too my babys," he screams at a crowd of children far to the right. He starts throwing some meat bones from the boxes. His voice is giving in. We must get him home, get him a hot toddy and let Esmie Phumzile work on him.

Look now. The children jump up and down and hop in circles like rabbits, the madness of the evening has taken hold of them. Behind the bakkie people are at it too, and jump and grab to get hold of the flying meat bones.

"We must go," Pilot warns again.

"What are you scared of, Pilot?" I hide my hands under my legs so that he won't see I'm shaking myself.

"I am not scared."

"So why do you keep saying: go, go. Why must we rush off?" The people dam up in front of us, seeking their reward. There won't be nearly enough meat bones for everyone. I freeze.

"You are just talking, Marlo'tjie. You do not know me, and you do not know this place where we live. You do not know what the people want. You do not live here, your people farmed on Ouplaas, but you and your sister ran away. Tomorrow you will also be gone and you will forget about us. We are out of your head; you won't even remember Pilot any more."

"I can tell you're afraid," I persist in projecting my own fear.

"Afraid? What is afraid? Why do you sit here and let other people do your work? What do you want? That they break up your father and mother's graves? Then you ought to get out and take the hammer and smash them yourself. You hide away here like a house cat."

"And you? Why did you come along? For a joyride? To see

a circus? For a bit of light relief? Now you've lost your Nintendo. Now your life will be *really* boring. You've got nothing, man, nothing."

People rush, shove one another to grab themselves a meat bone. There are very few bones left: their expectations won't be met. The whole plan is going awry.

"We must go. Why don't you go when I say you must go?"

"We have to wait for Koert. We'll go when *he* says."

"Koert," Pilot snorts as he fiddles with the 9 mm. "Now I hear how obedient you are."

"Are you going to shoot someone? That's something I'd still like to see, you're too scared to do it."

"You must not tease me." He's shaking uncontrollably: he can be so fragile.

"I take my words back." I test him for a bit of kindness, laugh uneasily.

He laughs with me, terrified, finger still on the trigger. Koert hasn't got anything left to give the people. They wait. I can tell they're not at all pleased. It's as Pilot said: you can't tell what their expectations are.

The brawny guy has remained next to Pappie and Mammie's smashed graves, the hammer still swinging in his hand. His work's done. The skin along his arm muscles tightens; he swings the sledgehammer this way and that, the momentum of the action remains in him. Everyone who didn't get a meat bone grumbles at him. They've claimed him as their leader, and his hand indicates what will happen next. Koert is silent.

I stick my head out of the window and call into a night filled with other sounds, "What now, Koert? You must say, man."

The first stone, a piece of granite from one of the tombstones, leaves a hand and arcs through the air. Onto the bonnet. There comes the next, then another, they follow fast. There are more stones and missiles than the crowd needs. People surge forward, some in front of the circular wall, metres from the bonnet. Suddenly a gang of teenaged boys breaks loose and runs round the bakkie. They jeer at Koert, at me and Pilot, showing their gums in the light of the headlamps. They form a sickle around us: the bakkie's trapped. Stones and slate hail down, even the children chuck little marbles of granite. One of the headlamps shatters.

"Who is he?" the leader with shiny arms taunts. "Who is this great white master? We know him, don't we? He's bigger than five of our men together. Our master is the man who gives meat to all the people of the dorp. He can embrace us in his arms and drop crackling in our mouths. Who would refuse this in these days of empty plates? Come closer, all of you. If he doesn't give tonight, then maybe tomorrow night. But he needs to know that we won't grow fat on stones. We will bow before him, we will sell our souls to him, as long as he provides. The great white master must reward us tonight. Look at everything we've done for him."

Koert bangs against the bakkie's roof, the signal for me to go, and bellows against the crowd. They're out of control. Furious, they show their empty hands: what's this?

Let's go, I step on the accelerator. Then I shove the bakkie into reverse and race backwards. The boys scatter. Forward again, I try to get us free. When I look back I see stones fly past Koert. He tries to ward off the stone throwers with his shouts, but there's very little he can do to save us. There's no way out. Koert Spies puffs himself up until he fills the whole bakkie, flays his arms about and performs karate kicks. Amazing. Between all this, he quivers and uses his rolls of fat as shields. The stone throwers dodge and retreat; some gape at the spectacle and stop throwing. Over there, there a stone hits Koert on the head.

"Youz people forget the great white master? All the presents he gives youz forever; and jetzt and jetzt?" he screams over the roar of the crowd and the straining engine, as I brake, accelerate and push forward, change gear and reverse with screeching tyres.

"They have got him," Pilot shouts. He's desperate. He jumps back and forth on his seat, sinks down so no one can see him, clutches my arm so that I lose control of the steering wheel.

"If I hit someone tonight and kill them, it's not my fault."

"Go, Marlo'tjie," he encourages me. "Let them get under the tyres."

I look back and fear for Koert. A mongrel with nasty fangs has been flung into the back of the bakkie. The animal, terrified, is snapping at Koert's thigh, and its owner spurs it on. The master has been hit, there are cuts on his arms and legs, a wound throbs in the spongy flesh of his belly. Blood streams out, as thin as water. He is beside himself with mindless indignation. He kicks the dog's skull, but the staggering animal continues to bite. It's become as crazy as Koert.

"Tha' gun!" Koert bangs against Pilot's window and the whole bakkie rattles. He wants the 9 mm. We won't be getting out of here tonight. Even Koert has become panicky – it's a disastrous sign. Exactly what Pilot feared would happen. Tonight his own people will slaughter him alive.

"Drive, Marlo'tjie," is all he keeps saying. He smells of his own fear.

Township whores pack against my window. They run backwards and forwards with the bakkie, pull up their shirts and press their tits against the window. "You," they scream at me. The one with the glasses, they gesture, and make owl eyes with their thumbs and forefingers, "You! Get out."

Backwards and forwards. The boys have grabbed the bakkie from behind. When I manage to reverse, they let go and fall away on either side. "We *will* get out," I tell myself. "I will not die here. Don't be afraid, Pilot. *Voertsek*," I scream against the window at the whores. One of them has obscene pink nipples.

"King Pharaoh," they taunt Koert and make lewd signs. Again and again the witches' chorus sounds, "King Pharoah." They are enraged, and the night awaits them with empty hands.

"Wrong, mine brudders, youz caused Kingk Koert unnecessary wrong." His voice rings out loudly over the mob. As the bakkie gains ground at the back, Pilot claps his hands and kicks his feet. The last of the boys' hands cling to the body of the bakkie. Backwards, just a few more metres, and I'll be able to turn right, push into first gear and break away to the front. Farewell, my beloved Pappie and Mammie. Farewell, Oom Andries, Oupa and Ouma Rhynie, Oumatjie Attie. My dear step-oumatjie, your liver-spotted hand on the silver bell called us to the table. Pumpkin fritters with cinnamon – what are my thoughts turning to in this evil hour?

"Pilot, will we make it? We *will* make it, you and me, Pilot, we're not so alienated from each other, or you'd have jumped out long ago. You chose sides tonight. My side." He hasn't been listening for a long time. With his head between his knees, he rubs the gold Nikes, and his tears fall.

And me: I must escape this fear. Imitate Koert Spies when he's angry. His big body doesn't have an ounce of fear. Tonight this master has become my teacher.

Koert bellows, and bestrides the bakkie. He sweeps his arms powerfully from on high and grabs the snapping mongrel by the tail. With a rush of adrenalin he swings the animal around, like someone possessed. It bares its fangs and snaps at the faces of the bystanders as it whirls about.

People back off; they've stopped their stone-throwing. They hold back, including the leader with the brawny forearms. Who dares attack the master?

"We're out. We're out. Where to, Pilot? Look up, man, we won't get stuck here. Who got us out? Koert. Koert Spies."

I reach a position where I can turn, swing the bakkie back, push it into first gear and put foot. Koert stands his ground, still swinging the mad dog. As we accelerate, the dog spins ever faster; Koert lets go and slings it into the crowd. All teeth, it snaps as it flies through the air – there'll be blood wherever it lands. Next to me, Pilot giggles like someone who's just had a screw and gone soft. He's moist around the eyes and mouth and has nothing to say.

"Did you piss yourself?" I look at his trousers. We laugh, weak with relief. "What are we afraid of, that they'll kill us?" I accelerate and drive off. Everyone in this county is constantly delivered to death. Here you are taught to feel a distaste for life.

Pilot rolls up his window and gets ready for an enjoyable bakkie ride, doesn't give a damn about a damn.

I glance at the rear-view mirror, "Are you all right, Koert?" It's wonderful on the open road, we're free. Once again, I look at the dark patch at Pilot's crotch.

"Are you all right, Koert?" I shout again.

Koert has sunk back on his mattress and pulled up the blanket. The mountain of his belly is visible. He can't cover himself properly, as Esmie Phumzile had arranged the blanket. All over it, blood stains have seeped through.

Headman runs out as we stop. Right up to the bakkie. Esmie and the others also come to help with Koert. Esmie has brought blankets and the thermos flask with a hot drink.

"What is it, Headman?" But he looks suspiciously at me and walks towards Pilot.

"*Le windpipe yophukile*! The windmill is broken. The last one that was still working is broken now. It's broken. The pipes have to be pulled up. There are holes in those pipes. The water that's in the tank at the house is the last water on the farm," Headman announces.

"Pilot?"

"It's finished for the people on Ouplaas. *Ebesingayo iphe-lile*! Everything's finished." Pilot and Headman laugh together. Headman has turned away from me so that I can't see his face.

"Is that really what Headman said?" Headman shakes his head when he hears my question and walks off a short distance, then comes back and licks his lips at Esmie who's busy with Koert.

"What's going on, Pilot?"

"Water, my baas," he taunts me. "We do not have any more water."

"We don't have water?"

"Who is your 'we'?" Pilot is rebellious now that we're back on the farm. It's to do with me seeing his wet crotch; there's no way he'll get out until everyone's gone inside.

"So what happened to the water, Headman?" I taunt back. "Isn't there water underground? It's the windmill. I saw it coming."

"I saw it coming," Pilot parrots me. I know it's over between him and me. Whatever was good in our relationship has turned bad.

Esmie gives instructions; everyone helps unload the stretcher carrying Koert. The thing lands on the earth with a thud, dust billows. Right away, Esmie covers Koert's head with a baby blanket as she likes to do.

Mildred has also come out and I know why she's watching me: it's about the water issue. I know her by now. When I catch her eye, she clasps her motherly hands together. "Water, Marlo'tjie. Immediate action is required," she tries to imitate Mammie and takes my arm. "You *must* help us." She's desperate.

The garage doors open and the two guards step forward and bend down under Koert's armpits to drag him along. Esmie is exhausted by all the instructions. She's especially exhausted at the sight of Koert's wounds, but forces herself to dab up the blood on his cheek. Koert's eyes stare glassily ahead of him. Before the doors close behind them and he disappears – no one knows for how long this time, his wounds could go septic – I hobble to his blanketed head as fast as I can. I lift the edge. Esmie slaps my hands, I ignore her.

"Koert, what are you going to do, my friend? All your windmills are broken now. You're drinking the last water on the farm. What about the sheep? November?" I see him out of the corner of my eye and turn towards him. November points a torch to where Esmie and the two guards have come to a halt with the bundle between them.

Koert opens his eyelids, a weak spirit in an abused body. He raises himself, can't get me into focus: I'm nothing but another presence in his line of vision. "Iffe water iz caput, dere iz always

Bells forever, and for de babies, Koert will buy Fanta." Everyone stares: a swollen tongue lolls in his mouth, an organ that distorts his words. There's blood on both cheeks.

"Tomollow night we'll throw the biggest party de Platz has ever made. Slaughter two sheepies for us, November," he says and licks his inner lip with its cuts. "Two sheepies, right? Right! Invite his worshipz the mayor, Esmie, an de Polizei ande zupreme sirs of the syndicates, everyone cumin celebrate. Esmie, let me go in now. Wij hebben het onslaught survived, reason to celebrate. Huh, Mister Marlouw?" he manages to call out as he's being helped in.

That was the first time Koert called me by my name. And it moved me. Later, I was no longer quite sure how to interpret my name on his lips.

10

These little things make all the great difference.
When they are gone you must fall back upon your own innate strength,
upon your own capacity for faithfulness.

NOVEMBER IS ALREADY awake, singing his morning psalm. Head under the blanket – I've taught myself to sleep like the others in this house – I try to escape the voices. I stick my fingers in my ears. I'm not getting up today. There's shouting outside my blanket and also beyond the walls of November's quarters. Even though I press my ears tightly closed, I still hear everything. I don't care.

The old man next to me stumbles, seems to lose his footing, and knocks my leg that is under the blanket. "The winter's not being good to November," I hear his voice somewhere above me. "For many years the Lord gave me strong legs, I could catch a lamb," he says.

What's he singing this morning? By now I know his simple routine: the shoes pulled on over the socks he's slept in the previous night. Then the curtain-fabric jacket over the pyjama top and shirt that have also been slept in.

Water. That's what the people are going on about outside. Anxious cries, or I wouldn't be hearing them under my blanket.

In a minute they'll be digging me out – and not to ask for advice. I'm the only one with money. Koert may have some in reserve, but he's out of action. I suspect that not much more will be said between Koert and me. The wounds must be disinfected. The wateriness of his blood didn't look too healthy to me. Esmie Phumzile will know what the best treatment is in the circumstances. The bad foot also needs to be bandaged up again; I'm concerned that the shin might have to be amputated along with the foot.

There's not much time left; and what remains I must use wisely to talk to them all like the patron of old. I don't want to. I remain on my mattress, covered from head to toe. Snuggle up in a warm bed until I'm completely rested – that's the first thing I'll do on my return. Woolly blankets and feather duvets and mohair covers on my flannel sheets – everything I can haul out from my linen cupboard. And I'll lie there in my flannel pyjamas for as long as I like. Remember to do it, Marlouw, remember this cold bed in November's quarters so that you can forget it for good.

The quarters become quiet. November and his psalm have disappeared, everyone's at the kitchen door to collect their plate of pap. On Ouplaas the day has begun. Mildred will have pity on me and set my pap aside. There won't be much; I have to go to the dorp again to get provisions. I don't want to at all.

There it is again, the psalm November has chosen for this morning: In pastures green he leadeth me. I remember the tune, the words return of their own accord and sift through the blanket; I can't close my ears tightly enough. It's an uplifting psalm.

A new pipe for the windmill. I breathe out under the blanket to generate more warmth. Muffled voices drift in from outside, and closer they come to where I'm hiding. They want to dig me out and explain to me what's gone wrong with the windmill: tiny hole in the pipe, worn-out cylinder, worn-out copper valve in the cylinder, worn-out foot-valve. Anything can go wrong with windmills. And what about the one that broke shortly after my arrival, has it been checked and fixed? No? No. You'll land up in hell, the lot of you. I don't want to get up. The moment I do, I'll have to help.

The voices are right at the door of November's quarters, there are deliberations. I hear the sounds of a tussle. They're anxious. The windmill has been dismantled and checked, the problem and solution are obvious. Marlo'tjie will open up his wallet and help.

"*Kufuneka siye kumbiza*. We must call him," someone says. It's Headman, who never says boo or baa – and now he's too big for his boots.

"Marlo'tjie?" that's Mildred. "Lying in bed this time of day?"

I'm as quiet as a mouse.

"I'm sure I hear something in there," she says.

Inside. Here they come to fetch me, they're capable of anything. "What do you want?" I ask before they can hassle me any more.

"Marlo'tjie, we here on the farm have a big problem now. The windmill has broken and stuff needs to be bought. What is it, again?" She turns to Headman, the windmill specialist.

"New iron pipes and leather washers. But you can't get them in Maitland. You'll have to drive to another place. Bloemfontein will have them."

I fly out of my bed and speak, my back towards them, as I quickly pull my trousers over my sleeping shorts, tie my laces, take my jersey from the bed, and pull it over my head. Then my jacket.

"Forget it. If you think I'm rushing to Bloemfontein to buy windmill parts for you and then driving back with those same parts – Mildred, listen to me now: if I get to Bloemfontein again, I'm finished with this country. I'll be flying away in an aeroplane. I'll never come back."

"There's only a little water left for the house. What will the farm people drink? The trough's last water is being drunk in the veld right now. Very soon the sheep will come looking and find dry troughs. They'll all be dead before the rain comes. Every one of them."

"It's not my fault." I keep my back turned to them; I don't want to expose myself to their eyes. "Where's November?"

"He's here."

"He must sing for me again."

"Will you help us? You said you wouldn't throw us away, Marlo'tjie."

"Goodness and mercy all my life shall surely follow me; and in God's house for evermore my dwelling place shall be," November sings with all his might; others join in, in dribs and drabs.

I straighten my jacket collar and walk through the gathering, I'll find my way somehow. As I pass, Headman jumps aside so that I don't perhaps touch him.

"Marlo'tjie, we're going to pay for this," Mildred calls after me.

I could weep. Away, I'm walking away from here. I'll walk and sing the whole day, the rest of the whole morning and all afternoon until it gets too cold outside: yea though I walk through death's dark vale.

I choose a north-westerly direction, away from the werf. The people stand about, downcast. I head on across the veld, careful not to step on the bossies, across bare patches where nothing grows, across the stones there. At times a sheep's trail opens up before me and I happily follow it, one foot cautiously in front of the other in order to remain on the path. Then I'm delivered to the endless monotony of the veld once again. I hum to console myself, and eventually come to an ant heap. Here, where the chocolate brown of the ant heap interrupts the veld's uniformity, I call a halt.

I sit on the ant heap. The silence is complete: no faraway bleating, no bird or insect, no sighing across the veld. The farm has stopped breathing.

God have mercy, I whisper into the silence, and look up at the sun, chilly behind fleecy clouds: today is my last day.

11

But the wilderness had found him out early,
and had taken on him a terrible vengeance
for the fantastic invasion.

FROM EARLY ON, people start arriving on the werf. Some are on foot, others have ordered taxis to drive them the fifteen kilometres or so from the dorp. The taxi man pulls up in front of the kitchen, the doors open in a cloud of dust, and a small crowd tumbles out. Crates of beer bulge from the boot, boxes of wine, whole braaied pigs' heads wrapped in dishcloths, bags of oranges for the children, and cans of water. Mildred must have sent a message about the water shortage.

She and I stand on the kitchen step and watch the guests arrive. Now and again she clutches my arm as she recognises someone or other. I do love Mildred. I'll remember her and miss her sayings and her moods and her pap. She's been motherly and honest towards me throughout my time on Ouplaas. She won't forgive me that at the end of my stay I betrayed them, though she's conveniently forgotten it for now.

The sun is shining today and we're all grateful for that. A sense of cheerfulness, of abundance – rare in *these* times – arrives with the guests. Chickens scratch in the soil, turkeys fan their feathers out until the children chase them off.

Here's Mildred's sister, Ouma Lindiwe. Panting, she gets out of the taxi. "Ouplaas." Her mouth's full of saliva. The food and booze being carried out recalls the times of plenty on the farm. Koert's time. She's excited. I remember Ouma Lindiwe: she was really plump then, but now her breasts and bottom are all that remain of her former fleshiness.

Chatting away, Ouma Lindiwe lands in Mildred's open arms. But first she's on about her three grandchildren who she has to care for day and night, how she's not been able to afford any soap for months because she saves every cent for their medication. The nurse says the bugs attacking the children from inside must be fought with medicine every week, and once a month is as good as nothing. How is she supposed to afford it? That's what she wants to know. The three orphans she's brought with her fidget on the back seat of the taxi. Clothes hang like sacks from their bodies, no matter how much food you cram into them.

"Cram in, how much? And what! What nonsense I'm talking," she's let slip too much. One by one she gathers the children from the back seat and hands the bundles of skin and bone to her sister. "Here," she calls to me to lend a hand. Mildred and I carry them, Mildred's arms more tenderly than mine. We prop them up on their feet in the sun. Not one of them makes the slightest squeak.

Ouma Lindiwe greets me warmly. I don't know whether she recognises me, she greets everyone in the same way. She reckons she's talked enough about her domestic woes and takes a half-jack of brandy from the folds of her bosom. She laughs heartily.

"Wait a moment," Mildred says, "I'll get the children something to keep them happy. I follow along after her; I've no role to fulfil now that the *umgidi*, the party, has all but begun.

Under the circumstances, Mildred's done well in the kitchen: a pot of fluffy ghoe-ghoe mealies has been cooked with sugar beans, and the last of the greens that she could still find in my vegetable patch have been put in as well.

"They'll die one of these days," Mildred says matter-of-factly as she dishes up the three portions.

The children take the food, meekly rolling it into little balls and stuffing it into their mouths. After a while one brings up some phlegm. I walk off to where the campfire's been stacked at the front of the house – more or less where Mammie's rose garden used to be, I say, being silly right to the end.

Pilot is skilfully making the fires. Wood is piled into small pyramids, and clumps of dry grass are stuffed between the stumps. Many of his and Esmie Phumzile's peers have already gathered, young people I've seen before on Ouplaas. They're mostly men, and also a few girls who have survived the virus. Many of the young men wear the black and red or black and silver balaclava that signals their association with a syndicate. Pilot doesn't introduce me to any of them.

A dagga joint the size of a child's arm does the rounds, and long-necked bottles of beer and boxes of wine are passed from hand to hand. Whether they're wearing balaclavas or not, none of the young people makes eye contact with me, and none of the dagga or drink is passed my way. I no longer give a damn. In any case, I look way out of place: lame foot, cheekbones that have become prominent over the past few weeks, and bags under the eyes. Resignedly, I walk among the people, observe and make a last few notes in my memory. To them I'm nothing more than a breath.

"I'm leaving tomorrow, Pilot," I tell him.

At least he condescends to look up from his crouching position. He breaks dry *besembos* branches into equal lengths, makes them into bundles, and places these under the stacked wood. Three fires have been made for the festivities.

"I know. You are pushing off because the water is finished on this farm. You will buy a can of water in the dorp and drive happily on to Bloemfontein," he says unkindly, but his eyes speak another, melancholy language.

"I want to give you something before I leave."

He gets up, flashes his eyes at me once, his chin held high: he doesn't believe anything I say any more. "This is a good fire, this." His mouth breaks into a smile and those amazing teeth of his sparkle.

"I'll miss you too, Pilot. You were good to me." He doesn't answer, and walks off to the next fire with his grass and *besembos* branches to ensure that it will ignite as well as the first.

I would never really know what he thought of me that night or before, and later it didn't matter to me any more. Back in Melbourne, no news of these people ever reached me.

I go and sit against the north wall of the house, pull up my trouser leg so that my lame foot can bathe in the sun. No one notices me. I've become an ant.

A constant stream of young men bursts in around the corner of the house. The new arrivals are all jolly. Some wear ostrich feathers and cheap Chinese costume jewellery that shimmers in the sun. Oxhide drums are set up at the third fire, the one furthest from the house. A muscular, well-fed man – a rare sight –

is in charge there. Once the horse-shoe of drums has been arranged, he tests each with his fingertips and palm.

My spot is not too far from Koert's quarters. As usual, his
door is tightly closed. Esmie Phumzile hasn't made her appearance yet. If Koert comes out tonight – and I expect he will – I'll
ask him one more time whether he wants to return home. I refuse
to beg, and he will not hear another word about his mother from
my mouth.

Today I'm not shivering and my heart is beating steadily. My
hands are relaxed, palms facing upwards. Through slit-eyes I
gaze at the shenanigans going on around me. If it weren't for the
emaciated guests, those shuffling around deliriously, or collapsing in the sun, you'd almost be able to say that peace and plenty
reigned on this piece of earth. I must admit: it's blissful in the
sunlight, there's very little left to fear. I look up – Ouma Zuka is
keeping to the western side of the koppies. She'll have spied the
goings-on on the werf by now.

And Koert. It always comes back to Koert. Soon his gangrenous foot will have to be amputated. What's going on in his
thoughts? He must know that the good times on Ouplaas are
coming to an end. Without some sort of intervention, planning
and funding, no one will be able to stay on here for much longer.
Water and mutton – I'm afraid there's not much left, my friend.
Is *he* afraid? I doubt it.

Can you hear me, Mildred and November and Headman and
all of you who have turned up for the festivities, can you hear the
bitter-sweet tone of my voice? It's because I have been face to face
with fear. It doesn't make my heart race any more, doesn't make
my blood freeze.

There, one of the balaclavas looks at me, after all. The eyes

shine for a moment through the slit of his balaclava. He leans to
the right and says something to his friend. If I land up in a life-
threatening situation tonight, or perhaps tomorrow, or some day
in the future, will my survival instinct awaken me, will my grey
matter give the signal to flee in time? Perhaps I'll succumb in
the face of the violence of the assault. And if I fall, will I crawl
forward, stand up and carry on running? Is that how I'll respond
to fear – now, after everything I've been through? I doubt it. I
shudder at the thought of a panic-stricken flight. Except for one
individual, we Louws have all left; even our graveyard has been
levelled to the ground. Survival has become irrelevant, there's
nothing left to survive. I mean, there's no reason for me to want
to survive here. Thirteen generations and three and a half centuries on the continent have come to an end. Others will procreate
and live here, but not us. My people and I have disappeared from
here forever.

Calm now, calmer still. I breathe in the dry, pure air of Ouplaas, the air that belongs to everyone, calmly in, calmly out.
Here's November to tell me something. He's wearing a double-
breasted suit with a waistcoat and a bright tie that he's dug up
from who knows where. Nothing on this earth terrifies me more
than the idea that I'll allow myself to be overwhelmed by fears
like yesterday and the day before, like in the old days.

"Hello, November. You're looking smart today."

"The Lord has blessed us with the *umgidi* tonight. We can
drink and eat. And the Lord will send rain too. Before we are
forced to leave this farm, the rain will come. Look, there to the
west, it's building up. And it's warm today, tortoise is heading for
the mountains, there are the first signs of rain. The Lord will not

throw us away, we are his people. There's pudding tonight too, for the children and old people."

"What kind of pudding?"

"Sweet pudding. Mildred has made it nice and sweet. *Ipudini.*" He laughs and starts his measured ritual of rolling a Boxer cigarette.

"You're contented tonight, November. You're happy."

"It is as the Lord says, we must all be happy from head to toe. You could also be happy, Marlo'tjie."

The day ends, cold, and the old people and dogs move with the sun. Pale orange lines lie across the western skyline. Proudly, Pilot walks between his stacks of firewood. Within a few moments, he'll light the first match.

"*Ina.* Here." His friends pass him bottles of beer. He's boozing non-stop. He rubs his stomach. He quivers in anticipation of the party this night promises. It's the kind of night he likes best. He claps his hands, laughs loudly, and jumps up, to the other side. For no reason at all. When I look again, he's back in his place. He's happy, like the others, I can see he is, and I am happy with him. Wish I could tell him this. He hasn't looked in my direction again, nor do I expect him to. Pilot and I have said our goodbyes. Whatever happens, my suitcase is packed. I'm leaving at dawn, with or without Koert Spies.

Behind the house more cars stop, doors shut, and hard, strange voices ring through the night. Women, men.

✷

It's about ten o' clock. The drummer lifts his arms above the taut cow-hide and lowers his palms onto the membrane. Close to the flames, he's sweating. Faster, faster. You can sense the vibration in your guts. Some of the guests have already collapsed and curled up at the furthest fire. Koert and Esmie Phumzile haven't made their appearance yet; his quarters are shrouded in utter darkness. I know they'll come. Koert is power; he's pure spectacle. He's waiting for his moment.

The balaclavas have also joined in. They stomp rhythmically to the beat of the drum and call to the girls who've come from the dorp. From nowhere, one with a lovely slender body confronts an old man. Till now, he's been glued to the same spot, his eyes watery and his knuckles knobbly on his *kierie*; she wants to animate him with her warm-bloodedness but he fails to rise to the occasion. The fist loses its grip on the *kierie*, he's about to drop. She dances away.

Now she weaves a snake coil around all three fires. Some of the young people follow. The snake slips through the flames, past the feet of the old people. Follow her, follow her, a hundred twists and turns. She's a jackal's tail, a whip. Ever faster, the snake of people spirals to the beat of the drums under the soles of their feet.

Gone. She leads them away from the fire. Everyone follows blindly. Closer to Koert's quarters, she claps, hisses with a pointed tongue and peers over her shoulder until the snake tail also claps and hisses. The hissing becomes a counterpoint to the bass drum, "*Vuka mhle Koert. Vuka!* Get up, Mister Koert. Get up! Show your face, we want to see our master. Come and greet us, Master Koert." The coil moves back to the fires and the hissing and clapping sound even louder, "*Vuka mhle Koert. Vuka!*"

Mildred stands next to me with a cup of dark-brown sherry. She sips and licks her lips, "It's going to be a long night before morning comes. Oh, if only it never comes, we don't need it any more."

"What are you saying now, Mildred?" I'm a little tipsy.

"I'm saying you must also be happy tonight, you, our Mar-lo'tjie."

"But I am, I am." And suddenly an image flashes in front of me. It's late afternoon, the temperature is about forty degrees, Mammie and I are driving back to Ouplaas. I'm about to pass out from the heat in the front of the bakkie. I call out, and before Mammie's even stopped I've stripped off my shirt and jumped onto the back, and Mammie drives, she drives as fast as she can, and the wind takes me and forces my throat open and brushes my hair back and presses my eyes so that they begin to water sweetly and I live that single moment in the divine, icy wind and there's nothing, only the seduction of the wind on my young skin, and me. Mildred's voice jolts me away from my romancing with the past.

"Oh my, oh dear," she points.

From the north-west, where the koppies form a ridge against the horizon and you can't make anything else out, the creature appears on all fours, at first like a phantom in the furthest glow of the fire, then more visibly, with more bravado. She *has* seen the fire, heard the drum. And here she is. She screams in terror – or to terrify – and creeps up, unsure of the reception awaiting her, yet audacious so that the snake of dancers gives way and yields to her the space in front of the middle fire. Go forward, they en-courage her, towards the fire and the heat and the people, blood and flesh like you.

Three-legged, three-legged, Ouma Zuka closes in, holding a stick in her right hand. A porcupine has been impaled on it.

Blood drips from the ripped neck, down the stick and onto her claw. She's right up against the flames now; you can smell the singed porcupine bristles.

The beat of the drums breaks off, then a loud bass beats, pauses again to give the new guest a chance. She rears up a little, and there's porcupine blood on her breasts. The rising action, the natural inclination after a long while to stand on your own legs, spurs her on. She screams in ecstasy and shakes the stick with the porcupine head at the bystanders, "Look, look."

These first words of Ouma Zuka drift towards me through the people and the flames. My skin is flushed; I feel as if I'm boiling, someone shoves a cold bottle of beer against my cheek. It's Mildred, no, it's Pilot.

Ouma Zuka has risen from being on all fours to almost three quarters of her height. There, she's up now, supporting herself with her stick, her head level with the porcupine's. They both grimace. "Give her wine," Headman shouts and rushes to the crates, grabs a box and opens the tap as he hurries back so that wine makes a trail all the way to Ouma Zuka. He cups his hand, forces her head back, and pours the wine into her open mouth. Wine streams over her cheeks.

The man beats the drum and the dance begins again. Wilder, this time, no one holds hands, everyone sways and shrieks, and more wood is thrown on the fire. "*Ipudini*," November calls from somewhere among the dusty tracks of the dancers. The stick with the porcupine's head is stuck into the ground near the fire, and that's Ouma Zuka's spot now. Some of the children touch the head and flee shrieking from the beast that rises from the fire and will bite, bite.

The balaclava men have begun to ape Ouma Zuka's gait: they

creep forward, withdraw, creep forward, and withdraw from the flames. They stick their fingers in the flames and grope at the ankles of the girls, or at a breast, before the dancer can whip it away.

I swim between reeds of arms and legs to where I'd heard Mildred's voice; I don't want to drift away from her. "Mildred." Just then, I notice Esmie Phumzile entering the circle of light from Koert's quarters. It can only be her, with those high heels and purple lips; only she wears jewels like that, and a silver belt. Tonight she's also tied a scarf around her head. An inventive headdress, its only flaw is a piece of cloth that should have been tucked in but hangs loose. Children skip up to admire the jewels of the princess of the werf. I push someone out of my way to get a proper view of Esmie. She's saying something, gesticulating, no one listens to her, no one hears her.

"Look, the lipstick," Mildred says. Then looks at me surprised. "What are you doing?"

I look at my feet: I'm jumping up and down. I'm still trying to hear what Esmie's saying – what? I try to cheer up my thoughts to make the best of these last hours; the sands of my memory are running out. I notice a hand beckoning, enticing me towards the circle of dancers. I'm the cripple who can't dance, who up till now has made sure he stays close to Mildred.

I dance.

All those long nights next to November and the others – the bodies – that's what I smell like now, and I don't resist it. When last did I have a bath? My underpants are brown like the veld. I have become one with everyone on Ouplaas. My people. I am one of them. Mildred offers me more wine; I choke on its glorious sweetness. I dance, I dance. Flare my nostrils to breathe; my sweat smells like frog slime, like cow dung. Like soil. Human.

Koert will not return with me – I've known that for a while now. He belongs here, where would he go if he were to leave? I've achieved my goal. I never really came for Koert's sake. I came to live. My dusty brain can't even form or recall the most beautiful memories. Nothing has been in vain. Impostor, lame brain, clubfoot, I'm glad I've come. At last I can name myself. I sink to the ground.

"Why are you falling down?" Mildred grabs my hand.

"Need water."

"But my goodness, why are you only telling me now? I'll send a little one to fetch some from the drum."

I spend the last hours on this farm in a daze. I drink, I dance. By morning only ash and dust will remain, the dancers spat out, cold and hungry. But I won't be here to see it all.

"Oh shit, she's bringing Koert," Mildred says beside me. "Esmie Phumzile has cleared a path for him. Look!"

I open my eyes. Here he comes. Koert Spies is approaching. It is him. And he's crawling, dragging himself along the path Esmie's opened up for him. Ouma Zuka also steps closer and stamps the stick she's pulled from the stack next to the fire. The wine's been wiped from her face, she's standing upright, prepared, she no longer looks like the wretch from out there, from the koppies.

Koert is coming. Koert's hands seek a grip in front of him, his elbows press on the earth, he worms his way forward, inch by inch. The white master is coming. There's a murmur and the drums quieten to a rumble that I feel in the pit of my stomach: nothing has been in vain. On my last night, Koert is my inspiration. Presented on a tray: all I need do is reach out and take it. I'm so glad I came.

"Koert, Koert, Koert," the volume rises. No one moves; no one dares speak above the monosyllabic chorus. The fire crackles and the bass drum thrums, and then the chorus quietens as Koert approaches. And now, vulnerable as the threadbare loincloth and bandages tied around it, the scraping sounds of the body dragging itself across the earth.

Mildred pushes me even closer to be part of the spectacle. I've had some water, a puff on November's Boxer cigarette. I'm standing there strong.

"Oh, he's not going to make it," Mildred snorts.

"The ice has been broken," November adds. A child whines, a mossie chirps in its night nest, feet lift up then stamp the ground, the drums rise again, and – still addressing the crawler – the people shout encouragement.

The wounds from the graveyard massacre are evident all over Koert's body. Pus glistens in the flames – he's come close – some wounds have turned into mouldy green patches. Koert keeps his crotch low and his gaze straight ahead of himself. Ouma Zuka edges in, doesn't take her eyes off Koert. She looks clever, cunning, not at all like a baboon any more.

The effort of the activity forms beads of sweat on Koert's back, that swell and drip down his flanks. He looks ahead, always ahead. Even though he's only crawling on the ground, you can sense his perseverance. "Dig into the soil just ahead of you," I too encourage him, "pull yourself up, man. Hang in there!"

The left thigh and leg shuffle, then the other thigh follows, the one that gangrenous foot and shin hang from. Some of the bandages have come undone and stream like wedding-car decorations in the wake of his body.

"That man's strong," Mildred says with a mouth full of wine.

"Oh Lord. Oh dear." She seems to be enjoying the difficulty Koert is experiencing. She never liked him much.

Pilot steps past Ouma Zuka and offers Koert a hand, but Koert slaps him away. He'll use his own strength, this is *his* path and he will take it right up to the fire. The people have closed in a circle behind him; they clap rhythmically, palm to palm, in time with the thrusting master.

"He had so much faith, Koert did – don't you see? – he had such faith. He could get himself to believe anything – anything." I talk to myself. No one dares touch him. Rather keep their ears close to the ground in case he speaks. If only he'd give the word, they would obey. If he wanted to, he could still rise up and take command of the whole crowd. If he wanted to. And I do so wish that he still had the will, that he could still give the people what they wanted.

"What are you saying?" Mildred wants to know. "See how stubborn Koert is, won't let Pilot help him."

With shudders and groans, he pushes on. His elbows are scuffed. He'll make it after all. He is the authentic white master, the one who enforces his will to the bitter end. Without knowing it, that's what he'd come here to be. Too stubborn ever to give up. That's what he's come to show the people. It doesn't matter *how*, just as long as they see it. And here he is anyway, before them with his urge, his will to terrify.

Esmie Phumzile goes up to the crawling man and stretches out her arm to prevent anyone from blocking his way. She even forces Ouma Zuka with her stick to one side. Koert is so close to the fire that the ground he's pressing on must be hot. His body is ruddy in its glow. He heaves his torso onto his tree-stump arms, looks right, left, then straight into Ouma Zuka's eyes. With the porcupine head, she pushes Esmie out of the way. Esmie doesn't have the strength to resist.

"He's the *mzungu*. He's not one of us," Ouma Zuka points her claw at the man on the ground. "Open your ears, people. Listen, before it's too late. This *mzungu* is vermin that's come to live on your werf, meant for humans only. He's hungry, the hunger in his belly is driving him mad, and he needs meat, night and day. You've seen it with your own eyes, haven't you? Mildred, *you* tell the people." Ouma Zuka tries to sniff Mildred out.

"Filth," Mildred hits back and hides behind me and November to get out of the light of the fire. She refuses to be drawn in.

Ouma Zuka looks down at Koert and twists her mouth to display her disgust, "He's devoured all the meat on this farm. And no, that wasn't enough for the *mzungu*. He went to the graves of his father and mother to eat the meat off their bones. Those graves were dug open, the bones of his people trampled. The *mzungu's* stomach is never filled. You think he came to help you grow a big flock of sheep on this farm? Where are they now? Where are the rams with the seed that's supposed to make the lambs? Look at Esmie Phumzile here, young woman that she is, how can she possibly make a child for the farm? The *mzungu* has fouled her womb: the *mzungu* has come and fouled everyone who's supposed to make babies on this farm. You think he's brought you drink and nice food? You, Pilot, you, Headman, you think he's brought you a machine to play games on? Where's everything tonight? He's stored all your house stuff in his dark place – all for himself. You've got nothing.

"And you men," – she sticks out her claw and rips a balaclava from a head – "your legs become weak before the *mzungu*. What

can he give you? Let him give if he can, or you must decide what
to do with him tonight."

With remarkable strength, Koert props his body up on his
arms. He's long stopped looking at Ouma Zuka, who's been carried away by her tirade. His head hangs listlessly, rolls to the left
then to the right. The corner of his mouth, too, has fallen open,
spittle dribbles from it.

Few of the bystanders know what to make of Ouma Zuka's
words. Hadn't they come to Ouplaas for the *umgidi*? "*Tsi, tsi*,"
November expresses his displeasure. Esmie is alarmed, her headscarf has slid down. She's taken hold of Pilot's hand.

Headman make sure he's part of the inner circle. Ouma Zuka
has already put him in his place with the porcupine head a few
times, "Down, down, you don't stand higher than your Ouma
Zuka." Still, his pricked-up ear remains turned to his ouma.

As Ouma Zuka continues, some of the balaclavas also push
torwards the fire and the white man on the ground. From here, I
can tell the mouths in the balaclavas are talking. Hard words not
intended to reach me and Mildred and November. They can say
what they like, Ouma Zuka can say what she likes; everyone is
waiting for Koert. As always. He's the one who must speak the
word. The sound of the cow-hide drum has almost died away;
only a low buzz is audible.

"We must give him a chance," November announces.

Koert holds his head still, lifts his eyelids. He wants to say
something, I can tell. He raises himself again. "Whaz the old
witch croakee-ing on about?" he bursts out. "Don't belief ein
Wort, my people, she's shitting a trap." He laughs, shakes. It
hurts. He drags his gangrenous foot into view and points to it,
searches for my eye especially. Enraged, I push my way through

the people to get closer. Mildred follows me protectively. "Leave me, fuckit," I shake a hand from my arm. "Koert?" He recognises me.

"I am the trencherman, Marlouw. I am he," he mouths the words. "I have devoured you and your language. I have cut you up into pieces." I make sure that he sees me nod, that I have understood.

Mildred was first to notice. "Watch out," I remembered her whispered warning afterwards and the force with which she pulled me back. We both stumbled; she was the one who got us onto our feet again, and dragged us from the inner circle.

One of the balaclavas steps forward into the glow, grabs Esmie – she was holding her hand in benediction over the big white rump – and, in a single movement, slings her into the crowd. From the balaclava's camouflage pants, somewhere from within a zipped pouch – it happens so suddenly that no one can say exactly from where – a long knife appears. The flames glint on the blade; I gasp, grab Mildred's arm.

Softly, as if into melted butter, he slips the knife into Koert's middle, right where the body folds in two, and jerks him upwards. Koert looks down his flank at the man, his eyes narrowed like never before, contemptuous, sharp as whetted jet.

Softly, as if from melted butter, the man withdraws the knife – I wonder whether Koert felt any pain, as it happened without resistance – and then plunges the knife in just past the shoulder, this time deeply.

Koert looks at the balaclava once more. His hatred is concentrated in the sharp point of the knife itself, then his elbow wobbles and he falls onto the side of his face. A second balaclava is at hand right away, a third and fourth await their chance. The knife passes from one hand to another as if they'd practised for this: each drives the knife cleanly and accurately into the flesh of the master. Some of the women and children scream, the drums thunder. The men come forward for their turn; they're without balaclavas now, without shame. Headman shrieks like a banshee. When he gets his chance he chooses the weakest spot, where the neck joins the back, and as he pulls the knife out he immediately lets go of it. He's pissed himself.

Then he's also there, the golden Nikes dancing in the flames, the only knifeman whose deed shocked me. I gulp. "Here, drink," Ouma Lindiwe dribbles the last of her brandy into my mouth when she sees me struggling against the gruesome sight of Pilot with Koert.

Pilot quivers like a rodent, just manages to drive in the tip of the knife. He has chosen the upper leg. When he sees the first trickle of blood from the wound, he retreats.

The last I'd seen of him was when he left the inner circle and disappeared into the darkness. He'd hugged himself, his shoulders as vulnerable as a boy's.

Blood flows from the freshest stab wound, Pilot's, and also from each of the others. A dark pool forms under the body. Blood on the knife and on its handle – the knife disappears as suddenly as it had appeared.

Once again Koert raises himself up on his elbows so that the bystanders recoil at the death throes. He lifts his head and utters a last mighty cry: "De horror. I am de horror," and thuds onto his cheek in the pool of blood that has by now spread wider than his body.

Ouma Zuka grabs her stick with the porcupine head still impaled on it, then runs around the carcass imitating the death rattle, foam pouring from her mouth just like Koert's, and points her claw at the wounds. She ululates and capers about, arse in the air. Towards the back of the group I notice Esmie's pathetic movements among the spectators who'd withdrawn, stunned. Esmie grabs hold of her head, shakes her wrists, and vibrates all over as if she's in the back of a bakkie, clinging on for dear life along a corrugated road.

Ouma Zuka sticks the porcupine head in the fire for the bristles to catch alight, then forces Headman's hands around the stick. "There!" she points, "quickly." Headman scuttles down the dark pathway to Koert's quarters, lifts the burning porcupine's head high and slings it through the window. When it bursts into flames behind them, the people step back from the pierced body in horror, make way for Ouma Zuka, move out of reach of her provocations, mill about dumbly.

Mildred slaps me through the face with a dishcloth to bring me to my senses. "You must go, Marlo'tjie. Right away. I've sent November to fetch your stuff."

"That's right," November hugs my suitcase. He'll carry it for me.

"This way, quickly, to your bakkie. This way. *Khawulezi-sa*! Hurry up!" Mildred becomes impatient when I turn in the wrong direction. She points to the east, away from the fires and the milling people, to where it's dark. "Get into your bakkie and drive to the back of the house, past the kraal, away, no one will hear you. Everyone's still busy here in front. *Baleka usindise ubomi bakho mntwana wam*. Flee for your life, my son."

I hobble on with Mildred to the left of me and November to the right. The spectacle of the slaughter and Ouma Zuka's victory dance is still engrossing the people; they don't turn around to see if they're missing anything more. Only the one who threw the burning porcupine head notices us. It is Headman. November grabs his stick from him and drives him away with its sharp end. Headman protests like a female baboon, his eyes bloodshot. When he persists in coming after us, November swings around and pummels his head.

The bakkie comes into view. Mildred supports me on my crippled side and pushes me forward; she realises I don't have much strength left. "Don't give up now, Marlo'tjie. You must drive like the wind, the gate that takes you from the farm will be open, then there's just the short stretch of road till you're on the big road. They've become heathens on this farm. All of them, godless." She shrieks as we run on, as shocked as I am. "What are they going to do when the sun rises tomorrow and they see what's lying next to the fire? And where will they find water to wash their murderers' hands?"

"The Lord is angry with us," November says. We've arrived at the bakkie and hurriedly say goodbye. I hug November's bony body, and he holds me tight. "The Lord bless you and keep you, the Lord make his face to shine upon you. The Lord lift up his countenance upon you and give you peace," he calls down the blessing upon me. Then he pushes me away.

Briefly I land in the warmth of Mildred's motherly body. It is finished. They help me into the bakkie and once again bestow on me the Lord's blessing.

Someone is with them, at my door. Esmie Phumzile, out of breath. She shakes her wrists, "They're coming to get me too, they're going to rip me apart." There's a cut at the corner of her mouth and her clothes are in tatters. All the jewels are gone.

"You have to take me, Marlouw. Mister Koert is dead. I

can't stay here any more." She pulls on my door, she's hysterical. "They're coming to get me." She runs around the bakkie to try to get in at the passenger side. Quickly I lean over, lock the door, and am startled at the evil of doing such a thing before the very eyes of a refugee. The engine's running: I can reach 100 km/h within minutes.

"I can't, Esmie, you're mad. They'll never let you in. Where's your passport? You don't even have a passport. I can't, I can't," I scream.

"Take me with." She throws herself against the passenger door that's now firmly locked. November and Mildred go and fetch her and take hold of her arms, but she sinks her teeth into November's old man's skin, pulls loose, and screams herself hoarse. She shoves her head through the half-open window on my side, her breath blows feverishly over me.

"You *have* to take me, I've got Koert's child." It's her trump card. She pulls back, grabs her belly and points to herself. "I'm family, Marlouw, I'm carrying your family's child. Koert said I must stay on the farm and plant your people on this soil again. Here he is," – she grabs her belly again – "here is your child, it is the future of your race."

"Impossible. You're mad. It's impossible to take you. Besides, you're positive. They'll never even let you in." I pull away.

She clings onto the window for dear life. As the bakkie starts moving, she's forced to let go of the window and grabs the door handle, then the rim of the back. The increasing speed of the vehicle jerks her hand loose, then her nail hooks on one of the bakkie's steel loops and rips off. She's thrown aside.

The progenitor, Esmie Phumzile, Lord forgive me. She with her deer-like arms and orphan's eyes. She accompanies me on my

journey and so do her reproaches, long after I've left Maitland
and am on my way to Bloemfontein. Esmie has become family.
The fourteenth generation will be born in this land, will live,
prattle away and die.

12

I found myself back in the sepulchral city resenting the sight of
people hurrying through the streets to filch a little money from each other,
to devour their infamous cookery, to gulp their unwholesome beer,
to dream their insignificant and silly dreams.

HELEEN DOESN'T KNOW that I've returned, nor do I phone to report back. The clinical orderliness of the city smothers me. In my own eyes I've become a thing of horror to others. I've washed my hair, but not had it cut yet. My bushy beard is matted: I'm delaying a visit to the barber. Since my return I've been dreaming of a wandering, hairy bag. I imagine it's got something to do with Esmie Phumzile's foetus. There's no one to interpret my dream with any accuracy.

Two days later when I do phone her, Heleen is dead calm. Don't ask me how she knew, but the moment I said: "Heleen, I'm back," she replied: "Koert's not with you, is he?"

She doesn't lay any blame on me. She'd like to treat me to lunch in a new restaurant. I don't tell her I haven't any money left – I used my last cent on a bribe to get an earlier flight out.

Nothing's said about my physical condition when we meet at the restaurant, though she does gasp at the sight of me.

She kisses me lightly – her lips feel icy on mine – and shudders at my beard and the throbbing cold sore on my lip. I know

Heleen. She's already on about Henrie's fits before we've even sat down at the table.

"Foaming at the mouth, oh my God, Marlouw. That too." She'd suddenly remembered Mammie's cure for the mad woman on the farm. Everything had come back to her, and this helped to calm her down. So she wrapped one of her silver teaspoons in a cloth and pushed it into his mouth so he wouldn't swallow his tongue.

Our wine arrives. Heleen tastes to see whether it's corked or not; she uses the extravagant white napkin to dab imaginary drops from her mouth. She's so composed that her movements seem slightly retarded to me.

The dog apparently carried on shuddering, and when he eventually stopped, he collapsed in her lap. Jocelyn had phoned the vet a long time before, but this time Henrie didn't survive the fit. Strangely, the vet didn't hurry back to his practice; he stayed for tea and Hertzog cookies.

"He had the most beautiful hands, that man, but you know the smell in vets' surgeries." For the first time today, an archness hovers around her mouth. "Well, that smell also clung to the man, as true as I'm sitting here. I suppose it eventually seeps into your skin if you're injecting and cutting all day long like that, don't you think, Marlouw?"

I order the most expensive steak on the menu. Marbled Black Angus rib-eye steak with porcini dust in a light sauce of parsley, oyster mushrooms and garlic. Heleen takes three white tablets with a glass of the Italian sparkling water that's been placed on our table without us ordering it.

"I don't have any appetite."

"Have the salad, come on, Heleen. Just to keep me company." I point to the menu: arugula and shavings of Grana Padano parmesan drizzled with extra virgin olive oil and fresh lemon juice.

"He died happy, I'm sure of that. He was the sweetest dog. I wrapped the remains in one of the silk scarves JP is forever bringing me from his travels. Poor JP," she giggles, less guarded now. She tells the whole story about Henrie without a hint of cynicism, and so sincerely that after a while I get up to put my arm around her shoulders.

Only then does she say, "Oh my God, Marlouw. Just look at you, my poor, poor little brother." She whispers, "It must have been horrific," and draws me closer, right up to the scent of her neck. "Order me a brandy and Coke, will you?"

I understand. Heleen is too embarrassed to order brandy and Coke here. The overwhelming effect of the restaurant's interior is of an ivory and ice-white mausoleum. The chairs have high, stiff tombstone backs and are covered in white damask. Heleen has booked one of the low tables with sofas upholstered in cream chamois. Every one of the waiters has an exotic appearance, they're from Sri Lanka or Mauritius, I suspect. The girls with the thick braids come from Fiji. They all wear cream shirts and long white aprons that offset their dark skins.

The one who'd taken the drinks order – here she is now with the floppy wing of a linen cloth over her left forearm – delivers it to me with an upturned nose.

"You see?" Heleen says. She lets the drink stand in front of me for ages before she allows me – imperceptibly, please – to slide it across to her.

"When the vet eventually left – he'd eaten five cookies and spoken so sadly about his autistic child – I asked Jocelyn to dig a grave for Henrie. Jocelyn couldn't believe her ears, she's not used to that kind of work, you know."

The dog was buried by five o' clock that afternoon, with one of Heleen's silver crosses stuck at its head. "I can't tell you how relieved I was when everything was over."

I eat my fillet, order potatoes as a side dish, which appear as identical balls on a white plate, delivered without my even noticing. I eat everything, Heleen's salad too. In between, I also devour all the Italian ciabatta. Heleen is amazed at my appetite, and when I have the breadbasket refilled, tears of laughter fill her eyes.

"Order me another one, please, Marlouw," and she points to her glass.

Around us, business lunches are being concluded, the elegant chairs silently pushed back, the men in designer suits getting up so athletically that the waiters aren't in time to help them with their chairs. A last sip of wine left in a glass is noticed. A manicured man's hand lifts it by the stem and finishes it. At the door the manager slips the gold credit card into the hand of the one who's obviously the alpha-male of the pack. *Parfum pour homme* wafts in the air around their table. Cellphones and car keys appear as they leave the establishment through automatic glass doors.

While I stare at the businessmen, Heleen gazes out intently ahead of her. "Did Koert ask about me?" she surprises me.

"He wanted to know how you were."

"What did he want to know? What *exactly* did he ask?" And the anxiety of the old Heleen is evident, the perfect nails clutching the ball of the glass.

"Oh, Heleen, he just wanted to know whether you were still in good health. If things were going well with you."

My report makes her think for a while. She doesn't ask anything more, and I don't say anything. Nothing about Koert's appearance, nothing about the circumstances in which he lived and died, nothing about his hubris. Heleen doesn't need to know any of it.

For dessert I decide on delicate vanilla-flavoured waffles with real clotted cream and persimmon crystals. After her third drink, Heleen doesn't give a damn any more and has her ball-shaped glass refilled herself. She gulps it down and immediately signals for two cognacs as an afterthought to the meal. When they arrive, she gets up from the cream sofa and climbs the marble flight of stairs that takes smokers to the roof garden. She doesn't invite me to join her.

I ask for my dessert to be served on the roof garden and follow her. As she climbs the stairs – there are lots of them – she has to stop twice to hold onto the wrought-iron handrail. She looks at me waiting just behind her on the steps – her grip is bone-white – and climbs further up. We arrive in a paradise of St Joseph lilies; the space under the glass dome is completely filled with white petals. The scent is intoxicating. I imagine that I can even smell the yellow pollen on the stamens.

"He's dead, isn't he?"

"Yes, Heleen." I don't avoid the question. It was only a matter of time before it came. I'm still amazed by the lilies. It's been an eternity since I've seen anything like it. I walk over to Heleen and she allows me to hug her. The lobe of her ear is transparent, and a tear drips from her nose.

"Were you with him when he died?"

"I was there." The question has tripped me up, after all, and I have to sit on one of the sofas. The waiter arrives with a fluttering apron and places the dessert on a white napkin on the table next to me. He arranges the cutlery professionally, in the exact spot where my right thumb and index finger will pick it up.

"Did he ask for me when he died?" She moves lightly across the marble floor as if on a mirror of water, until she stands right before me. "Did he say my name?" There's a ripple of expectation. Her profound love for her son must now be consummated. She waits patiently for it, her mouth begins to tremble.

The white throat and pistil of a lily reflect in the silver of my dessertspoon. I place the spoon on the plate and cover my mouth with my napkin as I look up at her. I shake my head lightly enough for her to think I'm just wiping my mouth. There's no one else on the roof garden. Rays of sunlight fall between the stalks and petals of the lilies, all the way down to our feet, directly onto the almond-shaped toes of Heleen's Manolo Blahnik shoes.

My hands shake beneath and on top of the napkin at my mouth. The little bit of courage I had quickly sinks to my feet in their pure wool socks. I can hear a bee, and the sound of Heleen's nails touching her glass, and from below, the rushing sound of the city floats up. She will remain loyal to her only child to the bitter end.

I place the napkin on my lap, then I fold it up and put it next to the untouched dessert: I have reached the end of my meditation on my mission. I have to make a last decision, and as soon as that's done, the stamp of the impostor will come down on my report. Thus it was suspected from the beginning, thus it was determined, thus it is: "He was already very far gone, you must understand, Heleen. All sorts of words came out of his mouth. You could almost say bubbled out. And yes, one of those words was your name." I get up quickly and step away from her and my white lie and try, without success, to forgive myself.

When I turn around, Heleen has stepped closer. She stands under the host of lilies, her glass neatly in her hands in front of her crotch. Her shoulders droop, both are at exactly the same level. She stares ahead without seeing, her left and right cheeks rouged in exactly the same way. Her parting cleaves her hair into the two identical halves of a bob. The symmetry to which she remains captive makes her sickly pale. Willingly, she receives the poison from my hand.

"My son," she murmurs, and a smile like a black winter frost falls across her face.

13

Marlow ceased, and sat apart, indistinct and silent,
in the pose of a meditating Buddha.

IMAGES OF OUPLAAS came to me often. Clear and perfectly pure like in the beginning, as it was when my first forefathers saw it: as wide as the vulture flies, as far as the veld stretches. Shimmering koppies of ironstone, mountains and cliffs where animals shelter against the cold in winter and ewes seek out the coolness of the *besembos* bush to give birth in the heat of the lambing season.

In fact, the images took me further back, to before the time when there were lambs on Ouplaas. I saw Ouplaas as it was in the days when the San trekked through the wild, fragrant landscape. Stopping here to slaughter a buck, or there under the overhang of a cliff for a few days until the landscape painting of the red eland was finished.

And then came the wind. Purifying. And more persistent and stronger than ever, yet who could say, who was there to compare and to measure the wind? That's the thing. It suddenly sprang up from the west, as a man might leap from his bed in terror. The west wind. But no shepherd or farmer, not a single human being to announce that such a wind might be a drought wind. And because there were no people left on the farm, the direction of the wind did not matter.

This is how it began: the first colony of bats moved into the quarters. Darting this way and that, they danced after gnats and mosquitoes at night. Once all the roof sheets had been worked loose and carted away, ants marched into the farmstead and made their ant heaps in the corners – whether November's quarters or Pappie's study, it doesn't really matter. Beautiful ones, dark brown like fresh baboon droppings.

Then the wind raced from the koppies towards the ruined farmstead carrying the scent of bossies. Of course, the bossies had also returned: the witblommetjie, the ankerkaroo and the *kerriebossie*. Rock pigeons, too, were carried in on the wind: so playful, so merry. They nested under an abandoned piece of rusted roofing and cooed to themselves at sunset. Swarms of bees busied themselves below in the ventilation holes. The honey they made was sweet with a heavenly scent. And the queen bee was also beautifully fat.

It sometimes rained on this wide but finite piece of earth and sometimes the rain stayed away. One day, amid the fresh *rooigras* – so precious for fattening livestock in the former days – a first springhare appeared as if from nowhere. Springbuck with their brown and white jackets, veld grasshoppers, *rooigras* – but I've mentioned that already – the whole lot arrived and lived quietly, lived and then died. Platannas and toads also hopped about because the vleis filled up again. And through the vleis up towards the mountains, shuffling onwards, cheerful mountain tortoises. And so on.

But no human footprint or human voice ever again existed on

that piece of land. The name of the farm was also long forgotten. Imagine: wind blowing through the ruins of the farmstead as if no one had ever lived there.

*

Acknowledgements

My grateful thanks to E K M Dido for her creative translations into isiXhosa; Prof Fred van Staden and James Kitching who provided me with the latest research on fear and anxiety; Louise Viljoen, Ina Gräbe, Lynda Gilfillan and Riana Barnard; my late father, W F Venter, for his sketch of a windmill and his explanation of how it works; and for the empathy and support from my life partner, Gerard Dunlop.

All quotations from: Conrad, J. *Heart of Darkness*. New York: Signet Classics, 1997. Certain characters, scenes and sentences in the text are reinterpretations and paraphrasings of Conrad's original text.

   The quotation on page (vii) is from Paul J Whalen. *Fear, Vigilance, and Ambiguity: Initial Neuroimaging Studies of the Human Amygdala*. In American Psychological Society, Vol. 7, No. 6, p. 182. Cambridge: Cambridge University Press, 1998.

   I have consulted the work of the following neuro-psychologists: Davis, Michael; Grant, Steven; Heinrichs, Nina; Hofmann, Stefan G; Kolb, Bryan; Lang, Peter J; Moscovitch, David A; Öhman, Arne; Rosen, Jeffrey B; Smith, EDL; Schulkin, Jay; Webster, Daniel G; Whalen, Paul J; Whishaw, Ian Q.

   I have also consulted the following: Comaroff, J. *Modernity and it Malcontents. Ritual and Power in Postcolonial Africa*. Chicago: The University of Chicago Press, 1993; Hund, J (ed.). *Witchcraft, Violence and the Law in South Africa*. Pretoria: Protea, 2003; Ashforth, Adam. *AIDS, Witchcraft, and the Problem of Power in Post-Apartheid South Africa*.

GLOSSARY

Afrikaner cattle indigenous red-brown long-horned African cattle

aikona no; not at all (Xhosa)

Alexis Preller prominent South African artist (1911–1975)

ankerkaroo small Karoo bush

baas boss, sir; subservient form of address to a white male, sometimes used ironically

bakkie pick-up truck

besembos/se broombush/es; a large shrub that grows in the Eastern Cape, from which brooms are frequently made

biltong salted meat that is dried in strips

blesbuck medium-sized antelope

bobotie traditional dish of spicy curried minced meat baked with a savoury custard topping

boer/boere farmer/farmers; affectionate or pejorative name for Afrikaners

boere-anties Afrikaner women

boerbull South African cross-bred guard dog

boerpampoen large white pumpkin

boerseun farmer's son

boetman an affectionate form of address for a young man

bossie small bush

bossieveld veld where mostly small bushes grow

braaipot a saucepan or cast-iron pot used over open coals

Damkamp name given to fenced-off pasture that contains a dam

dimmas sunglasses (township slang)

dinges thingamajig/whatsisname

dominee minister in the one of the three Dutch Reformed churches

dorp country town or village

eland large African antelope

ghoe-ghoe mealies large dried white maize that is soaked and boiled

graaitjiemeerkat slender-tailed meerkat

Hertzog cookies jam tartlet named after General J B M Hertzog

intombi young girl of marriageable age (Xhosa)

ja-nee vague expression indicating resignation, dejection, etc.

Japara Australian oilskin coat

karee evergreen tree

kerriebossie small Karoo bush that has a strong curry smell

kierie stick with a knobbed head, used for walking or fighting

kleinbasie little master/boss, used to address a young white male

koppie small hill; hillock

laaitie young boy or adolescent male

Langenhoven, C J (1873–1932) important Afrikaans writer who promoted the Afrikaans language

lobola goods or cattle given to a woman's parents to secure her hand in marriage (Xhosa)

majitas township slang for a group of youth or men

mammie mommy

Marlo'tjie diminutive of "Marlouw", used in an affectionate or mocking way

meneer mister/sir

mevrou madam; mistress

miesies subservient form of address to a white woman

Môreson Morning Sun

mossie sparrow

muthi traditional African medicine, sometimes believed to have magical properties (Zulu)

neef nephew, affectionate form of address for a young boy or man

nooi/nooiens young lady/ladies

oom uncle; a respectful form of address for an older man

oubaas deferential form of address for an elderly master/boss

Ouplaas Old Farm

pappie daddy

perdekaroobossie small Karoo bush with dark green foliage

platanna clawed toad

platteland the rural areas

Prinsdom Principality

Reddersburg a small town in the Free State

Reformed Church one of the Dutch Reformed churches (Calvinist)

riempie a leather thong that can be woven into a seat or panel for a piece of furniture

rooikat lynx

rooigras a type of grass providing good grazing, the leaves of which go red in autumn

slap pap a type of maize porridge

Springbokkamp a fenced-off pasture named after the springbuck

stoep veranda

stofdakkie a small round crawling insect

tannie auntie; a respectful form of address for an older woman

taal language; Afrikaans is sometimes referred to as "die taal" (the language)

tierboskatjies coarse term for girls or women connoting wildness and sexuality (literally: servals)

trompie Jewish harp

Tweewindpompkamp name given to a fenced-off pasture where there are two windmills

veld open countryside with natural vegetation such as grass and small bushes

Versamelde Werke Collected Works

vlei low-lying ground that is covered with water during the rainy season

voertsek scram, go away, as spoken to a dog or as an insult to a person

volk people; members of a particular group, or citizens of a country

Volksblad an Afrikaans newspaper in the Free State

Vrouemonument the Women's Monument in Bloemfontein that commemorates the women and children who died in British concentration camps during the Anglo-Boer War (1899-1902)

werf farmyard, usually fenced off

witblommetjie a small Karoo bush with white flowers